Oates, Joyce Carol, 1938-
   The wheel of love, and other stories.
New York, Vanguard Press [1970]
   440 p. 23cm.

    I. Title.

Books by Joyce Carol Oates

Them

Expensive People

A Garden of Earthly Delights

With Shuddering Fall

Upon the Sweeping Flood

By the North Gate

Anonymous Sins (poems)

Wee can dye by it, if not live by love,
  And if unfit for tombes and hearse
Our legend bee, it will be fit for verse;
  And if no peece of Chronicle wee prove,
    We'll build in sonnets pretty roomes;
    As well a well wrought urne becomes
The greatest ashes, as halfe-acre tombes,
  And by these hymnes, all shall approve
Us Canoniz'd for Love:

—JOHN DONNE, "THE CANONIZATION"

The Wheel of Love

AND OTHER STORIES BY

Joyce Carol Oates

THE VANGUARD PRESS, NEW YORK

Manufactured in the United States of America by
H. Wolff Book Manufacturing Company, New York

Library of Congress Catalogue Card Number: 79–134661
SBN 8149–0676–1

Designer: Ernst Reichl

ACKNOWLEDGMENTS   "In The Region of Ice" was first published in THE ATLANTIC MONTHLY, August 1965, and was First Prize Winner in the *Prize Stories: the O. Henry Awards* 1967.

"Where Are You Going, Where Have You Been?" was first published in EPOCH, Fall 1966, and was included in *Prize Stories: the O. Henry Awards* 1968 and *The Best American Short Stories* 1967.

"Unmailed, Unwritten Letters" was first published in THE HUDSON REVIEW, Spring 1969, and was included in *Prize Stories: the O. Henry Awards* 1970.

"Convalescing" was first published in THE VIRGINIA QUARTERLY REVIEW, Summer 1969, and was First Prize Winner of the Emily Clark Balch Short Story Competition, 1969.

"Shame" was first published in THE ATLANTIC MONTHLY, June 1968.

"Accomplished Desires" was first published in ESQUIRE, May 1968, and was Second Prize Winner in *Prize Stories: the O. Henry Awards* 1969.

"Wild Saturday" was first published in MADEMOISELLE, September 1970.

"How I Contemplated the World from the Detroit House of Correction and Began My Life Over Again" was first published in TRIQUARTERLY, Spring 1969, and was included in *Prize Stories: the O. Henry Awards* 1970.

"The Wheel of Love" was first published in ESQUIRE, October 1967.

"Four Summers" was first published in THE YALE REVIEW, Spring 1967, and was included in *The American Literary Anthology*, 1968.

"Demons" was first published in THE SOUTHERN REVIEW, Winter 1970.

"Bodies" was first published in HARPER'S BAZAAR, February 1970.

"Boy and Girl" was first published in PRISM INTERNATIONAL, Spring 1969.

"The Assailant" was first published in PRAIRIE SCHOONER, Winter 1965–66.

"The Heavy Sorrow of the Body" was first published in THE NORTHWEST REVIEW, Summer 1968.

"Matter and Energy" was first published in PARTISAN REVIEW, Volume 36, 1969.

"You" was first published in COSMOPOLITAN, February 1970.

"I Was in Love" was first published in SHENANDOAH, Spring 1970.

"An Interior Dialogue" was first published in ESQUIRE, February 1969.

"What Is the Connection Between Men and Women?" was first published in MADEMOISELLE, February 1970.

The lines from "Lovers Relentlessly" by Stanley Kunetz which appeared in his *Selected Poems/1928–1958* are reprinted courtesy of Atlantic-Little, Brown, © Stanley Kunetz 1958.

for Helen and Milton Covensky

Contents

The Wheel of Love

In the Region of Ice

Sister Irene was a tall, deft woman in her early thirties. What one could see of her face made a striking impression—serious, hard gray eyes, a long slender nose, a face waxen with thought. Seen at the right time, from the right angle, she was almost handsome. In her past teaching positions she had drawn a little upon the fact of her being young and brilliant and also a nun, but she was beginning to grow out of that.

This was a new university and an entirely new world. She had heard—of course it was true—that the Jesuit administration of this school had hired her at the last moment to save money and to head off the appointment of a man of dubious religious commitment. She had prayed for the necessary energy to get her through this first semester. She had no trouble with teaching itself; once she stood before a classroom she felt herself capable of anything. It was the world immediately outside the classroom that confused and alarmed her, though she let none of this show—the cynicism of her colleagues, the indifference of many of the students, and, above all, the looks she got that told her nothing much would be expected of her because she was a nun. This took energy, strength. At times she had the idea that she was on trial and that the excuses she made to herself about her discomfort were only the common excuses made by guilty people. But in front of a class she had no time to worry about herself or the conflicts in her mind. She became, once and for all, a figure existing only for the benefit of others, an instrument by which facts were communicated.

About two weeks after the semester began, Sister Irene noticed a new student in her class. He was slight and fair-haired, and his face was blank, but not blank by accident, blank on purpose, suppressed and restricted into a dumbness that looked hysterical. She was prepared for him before he raised his hand, and when she saw his arm jerk, as if he had at last lost control of it, she nodded to him without hesitation.

"Sister, how can this be reconciled with Shakespeare's vision in *Hamlet?* How can these opposing views be in the same mind?"

Students glanced at him, mildly surprised. He did not belong in the class, and this was mysterious, but his manner was urgent and blind.

"There is no need to reconcile opposing views," Sister Irene said, leaning forward against the podium. "In one play Shakespeare suggests one vision, in another play another; the plays are not simultaneous creations, and even if they were, we never demand a logical—"

"We must demand a logical consistency," the young man said.

"The idea of education is itself predicated upon consistency, order, sanity—"

He had interrupted her, and she hardened her face against him—for his sake, not her own, since she did not really care. But he noticed nothing. "Please see me after class," she said.

After class the young man hurried up to her.

"Sister Irene, I hope you didn't mind my visiting today. I'd heard some things, interesting things," he said. He stared at her, and something in her face allowed him to smile. "I . . . could we talk in your office? Do you have time?"

They walked down to her office. Sister Irene sat at her desk, and the young man sat facing her; for a moment they were self-conscious and silent.

"Well, I suppose you know—I'm a Jew," he said.

Sister Irene stared at him. "Yes?" she said.

"What am I doing at a Catholic university, huh?" He grinned. "That's what you want to know."

She made a vague movement of her hand to show that she had no thoughts on this, nothing at all, but he seemed not to catch it. He was sitting on the edge of the straight-backed chair. She saw that he was young but did not really look young. There were harsh lines on either side of his mouth, as if he had misused that youthful mouth somehow. His skin was almost as pale as hers, his eyes were dark and not quite in focus. He looked at her and through her and around her, as his voice surrounded them both. His voice was a little shrill at times.

"Listen, I did the right thing today—visiting your class! God, what a lucky accident it was; some jerk mentioned you, said you were a good teacher—I thought, what a laugh! These people know about good teachers here? But yes, listen, yes, I'm not kidding—you are good. I mean that."

Sister Irene frowned. "I don't quite understand what all this means."

He smiled and waved aside her formality, as if he knew better. "Listen, I got my B.A. at Columbia, then I came back here to this crappy city. I mean, I did it on purpose, I wanted to come back. I wanted to. I have my reasons for doing things. I'm on a three-thousand-dollar fellowship," he said, and waited for that to impress her. "You know, I could have gone almost anywhere with that fellowship, and I came back home here—my home's in the city—and enrolled here. This was last year. This is my second year. I'm working on a thesis, I mean I was, my master's thesis— but the hell with that. What I want to ask you is this: Can I enroll in your class, is it too late? We have to get special permission if we're late."

Sister Irene felt something nudging her, some uneasiness in him that was pleading with her not to be offended by his abrupt, familiar manner. He seemed to be promising another self, a better self, as if his fair, childish, almost cherubic face were doing tricks to distract her from what his words said.

"Are you in English studies?" she asked.

"I was in history. Listen," he said, and his mouth did something odd, drawing itself down into a smile that made the lines about it deepen like knives, "listen, they kicked me out."

He sat back, watching her. He crossed his legs. He took out a package of cigarettes and offered her one. Sister Irene shook her head, staring at his hands. They were small and stubby and might have belonged to a ten-year-old, and the nails were a strange near-violet color. It took him awhile to extract a cigarette.

"Yeah, kicked me out. What do you think of that?"

"I don't understand."

"My master's thesis was coming along beautifully, and then this bastard—I mean, excuse me, this professor, I won't pollute your office with his name—he started making criticisms, he said some things were unacceptable, he—" The boy leaned forward and hunched his narrow shoulders in a parody of secrecy. "We had an argument. I told him some frank things, things only a broad-minded person could hear about himself. That takes courage, right? He didn't have it! He kicked me out of the master's program, so now I'm coming into English. Literature is greater than history; European history is one big pile of garbage. Sky-high. Filth and rotting corpses, right? Aristotle says that poetry is higher than history; he's right; in your class today I suddenly realized that this is my field, Shakespeare, only Shakespeare is—"

Sister Irene guessed that he was going to say that only Shakespeare was equal to him, and she caught the moment of recognition and hesitation, the half-raised arm, the keen, frowning forehead, the narrowed eyes; then he thought better of it and did not end the sentence. "The students in your class are mainly negligible, I can tell you that. You're new here, and I've been here a year—I would have finished my studies last year but my father got sick, he was hospitalized, I couldn't take exams and it was a mess—but I'll make it through English in one year or drop dead. I can do it, I can do anything. I'll take six courses at once—" He broke off, breathless. Sister Irene tried to smile. "All right then, it's settled? You'll let me in? Have I missed anything so far?"

He had no idea of the rudeness of his question. Sister Irene, feeling suddenly exhausted, said, "I'll give you a syllabus of the course."

"Fine! Wonderful!"

He got to his feet eagerly. He looked through the schedule, muttering to himself, making favorable noises. It struck Sister Irene that she was making a mistake to let him in. There were these moments when one had to make an intelligent decision. . . . But she was sympathetic with him, yes. She was sympathetic with something about him.

She found out his name the next day: Allen Weinstein.

After this she came to her Shakespeare class with a sense of excitement. It became clear to her at once that Weinstein was the most intelligent student in the class. Until he had enrolled, she had not understood what was lacking, a mind that could appreciate her own. Within a week his jagged, protean mind had alienated the other students, and though he sat in the center of the class, he seemed totally alone, encased by a miniature world of his own. When he spoke of the "frenetic humanism of the High Renaissance," Sister Irene dreaded the raised eyebrows and mocking smiles of the other students, who no longer bothered to look at Weinstein. She wanted to defend him, but she never did, because there was something rude and dismal about his knowledge; he used it like a weapon, talking passionately of Nietzsche and Goethe and Freud until Sister Irene would be forced to close discussion.

In meditation, alone, she often thought of him. When she tried to talk about him to a young nun, Sister Carlotta, everything sounded gross. "But no, he's an excellent student," she insisted. "I'm very grateful to have him in class. It's just that . . . he thinks ideas are real." Sister Carlotta, who loved literature also, had been forced to teach grade-school arithmetic for the last four years. That might have been why she said, a little sharply, "You don't think ideas are real?"

Sister Irene acquiesced with a smile, but of course she did not think so: only reality is real.

When Weinstein did not show up for class on the day the first paper was due, Sister Irene's heart sank, and the sensation was somehow a familiar one. She began her lecture and kept waiting for the door to open and for him to hurry noisily back to his seat, grinning an apology toward her—but nothing happened.

If she had been deceived by him, she made herself think angrily, it was as a teacher and not as a woman. He had promised her nothing.

Weinstein appeared the next day near the steps of the liberal arts building. She heard someone running behind her, a breathless exclamation: "Sister Irene!" She turned and saw him, panting and grinning in embarrassment. He wore a dark-blue suit with a necktie, and he looked, despite his childish face, like a little old man; there was something oddly precarious and fragile about him. "Sister Irene, I owe you an apology, right?" He raised his eyebrows and smiled a sad, forlorn, yet irritatingly conspiratorial smile. "The first paper—not in on time, and I know what your rules are. . . . You won't accept late papers, I know— that's good discipline, I'll do that when I teach too. But, unavoidably, I was unable to come to school yesterday. There are many —many—" He gulped for breath, and Sister Irene had the startling sense of seeing the real Weinstein stare out at her, a terrified prisoner behind the confident voice. "There are many complications in family life. Perhaps you are unaware—I mean—"

She did not like him, but she felt this sympathy, something tugging and nagging at her the way her parents had competed for her love so many years before. They had been whining, weak people, and out of their wet need for affection, the girl she had been (her name was Yvonne) had emerged stronger than either of them, contemptuous of tears because she had seen so many. But Weinstein was different; he was not simply weak—perhaps he was not weak at all—but his strength was confused and hysterical. She felt her customary rigidity as a teacher begin to falter. "You may turn your paper in today if you have it," she said, frowning.

Weinstein's mouth jerked into an incredulous grin. "Wonderful! Marvelous!" he said. "You are very understanding, Sister Irene, I must say. I must say . . . I didn't expect, really . . ." He was fumbling in a shabby old briefcase for the paper. Sister Irene waited. She was prepared for another of his excuses, certain that he did not have the paper, when he suddenly straightened up and handed her something. "Here! I took the liberty of writing thirty pages instead of just fifteen," he said. He was obviously quite excited; his cheeks were mottled pink and white. "You may disagree violently with my interpretation—I expect you to, in fact I'm counting on it—but let me warn you, I have

the exact proof, right here in the play itself!" He was thumping
at a book, his voice growing louder and shriller. Sister Irene, startled, wanted to put her hand over his mouth and soothe him.

"Look," he said breathlessly, "may I talk with you? I have a
class now I hate, I loathe, I can't bear to sit through! Can I talk
with you instead?"

Because she was nervous, she stared at the title page of the
paper: " 'Erotic Melodies in *Romeo and Juliet*' by Allen Weinstein, Jr."

"All right?" he said. "Can we walk around here? Is it all right?
I've been anxious to talk with you about some things you said in
class."

She was reluctant, but he seemed not to notice. They walked
slowly along the shaded campus paths. Weinstein did all the talking, of course, and Sister Irene recognized nothing in his cascade
of words that she had mentioned in class. "The humanist must be
committed to the totality of life," he said passionately. "This is
the failing one finds everywhere in the academic world! I found
it in New York and I found it here and I'm no ingénu, I don't go
around with my mouth hanging open—I'm experienced, look,
I've been to Europe, I've lived in Rome! I went everywhere in
Europe except Germany, I don't talk about Germany . . . Sister Irene, think of the significant men in the last century, the
men who've changed the world! Jews, right? Marx, Freud, Ein-
stein! Not that I believe Marx, Marx is a madman . . . and
Freud, no, my sympathies are with spiritual humanism. I believe
that the Jewish race is the exclusive . . . the exclusive, what's
the word, the exclusive means by which humanism will be extended. . . . Humanism begins by excluding the Jew, and
now," he said with a high, surprised laugh, "the Jew will perfect
it. After the Nazis, only the Jew is authorized to understand humanism, its limitations and its possibilities. So, I say that the humanist is committed to life in its totality and not just to his profession! The religious person is totally religious, he is his religion!

What else? I recognize in you a humanist and a religious person—"

But he did not seem to be talking to her or even looking at her.

"Here, read this," he said. "I wrote it last night." It was a long free-verse poem, typed on a typewriter whose ribbon was worn out.

"There's this trouble with my father, a wonderful man, a lovely man, but his health—his strength is fading, do you see? What must it be to him to see his son growing up? I mean, I'm a man now, he's getting old, weak, his health is bad—it's hell, right? I sympathize with him. I'd do anything for him, I'd cut open my veins, anything for a father—right? That's why I wasn't in school yesterday," he said, and his voice dropped for the last sentence, as if he had been dragged back to earth by a fact.

Sister Irene tried to read the poem, then pretended to read it. A jumble of words dealing with "life" and "death" and "darkness" and "love." "What do you think?" Weinstein said nervously, trying to read it over her shoulder and crowding against her.

"It's very . . . passionate," Sister Irene said.

This was the right comment; he took the poem back from her in silence, his face flushed with excitement. "Here, at this school, I have few people to talk with. I haven't shown anyone else that poem." He looked at her with his dark, intense eyes, and Sister Irene felt them focus upon her. She was terrified at what he was trying to do—he was trying to force her into a human relationship.

"Thank you for your paper," she said, turning away.

When he came the next day, ten minutes late, he was haughty and disdainful. He had nothing to say and sat with his arms folded. Sister Irene took back with her to the convent a feeling of betrayal and confusion. She had been hurt. It was absurd, and yet— She spent too much time thinking about him, as if he were somehow a kind of crystallization of her own loneliness; but she had no right to think so much of him. She did not want to think of him or of her loneliness. But Weinstein did so much more than think of his predicament: he embodied it, he acted it out, and that was perhaps why he fascinated her. It was as if he were doing a dance for her, a dance of shame and agony and delight, and so long as he did it, she was safe. She felt embarrassment for him, but also anxiety; she wanted to protect him. When the dean of the graduate school questioned her about Weinstein's work, she insisted that he was an "excellent" student, though she knew the dean had not wanted to hear that.

She prayed for guidance, she spent hours on her devotions, she was closer to her vocation than she had been for some years. Life at the convent became tinged with unreality, a misty distortion that took its tone from the glowering skies of the city at night, identical smokestacks ranged against the clouds and giving to the sky the excrement of the populated and successful earth. This city was not her city, this world was not her world. She felt no pride in knowing this, it was a fact. The little convent was not like an island in the center of this noisy world, but rather a kind of hole or crevice the world did not bother with, something of no interest. The convent's rhythm of life had nothing to do with the world's rhythm, it did not violate or alarm it in any way. Sister Irene tried to draw together the fragments of her life and synthesize them somehow in her vocation as a nun: she was a nun, she was recognized as a nun and had given herself happily to that life, she had a name, a place, she had dedicated her superior intelligence to the Church, she worked without pay and without expecting gratitude, she had given up pride, she did not think of herself but only of her work and her vocation, she did not think of anything external to these, she saturated herself daily in the knowledge that she was involved in the mystery of Christianity.

A daily terror attended this knowledge, however, for she sensed herself being drawn by that student, that Jewish boy, into a relationship she was not ready for. She wanted to cry out in fear that she was being forced into the role of a Christian, and what did that mean? What could her studies tell her? What could the other nuns tell her? She was alone, no one could help; he was making her into a Christian, and to her that was a mystery, a thing of terror, something others slipped on the way they slipped on their clothes, casually and thoughtlessly, but to her a magnificent and terrifying wonder.

For days she carried Weinstein's paper, marked A, around with her; he did not come to class. One day she checked with the graduate office and was told that Weinstein had called in to say his father was ill and that he would not be able to attend classes for a while. "He's strange, I remember him," the secretary said. "He missed all his exams last spring and made a lot of trouble. He was in and out of here every day."

So there was no more of Weinstein for a while, and Sister Irene stopped expecting him to hurry into class. Then, one morning, she found a letter from him in her mailbox.

He had printed it in black ink, very carefully, as if he had not trusted handwriting. The return address was in bold letters that, like his voice, tried to grab onto her: Birchcrest Manor. Somewhere north of the city. "Dear Sister Irene," the block letters said, "I am doing well here and have time for reading and relaxing. The Manor is delightful. My doctor here is an excellent, intelligent man who has time for me, unlike my former doctor. If you have time, you might drop in on my father, who worries about me too much, I think, and explain to him what my condition is. He doesn't seem to understand. I feel about this new life the way that boy, what's his name, in *Measure for Measure*, feels about the prospects of a different life; you remember what he says to his sister when she visits him in prison, how he is looking forward to an escape into another world. Perhaps you could *explain* this to my father and he would stop worrying." The letter ended with the father's name and address, in letters that were just a little too big. Sister Irene, walking slowly down the corridor as she read the letter, felt her eyes cloud over with tears. She was cold with fear, it was something she had never experienced before. She knew what Weinstein was trying to tell her, and the desperation of his attempt made it all the more pathetic; he did not deserve this, why did God allow him to suffer so?

She read through Claudio's speech to his sister, in *Measure for Measure:*

> *Ay, but to die, and go we know not where;*
> *To lie in cold obstruction and to rot;*
> *This sensible warm motion to become*
> *A kneaded clod; and the delighted spirit*
> *To bathe in fiery floods, or to reside*
> *In thrilling region of thick-ribbed ice,*
> *To be imprison'd in the viewless winds*
> *And blown with restless violence round about*
> *The pendent world; or to be worse than worst*
> *Of those that lawless and incertain thought*
> *Imagines howling! 'Tis too horrible!*
> *The weariest and most loathed worldly life*
> *That age, ache, penury, and imprisonment*
> *Can lay on nature is a paradise*
> *To what we fear of death.*

Sister Irene called the father's number that day. "Allen Weinstein residence, who may I say is calling?" a woman said, bored. "May I speak to Mr. Weinstein? It's urgent—about his son," Sister Irene said. There was a pause at the other end. "You want to talk to his mother, maybe?" the woman said. "His mother? Yes, his mother, then. Please. It's very important."

She talked with this strange, unsuspected woman, a disembodied voice that suggested absolutely no face, and insisted upon going over that afternoon. The woman was nervous, but Sister Irene, who was a university professor, after all, knew enough to hide her own nervousness. She kept waiting for the woman to say, "Yes, Allen has mentioned you . . ." but nothing happened.

She persuaded Sister Carlotta to ride over with her. This urgency of hers was something they were all amazed by. They hadn't suspected that the set of her gray eyes could change to this blurred, distracted alarm, this sense of mission that seemed to have come to her from nowhere. Sister Irene drove across the city in the late afternoon traffic, with the high whining noises from residential streets where trees were being sawed down in pieces. She understood now the secret, sweet wildness that Christ must have felt, giving himself for man, dying for the billions of men who would never know of him and never understand the sacrifice. For the first time she approached the realization of that great act. In her troubled mind the city traffic was jumbled and yet oddly coherent, an image of the world that was always out of joint with what was happening in it, its inner history struggling with its external spectacle. This sacrifice of Christ's, so mysterious and legendary now, almost lost in time—it was that by which Christ transcended both God and man at one moment, more than man because of his fate to do what no other man could do, and more than God because no god could suffer as he did. She felt a flicker of something close to madness.

She drove nervously, uncertainly, afraid of missing the street and afraid of finding it too, for while one part of her rushed forward to confront these people who had betrayed their son, another part of her would have liked nothing so much as to be waiting as usual for the summons to dinner, safe in her room. . . . When she found the street and turned onto it, she was in a state of breathless excitement. Here lawns were bright green and marred with only a few leaves, magically clean, and the houses were enormous and pompous, a mixture of styles: ranch houses, colonial houses, French country houses, white-bricked wonders with curving glass and clumps of birch trees somehow encircled by white concrete. Sister Irene stared as if she had blundered into another world. This was a kind of heaven, and she was too shabby for it.

The Weinstein's house was the strangest one of all: it looked like a small Alpine lodge, with an inverted-V-shaped front entrance. Sister Irene drove up the black-topped driveway and let the car slow to a stop; she told Sister Carlotta she would not be long.

At the door she was met by Weinstein's mother, a small, nervous woman with hands like her son's. "Come in, come in," the woman said. She had once been beautiful, that was clear, but now in missing beauty she was not handsome or even attractive but looked ruined and perplexed, the misshapen swelling of her white-blond professionally set hair like a cap lifting up from her surprised face. "He'll be right in. Allen?" she called, "our visitor is here." They went into the living room. There was a grand piano at one end and an organ at the other. In between were scatterings of brilliant modern furniture in conversational groups, and several puffed-up white rugs on the polished floor. Sister Irene could not stop shivering.

"Professor, it's so strange, but let me say when the phone rang I had a feeling—I had a feeling," the woman said, with damp eyes. Sister Irene sat, and the woman hovered about her. "Should I call you Professor? We don't . . . you know . . . we don't understand the technicalities that go with—Allen, my son, wanted to go here to the Catholic school; I told my husband why not? Why fight? It's the thing these days, they do anything they want for knowledge. And he had to come home, you know. He couldn't take care of himself in New York, that was the beginning of the trouble. . . . Should I call you Professor?"

"You can call me Sister Irene."

"Sister Irene?" the woman said, touching her throat in awe, as if something intimate and unexpected had happened.

Then Weinstein's father appeared, hurrying. He took long, impatient strides. Sister Irene stared at him and in that instant doubted everything—he was in his fifties, a tall, sharply hand-some man, heavy but not fat, holding his shoulders back with what looked like an effort, but holding them back just the same. He wore a dark suit and his face was flushed, as if he had run a long distance.

"Now," he said, coming to Sister Irene and with a precise wave of his hand motioning his wife off, "now, let's straighten this out. A lot of confusion over that kid, eh?" He pulled a chair over, scraping it across a rug and pulling one corner over, so that its brown underside was exposed. "I came home early just for this, Libby phoned me. Sister, you got a letter from him, right?"

The wife looked at Sister Irene over her husband's head as if trying somehow to coach her, knowing that this man was so loud and impatient that no one could remember anything in his pres-ence.

"A letter—yes—today—"

"He says what in it? You got the letter, eh? Can I see it?"

She gave it to him and wanted to explain, but he silenced her with a flick of his hand. He read through the letter so quickly that Sister Irene thought perhaps he was trying to impress her with his skill at reading. "So?" he said, raising his eyes, smiling, "so what is this? He's happy out there, he says. He doesn't com-municate with us any more, but he writes to you and says he's happy—what's that? I mean, what the hell is that?"

"But he isn't happy. He wants to come home," Sister Irene said. It was so important that she make him understand that she could not trust her voice; goaded by this man, it might suddenly turn shrill, as his son's did. "Someone must read their letters be-fore they're mailed, so he tried to tell me something by making an allusion to—"

"What?"

"—an allusion to a play, so that I would know. He may be thinking suicide, he must be very unhappy—"

She ran out of breath. Weinstein's mother had begun to cry,

but the father was shaking his head jerkily back and forth. "Forgive me, Sister, but it's a lot of crap, he needs the hospital, he needs help—right? It costs me fifty a day out there, and they've got the best place in the state, I figure it's worth it. He needs help, that kid, what do I care if he's unhappy? He's unbalanced!" he said angrily. "You want us to get him out again? We argued with the judge for two hours to get him in, an acquaintance of mine. Look, he can't control himself—he was smashing things here, he was hysterical. They need help, lady, and you do something about it fast! You do something! We made up our minds to do something and we did it! This letter—what the hell is this letter? He never talked like that to us!"

"But he means the opposite of what he says—"

"Then he's crazy! I'm the first to admit it." He was perspiring, and his face had darkened. "I've got no pride left this late. He's a little bastard, you want to know? He calls me names, he's filthy, got a filthy mouth—that's being smart, huh? They give him a big scholarship for his filthy mouth? I went to college too, and I got out and knew something, and I for Christ's sake did something with it; my wife is an intelligent woman, a learned woman, would you guess she does book reviews for the little newspaper out here? Intelligent isn't crazy—crazy isn't intelligent. Maybe for you at the school he writes nice papers and gets an A, but out here, around the house, he can't control himself, and we got him committed!"

"But—"

"We're fixing him up, don't worry about it!" He turned to his wife. "Libby, get out of here, I mean it. I'm sorry, but get out of here, you're making a fool of yourself, go stand in the kitchen or something, you and the goddamn maid can cry on each other's shoulders. That one in the kitchen is nuts too, they're all nuts. Sister," he said, his voice lowering, "I thank you immensely for coming out here. This is wonderful, your interest in my son. And I see he admires you—that letter there. But what about that letter? If he did want to get out, which I don't admit—he was willing to be committed, in the end he said okay himself—if he wanted out I wouldn't do it. Why? So what if he wants to come back? The next day he wants something else, what then? He's a sick kid, and I'm the first to admit it."

Sister Irene felt that sickness spread to her. She stood. The room was so big it seemed it must be a public place; there had been nothing personal or private about their conversation. Weinstein's mother was standing by the fireplace, sobbing. The father jumped to his feet and wiped his forehead in a gesture that was meant to help Sister Irene on her way out. "God, what a day," he said, his eyes snatching at hers for understanding, "you know— one of those days all day long? Sister, I thank you a lot. There should be more people in the world who care about others, like you. I mean that."

On the way back to the convent, the man's words returned to her, and she could not get control of them; she could not even feel anger. She had been pressed down, forced back, what could she do? Weinstein might have been watching her somehow from a barred window, and he surely would have understood. The strange idea she had had on the way over, something about understanding Christ, came back to her now and sickened her. But the sickness was small. It could be contained.

About a month after her visit to his father, Weinstein himself showed up. He was dressed in a suit as before, even the necktie was the same. He came right into her office as if he had been pushed and could not stop.

"Sister," he said, and shook her hand. He must have seen fear in her because he smiled ironically. "Look, I'm released. I'm let out of the nut house. Can I sit down?"

He sat. Sister Irene was breathing quickly, as if in the presence of an enemy who does not know he is an enemy.

"So, they finally let me out. I heard what you did. You talked with him, that was all I wanted. You're the only one who gave a

damn. Because you're a humanist and a religious person, you respect . . . the individual. Listen," he said, whispering, "it was
hell out there! Hell Birchcrest Manor! All fixed up with fancy
chairs and *Life* magazines lying around—and what do they do to
you? They locked me up, they gave me shock treatments! Shock
treatments, how do you like that, it's discredited by everybody
now—they're crazy out there themselves, sadists. They locked
me up, they gave me hypodermic shots, they didn't treat me like
a human being! Do you know what that is," Weinstein demanded
savagely, "not to be treated like a human being? They made me
an animal—for fifty dollars a day! Dirty filthy swine! Now I'm an
outpatient because I stopped swearing at them. I found somebody's bobby pin, and when I wanted to scream I pressed it under my fingernail and it stopped me—the screaming went inside
and not out—so they gave me good reports, those sick bastards.
Now I'm an outpatient and I can walk along the street and
breathe in the same filthy exhaust from the buses like all you
normal people! Christ," he said, and threw himself back against
the chair.

Sister Irene stared at him. She wanted to take his hand, to
make some gesture that would close the aching distance between
them. "Mr. Weinstein—"

"Call me Allen!" he said sharply.

"I'm very sorry—I'm terribly sorry—"

"My own parents committed me, but of course they didn't
know what it was like. It was hell," he said thickly, "and there
isn't any hell except what other people do to you. The psychiatrist out there, the main shrink, he hates Jews too, some of us
were positive of that, and he's got a bigger nose than I do, a real
beak." He made a noise of disgust. "A dirty bastard, a sick, dirty,
pathetic bastard—all of them. Anyway, I'm getting out of here,
and I came to ask you a favor."

"What do you mean?"

"I'm getting out. I'm leaving. I'm going up to Canada and lose

the sweep of the Great Lakes up to the silence of Canada. But she called that part of herself back. She could only be one person in her lifetime. That was the ugly truth, she thought, that she could not really regret Weinstein's suffering and death; she had only one life and had already given it to someone else. He had come too late to her. Fifteen years ago, perhaps, but not now.

She was only one person, she thought, walking down the corridor in a dream. Was she safe in this single person, or was she trapped? She had only one identity. She could make only one choice. What she had done or hadn't done was the result of that choice, and how was she guilty? If she could have felt guilt, she thought, she might at least have been able to feel something.

Where Are You Going, Where Have You Been?

FOR BOB DYLAN

Her name was Connie. She was fifteen and she had a quick, nervous giggling habit of craning her neck to glance into mirrors or checking other people's faces to make sure her own was all right. Her mother, who noticed everything and knew everything and who hadn't much reason any longer to look at her own face, always scolded Connie about it. "Stop gawking at yourself. Who are you? You think you're so pretty?" she would say. Connie would raise her eyebrows at these familiar old complaints and look right through her mother, into a shadowy vision of herself as she was right at that moment: she knew she was pretty and that was everything. Her mother had been pretty once too, if you could believe those old snapshots in the album, but now her looks were gone and that was why she was always after Connie.

"Why don't you keep your room clean like your sister? How've you got your hair fixed—what the hell stinks? Hair spray? You don't see your sister using that junk."

Her sister June was twenty-four and still lived at home. She was a secretary in the high school Connie attended, and if that wasn't bad enough—with her in the same building—she was so plain and chunky and steady that Connie had to hear her praised all the time by her mother and her mother's sisters. June did this, June did that, she saved money and helped clean the house and cooked and Connie couldn't do a thing, her mind was all filled with trashy daydreams. Their father was away at work most of the time and when he came home he wanted supper and he read the newspaper at supper and after supper he went to bed. He didn't bother talking much to them, but around his bent head Connie's mother kept picking at her until Connie wished her mother was dead and she herself was dead and it was all over. "She makes me want to throw up sometimes," she complained to her friends. She had a high, breathless, amused voice that made everything she said sound a little forced, whether it was sincere or not.

There was one good thing: June went places with girl friends of hers, girls who were just as plain and steady as she, and so when Connie wanted to do that her mother had no objections. The father of Connie's best girl friend drove the girls the three miles to town and left them at a shopping plaza so they could walk through the stores or go to a movie, and when he came to pick them up again at eleven he never bothered to ask what they had done.

They must have been familiar sights, walking around the shopping plaza in their shorts and flat ballerina slippers that always scuffed the sidewalk, with charm bracelets jingling on their

thin wrists; they would lean together to whisper and laugh secretly if someone passed who amused or interested them. Connie had long dark blond hair that drew anyone's eye to it, and she
wore part of it pulled up on her head and puffed out and the rest
of it she let fall down her back. She wore a pull-over jersey blouse
that looked one way when she was at home and another way
when she was away from home. Everything about her had two
sides to it, one for home and one for anywhere that was not
home: her walk, which could be childlike and bobbing, or languid enough to make anyone think she was hearing music in her
head; her mouth, which was pale and smirking most of the time,
but bright and pink on these evenings out; her laugh, which was
cynical and drawling at home—"Ha, ha, very funny,"—but high-
pitched and nervous anywhere else, like the jingling of the
charms on her bracelet.

Sometimes they did go shopping or to a movie, but sometimes
they went across the highway, ducking fast across the busy road,
to a drive-in restaurant where older kids hung out. The restaurant was shaped like a big bottle, though squatter than a real
bottle, and on its cap was a revolving figure of a grinning boy
holding a hamburger aloft. One night in midsummer they ran
across, breathless with daring, and right away someone leaned
out a car window and invited them over, but it was just a boy
from high school they didn't like. It made them feel good to be
able to ignore him. They went up through the maze of parked
and cruising cars to the bright-lit, fly-infested restaurant, their
faces pleased and expectant as if they were entering a sacred
building that loomed up out of the night to give them what haven and blessing they yearned for. They sat at the counter and
crossed their legs at the ankles, their thin shoulders rigid with
excitement, and listened to the music that made everything so
good: the music was always in the background, like music at a
church service; it was something to depend upon.

A boy named Eddie came in to talk with them. He sat backwards on his stool, turning himself jerkily around in semicircles and then stopping and turning back again, and after a while he asked Connie if she would like something to eat. She said she would and so she tapped her friend's arm on her way out—her friend pulled her face up into a brave, droll look—and Connie said she would meet her at eleven, across the way. "I just hate to leave her like that," Connie said earnestly, but the boy said that she wouldn't be alone for long. So they went out to his car, and on the way Connie couldn't help but let her eyes wander over the windshields and faces all around her, her face gleaming with a joy that had nothing to do with Eddie or even this place; it might have been the music. She drew her shoulders up and sucked in her breath with the pure pleasure of being alive, and just at that moment she happened to glance at a face just a few feet from hers. It was a boy with shaggy black hair, in a convertible jalopy painted gold. He stared at her and then his lips widened into a grin. Connie slit her eyes at him and turned away, but she couldn't help glancing back and there he was, still watching her. He wagged a finger and laughed and said, "Gonna get you, baby," and Connie turned away again without Eddie noticing anything.

She spent three hours with him, at the restaurant where they ate hamburgers and drank Cokes in wax cups that were always sweating, and then down an alley a mile or so away, and when he left her off at five to eleven only the movie house was still open at the plaza. Her girl friend was there, talking with a boy. When Connie came up, the two girls smiled at each other and Connie said, "How was the movie?" and the girl said, "*You* should know." They rode off with the girl's father, sleepy and pleased, and Connie couldn't help but look back at the darkened shopping plaza with its big empty parking lot and its signs that were faded and ghostly now, and over at the drive-in restaurant where cars were still circling tirelessly. She couldn't hear the music at this distance.

Next morning June asked her how the movie was and Connie said, "So-so."

She and that girl and occasionally another girl went out several times a week, and the rest of the time Connie spent around the house—it was summer vacation—getting in her mother's way and thinking, dreaming about the boys she met. But all the boys fell back and dissolved into a single face that was not even a face but an idea, a feeling, mixed up with the urgent insistent pounding of the music and the humid night air of July. Connie's mother kept dragging her back to the daylight by finding things for her to do or saying suddenly, "What's this about the Pettinger girl?"

And Connie would say nervously, "Oh, her. That dope." She always drew thick clear lines between herself and such girls, and her mother was simple and kind enough to believe it. Her mother was so simple, Connie thought, that it was maybe cruel to fool her so much. Her mother went scuffling around the house in old bedroom slippers and complained over the telephone to one sister about the other, then the other called up and the two of them complained about the third one. If June's name was mentioned her mother's tone was approving, and if Connie's name was mentioned it was disapproving. This did not really mean she disliked Connie, and actually Connie thought that her mother preferred her to June just because she was prettier, but the two of them kept up a pretense of exasperation, a sense that they were tugging and struggling over something of little value to either of them. Sometimes, over coffee, they were almost friends, but something would come up—some vexation that was like a fly buzzing suddenly around their heads—and their faces went hard with contempt.

One Sunday Connie got up at eleven—none of them bothered with church—and washed her hair so that it could dry all day long in the sun. Her parents and sister were going to a barbecue at an aunt's house and Connie said no, she wasn't interested, rolling her eyes to let her mother know just what she thought of it. "Stay home alone then," her mother said sharply. Connie sat out back in a lawn chair and watched them drive away, her father quiet and bald, hunched around so that he could back the car out, her mother with a look that was still angry and not at all softened through the windshield, and in the back seat poor old June, all dressed up as if she didn't know what a barbecue was, with all the running yelling kids and the flies. Connie sat with her eyes closed in the sun, dreaming and dazed with the warmth about her as if this were a kind of love, the caresses of love, and her mind slipped over onto thoughts of the boy she had been with the night before and how nice he had been, how sweet it always was, not the way someone like June would suppose but sweet, gentle, the way it was in movies and promised in songs; and when she opened her eyes she hardly knew where she was, the back yard ran off into weeds and a fence-like line of trees and behind it the sky was perfectly blue and still. The asbestos "ranch house" that was now three years old startled her—it looked small. She shook her head as if to get awake.

It was too hot. She went inside the house and turned on the radio to drown out the quiet. She sat on the edge of her bed, barefoot, and listened for an hour and a half to a program called XYZ Sunday Jamboree, record after record of hard, fast, shrieking songs she sang along with, interspersed by exclamations from "Bobby King": "An' look here, you girls at Napoleon's—Son and Charley want you to pay real close attention to this song coming up!"

And Connie paid close attention herself, bathed in a glow of slow-pulsed joy that seemed to rise mysteriously out of the music itself and lay languidly about the airless little room, breathed in and breathed out with each gentle rise and fall of her chest.

After a while she heard a car coming up the drive. She sat up at once, startled, because it couldn't be her father so soon. The gravel kept crunching all the way in from the road—the driveway was long—and Connie ran to the window. It was a car she didn't know. It was an open jalopy, painted a bright gold that caught the sunlight opaquely. Her heart began to pound and her fingers snatched at her hair, checking it, and she whispered, "Christ. Christ," wondering how bad she looked. The car came to a stop at the side door and the horn sounded four short taps, as if this were a signal Connie knew.

She went into the kitchen and approached the door slowly, then hung out the screen door, her bare toes curling down off the step. There were two boys in the car and now she recognized the driver: he had shaggy, shabby black hair that looked crazy as a wig and he was grinning at her.

"I ain't late, am I?" he said.

"Who the hell do you think you are?" Connie said.

"Toldja I'd be out, didn't I?"

"I don't even know who you are."

She spoke sullenly, careful to show no interest or pleasure, and he spoke in a fast, bright monotone. Connie looked past him to the other boy, taking her time. He had fair brown hair, with a lock that fell onto his forehead. His sideburns gave him a fierce, embarrassed look, but so far he hadn't even bothered to glance at her. Both boys wore sunglasses. The driver's glasses were metallic and mirrored everything in miniature.

"You wanta come for a ride?" he said.

Connie smirked and let her hair fall loose over one shoulder.

"Don'tcha like my car? New paint job," he said. "Hey."

"What?"

"You're cute."

She pretended to fidget, chasing flies away from the door.

"Don'tcha believe me, or what?" he said.

"Look, I don't even know who you are," Connie said in disgust.

"Hey, Ellie's got a radio, see. Mine broke down." He lifted his friend's arm and showed her the little transistor radio the boy was holding, and now Connie began to hear the music. It was the same program that was playing inside the house.

"Bobby King?" she said.

"I listen to him all the time. I think he's great."

"He's kind of great," Connie said reluctantly.

"Listen, that guy's *great*. He knows where the action is."

Connie blushed a little, because the glasses made it impossible for her to see just what this boy was looking at. She couldn't decide if she liked him or if he was just a jerk, and so she dawdled in the doorway and wouldn't come down or go back inside. She said, "What's all that stuff painted on your car?"

"Can'tcha read it?" He opened the door very carefully, as if he were afraid it might fall off. He slid out just as carefully, planting his feet firmly on the ground, the tiny metallic world in his glasses slowing down like gelatine hardening, and in the midst of it Connie's bright green blouse. "This here is my name, to begin with," he said. ARNOLD FRIEND was written in tarlike black letters on the side, with a drawing of a round, grinning face that reminded Connie of a pumpkin, except it wore sunglasses. "I wanta introduce myself, I'm Arnold Friend and that's my real name and I'm gonna be your friend, honey, and inside the car's Ellie Oscar, he's kinda shy." Ellie brought his transistor radio up to his shoulder and balanced it there. "Now, these numbers are a secret code, honey," Arnold Friend explained. He read off the numbers 33, 19, 17 and raised his eyebrows at her to see what she thought of that, but she didn't think much of it. The left rear fender had been smashed and around it was written, on the gleaming gold background: DONE BY CRAZY WOMAN DRIVER. Connie had to laugh at that. Arnold Friend was pleased at her laughter and looked up at her. "Around the other side's a lot more —you wanta come and see them?"

"No."

"Why not?"

"Why should I?"

"Don'tcha wanta see what's on the car? Don'tcha wanta go for a ride?"

"I don't know."

"Why not?"

"I got things to do."

"Like what?"

"Things."

He laughed as if she had said something funny. He slapped his thighs. He was standing in a strange way, leaning back against the car as if he were balancing himself. He wasn't tall, only an inch or so taller than she would be if she came down to him. Connie liked the way he was dressed, which was the way all of them dressed: tight faded jeans stuffed into black, scuffed boots, a belt that pulled his waist in and showed how lean he was, and a white pull-over shirt that was a little soiled and showed the hard small muscles of his arms and shoulders. He looked as if he probably did hard work, lifting and carrying things. Even his neck looked muscular. And his face was a familiar face, somehow: the jaw and chin and cheeks slightly darkened because he hadn't shaved for a day or two, and the nose long and hawklike, sniffing as if she were a treat he was going to gobble up and it was all a joke.

"Connie, you ain't telling the truth. This is your day set aside for a ride with me and you know it," he said, still laughing. The way he straightened and recovered from his fit of laughing showed that it had been all fake.

"How do you know what my name is?" she said suspiciously.

"It's Connie."

"Maybe and maybe not."

"I know my Connie," he said, wagging his finger. Now she remembered him even better, back at the restaurant, and her cheeks warmed at the thought of how she had sucked in her breath just at the moment she passed him—how she must have looked to him. And he had remembered her. "Ellie and I come out here especially for you," he said. "Ellie can sit in back. How about it?"

"Where?"

"Where what?"

"Where're we going?"

He looked at her. He took off the sunglasses and she saw how pale the skin around his eyes was, like holes that were not in shadow but instead in light. His eyes were like chips of broken glass that catch the light in an amiable way. He smiled. It was as if the idea of going for a ride somewhere, to someplace, was a new idea to him.

"Just for a ride, Connie sweetheart."

"I never said my name was Connie," she said.

"But I know what it is. I know your name and all about you, lots of things," Arnold Friend said. He had not moved yet but stood still leaning back against the side of his jalopy. "I took a special interest in you, such a pretty girl, and found out all about you—like I know your parents and sister are gone somewheres and I know where and how long they're going to be gone, and I know who you were with last night, and your best girl friend's name is Betty. Right?"

He spoke in a simple lilting voice, exactly as if he were reciting the words to a song. His smile assured her that everything was fine. In the car Ellie turned up the volume on his radio and did not bother to look around at them.

"Ellie can sit in the back seat," Arnold Friend said. He indicated his friend with a casual jerk of his chin, as if Ellie did not count and she should not bother with him.

"How'd you find out all that stuff?" Connie said.

"Listen: Betty Schultz and Tony Fitch and Jimmy Pettinger and Nancy Pettinger," he said in a chant. "Raymond Stanley and Bob Hutter—"

"Do you know all those kids?"

"I know everybody."

"Look, you're kidding. You're not from around here."

"Sure."

"But—how come we never saw you before?"

"Sure you saw me before," he said. He looked down at his boots, as if he were a little offended. "You just don't remember."

"I guess I'd remember you," Connie said.

"Yeah?" He looked up at this, beaming. He was pleased. He began to mark time with the music from Ellie's radio, tapping his fists lightly together. Connie looked away from his smile to the car, which was painted so bright it almost hurt her eyes to look at it. She looked at that name, ARNOLD FRIEND. And up at the front fender was an expression that was familiar—MAN THE FLYING SAUCERS. It was an expression kids had used the year before but didn't use this year. She looked at it for a while as if the words meant something to her that she did not yet know.

"What're you thinking about? Huh?" Arnold Friend demanded. "Not worried about your hair blowing around in the car, are you?"

"No."

"Think I maybe can't drive good?"

"How do I know?"

"You're a hard girl to handle. How come?" he said. "Don't you know I'm your friend? Didn't you see me put my sign in the air when you walked by?"

"What sign?"

"My sign." And he drew an X in the air, leaning out toward her. They were maybe ten feet apart. After his hand fell back to his side the X was still in the air, almost visible. Connie let the screen door close and stood perfectly still inside it, listening to the music from her radio and the boy's blend together. She stared at Arnold Friend. He stood there so stiffly relaxed, pretending to be relaxed, with one hand idly on the door handle as if he were keeping himself up that way and had no intention of ever moving again. She recognized most things about him, the tight jeans that showed his thighs and buttocks and the greasy leather boots and the tight shirt, and even that slippery friendly smile of his, that sleepy dreamy smile that all the boys used to get across ideas they didn't want to put into words. She recognized all this and also the singsong way he talked, slightly mocking, kidding, but serious and a little melancholy, and she recognized the way he tapped one fist against the other in homage to the perpetual music behind him. But all these things did not come together.

She said suddenly, "Hey, how old are you?"

His smiled faded. She could see then that he wasn't a kid, he was much older—thirty, maybe more. At this knowledge her heart began to pound faster.

"That's a crazy thing to ask. Can'tcha see I'm your own age?"

"Like hell you are."

"Or maybe a coupla years older. I'm eighteen."

"Eighteen?" she said doubtfully.

He grinned to reassure her and lines appeared at the corners of his mouth. His teeth were big and white. He grinned so broadly his eyes became slits and she saw how thick the lashes were, thick and black as if painted with a black tarlike material. Then, abruptly, he seemed to become embarrassed and looked over his shoulder at Ellie. "*Him,* he's crazy," he said. "Ain't he a riot? He's a nut, a real character." Ellie was still listening to the music. His sunglasses told nothing about what he was thinking. He wore a bright orange shirt unbuttoned halfway to show his chest, which was a pale, bluish chest and not muscular like Arnold Friend's. His shirt collar was turned up all around and the very tips of the collar pointed out past his chin as if they were protecting him. He was pressing the transistor radio up against his ear and sat there in a kind of daze, right in the sun.

"He's kinda strange," Connie said.

"Hey, she says you're kinda strange! Kinda strange!" Arnold Friend cried. He pounded on the car to get Ellie's attention. Ellie turned for the first time and Connie saw with shock that he wasn't a kid either—he had a fair, hairless face, cheeks reddened slightly as if the veins grew too close to the surface of his skin, the face of a forty-year-old baby. Connie felt a wave of dizziness rise in her at this sight and she stared at him as if waiting for something to change the shock of the moment, make it all right again. Ellie's lips kept shaping words, mumbling along with the words blasting in his ear.

"Maybe you two better go away," Connie said faintly.

"What? How come?" Arnold Friend cried. "We come out here to take you for a ride. It's Sunday." He had the voice of the man on the radio now. It was the same voice, Connie thought. "Don'tcha know it's Sunday all day? And honey, no matter who you were with last night, today you're with Arnold Friend and don't you forget it! Maybe you better step out here," he said, and this last was in a different voice. It was a little flatter, as if the heat was finally getting to him.

"No. I got things to do."

"Hey."

"You two better leave."

"We ain't leaving until you come with us."

"Like hell I am—"

"Connie, don't fool around with me. I mean—I mean, don't fool *around*," he said, shaking his head. He laughed incredulously. He placed his sunglasses on top of his head, carefully, as if he were indeed wearing a wig, and brought the stems down behind his ears. Connie stared at him, another wave of dizziness and fear rising in her so that for a moment he wasn't even in focus but was just a blur standing there against his gold car, and she had the idea that he had driven up the driveway all right but had come from nowhere before that and belonged nowhere and that everything about him and even about the music that was so familiar to her was only half real.

"If my father comes and sees you—"

"He ain't coming. He's at a barbecue."

"How do you know that?"

"Aunt Tillie's. Right now they're—uh—they're drinking. Sitting around," he said vaguely, squinting as if he were staring all the way to town and over to Aunt Tillie's back yard. Then the vision seemed to get clear and he nodded energetically. "Yeah. Sitting around. There's your sister in a blue dress, huh? And high heels, the poor sad bitch—nothing like you, sweetheart! And your mother's helping some fat woman with the corn, they're cleaning the corn—husking the corn—"

"What fat woman?" Connie cried.

"How do I know what fat woman, I don't know every goddamn fat woman in the world!" Arnold Friend laughed.

"Oh, that's Mrs. Hornsby. . . . Who invited her?" Connie said. She felt a little lightheaded. Her breath was coming quickly.

"She's too fat. I don't like them fat. I like them the way you are, honey," he said, smiling sleepily at her. They stared at each other for a while through the screen door. He said softly, "Now, what you're going to do is this: you're going to come out that door. You're going to sit up front with me and Ellie's going to sit in the back, the hell with Ellie, right? This isn't Ellie's date. You're my date. I'm your lover, honey."

"What? You're crazy—"

"Yes, I'm your lover. You don't know what that is but you will," he said. "I know that too. I know all about you. But look: it's real nice and you couldn't ask for nobody better than me, or more polite. I always keep my word. I'll tell you how it is, I'm always nice at first, the first time. I'll hold you so tight you won't think you have to try to get away or pretend anything because you'll know you can't. And I'll come inside you where it's all secret and you'll give in to me and you'll love me—"

"Shut up! You're crazy!" Connie said. She backed away from the door. She put her hands up against her ears as if she'd heard something terrible, something not meant for her. "People don't talk like that, you're crazy," she muttered. Her heart was almost too big now for her chest and its pumping made sweat break out all over her. She looked out to see Arnold Friend pause and then take a step toward the porch, lurching. He almost fell. But, like clever drunken man, he managed to catch his balance. He wobbled in his high boots and grabbed hold of one of the porch posts.

"Honey?" he said. "You still listening?"

"Get the hell out of here!"

"Be nice, honey. Listen."

"I'm going to call the police—"

He wobbled again and out of the side of his mouth came a fast spat curse, an aside not meant for her to hear. But even this "Christ!" sounded forced. Then he began to smile again. She watched this smile come, awkward as if he were smiling from inside a mask. His whole face was a mask, she thought wildly, tanned down to his throat but then running out as if he had plastered make-up on his face but had forgotten about his throat.

"Honey—? Listen, here's how it is. I always tell the truth and I promise you this: I ain't coming in that house after you."

"You better not! I'm going to call the police if you—if you don't—"

"Honey," he said, talking right through her voice, "honey, I'm not coming in there but you are coming out here. You know why?"

She was panting. The kitchen looked like a place she had never seen before, some room she had run inside but that wasn't good enough, wasn't going to help her. The kitchen window had never had a curtain, after three years, and there were dishes in the sink for her to do—probably—and if you ran your hand across the table you'd probably feel something sticky there.

"You listening, honey? Hey?"

"—going to call the police—"

"Soon as you touch the phone I don't need to keep my promise and can come inside. You won't want that."

She rushed forward and tried to lock the door. Her fingers were shaking. "But why lock it," Arnold Friend said gently, talking right into her face. "It's just a screen door. It's just nothing." One of his boots was at a strange angle, as if his foot wasn't in it. It pointed out to the left, bent at the ankle. "I mean, anybody can break through a screen door and glass and wood and iron or anything else if he needs to, anybody at all, and specially Arnold Friend. If the place got lit up with a fire, honey, you'd come runnin' out into my arms, right into my arms an' safe at home— like you knew I was your lover and'd stopped fooling around. I don't mind a nice shy girl but I don't like no fooling around." Part of those words were spoken with a slight rhythmic lilt, and Connie somehow recognized them—the echo of a song from last year, about a girl rushing into her boy friend's arms and coming home again—

Connie stood barefoot on the linoleum floor, staring at him. "What do you want?" she whispered.

"I want you," he said.

"What?"

"Seen you that night and thought, that's the one, yes sir. I never needed to look anymore."

"But my father's coming back. He's coming to get me. I had to wash my hair first—" She spoke in a dry, rapid voice, hardly raising it for him to hear.

"No, your daddy is not coming and yes, you had to wash your hair and you washed it for me. It's nice and shining and all for me. I thank you sweetheart," he said with a mock bow, but again he almost lost his balance. He had to bend and adjust his boots. Evidently his feet did not go all the way down; the boots must have been stuffed with something so that he would seem taller. Connie stared out at him and behind him at Ellie in the car, who seemed to be looking off toward Connie's right, into nothing. This Ellie said, pulling the words out of the air one after another as if he were just discovering them, "You want me to pull out the phone?"

"Shut your mouth and keep it shut," Arnold Friend said, his face red from bending over or maybe from embarrassment because Connie had seen his boots. "This ain't none of your business."

"What—what are you doing? What do you want?" Connie said. "If I call the police they'll get you, they'll arrest you—"

"Promise was not to come in unless you touch that phone, and I'll keep that promise," he said. He resumed his erect position and tried to force his shoulders back. He sounded like a hero in a movie, declaring something important. But he spoke too loudly and it was as if he were speaking to someone behind Connie. "I ain't made plans for coming in that house where I don't belong but just for you to come out to me, the way you should. Don't you know who I am?"

"You're crazy," she whispered. She backed away from the door but did not want to go into another part of the house, as if this would give him permission to come through the door. "What do you . . . you're crazy, you. . . ."

"Huh? What're you saying, honey?"

Her eyes darted everywhere in the kitchen. She could not remember what it was, this room.

"This is how it is, honey: you come out and we'll drive away, have a nice ride. But if you don't come out we're gonna wait till your people come home and then they're all going to get it."

"You want that telephone pulled out?" Ellie said. He held the radio away from his ear and grimaced, as if without the radio the air was too much for him.

"I toldja shut up, Ellie," Arnold Friend said, "you're deaf, get a hearing aid, right? Fix yourself up. This little girl's no trouble and's gonna be nice to me, so Ellie keep to yourself, this ain't your date—right? Don't hem in on me, don't hog, don't crush, don't bird dog, don't trail me," he said in a rapid, meaningless voice, as if he were running through all the expressions he'd learned but was no longer sure which of them was in style, then rushing on to new ones, making them up with his eyes closed. "Don't crawl under my fence, don't squeeze in my chipmunk hole, don't sniff my glue, suck my popsicle, keep your own greasy fingers on yourself!" He shaded his eyes and peered in at Connie, who was backed against the kitchen table. "Don't mind him, honey, he's just a creep. He's a dope. Right? I'm the boy for you and like I said, you come out here nice like a lady and give me your hand, and nobody else gets hurt, I mean, your nice old bald-headed daddy and your mummy and your sister in her high heels. Because listen: why bring them in this?"

"Leave me alone," Connie whispered.

"Hey, you know that old woman down the road, the one with the chickens and stuff—you know her?"

"She's dead!"

"Dead? What? You know her?" Arnold Friend said.

"She's dead—"

"Don't you like her?"

"She's dead—she's—she isn't here any more—"

"But don't you like her, I mean, you got something against her? Some grudge or something?" Then his voice dipped as if he were conscious of a rudeness. He touched the sunglasses perched up on top of his head as if to make sure they were still there. "Now, you be a good girl."

"What are you going to do?"

"Just two things, or maybe three," Arnold Friend said. "But I promise it won't last long and you'll like me the way you get to like people you're close to. You will. It's all over for you here, so come on out. You don't want your people in any trouble, do you?"

She turned and bumped against a chair or something, hurting

her leg, but she ran into the back room and picked up the tele-phone. Something roared in her ear, a tiny roaring, and she was so sick with fear that she could do nothing but listen to it—the telephone was clammy and very heavy and her fingers groped down to the dial but were too weak to touch it. She began to scream into the phone, into the roaring. She cried out, she cried for her mother, she felt her breath start jerking back and forth in her lungs as if it were something Arnold Friend was stabbing her with again and again with no tenderness. A noisy sorrowful wail-ing rose all about her and she was locked inside it the way she was locked inside this house.

After a while she could hear again. She was sitting on the floor with her wet back against the wall.

Arnold Friend was saying from the door, "That's a good girl. Put the phone back."

She kicked the phone away from her.

"No, honey. Pick it up. Put it back right."

She picked it up and put it back. The dial tone stopped.

"That's a good girl. Now, you come outside."

She was hollow with what had been fear but what was now just an emptiness. All that screaming had blasted it out of her. She sat, one leg cramped under her, and deep inside her brain was something like a pinpoint of light that kept going and would not let her relax. She thought, I'm not going to see my mother again. She thought, I'm not going to sleep in my bed again. Her bright green blouse was all wet.

Arnold Friend said, in a gentle-loud voice that was like a stage voice, "The place where you came from ain't there any more, and where you had in mind to go is cancelled out. This place you are now—inside your daddy's house—is nothing but a cardboard box I can knock down any time. You know that and always did know it. You hear me?"

She thought, I have got to think. I have got to know what to do.

"We'll go out to a nice field, out in the country here where it smells so nice and it's sunny," Arnold Friend said. "I'll have my arms tight around you so you won't need to try to get away and I'll show you what love is like, what it does. The hell with this house! It looks solid all right," he said. He ran a fingernail down the screen and the noise did not make Connie shiver, as it would have the day before. "Now, put your hand on your heart, honey. Feel that? That feels solid too but we know better. Be nice to me, be sweet like you can because what else is there for a girl like you but to be sweet and pretty and give in?—and get away before her people come back?"

She felt her pounding heart. Her hand seemed to enclose it. She thought for the first time in her life that it was nothing that was hers, that belonged to her, but just a pounding, living thing inside this body that wasn't really hers either.

"You don't want them to get hurt," Arnold Friend went on. "Now, get up, honey. Get up all by yourself."

She stood.

"Now, turn this way. That's right. Come over here to me.— Ellie, put that away, didn't I tell you? You dope. You miserable creepy dope," Arnold Friend said. His words were not angry but only part of an incantation. The incantation was kindly. "Now, come out through the kitchen to me, honey, and let's see a smile, try it, you're a brave, sweet little girl and now they're eating corn and hot dogs cooked to bursting over an outdoor fire, and they don't know one thing about you and never did and honey, you're better than them because not a one of them would have done this for you."

Connie felt the linoleum under her feet; it was cool. She brushed her hair back out of her eyes. Arnold Friend let go of the post tentatively and opened his arms for her, his elbows pointing in toward each other and his wrists limp, to show that this was an embarrassed embrace and a little mocking, he didn't want to make her self-conscious.

She put out her hand against the screen. She watched herself push the door slowly open as if she were back safe somewhere in the other doorway, watching this body and this head of long hair moving out into the sunlight where Arnold Friend waited.

"My sweet little blue-eyed girl," he said in a half-sung sigh that had nothing to do with her brown eyes but was taken up just the same by the vast sunlit reaches of the land behind him and on all sides of him—so much land that Connie had never seen before and did not recognize except to know that she was going to it.

Unmailed, Unwritten Letters

Dear Mother and Father,

The weather is lovely here. It rained yesterday. Today the sky is blue. The trees are changing colors, it is October 20, I have got to buy some new clothes sometime soon, we've changed dentists, doctors, everything is lovely here and I hope the same with you. Greg is working hard as usual. The doctor we took Father to see, that time he hurt his back visiting here, has died and so we must change doctors. Dentists also. I want to change dentists because I can't stand to go back to the same dentist any more. He is too much of a fixed point, a reference point. It is such a chore, changing doctors and dentists.

Why are you so far away in the Southwest? Is there something

about the Southwest that lures old people? Do they see images
there, shapes in the desert? Holy shapes? Why are you not closer
to me, or farther away? In an emergency it would take hours or
days for you to get to me. I think of the two of you in the Southwest, I see the highways going off into space and wonder at your
courage, so late in life, to take on space. Father had all he could
do to manage that big house of yours, and the lawn. Even with
workers to help him it was terrifying, all that space, because he
owned it. Maybe that was why it terrified him, because he owned
it. Out in the Southwest I assume that no one owns anything. Do
people even live there? Some people live there, I know. But I
think of the Southwest as an optical illusion, sunshine and sand
and a mountainous (mountainous?) horizon, with highways perfectly divided by their white center lines, leading off to Mars or
the moon, unhurried. And there are animals, the designs of animals, mashed into the highways! The shape of a dog, a dog's
pelty shadow, mashed into the hot, hot road—in mid-flight, so to
speak, mid-leap, run over again and again by big trucks and re-
tired people seeing America. That vastness would terrify me. I
think of you and I think of protoplasm being drawn off into
space, out there, out in the West, with no human limits to keep it
safe.

Dear Marsha Katz,
    Thank you for the flowers, white flowers, but why that delicate
hint of death, all that fragrance wasted on someone like myself
who is certain to go on living? Why are you pursuing me? Why
in secrecy? (I see all the letters you write to your father, don't
forget; and you never mention me in them.) Even if your father
were my lover, which is not true and cannot be verified, why
should you pursue me? Why did you sign the card with the
flowers *Trixie*? I don't know anyone named Trixie! How could I
know anyone named Trixie? It is a dog's name, a high school

cheerleader's name, an aunt's name . . . why do you play these games, why do you pursue me?

Only ten years old, and too young for evil thoughts—do you look in your precocious heart and see only grit, the remains of things, a crippled shadow of a child? Do you see in all this the defeat of your Daughterliness? Do you understand that a Daughter, like a Mistress, must be feminine or all is lost, must keep up the struggle with the demonic touch of matter-of-fact irony that loses us all our men . . . ? I think you have lost, yes. A ten-year-old cannot compete with a thirty-year-old. Send me all the flowers you want. I pick them apart one by one, getting bits of petals under my fingernails, I throw them out before my husband gets home.

Nor did I eat that box of candies you sent. Signed "Uncle Bumble"!

Are you beginning to feel terror at having lost? Your father and I are not lovers, we hardly see each other any more, since last Wednesday and today is Monday, still you've lost because I gather he plans on continuing the divorce proceedings, long distance, and what exactly can a child do about that . . . ? I see all the letters you write him. No secrets. Your Cape Cod sequence was especially charming. I like what you did with that kitten, the kitten that is found dead on the beach! Ah, you clever little girl, even with your I.Q. of uncharted heights, you couldn't quite conceal from your father and me your attempt to make him think 1) the kitten suggests a little girl, namely you 2) its death suggests your pending, possible death, if Father does not return. Ah, how we laughed over that! . . . Well, no, we didn't laugh, he did not laugh, perhaps he did not even understand the trick you were playing . . . your father can be a careless, abrupt man, but things stick in his mind, you know that and so you write of a little white kitten, alive one day and dead the next, so you send me flowers for a funeral parlor, you keep me in your thoughts

constantly so that I can feel a tug all the way here in Detroit, all
the way from Boston, and I hate it, I hate that invisible pulling,
tugging, that witch's touch of yours. . . .

Dear Greg,

We met about this time years ago. It makes me dizzy, it frightens me to think of that meeting. Did so much happen, and yet
nothing? Miscarriages, three or four, one loses count, and eight
or nine sweet bumbling years—why do I use the word *bumbling*,
it isn't a word I would ever use—and yet there is nothing there, if
I go to your closet and open the door your clothes tell me as much
as you do. You are a good man. A faithful husband. A subdued
and excellent husband. The way you handled my parents alone
would show how good you are, how excellent. . . . My friend
X, the one with the daughter said to be a genius and the wife no
one has ever seen, X couldn't handle my parents, couldn't put up
with my father's talk about principles, the Principles of an
Orderly Universe, which he sincerely believes in though he is an
intelligent man. . . . X couldn't handle anything, anyone. He
loses patience. He is vulgar. He watches himself swerve out of
control but can't stop. Once, returning to his car, we found a
ticket on the windshield. He snatched it and tore it up, very
angry, and then when he saw my surprise he thought to make a
joke of it—pretending to be tearing it with his teeth, a joke. And
he is weak, angry men are weak. He lets me close doors on him.
His face seems to crack with sorrow, but he lets me walk away,
why is he so careless and weak . . . ?

But I am thinking of us, our first meeting. An overheated
apartment, graduate school . . . a girl in dark stockings, myself,
frightened and eager, trying to be charming in a voice that didn't
carry, a man in a baggy sweater, gentle, intelligent, a little perplexed, the two of us gravitating together, fearful of love and
fearful of not loving, of not being loved. . . . So we met. The

evening falls away, years fall away. I count only three miscarriages, really. The fourth a sentimental miscalculation.

My darling,

I am out somewhere, I see a telephone booth on a corner, the
air is windy and too balmy for October. I won't go in the phone
booth. Crushed papers, a beer bottle, a close violent stench. . . .
I walk past it, not thinking of you. I am out of the house so that
you can't call me and so that I need not think of you. Do you talk
to your wife every night, still? Does she weep into your ear? How
many nights have you lain together, you and that woman now
halfway across the country, in Boston, weeping into a telephone?
Have you forgotten all those nights?

Last night I dreamed about you mashed into a highway. More
than dead. I had to wake Greg up, I couldn't stop trembling, I
wanted to tell him of the waste, the waste of joy and love, your
being mashed soundlessly into a road and pounded into a shape
no one would recognize as yours. . . . Your face was gone.
What will happen to me when your face is gone from this world?

I parked the car down here so that I could go shopping at Saks
but I've been walking, I'm almost lost. The streets are dirty. A tin
can lies on the sidewalk, near a vacant lot. Campbell's Tomato
Soup. I am dressed in the suit you like, though it is a little baggy
on me, it would be a surprise for someone driving past to see a
lady in such a suit bend to pick up a tin can. . . . I pick the can
up. The edge is jagged and rusty. No insects inside. Why would
insects be inside, why bother with an empty can? Idly I press the
edge of the lid against my wrist; it isn't sharp, it makes only a fine
white line on my skin, not sharp enough to penetrate the skin.

Dear Greg,

I hear you walking downstairs. You are going outside, out into
the back yard. I am tempted, heart pounding, to run to the win-

dow and spy on you. But everything is tepid, the universe is
dense with molecules, I can't get up. My legs won't move. You
said last night, "The Mayor told me to shut up in front of Arthur
Grant. He told me to shut up." You were amused and hurt at the
same time, while I was furious, wishing you were . . . were
someone else, someone who wouldn't be amused and hurt, a good
man, a subdued man, but someone else who would tell that bastard to go to hell. I am a wife, jealous for her husband.

Three years you've spent working for the Mayor, His Honor,
dodging reporters downtown. Luncheons, sudden trips, press
conferences, conferences with committees from angry parts of
Detroit, all of Detroit angry, white and black, bustling, ominous.
Three years. Now he tells you to shut up. All the lies you told for
him, not knowing how to lie with dignity, he tells you to shut up,
my body suffers as if on the brink of some terrible final expulsion
of our love, some blood-smear of a baby. When a marriage ends,
who is left to understand it? No witnesses. No young girl in
black stockings, no young man, all those witnesses gone, grown
up, moved on, lost.

Too many people know you now, your private life is dwin-
dling. You are dragged back again and again to hearings, commission meetings, secret meetings, desperate meetings, television
interviews, interviews with kids from college newspapers. Everyone has a right to know everything! *What Detroit Has Done to
Combat Slums. What Detroit Has Done To Prevent Riots,* up-
dated to *What Detroit Has Done to Prevent a Recurrence of the
1967 Riot.* You people are rewriting history as fast as history happens. I love you, I suffer for you, I lie here in a paralysis of love,
sorrow, density, idleness, lost in my love for you, my shame for
having betrayed you. . . . Why should slums be combatted?
Once I wept to see photographs of kids playing in garbage heaps,
now I weep at crazy sudden visions of my lover's body become
only a body, I have no tears left for anyone else, for anything
else. Driving in the city I have a sudden vision of my lover

dragged along by a stranger's car, his body somehow caught up under the bumper or the fender and dragged along, bleeding wildly in the street. . . .

My dear husband, betraying you was the most serious act of my life. Far more serious than marrying you. I knew my lover better when he finally became my lover than I knew you when you became my husband. I know him better now than I know you. You and I have lived together for eight years. Smooth coins, coins worn smooth by constant handling. . . . I am a woman trapped in love, in the terror of love. Paralysis of love. Like a great tortoise, trapped in a heavy deathlike shell, a mask of the body pressing the body down to earth. . . . I went for a week without seeing him, an experiment. The experiment failed. No husband can keep his wife's love. So you walk out in the back yard, admiring the leaves, the sky, the flagstone terrace, you are a man whom betrayal would destroy and yet your wife betrayed you, deliberately.

To The Editor:

Anonymously and shyly I want to ask—why are white men so weak, so feeble? The other day I left a friend at his hotel and walked quickly, alone, to my car, and the eyes of black men around me moved onto me with a strange hot perception, seeing everything. They knew, seeing me, what I was. Tension rose through the cracks in the sidewalk. Where are white men who are strong, who see women in this way? The molecules in the air of Detroit are humming. I wish I could take a knife and cut out an important piece of my body, my insides, and hold it up . . . on a street corner, an offering. Then will they let me alone? The black men jostle one another on street corners, out of work and not wanting work, content to stare at me, knowing everything in me, not surprised. My lover, a white man, remains back in the hotel, his head in his hands because I have walked out, but he won't run after me, he won't follow me. *They* follow me. One of them bumped into me, pretending it was an accident. I want to cut up my body, I can't live in this body.

Next door to us a boy is out in his driveway, sitting down, playing a drum. Beating on a drum. Is he crazy? A white boy of about sixteen pounding on a drum. He wants to bring the city down with that drum and I don't blame him. I understand that vicious throbbing.

Dear Marsha Katz,

Thank you for the baby clothes. Keep sending me things, test your imagination. I feel that you are drowning. I sense a tightness in your chest, your throat. Are your eyes leaden with defeat, you ten-year-old wonder? How many lives do children relive at the moment of death?

Dear Mother and Father,

The temperature today is ———. Yesterday at this time, ———. Greg has been very busy as usual with ———, ———, ———. This weekend we must see the ———'s, whom you have met. How is the weather there? How is your vacation? Thank you for the postcard from ———. I had not thought lawns would be green there.

. . . The Mayor will ask all his aides for resignations, signed. Some he will accept and others reject. A kingly man, plump and alcoholic. Divorced. Why can't I tell you about my husband's job, about my life, about anything real? Scandals fall on the head of my husband's boss, reading the paper is torture, yet my husband comes home and talks seriously about the future, about improvements, as if no chaos is waiting. No picketing ADC mothers, no stampede to buy guns, no strangled black babies found in public parks. In the midst of this my husband is clean and untouched, innocent, good. He has dedicated his life to helping others. I love him but cannot stop betraying him, again and again, having reclaimed my life as my own to throw away, to destroy, to lose. My life is my own. I keep on living.

My darling,

It is one-thirty and if you don't call by two, maybe you won't call; I know that you have a seminar from two to four, maybe you won't call; I know that you have a seminar from two to four, maybe you won't call today and everything will end. My heart pounds bitterly, in fear, in anticipation? Your daughter sent me some baby clothes, postmarked Boston. I understand her hatred, but one thing: how much did you tell your wife about me? About my wanting children? You told her you no longer loved her and couldn't live with her, that you loved another woman who could not marry you, but . . . did you tell her this other woman had no children? And what else?

I will get my revenge on you.

I walk through the house in a dream, in a daze. I am sinking slowly through the floor of this expensive house, a married woman in a body grown light as a shell, empty as a shell. My body has no other life in it, only its own. What you discharge in me is not life but despair. I can remember my body having life, holding it. It seemed a trick, a feat that couldn't possibly work: like trying to retain liquid up a reed, turning the reed upside down. The doctor said, "Babies are no trouble. Nothing." But the liquid ran out. All liquid runs out of me. That first week, meeting with you at the Statler, everything ran out of me like blood. I alarmed you, you with your nervous sense of fate, your fear of getting cancer, of having a nervous breakdown. I caused you to say stammering *But what if you get pregnant?* I am not pregnant but I feel a strange tingling of life, a tickling, life at a distance, as if the spirit of your daughter is somehow in me, lodged in me. She sucks at my insides with her pinched jealous lips, wanting blood. My body seeks to discharge her magically.

My dear husband,

I wanted to test being alone. I went downtown to the library, the old library. I walked past the hotel where he and I have met, my lover and I, but we were not meeting today and I was alone, testing myself as a woman alone, a human being alone. The library was filled with old men. Over seventy, dressed in black, with white shirts. Black and white: a reading room of old men, dressed in black and white.

I sat alone at a table. Some of the old men glanced at me. In a dream I began to leaf through a magazine, thinking, *Now I am leafing through a magazine: this is expected.* Why can't I be transformed to something else—to a mask, a shell, a statue? I glance around shyly, trying to gauge the nature of the story I am in. Is it tragic or only sad? The actors in this play all seem to be wearing masks, even I am wearing a mask, I am never naked. My nakedness, with my lover, is a kind of mask—something he sees, something I can't quite believe in. Women who are loved are in perpetual motion, dancing. We dance and men follow to the brink of madness and death, but what of us, the dancers?—when the dancing ends we stand back upon our heels, back upon our heels, dazed and hurt. Beneath the golden cloth on our thighs is flesh, and flesh hurts. Men are not interested in the body, which feels pain, but in the rhythm of the body as it goes about its dance, the body of a woman who cannot stop dancing.

A confession. In Ann Arbor last April, at the symposium, I fell in love with a man. The visiting professor from Boston University—a man with black-rimmed glasses, Jewish, dark-eyed, dark-haired, nervous and arrogant and restless. Drumming his fingers. Smoking too much. (And you, my husband, were sane enough to give up smoking five years ago.) A student stood up in the first row and shouted out something and it was he, my lover, the man who would become my lover, who stood up in turn and shouted something back . . . it all happened so fast, astounding everyone, even the kid who reported for the campus newspaper didn't

catch the exchange. How many men could handle a situation like
that, being wilder and more profane than a heckler? . . . He
was in the group at the party afterward, your friend Bryan's
house. All of you talked at once, excited and angry over the out-
come of the symposium, nervous at the sense of agitation in the
air, the danger, and he and I wandered to the hostess's table,
where food was set out. We made pigs of ourselves, eating. He
picked out the shrimp and I demurely picked out tiny flakes of
dough with miniature asparagus in them. Didn't you notice us?
Didn't you notice this dark-browed man with the glasses that
kept slipping down his nose, with the untidy black hair? We
talked. We ate. I could see in his bony knuckles a hunger that
would never be satisfied. And I, though I think I am starving
slowly to death now, I leaped upon the food as if it were a way of
getting at him, of drawing him into me. We talked. We wandered around the house. He looked out a window, drawing a curtain aside, at the early spring snowfall, falling gently outside, and
he said that he didn't know why he had come to this part of the
country, he was frightened of traveling, of strangers. He said that
he was very tired. He seduced me with the slump of his shoulders. And when he turned back to me we entered another stage
of the evening, having grown nervous and brittle with each
other, the two of us suddenly conscious of being together. My
eyes grew hot and searing. I said carelessly that he must come
over to Detroit sometime, we could have lunch, and he said at
once, "I'd like that very much. . . ." and then paused. Silence.

Later, in the hotel, in the cheap room he rented, he confessed
to me that seeing my face had been an experience for him—did
he believe in love at first sight, after all? Something so childish?
It had been some kind of love, anyway. We talked about our
lives, about his wife, about my husband, and then he swung onto
another subject, talking about his daughter for forty-five minutes
. . . a genius, a ten-year-old prodigy. I am brought low, as-
tounded. I want to cry out to him, *But what about me! Don't stop*

thinking about me! At the age of six his daughter was writing poems, tidy little poems, like Blake's. *Like Blake's? Yes.* At the age of eight she was publishing those poems.

No, I don't want to marry him. I'm not going to marry him. What we do to each other is too violent, I don't want it brought into marriage and domesticated, nor do I want him to see me at unflattering times of the day . . . getting up at three in the morning to be sick, a habit of mine. He drinks too much. He reads about the connection between smoking and death, and turns the page of the newspaper quickly. Superstitious, stubborn. In April he had a sore throat, that was why he spoke so hoarsely on the program . . . but a month later he was no better: "I'm afraid of doctors," he said. This is a brilliant man, the father of a brilliant child? We meet nowhere, at an unimaginative point X, in a hotel room, in the anonymous drafts of air from blowers that never stop blowing, the two of us yearning to be one, in this foreign dimension where anything is possible. Only later, hurrying to my car, do I feel resentment and fury at him . . . why doesn't he buy me anything, why doesn't he get a room for us, something permanent? And hatred for him rises in me in long shuddering surges, overwhelming me. I don't want to marry him. Let me admit the worst—anxious not to fall in love with him, I think of not loving him at the very moment he enters me, I think of him already boarding a plane and disappearing from my life, with relief, I think with pity of human beings and this sickness of theirs, this desire for unity. Why this desire for unity, why? We walk out afterward, into the sunshine or into the smog. Obviously we are lovers. Once I saw O'Leary, from the Highway Commission, he nodded and said a brisk hello to me, ignored my friend; obviously we are lovers, anyone could tell. We walked out in the daylight, looking for you. That day, feverish and aching, we were going to tell you everything. He was going to tell his wife everything. But nothing happened . . . we ended up in a cocktail lounge, we calmed down. The air conditioning calmed us. On the street we passed a Negro holding out pamphlets to other Negroes but drawing them back when whites passed. I saw the headline—*Muslim Killed in Miami Beach by Fascist Police.* A well-dressed Negro woman turned down a pamphlet with a toothy, amused smile—none of that junk for her! My lover didn't even notice.

Because he is not my husband I don't worry about him. I worry about my own husband, whom I own. I don't own this man. I am thirty and he is forty-one; to him I am young—what a laugh. I don't worry about his coughing, his drinking (sometimes over the telephone I can hear ice cubes tinkling in a glass—he drinks to get the courage to call me), his loss of weight, his professional standing. He didn't return to his job in Boston, but stayed on here. A strange move. The department at Michigan considered it a coup to get him, this disintegrating, arrogant man, they were willing to pay him well, a man who has already made enemies there. No, I don't worry about him.

On a television program he was moody and verbose, moody and silent by turns. Smokes too much. Someone asked him about the effect of something on something—Vietnam on the presidential election, I think—and he missed subtleties, he sounded distant, vague. Has lost passion for the truth. He has lost his passion for politics, discovering in himself a passion for me. It isn't my fault. On the street he doesn't notice things, he smiles slowly at me, complimenting me, someone brushes against him and he doesn't notice, what am I doing to this man? Lying in his arms I am inspired to hurt him. I say that we will have to give this up, these meetings; too much risk, shame. What about my husband, what about his wife? (A deliberate insult—I know he doesn't love his wife.) I can see at once that I've hurt him, his face shows everything, and as soon as this registers in both of us I am stunned with the injustice of what I've done to him, I must erase it, cancel it out, undo it; I caress his body in desperation. . . . Again and again. A pattern. What do I know about caressing the bodies of men? I've known only two men in my life. My husband and his successor. I have never wanted to love anyone, the strain and risk are too great, yet I have fallen in love for the second time in my life and this time the sensation is terrifying, bitter, violent. It ends the first cycle, supplants all that love, erases all that affection—destroys everything. I stand back dazed, flat on my heels, the dance being over. I will not move on into another marriage. I will die slowly in ths marriage rather than come to life in another.

Dear Mrs. Katz,
    I received your letter of October 25 and I can only say
    I don't know how to begin this letter except to tell you
    Your letter is here on my desk. I've read it over again and again all morning. It is true, yes, that I have made the acquaintance of a man who is evidently your husband, though he has not spoken of you. We met through mutual friends in Ann Arbor and Detroit. Your informant at the University is obviously trying to upset you, for her own reasons. I assume it is a woman—who else would write you such a letter? I know nothing of your personal affairs. Your husband and I have only met a few times, socially. What do you want from me?
    And your daughter, tell your daughter to let me alone!
    Thank you both for thinking of me. I wish I could be equal to your hatred. But the other day an old associate of my husband's, a bitch of a man, ran into me in the Fisher lobby and said, "What's happened to you—you look terrible! You've lost weight!" He pinched the waist of my dress, drawing it out to show how it hung loose on me, he kept marveling over how thin I am, not releasing me. A balding, pink-faced son of a bitch who has made himself rich by being on the board of supervisors for a country north of here, stuffing himself at the trough. I know all about him. A subpolitician, never elected. But I trust the eyes of these submen, their hot keen perception. Nothing escapes them. "One

month ago," he said, "you were a beautiful woman." Nothing in my life has hurt me as much as that remark, *One month ago you were a beautiful woman. . . .*

Were you ever beautiful? He says not. So he used you, he used you up. That isn't my fault. You say in your letter—thank you for typing it, by the way—that I could never understand your husband, his background of mental instability, his weaknesses, his penchant (your word) for blaming other people for his own faults. Why tell me this? He isn't going to be my husband. I have a husband. Why should I betray my husband for yours, your nervous, guilty, hypochrondriac husband? The first evening we met, believe it or not, he told me about his *hurts*— people who've hurt him deeply! "The higher you go in a career, the more people take after you, wanting to bring you down," he told me. And listen: "The worst hurt of my life was when my first book came out, and an old professor of mine, a man I had idolized at Columbia, reviewed it. He began by saying, *Bombarded as we are by prophecies in the guise of serious historical research* . . . and my heart was broken." We were at a party but apart from the other people, we ate, he drank, we played a game with each other that made my pulse leap, and certainly my pulse leaped to hear a man, a stranger, speak of his heart being broken—where I come from men don't talk like that! I told him a *hurt* of my own, which I've never told anyone before: "The first time my mother saw my husband, she took me aside and said, *Can't you tell him to stand up straighter?* and my heart was broken. . . ."

And so, with those words, I had already committed adultery, betraying my husband to a stranger.

Does he call you every night? I am jealous of those telephone calls. What if he changes his mind and returns to you, what then? When he went to the Chicago convention I'm sure he telephoned you constantly (he telephoned me only three times, the bastard) and joked to you about his fear of going out into the street. "Jesus, what if somebody smashes in my head, there goes my next book!" he said over the phone, but he wasn't kidding me. I began to cry, imagining him beaten up, bloody, far away from me. Why does he joke like that? Does he joke like that with you?

Dear Mother and Father,

My husband Greg is busy with ——————. Doing well. Not fired. Pressure on, pressure off. Played golf with ——————. I went to a new doctor yesterday, a woman. I had made an appointment to go to a man but lost my courage, didn't show up. Better a woman. She examined me, she looked at me critically and said, "Why are you trying to starve yourself?" *To keep myself from feeling love, from feeling lust, from feeling anything at all.* I told her I didn't know I was starving myself. I had no appetite. Food sickened me . . . how could I eat? She gave me a vitamin shot that burned me, like fire. Things good for you burn like fire, shot up into you, no escape. You would not like my lover, you would take me aside and say, *Jews are very brilliant and talented, yes, but.* . . .

I am surviving at half-tempo. A crippled waltz tempo. It is only my faith in the flimsiness of love that keeps me going—I know this will end. I've been waiting for it to end since April, having faith. Love can't last. Even lust can't last. I loved my husband and now I do not love him, we never sleep together, that's through. Since he isn't likely to tell you that, I will.

Lloyd Burt came to see my husband the other day, downtown. Eleven in the morning and already drunk. His kid had been stopped in Grosse Pointe, speeding. The girl with him knocked out on pills. *He* had no pills on him, luckily. Do you remember Lloyd? Do you remember any of us? I am your daughter. Do you regret having had a daughter? I do not regret having no children, not now. Children, more children, children upon children, protoplasm upon protoplasm. . . . Once I thought I couldn't bear to

live without having children, now I can't bear to live at all. I
must be the wife of a man I can't have, I don't even want children from him. I sit here in my room with my head and body
aching with a lust that has become metaphysical and skeptical
and bitter, living on month after month, cells dividing and heat-
ing endlessly. I don't regret having no children. I don't thank you
for having me. No gratitude in me, nothing. No, I feel no gratitude. I can't feel gratitude.

My dear husband,
   I want to tell you everything. I am in a motel room, I've just
taken a bath. How can I keep a straight face telling you this? Sat
in the bathtub for an hour, not awake, not asleep, the water was
very hot. . . .
   I seem to want to tell you something else, about Sally Rodgers.
I am lightheaded, don't be impatient. I met Sally at the airport
this afternoon, she was going to New York, and she saw me with
a man, a stranger to her, the man who is the topic of this letter,
the crucial reason for this letter. . . . Sally came right up to me
and started talking, exclaiming about her bad fortune, her car
had been stolen last week! Then, when she and a friend took her
boat out of the yacht club and docked it at a restaurant on the
Detroit River, she forgot to take the keys out and someone stole
her boat! Twenty thousand dollars' worth of boat, a parting gift
from her ex-husband, pirated away down-river. She wore silver
eyelids, silver stockings, attracting attention not from men but
from small children, who stared. My friend, my lover, did not
approve of her—her clanking jewelry made his eye twitch.
   I am thirty miles from Detroit. In Detroit the multiplication of
things is too brutal, I think it broke me down. Weak, thin,
selfish, a wreck, I have become oblivious to the deaths of other
people. (Robert Kennedy was murdered since I became this
man's mistress, but I had no time to think of him—I put the
thought of his death aside, to think of later. No time now.) Leav-

ing him and walking in Detroit, downtown, on those days we met
to make love, I began to understand what love is. Holding a man
between my thighs, my knees, in my arms, one single man out of
all this multiplication of men, this confusion, this din of human
beings. So it is we choose someone. Someone chooses us. I admit
that if he did not love me so much I couldn't love him. It would
pass. But a woman has no choice, let a man love her and she must
love him, if the man is strong enough. I stopped loving you, I am
a criminal. . . . I see myself sinking again and again beneath
his body, those heavy shoulders with tufts of dark hair on them,
again and again pressing my mouth against his, wanting something from him, betraying you, giving myself up to that throbbing that arises out of my heartbeat and builds to madness and
then subsides again, slowly, to become my ordinary heartbeat
again, the heartbeat of an ordinary body from which divinity has
fled.

Flesh with an insatiable soul. . . .

You would hear in a few weeks, through your innumerable far-
flung cronies, that my lover's daughter almost died of aspirin poison, a ten-year-old girl with an I.Q. of about 200. But she didn't
die. She took aspirin because her father was leaving her, divorc-
ing her mother. The only gratitude I can feel is for her not having died. . . . My lover, whom you hardly know (he's the man
of whom you said that evening, "He certainly can talk!") telephoned me to give me this news, weeping over the phone. A man
weeping. A man weeping turns a woman's heart to stone. I told
him I would drive out at once, I'd take him to the airport. He had
to catch the first plane home and would be on stand-by at the
airport. So I drove to Ann Arbor to get him. I felt that we were
already married and that passion had raced through us and left us
years ago, as soon as I saw him lumbering to the car, a man who
has lost weight in the last few months but who carries himself a
little clumsily, out of absent-mindedness. He wore a dark suit,

rumpled. His necktie pulled away from his throat. A father distraught over his daughter belongs to mythology. . . .

Like married people, like conspirators, like characters in a difficult scene hurrying their lines, uncertain of the meaning of lines . . . "It's very thoughtful of you to do this," he said, and I said, "What else can I do for you? Make telephone calls? Anything?" *Should I go along with you?* So I drive him to the airport. I let him out at the curb, he hesitates, not wanting to go without me. He says, "But aren't you coming in . . . ?" and I see fear in his face. I tell him yes, yes, but I must park the car. This man, so abrupt and insulting in his profession, a master of whining rhetoric, stares at me in bewilderment as if he cannot remember why I have brought him here to let him out at the United Air Lines terminal, why I am eager to drive away. "I can't park here," I tell him sanely, "I'll get a ticket." He respects all minor law; he nods and backs away. It takes me ten minutes to find a parking place. All this time I am sweating in the late October heat, thinking that his daughter is going to win after all, has already won. Shouldn't I just drive home and leave him, put an end to it? A bottle of aspirin was all it took. The tears I might almost shed are not tears of shame or regret but tears of anger—that child has taken my lover from me. That child! I don't cry, I don't allow myself to cry, I drive all the way through a parking lot without finding a place and say to the girl at the booth, who puts her hand out expecting a dime, "But I couldn't find a place! I've driven right through! This isn't fair!" Seeing my hysteria, she relents, opens the gate, lets me through. *Once a beautiful woman,* she is thinking. I try another parking lot.

Inside the terminal, a moment of panic—what if he has already left? Then he hurries to me. I take his arm. He squeezes my hand. Both of us very nervous, agitated. "They told me I can probably make the two-fifteen, can you wait with me?" he says. His face, now so pale, is a handsome man's face gone out of control; a pity to look upon it. In a rush I feel my old love for him, hopeless. I begin to cry. Silently, almost without tears. A girl in a very short skirt passes us with a smile—lovers, at their age! "You're not to blame," he says, very nervous, "she's just a child and didn't know what she was doing—please don't blame yourself! It's my fault—" But a child tried to commit suicide, shouldn't someone cry? I am to blame. She is hurting me across the country. I have tried to expel her from life and she, the baby, the embryo, stirs with a will of her own and chooses death calmly. . . . "But she's going to recover," I say to him for the twentieth time, "isn't she? You're sure of that?" He reassures me. We walk.

The airport is a small city. Outside the plate glass, airplanes rise and sink without effort. Great sucking vacuums of power, enormous wings, windows brilliant with sunlight. We look on unamazed. To us these airplanes are unspectacular. We walk around the little city, walking fast and then slowing down, wandering, holding hands. It is during one of those strange lucky moments that lovers have—he lighting a cigarette—that Sally comes up to us. We are not holding hands at that moment. She talks, bright with attention for my friend, she herself being divorced and not equipped to live without a man. He smiles nervously, ignoring her, watching people hurry by with their luggage. She leaves. We glance at each other, understanding each other. Nothing to say. *My darling!* . . .

Time does not move quickly. I am sweating again, I hope he won't notice, he is staring at me in that way . . . the way that frightens me. I am not equal to your love, I want to tell him. Not equal, not strong enough. I am ashamed. Better for us to say goodby. A child's corpse between us? A few hundred miles away, in Boston, are a woman and a child I have wronged, quite intentionally; aren't these people real? But he stares at me, the magazine covers on a newsstand blur and wink, I feel that everything is becoming a dream and I must get out of here, must escape from him, before it is too late. . . . "I should leave," I tell him. He seems not to hear. He is sick. Not sick; frightened. He shows too much. He takes my hand, caresses it, pleading in silence. A terrible sensation of desire rises in me, surprising me. I don't want to feel desire for him! I don't want to feel it for anyone, I don't want to feel anything at all! I don't want to be drawn to an act of love, or even to think about it; I want freedom, I want the smooth sterility of coins worn out from friendly handling, rubbing together, I want to say good-by to love at the age of thirty, not being strong enough for it. A woman in the act of love feels no joy but only terror, a parody of labor, giving birth. Torture. Heartbeat racing at 160, 180 beats a minute, where is joy in this, what is this deception, this joke. Isn't the body itself a joke?

He leads me somewhere, along a corridor. Doesn't know where he is going. People head toward us with suitcases. A soldier on leave from Vietnam, we don't notice, a Negro woman weeping over another soldier, obviously her son, my lover does not see. A man brushes against me and with exaggerated fear I jump to my lover's side . . . but the man keeps on walking, it is nothing. My lover strokes my damp hand. "You won't. . . . You're not thinking of. . . . What are you thinking of?" he whispers. Everything is open in him, everything. He is not ashamed of the words he says, of his fear, his pleading. No irony in him, this ironic man. And I can hear myself saying that we must put an end to this, it's driving us both crazy and there is no future, nothing ahead of us, but I don't say these words or anything like them. We walk along. I am stunned. I feel a heavy, ugly desire for him, for his body. I want him as I've wanted him many times before, when our lives seemed simpler, when we were both deluded about what we were doing . . . both of us thought, in the beginning, that no one would care if we fell in love . . . not my husband, not his family. I don't know why. Now I want to say good-by to him but nothing comes out, nothing. I am still crying a little. It is not a weapon of mine—it is an admission of defeat. I am not a woman who cries well. Crying is a confession of failure, a giving in. I tell him no, I am not thinking of anything, only of him. I love him. I am not thinking of anything else.

We find ourselves by Gate 10. What meaning has Gate 10 to us? People are lingering by it, obviously a plane has just taken off, a stewardess is shuffling papers together, everything is normal. I sense normality and am drawn to it. We wander on. We come to a doorway, a door held open by a large block of wood. Where does that lead to? A stairway. The stairway is evidently not open. We can see that it leads up to another level, a kind of runway, and though it is not open he takes my hand and leads me to the stairs. In a delirium I follow him, why not? The airport is so crowded that we are alone and anonymous. He kicks the block of wood away, wisely. We are alone. On this stairway— which smells of disinfectant and yet is not very clean—my lover embraces me eagerly, wildly, he kisses me, kisses my damp cheeks, rubs his face against mine. I half-fall, half-sit on the stairs. He begins to groan, or to weep. He presses his face against me, against my breasts, my body. It is like wartime—a battle is going on outside, in the corridor. Hundreds of people! A world of people jostling one another! Here, in a dim stairway, clutching each other, we are oblivious to their deaths. But I want to be good! What have I wanted in my life except to be good? To lead a simple, good, intelligent life? He kisses my knees, my thighs, my stomach. I embrace him against me. Everything has gone wild, I am seared with the desire to be unfaithful to a husband who no longer exists, nothing else matters except this act of unfaithfulness. I feel that I am a character in a story, a plot, who has not understood until now exactly what is going to happen to her. Selfish, eager, we come together and do not breathe, we are good friends and anxious to help each other, I am particularly anxious to help him, my soul is sweated out of me in those two or three minutes that we cling together in love. Then, moving from me, so quickly exhausted, he puts his hands to his face and seems to weep without tears, while I feel my eyelids closing slowly upon the mangled length of my body. . . .

This is a confession but part of it is blacked out. Minutes pass in silence, mysteriously. It is those few minutes that pass after we make love that are most mysterious to me, uncanny. And then we cling to each other again, like people too weak to stand by ourselves; we are sick in our limbs but warm with affection, very good friends, the kind of friends who tell each other only good news. He helps me to my feet. We laugh. Laughter weakens me, he has to hold me, I put my arms firmly around his neck and we kiss, I am ready to give up all my life for him, just to hold him like this. My body is all flesh. There is nothing empty about us, only a close space, what appears to be a stairway in some public place. . . . He draws my hair back from my face, he stares at me. It is obvious that he loves me.

When we return to the public corridor no one has missed us. It is strangely late, after three. This is a surprise, I am really surprised, but my lover is more businesslike and simply asks at the desk—the next plane? to Boston? what chance of his getting on? His skin is almost ruddy with pleasure. I can see what pleasure does to a man. But now I must say good-by, I must leave. He holds my hand. I linger. We talk seriously and quietly in the middle of the great crowded floor about his plans—he will stay in Boston as long as he must, until things are settled; he will see his lawyer; he will talk it over, *talk it over*, with his wife and his daughter, he will not leave until they understand why he has to leave. . . . I want to cry out at him, *Should you come back?* but I can't say anything. Everything in me is a curving to submission, in spite of what you, my husband, have always thought.

Finally . . . he boards a plane at four. I watch him leave. He looks back at me, I wave, the plane taxis out onto the runway and rises . . . no accident, no violent ending. There is nothing violent about us, everything is natural and gentle. Walking along the long corridor I bump into someone, a woman my own age. I am suddenly dizzy. She says, "Are you all right?" I turn away, ashamed. I am on fire! My body is on fire! I feel his semen stirring in my loins, that rush of heat that always makes me pause, staring into the sky or at a wall, at something blank to mirror the blankness in my mind . . . stunned, I feel myself so heavily a body, so lethargic with the aftermath of passion. How did I hope to turn myself into a statue, into the constancy of a soul? No hope. The throbbing in my loins has not yet resolved itself into the throbbing of my heart. A woman does not forget so quickly, nothing lets her forget. I am transparent with heat. I walk on, feeling my heart pound weakly, feeling the moisture between my legs, wondering if I will ever get home. My vision seems blotched. The air—air conditioning—is humming, unreal. It is not alien to me but a part of my own confusion, a long expulsion of my own breath. What do I look like making love? Is my face distorted, am I ugly? Does he see me? Does he judge? Or does he see nothing but beauty, transported in love as I am, helpless?

I can't find the car. Which parking lot? The sun is burning. A man watches me, studies me. I walk fast to show that I know what I'm doing. And if the car is missing, stolen . . . ? I search through my purse, noting how the lining is soiled, ripped. Fifty thousand dollars in the bank and no children and I can't get around to buying a new purse; everything is soiled, ripped, worn out . . . the keys are missing . . . only wadded tissue, a sweetish smell, liquid stiffening on the tissue . . . everything hypnotizes me. . . . I find the keys, my vision swims, I will never get home.

My knees are trembling. There is an ocean of cars here at Metropolitan Airport. Families stride happily to cars, get in, drive away. I wander around, staring. I must find my husband's car in order to get home. . . . I check in my purse again, panicked. No, I haven't lost the keys. I take the keys out of my purse to look at them. The key to the ignition, to the trunk, to the front door of the house. All there. I look around slyly and see, or think

I see, a man watching me. He moves behind a car. He is walking away. My body still throbs from the love of another man, I can't concentrate on a stranger, I lose interest and forget what I am afraid of. . . .

The heat gets worse. Thirty, forty, forty-five minutes pass . . . I have given up looking for the car . . . I am not lost, I am still heading home in my imagination, but I have given up looking for the car. I turn terror into logic. I ascend the stairway to the wire-guarded overpass that leads back to the terminal, walking sensibly, and keep on walking until I come to one of the airport motels. I ask them for a room. A single. Why not? Before I can go home I must bathe, I must get the odor of this man out of me, I must clean myself. I take a room, I close the door to the room behind me; alone, I go to the bathroom and run a tubful of water. . . .

And if he doesn't call me from Boston then all is finished, at an end. What good luck, to be free again and alone, the way I am alone in this marvelous empty motel room! the way I am alone in this bathtub, cleansing myself of him, of every cell of him!

My darling,
    You have made me so happy. . . .

Convalescing

She was a fair young woman in blue, her arms and legs tanned, lean, ready for grappling with the enormous problems of life he had gone blind to, her voice attractively raspy and yet professional, her blond hair pulled back like his wife's, though not so nice as his wife's—she eyed him with a small universal smile and said, "Do you prefer toothpaste or tooth powder?" He thought this over, giving it more thought than he should have. The two of them—the girl, a stranger to him, and the man, a kindly and amused stranger to himself—were standing in his side yard, a handsome green yard well-kept and unthreatening, on a Saturday afternoon when everyone else was out. He wanted to congratulate her on her pretty smile!—did she prefer toothpaste herself?

What was her secret? But her smile was not very pretty, only coaxing, and he had a vision of his wife's quick excited smile, superimposed upon hers; the girl seemed suddenly uninteresting.

"Toothpaste," he said. He did not know if this were true, but it was not quite a lie.

She checked something off on a paper stuck to her clip-board. Yes, her seriousness made her uninteresting. Life was a joke she hadn't caught. "About how many hours a week do you watch television?"

Though he was a *convalescent,* which is to say not an *invalid,* he did not watch television many hours a week. He did not watch television at all. His own catastrophe had been followed by the catastrophe of a leading American politician, and the networks had been crowded with dour fake-reluctant news and old film clips and reports and prophecies he had not wanted to note. In a pleasant stupor he had turned aside, and even "his" record collection did not interest him. It was "his" because he understood that it belonged to him and was the result of many years of collecting, replacing, hunting up of rare records, but he could not really recall these years nor could he recall the pleasure he must have had, sometime, in music or in life.

He smiled with the smile he had learned in imitation of his own smiling face in snapshots. To be polite, he said, "Oh, maybe ten hours a week?"

"Only ten?" The girl was disappointed.

"More like twenty."

"Twenty." She checked something off.

And so, while he fooled around with the hose and cast an admiring eye on the lawn, on the girl, and on the houses across the street with their new coats of paint and their newly sanded brick and their relaxed, welcoming air of approval, the girl went through a litany of mechanical raspy questions: Do you smoke? How many packs a day? Filter-tip or plain? Regular or king-size? Which magazines do you subscribe to? Do you own an American

car? Or two cars? Which makes? Standard or compact? Does
your car have an air conditioner and if not, would you be interested in one? Do you prefer beer in bottles or in cans? Do you
have an automatic can opener? Are you for, against, undecided
concerning the Vietnam war?

The first questions had panicked him because he did not know
the answers. But he was considerate enough not to show panic;
why alarm a young person? The girl was fifteen years younger
than he, not much older than his daughter. So he answered
slowly, seriously, giving the answers he imagined someone with
his name, David Scott, might give, the most pleasant answers to
come out of a house that looked like his—a colonial with a field-
stone front, a neat expensive house—for why disturb the harmony of a fine June day?

After about ten minutes the girl said, "Thank you very much!"

"Did you—have you come to any conclusions?"

"No, we don't come to conclusions." She blushed, holding the
clip-board up to her chest. "I mean, people like myself don't. We
just interview."

"You don't come to any conclusions?" he said, his heart sinking.

"What kind of conclusions did you want?"

"Are the answers at least normal? Convincing?"

The girl eyed him suspiciously, though she was still smiling.
But why disturb the harmony of the day? So he waved her on,
smiling himself to show that this was nothing important, she
should move on, go to the DeLillos' house next door and ask
them about toothpaste—

"Thank you very much," said the girl.

He returned to his lawn work, in a kind of sleep. Such stupor
has its deeper dimensions, its geography, not to be noted on a
chart; he felt safe in his inch or two of grass. He watered some
bushes with his clean green hose. Was this his hose, bought
when? The bushes, planted by another man, the head of another

household, perhaps fictitious, were not really his bushes but only in his keeping until he sold the house to another head of a family anxious to settle down on this good green street. And would he then become fictitious? Or was he fictitious already?

At two-thirty his daughter came home from her cello lesson, the cello in its dusty black case much too big for her. She looked victimized, a refugee from war, trudging along a country road toward some humiliating fate. His daughter, only thirteen. Her name was Eunice, not David's idea of a name for a baby girl, but now she had grown up into a Eunice and dragged her cello off to a music lesson every Saturday, keen and nervous about her music, her scrawny legs, her mother's forgetfulness, her father's vague suffering. She greeted him warmly. He greeted her. "How was it today?" he said, a standard question. Grown more awkward in his gaze, now dragging the case along the ground, she shifted her ninety pounds from one foot to another, pretending to think over his question, a little embarrassed maybe by—by what?—by his new sports shirt, which was too new, or too vivid a yellow?—too sporty for a convalescing man? "Oh, you know, coming along," she said. Her posture was bad, no nagging could improve it. Her legs were certainly too thin. What help could her father give her? He loved her but could not truly believe in this love. Eunice, her smile ironic from too many A's and too little joy, glanced at him with her dreamy dark eyes and seemed to be forgiving him for not loving her, for having forgotten her.

Sad to say, he had forgotten her.

Panic had arisen in him, to think that he had a child. They told him he had a daughter. A wife and a thirteen-year-old daughter. Nothing else? Many other things, they told him, being gentle and wise, speaking in the intonations of civilized men, exactly the intonations he had himself mastered for nearly thirty years, but had somehow forgotten. "Daughter? My daughter? Where, who?" he had cried, hysterical. But that hysteria had passed.

Now he was safe at home, convalescing. He went in to work
two afternoons a week, on the bus, and in a while he would go in
three afternoons. He had forgotten nothing of his work. His
memory for small, meager details had not deserted him, though it
seemed the memory of another man, somehow acquired by him.
He was being drawn back into life like a minor thread, drawn
into a complicated tapestry of vivid, major colors, a tapestry that
would tolerate him. He admired the tapestry and he feared for
his own destiny in it, that thin thread, a slowly strengthening
thread that might come to some destination. . . . In a few
weeks, a few months? When he remembered who he was? When
he woke up to find himself inhabiting his body again, returned to
himself, the *same person* he had been all along?

"Mother isn't back yet?" Eunice said.

"She'll be back soon," he said, glad to feel how all tension, all
concern shifted off onto his wife, his absent wife, and left him
free.

Alone, he felt the new, familiar numbness again. It was his
only emotion and it was not an emotion but the absence of one,
the tingling of nerves in anticipation of an emotion, the regret of
emotion lost, not clearly remembered. He was *in love* with his
wife but it was a condition he could not feel. From a close, intimate distance he admired her, this hurried, forgetful, busy
woman, a very attractive woman whose striking face made her
daughter withdraw out of shyness—a woman with the kind of
face he had always admired from a distance, not hoping to win
her. Yet he had won her. "He" had accomplished it, some fifteen
years ago, but he could not remember how and he could not remember, though he tried desperately, the enormous joy that must
have been his. . . .

She arrived home, in her own car. She smiled and waved to
him and he saw that her hair had been done, in anticipation of
Saturday night, and that she had immense patience and love for
him but no need for him, this sickly quiet man to whom she

found herself married. "I saw Tony Harper downtown," she said, gathering up packages from the back seat of the car, "and he asked after you, he wants us all to get together soon. . . . He didn't look too well himself."

David could not remember Tony Harper except for the name, a certain face, a certain nervous manner. They had gone to law school together at the University of Michigan, but he could not remember Tony Harper. His wife's smile showed that she did not catch on or had no time to catch on; she might have thought his convalescence could be speeded up by ignoring it.

"Where did you park downtown?" he said.

"In a garage, one of those places where you drive around and up onto different levels . . . you know."

He found her confidence astounding. He no longer drove a car; he took a bus, or his wife drove him. But she drove everywhere, downtown in terrible traffic, out to far-flung suburbs to visit women friends, at home on the road, on the telephone, in the two stories and basement of their complicated house. He felt the emptiness in him grow sharper, teased by her strength. He said, "You should be careful in a place like that. Those garages aren't very safe."

"Aren't safe, why not?"

"Someone could follow you up to your car, there aren't any watchmen or guards around. I mean it. You should be more careful."

The packages in her arms were gaily colored—pink, mint green, yellow. They spoke of mysterious silken things, of fragrant things, airy secrets from him. She knew what she wanted. She knew where to buy it. Since his accident he knew nothing. He spoke out of habit, using words automatically; perhaps if he tried to remember which words to use he would stand dumb. Catatonic, turned into a statue. He sensed that fate ahead and tried to dodge it by *taking an interest*. He was interested in the state of his lawn. He was interested in his daughter's music lessons. Friends

were coming over that evening for a quiet evening. An old familiar couple he could nearly remember. Old friends, safe friends.
Nothing alarming. He took an interest in his daughter and in his
wife, whom he feared a little, and he did worry about her parking
in an unattended garage deep in the heart of a hot crowded city.

"I can take care of myself," she said. But her voice sounded
suddenly lame, guilty. She was nearly his height, and he imagined that since the accident he had become shorter. He had lost
weight until his ribs showed and no doubt he had lost some
inches also, why not? Anything was possible. His lovely wife,
whom he had courted and won in the guise of another, younger,
more joyful self, now stood staring gloomily at him and must
have noticed the contrast between his bony, accusing face and
the healthy Saturday sunlight.

"It isn't always just a woman's purse they want," he said, as if
trying to break through his own numbness. "Sometimes there are
a bunch of them, no more than kids, and down there nobody will
bother coming if you scream for help. Oh, they'll come after a
while, after somebody tells a policeman, but by then it would be
too late. . . ."

"I'll be more careful," she said.

"Yes, please. Be more careful."

II

Look, look at that! An automobile is speeding along just under
the legal speed limit, on an expressway, at five-twenty on a
Wednesday afternoon in spring. The automobile is black and expensive but not outstanding. In four lanes of sparkling traffic it
does not especially catch the eye. Cars and trucks of all sizes,
trucks loaded down with evergreen snippings and dismembered
trees, trucks loaded with other trucks, great trucks hauling great
vans, bright blue, with *Chrysler Corporation* on their sides—all

rushing along with certain destinations, unswerving. At four minutes from the point of collision, point X, the black car is held in firm control by its driver, a man with thinning dark hair and a pleasant, undistinguished face, his brain taking in without excitement the various familiar sights of this expressway, billboards and embankments littered with paper and other trash, and in the sleepy dense sky contrails of jets appear—these lines of white smoke in the sky please him. What do they mean? The day hasn't been too bad, he is not exactly exhausted. Not worried. At the back of his mind something is trying to open and spread its wings, but the pain would be too great and he fights it down. He is not worried. He knows exactly how to drive this expressway, when to get into the right lane and when to exit.

A shape of black, softer than smoke but then hardening to something brittle, like a crow's wings—he fights it down, he does not acknowledge it.

At five twenty-one he passes the Cooley Avenue overpass, speeding into its shadow and out of its shadow, hardly aware of it, and at five twenty-two his attention is caught by a stalled car on the shoulder of the expressway, an angry-looking rusty car with rear fenders shaped into fins. An impulse of sympathy for the car's owner—who is nowhere around. Then the sympathy fades, he has driven past, on his way home and certain of his destination. He makes his way through the slightly smutty air, crashing through it with his heavy, expensive car, cleaving a way through with the ease of a hand turned sideways to make a casual gesture in the air—and the time, he notes, is now five twenty-three on the Goodyear Tire clock—and he imagines whimsically that somewhere in this city someone is thinking, maybe in the Adventure Lounge that looks sadly down upon the expressway onto point X, someone is thinking sullenly *I wish to hell they would burn this city down* because there is too much gravity in the city, too much noise, the planet is bloodstained and weary with cataclysms, especially in this city. A few hundred feet from point X a blue automobile with fins appears, leaping to life in the sunlight. Out of nowhere? The driver of the black car notices it, but only casually, since so many objects leap forward into one's attention in the space of only one minute—

All the rest is fiction, not remembered.

It became fiction because it was told to David, explained to him; he believed it the way he believed in the reality of Napoleon, Christ, Julius Caesar; the way he believed in the reality of impoverished Ozark families photographed for *Life Magazine;* the way he believed in his grandparents' parents, people who must have existed but were out of sight, X's that had to be postulated and accepted on faith. It was a more solid form of fiction than the fiction of novels and legends, but not much more solid.

What is missing, then? A point of view.

What is tragically missing? A personality. That is, a soul.

What happened at point X, that mysterious point X? If he made the trip back to that spot he would see nothing much. The Adventure Lounge, blocked off by the expressway and on a dead-end street, looks down upon the site but looks down without commitment. No witnesses to the accident. Hundreds of eyes but no witnesses. On the other side there is the usual wire fence, with dozens of yellowed newspaper pages flattened against it, and beyond the fence another street, and beyond that some vacated stores—nothing, no witnesses. It could not have been said that David himself was a witness. He witnessed nothing. So if he returned he would remember nothing, all the evidence has been cleared away and swept up. Traffic rushed past five minutes later. It rushed past two minutes later. In fact, except in the two lanes that were affected, traffic did not stop at all, but only slowed down. The planet flowed, the minute hand on the Goodyear Tire clock made its determined leap, a black car and a blue car swept together with a terrible grace as if decades of planning had led them to this impact, two minor threads in a mad, brilliant tapestry come together at last for a trivial climax. The cars slammed together, side to side, they shook, shuddered, gave way, came apart . . . and then what happened?

Was it an ordinary accident, with ordinary blood?

He did not want to force the accident out of his memory because he thought that might be dangerous. Repression was dangerous. So he tried to remember it. He knew he had had an accident—a fractured skull, broken ribs, multiple lacerations, wounds, scratches. These things had happened to *his own body*. He knew also that for twenty minutes, recorded faithfully on the Goodyear Tire clock, he had lain in the wreckage of his car, not unconscious, groaning aloud for help, probably, and no help had come. The other driver had died at once. Better not to think of that. But David had not died and had lain bleeding for twenty minutes in the hot searing metal of his car, among the expensive smashed gadgets and ripped upholstery, while traffic went on by. Yet he did not truly remember those twenty minutes.

People said, "My God, what a scandal! Twenty minutes!" and other people said, by way of explanation, "There must have been a communication breakdown." But these remarks did not mean anything. He could not remember those twenty minutes of agony and so, in a sense, they did not exist. But in those twenty minutes he had evidently died.

He thought about the accident, the "twenty minutes," trying to remember. He could not remember. Something blocked him off. He thought of himself as a character in a story, trying to remember himself in order to come alive. How to get out of this fiction? How to remember himself? What must he do to be saved?

III

In the hospital his wife came to him shyly. She had a criminal's anxiety to please, an expert liar's love of lying. He had forgotten her but, seeing her, some dim alarming recollection set him right. A lovely woman, a woman to be won. She looked at him and might have imagined him as he had been, before the accident, though the accident had not really damaged his face— slightly coarse skin now rather pale, dark, deep eyes, prominent eyebrows, dark hair grown a little thin at the crown and the temples—yes, her husband—but he looked back at her with no more than polite recognition. They talked about the house, about home. About Eunice. About friends, his work, whether his mother should be told. (Senile, she had forgotten him and he could not feel guilt at having forgotten her—an aged woman in an expensive nursing home.)

On the day before his release she had said, "So you'll be coming home tomorrow?"

He had felt panic at once.

"Home?"

"Yes, tomorrow, you'll be coming home tomorrow . . . ?"

"Yes."

"I'm so glad."

They had stared uneasily at each other. He said her name to himself, *Elaine,* but he could not believe in it. He knew that they had been married for nearly fifteen years, that they had a daughter whom they loved in the way in which daughters are loved, that they had lain together for years of darkness, sometimes asleep and sometimes awake, *in love,* thinking of their love or of other, quite ordinary things, harmlessly . . . but he could not quite believe it.

His own name was *David Scott.* The identification bracelet he wore, made up of beads, told him that and would not let him forget.

And so, back home, he lay upstairs in the handsome big bedroom, getting back his strength. Somewhere "his" strength existed, to be won back. He was resting. Convalescing. He could certainly remember this bedroom, but he had the idea he'd seen it in a movie or in a photograph. While Elaine chattered to him in the sure, friendly, impersonal tone of a hospital nurse, nudging him back to health, he answered her in the way a husband might, recovering from some terrible shock to his body and soul. But a certain blankness in him could not escape her, could it?— was she pretending? He asked to see the photograph album and for days looked at old snapshots, clever enough to know that he had to relearn everything. He stared at the pictures of a man said to be himself. He knew the man was himself because of the scribbled notations on the backs of the pictures, in Elaine's half-familiar handwriting, *David June 1958 . . . David Fall '61 . . . David, David, David. . . .* More interesting to him were snapshots of Eunice, growing up. A handful of snapshots, flicked, would show a girl growing up jerkily, unwillingly, forced into growth by the terrible mechanism of muscles and bones. And more interesting than these were the snapshots of Elaine, that charming woman, Elaine playing tennis with a friend, Elaine in her dark bathing suit (she did not bother noting her own name on the backs of such snapshots: certain of her own identity, it was enough for her to write *Nantucket Summer '66*), and occasionally *Elaine with David,* wife and husband.

From these snapshots he judged himself to have been a pleasant, kindly man, well liked by family and friends. The friends in the snapshots changed gradually, their places taken by other friends, but they all looked like pleasant, kindly people. He was grateful for them. Though they did not lift him out of his sleep, he had the hope that someday they would, just as Elaine would, bringing him back to life. . . .

She had awakened him once. One morning, quite casually, he remembered a conversation he'd had with her a month or so before, before the accident. He had come home for some papers, just after lunch, and while looking through his desk drawers he'd glanced out to see her hurrying into the house. Her spring coat was unbuttoned, her hair a little blown, but her face was lustrous, radiant, a face she no longer showed to him—and he had known, suddenly, that she was in love. He went downstairs. She opened the door with her own key and he stood there, in the dim back hallway, quietly waiting for her to enter, fearful of her happiness. She had been quite surprised to see him. He had wanted to get out, escape, but something made him linger. . . . She talked him into having a cup of coffee, she was so energetic and nervous and happy that he dared not contradict her; so they sat in the kitchen and she told him.

"I can't help it, I've fallen in love. I didn't want it to happen," she said.

He felt faint, though he had guessed her secret. He could not speak.

"Please don't hate me, what can I do?" she said. Her breath was rapid and sweet. In her glowing health, in the daring of her body and face, she had strength that he no longer had—she had his name, she had everything in their marriage, and something secret beside, something that went beyond all that he could offer her. She had gone beyond him, outlived him.

"What do you want to do?" he had asked, suddenly afraid.

"I have to marry him. Can't I—can't we— Is it too awful? You don't want me now anyway, do you, after this?—won't you want to divorce me?"

"Is that what you want?"

"I don't know what I want. Please don't hate me. Yes, I want to marry him, I can't do anything about my feelings. I can't help myself."

He had sat staring toward her, appalled and numb. She did not seem familiar to him. Her rapid, fluttery voice—her nervous hands, lighting a cigarette—her flushed cheeks and brilliant eyes that indicated how beautiful she was elsewhere, made beautiful by someone else's existence—these things were a shock to him, the features of a stranger. She was a woman he could never win. Drawn to her, at a party, he might engage her in ordinary conversation for a few minutes and get her to smile that charming smile, but he could never hold her.

"Who is it?" he said.

"I don't want to tell you yet. Please. Can you understand?"

"Is he married? Do I know him?"

"Yes, you know him very well, and he's married—yes—he has children—I'm sorry—I don't know how it happened but we can't change anything; we've waited and thought about this for almost a year but there's nothing we can do, we love each other. I can't explain except by coming back again and again to that—"

"You're in love, I understand. I think I understand," he said slowly.

"Do you hate me?"

"No."

"But what—what do you feel? What do you feel?" And she stared at him as if really seeing him for the first time, alarmed at his silence.

"I don't feel anything," he said. What was strange was that her disclosure seemed more than personal, more than private—it was like a door suddenly opening to show him the unsettled landscape of the world, something beyond his control and indifferent to him, knowing no laws, opaque and mysterious and terrifying.

Two days later, on a Wednesday afternoon, he had had his "accident."

Now he spoke to her gravely of parking downtown, of being cautious. "You know how people in trouble are ignored," he said, drawing upon his own trouble to bully her into submission, into a look of guilt. Dressed for Saturday shopping, long-legged and lively, she had been cowed by something dark in his eye and he wondered if she was recalling that conversation, that unforgotten conversation, and whether she knew that he remembered everything or whether she knew nothing, absolutely innocent in her own honesty. She would never bring the subject up again, he felt sure. He was safe in her kindliness. But she was so frank and honest herself. In conversations with friends she would say, *But I myself, I have to fight prejudice in myself,* or she would say, though such a remark was unpleasant, *I really don't agree with you.* . . . David, made complex and subtle by his years of training, never committed himself clearly to one side or another, reluctant to take a stand and not sure of the wisdom of taking a stand. Why?

He took some of her packages from her and they went into the house, into the kitchen. Eunice was there, drinking a glass of milk. Elaine complained about Eunice's untidy room, and about the lateness of the hour, and with her deft quick fingers she brushed strands of hair back out of her eyes. "Did anyone call or stop by?" she asked. David had heard the telephone ring, that was true, but hadn't had the energy to answer it. So he told her only, "Yes, somebody stopped by, just a girl interviewer for a marketing survey. She asked me various questions like 'Do you have an automatic can opener?' "

"And what did you answer?" Elaine said, teasing.

"I said yes."

She laughed and went to the sink, where the automatic can opener was fastened to the wall. "Yes, here it is, you remembered —but we never use it. It's broken."

"I remembered it very clearly," he said with a fake, strained smile.

"And in this drawer," she said, opening a drawer, "we have a collection of can openers—this gadget here, which is broken, and this one here, which I bought only the other week, and this old-fashioned thing—here—and even this grimy bottle opener, the handiest of all for opening bottles." She showed him a small rusted bottle opener, three or four inches long. He could remember none of these things, but their shapes intrigued him. Just such things—bottle and can openers of all makes, simple and ingenious, broken, rusted, new, guaranteed, unused, hand-run or automatic—such things were the property of homeowners up and down the block, everywhere in this lovely green neighborhood, everywhere in the country. Their kitchen junk drawer itself, cluttered with such innocent objects, was American and proved that he was a normal American because he owned it.

"I'm glad you remembered," Elaine said.

She had come home safely, she had returned. Safe from downtown, safe from the expressway and its dangers—home to him and her daughter, home to keep them safe. He felt an enlargement of his numbness, suddenly, to think of her lost to him. It was like a sack of compressed cold air, this numbness, in a space just beneath his heart. It was perhaps the space in which his soul had resided, when he had had a soul.

IV

"So now they have assassination flags for sale, special flags," their friend Taylor was saying. "They can be lowered on a string to half-mast, that's their unique value. I saw them for sale in the discount drugstore." Taylor had an ironic, helpless smirk, his intellectual smirk; he used it when talking about ironic and helpless things, like the assassinations of American leaders or the fate of the middle class. He himself was in real estate, a business his father had left him, and he was watching it dwindle in his grasp, shrink unaccountably in spite of his superior brains and good looks. His wife, maternal and tolerant, watched him with her usual smile; she was a solid woman, as Elaine liked to say in lackluster defense of her, a sensible woman and just the wife for Taylor. Withdrawn slightly, David listened to everything that was said. He made an attempt to listen to things that were not said, but he could not decipher them. Taylor and Brenda MacIntyre were old friends of theirs, going back a decade to simpler and warmer times, when David had been on the way up and Taylor not yet on the way down. Between Elaine and Brenda there was a kind of friendship, mysterious like the friendships of all women with women—what had they in common, Brenda with her bland smile, Elaine with her alert, quizzical look?

"Civilization is coming to an end maybe," Elaine said. "People can't always be wrong about predicting the end. There have been final generations, the very end of epochs, and there must have been—there must be—individuals who are the last survivors of their worlds—isn't that plausible?"

They laughed at her seriousness, but she did not release them. She fixed Taylor with an accusing look so that David wondered, for an instant, whether he was the one—then he rejected this thought, Taylor was too obvious—and said, "No one wants to think about the end. People want to talk about it for conversation. But no one is prepared for a real ending because they haven't done anything yet, they're still waiting. . . ."

"Waiting for what?" Brenda said.

"To live. To wake up. They can't admit that their lives are coming to an end when they haven't yet lived."

Though the living room was large, they were sitting close together. Elaine's manner was slightly aggressive, argumentative, intimate, her long legs tucked under her, strangely feminine and persistent at the same time; she looked younger than thirty-four. David understood that he was not talking enough. He had to be intimate with these people, he had to draw them all together, be in harmony with them. His friends—and he was willing to call them friends and be grateful for their existence—would speak of him the next day to other friends, saying, *David still isn't well; I worry about him.* He finished his drink. Did he drink too much, or not enough? Would they wonder why he wasn't drinking as much as he had previously, the old, lively, cuckolded David, or would they wonder why he was drinking so much? He thought idly of people gossiping about him, secretaries at his office, his partners, his partners' wives, his friends—with nothing better to do than to gossip about him, marveling at the seams in his personality, glued together, patched up, a stand-in for the other David and not convincing. Now Brenda and Taylor were talking heatedly. Brenda was talking and Taylor was trying to wrench the conversation away from her.

"No, please, let me tell Elaine," Brenda was saying, "she has a daughter herself and she knows—"

"Why the hell are you bringing this up?"

"Elaine and David can give us advice. I don't care who knows. I don't have secrets." Brenda leaned forward to entrust her secret to Elaine, who would certainly run out and tell everyone the next morning. . . . "It's Judy. She got caught shoplifting. I had to go down to the store, Steinboch's, and talk with the manager. How do you like that? Fifteen years old and she has an allowance, and she goes out and steals."

"What did she steal?" Elaine asked.

"It doesn't matter what she stole," Taylor said.

"She took some stockings. But only because they were out on the counter, she would have taken anything. She told me," Brenda said. The hour was late. She had a slightly self-righteous, smug, drunken smile; David wondered suddenly if perhaps he had never seen this woman before, really. It might be that they were all strangers. Watching her, alarmed at her admission of so private a secret, he wondered also whether he ought to escape. Before it was too late and too many secrets were told, so that the four of them would be bound together for eternity. . . .

"I'm very sorry to hear that," Elaine said.

"Yes, that's . . . that's bad news," David said.

"Well, it's happening. Not just Judy. It's happening all over and nobody knows what to do."

"What did you do?" Elaine asked.

"I told you, nobody knows what to do. I talked to her. She said she wouldn't do it again, that's what she said. I chose to believe her, so did Taylor. What else can you do?"

"With Eunice something different came up," Elaine said, and

David dreaded hearing what might come next—he did not remember anything coming up about her, any trouble. "She went
to a birthday party for a friend of hers, and about ten other girls
were invited. She left her purse with her coat, upstairs in the
girl's bedroom. Then, when she went to go home, she found that
someone had taken her money—took the money out of her billfold. But she was afraid to say anything to the girl or her mother
because—because she was afraid—"

"Of what?" said Taylor.

"Of never being asked back again, I think."

"What? Really?"

"Or afraid of losing her friends. Afraid of complaining at all,
making any fuss," Elaine said. She looked so stricken, so ashamed
of her daughter and weary over such daughterly weaknesses, that
Taylor reached over to stroke her hand. In this instant David was
reminded of his wife's lover, her secret, second husband, a more
satisfying and demanding man than David himself.

"Well—don't forget when you were that age," Brenda said.

Taylor brought Elaine's hand up to his lips and kissed it.
"You're so demanding. It's you who demand too much of people,
you," he said fondly.

David saw them through a kind of mist, these people in a photograph, people who had had a hand in his fate. Through them
he might know himself. But the way into knowing himself had
something to do also with the coming together of two cars, of tons
of steel, the pulsating pain of twenty minutes' wait on the shoulder of an expressway and an hour's wait in the emergency ward
of a noisy hospital—it had too much to do with knowing his
daughter and her precocious failure, her cowardice that was his
own cowardice, inherited. He thought of his wife in the kitchen,
weeks ago, through the excitement of her words reliving an exquisite passion he could never again evoke in her. He pressed his
hands against his forehead, baffled by the mystery of personality.
Who were these people? Who was this woman, that she had

come to mean so much to him? It was not just his own soul that was opaque, lost, but the souls of people he loved and had believed he knew, had trusted. . . . And, beyond them, the shadowy souls of people known to him only over the television screen or in newspaper photographs, the famous and notorious, monumental figures, shadowy nubs of being as mysterious to him as his own past.

"I read in a magazine about these teen-age clubs in, where was it, Sacramento," Brenda said in a shocked, hushed voice, as if teen-agers might be listening, "and my God you wouldn't believe—"

David got up. With a gesture he indicated that he was going to refill his drink. "Here, take mine," Taylor said. David took it and went out to the kitchen, a partly familiar room, safe. He sat down. Then, nervous, he got up and walked beside the very clean, clean counter, running his knuckles along it. He wondered in a daze who he was and to whose country he had come. It was true that he was married—there was a certificate to prove it—and he did own this house, he had ten thousand dollars yet to pay on the mortgage—and he had contributed toward bringing another person into the world, though he hadn't the slightest knowledge of what that meant—and so—and so it was certain that he had a specific identity. But the identity was empty, numb. His body was paralyzed as if by a dentist's giant needle, expelling forgetfulness and silence into his spine.

He studied the spices in Elaine's spice rack. For a while she had taken cooking lessons—she'd been domestic for years, then switched to outward, intellectual, humanistic interests like integration and voting reform—and she had collected a number of spices, all in identical green jars, *parsley, oregano, clove, ginger, sweet basil, nutmeg,* even *white pepper,* even *saffron*— Inside his body he felt something straining to open itself, to spread its wings. Its muscles ached for freedom. He leaned against the counter and gripped his skull. He was going mad. The slowness of his bones was driving him mad. Kennedy had been assassinated just the other day, the second Kennedy, shot in the back of the skull and killed, and David's own life made no more sense than that death. Yet he had the glancing notion that he might have pulled the trigger himself, granted a certain immunity. Granted safety, invisibility. . . .

On the counter, lying on the clean-wiped counter, was the bottle opener Elaine had held up to him that afternoon, as if showing him something important. He picked it up. Bottle caps were scattered around it, from bottles of bitter lemon. This bottle opener was the cheapest kind, sold for a nickel or given away for advertising purposes . . . it had rusted and only part of its legend was readable: *Hamm's—from the land of sky blue waters.* The opener was very sharp at one point; David tested it on his thumb. Very sharp. It should have been enough to wake him. He pressed the point against his wrist, thinking. For all of his life he had been certain of himself, beginning with his name; nothing had escaped him. And yet everything had escaped him. He had felt certain emotions—love and hate—and had been swept along in violence by these emotions, purified by them like his wife Elaine, justified by them as the assassin of Kennedy and the assassins of other men are justified by emotions. But it had all been without meaning. The emotions faded, the events could not be remembered—and where, in such a puzzle, was a fixed point? He stared at the dingy little bottle opener and wondered if so meager an object might have a soul of its own, a center of gravity firmly fixed and measurable.

"What's wrong? What are you doing?"

Elaine stood staring at him. She was nervous, her voice uneasy. He saw that her clear, handsome brow was damp with droplets of worry—from the tense discussion of daughters or worry over this strange husband? She was looking at the can opener in his hand. Perhaps she thought he was holding it as a weapon, imagining it as a weapon?—perhaps he was contemplating a sudden surprise for her, raking the point down across the skin of her cheek?

He shivered, thinking of that.

"What are you doing out here? I've been waiting for you to come back—I didn't think you felt well—"

She put her hand on his arm.

Again he thought of the can opener, its sharp little point. . . .

"Please, please don't be sick," she said. She looked into his face. For a moment he remained rigid, secretive in thought. Then he pressed his hands against his forehead.

"You won't leave me?" he said.

"No."

"You'll never leave me?" He was sweating.

She put her arms around him. "I'll never leave you. Please don't think of it." She spoke gently and yet with an air of certainty, as if making a public vow, a vow of commitment and energy. He was weak with relief but he felt no shame, nothing. Emotions faded. Events could not be remembered. Perhaps his wife had not committed adultery, perhaps he had imagined everything? He was still a convalescent and people must treat him with gentleness.

Shame

Much change here? No, not much. He had been worried about that, but really there was little sign of change. Things were older, houses looked meeker, stores were crowded absurdly together along this familiar block. He felt a little perplexed, coming back here, as if he had been presented a gift he could not understand.

At one time this neighborhood had been his entire world, bounded on the north by the tire factory and its great, dangerous parking lots, and on the east by Grand Boulevard, and on the west by Lincoln Park; the southern end of the neighborhood just dwindled off into a twilight of street after street of ordinary shabby houses. Much of the neighborhood was now occupied by Negro families but still things looked the same. He stood on the sidewalk where the bus had left him, staring with a foolish fondness at the old grocery store. Its interior looked murky as always, but detailed and promising, and "Salada Tea" on the window had the same trim white letters as always, the word "Salada" arranged in a semicircle above the word "Tea." Good, that was the same. He was pleased. And the gas station at the corner, not much different, with three or four old cars in its weedy grease-splattered side lot; they looked like the same old cars he had played in as a child, in that very lot.

He seemed at first to see no people at all, only the street and the buildings. It was important that he see them and understand what they were. But gradually, as if awakening, he noticed crowds of school children and women with babies and men in baggy trousers, old men who were a sign of big cities: they wandered along the sidewalks to Lincoln Park, where they played cards all day long, arguing with one another in languages—Polish? Hungarian?—no one else could understand. The school children were in a hurry and noisy. They reminded him of his classmates years ago, who had always seemed to know where they were going, who had the noise and bustle of adults. He glanced at the young women with their babies, wondering if they were the girls of his childhood now grown up and married and, like him, committed to another life; he was a little shy before their smiles. Smiles were frequent in his life, not because anyone recognized him but because he was a priest. Wearing the collar and the black suit did it, it was a complete transformation, and it pleased him because he was able to learn tenderness from the smiles of such people and that was good. His name was Andrew Rollins but he was called Father Rollins and sometimes just "Father," which was a magical name, and he felt complicated in coming back here. His life was a clutter of events that had somehow marked him for success in the competitive life he had chosen. This neighborhood looked untouched by complications. Time must have rushed through it, generations after generations, and yet the buildings still faced one another in that resigned, hunched way, and the thirteen-year-old girls with long swinging hair who passed giggling by him seemed the same girls he had known twenty years before.

The address he wanted was not far from the corner. It was a nondescript house with a wide, sagging veranda spanning its front. After ringing the doorbell a few times, he knocked. He knew someone was inside because he could hear a child crying and another sputtery noise, probably a television set.

The curtain at the door window was moved suspiciously aside and a woman of about forty squinted out at him. Then she opened the door quickly. "Yes, hello?" she said. She stood flat-footed in bedroom slippers, a messy, hopeful woman. "What did you want, Father?"

"Does Frank Taylor live here? I have this address—"

"Frank Taylor, oh, him—they moved away— I mean she moved away, his wife—" The woman stared at Andrew with a look of alarm and pity. She was very confused. "I'm terrible sorry to tell you this, Father, if you're a friend of his or a relative or something, but Frank is dead. I mean, he died, he had a accident, he's dead. . . ."

"Dead?"

"Yes, dead. He died," she said, shaking her head.

Andrew stepped back. "But when did it happen? I hadn't heard about it. . . ."

"Oh, a few months ago, I don't know, it was real terrible—the two of them like that—I'm a friend of her mother's, I mean Frank's wife, her mother. I'm a friend of her mother's and I moved right in here when Toni—that's the wife, you know her —when she didn't want to stay here— I moved in, it was real convenient for me—"

"He's dead?"

"I'm awful sorry, Father, were you a friend of his?"

"Yes, but we were out of touch. . . ."

"He was a real nice boy. I'm sorry. I just don't know what to say," she said, looking up at him as if he had to think of something, had to make things right. As a priest he was always being tossed things, even in the midst of his own private grief, burdened with clumsiness and pain he had to make right through magic words.

"I'm sorry to have troubled you," he said shakily.

"If you want Toni's address, it's right down the street here—"

He had never met Frank's wife and her name offended him. "Toni" was a name that made death seem cheap.

"I don't want to bother her."

"Oh, it's no bother, she'd like to talk to you. I know she'd like to talk to you, Father. It would be good for her," the woman said with a sharp downward twist of her lips, which Andrew interpreted as: the girl has stopped going to church. Or, the girl is getting into trouble. "Her mother don't live up here now and she'd be real glad if you went. I know that."

"How did Frank die?"

The question was too blunt and he regretted having asked it. The woman, confused, muttered something about a car accident, two cars. She flinched away from that topic and latched onto the female topic, the wife, who was just down the street. And so he finally agreed to see the wife. The woman would have talked on but he backed away, smiling, polite, thanking her and saying good-by. Good-by. Her solid, sloppy, friendly body reminded him of his mother and his mother's world of female friends and relatives; he felt a kind of affection for her.

Out on the sidewalk, he was in the midst of a sudden gang of children. They rushed around him, on either side, and ran past and did not touch him. Their hard stamping feet and their cries mixed with the clamor in his head.

Frank had died?

Frank was his own age and had been his closest friend for many years, at a time in Andrew's life when he had needed a friend and had not understood what his life was to be. Frank's role in his life was magical; it was hard to explain how closely they were related, though for years they had had little in common and Frank had never answered Andrew's last several letters. . . . They had been friends as children and as young teenagers and in a way they were closer than brothers; Andrew was sure that he had loved Frank more than he would have loved any brother of his own.

Disturbed, he walked down the street. His legs felt weak. The neighborhood did not seem so familiar and friendly now. It was a great shock to him that Frank was dead. The fact that he would not see Frank but only hear of him from other people, from strangers, was a puzzling fact. He felt a surge of anger, as if he had been cheated.

He arrived at the old mustard-yellow apartment building and stood out front for a while, thinking, a tall, lean priest with a look of being lost. This apartment building was a familiar landmark; he remembered its ugly bulk from childhood. Hadn't the kids had some vulgar name for it? The desire to go inside had left him completely. A woman with a full shopping bag passed by him on her way in and said, "Hello, Father."

His head ached slightly, as if he had been studying too much or thinking too much of hopeless things. He did not want to see this wife of Frank's, this widow—he had never met her, knew nothing about her—and so he had to go in, for he never let himself off easily. He climbed up the three flights of stairs, sensing how fatally he was being drawn back to this neighborhood, back to the smells and noises and faces he had left behind; it was no oddity being back, nothing to enjoy, but only a burden. What vulgar name had the kids made up for this building? He could not remember it and was disturbed at his inability to remember.

The door was opened quickly upon his knock and a woman stared out at him, not speaking. He said, "I was a friend of Frank's. Your husband?"

Despite the gentleness of his voice, the woman looked frightened. A blast of music behind her must have confused her
thoughts. She said finally, "You heard what happened?"

"I was just told that he had died. Just now."

"You want to come in?"

She was thin and banally pretty; her voice had no depth to it
but sounded like another voice from the radio. She stood aside
awkwardly and he entered, prepared for the cramped living room
and its bargain-basement furniture, the quilt fixed primly over
the back of the sofa, the remnant rugs in doorways to protect the
ugly brown rug beneath. Familiar, familiar. Andrew felt absurdly
sorry for both himself and this woman.

"So you were Frank's friend? You're Andrew?" she said nervously. "He talked about you a lot, he liked you." She paused and
shot a shy, inquisitive look at him. "What kind of priest are you?
—I can't remember."

"A Jesuit. I teach in Chicago."

"Yeah, what do you teach?"

"History."

She sucked her lower lip and considered this. She was a
daughter of this neighborhood, from her painted nails to her
plucked eyebrows and the long, smooth, naked expanse of her
legs beneath a house dress, but this hesitation belonged to a
newer generation; she read the newspapers, she had opinions.
"Yeah, do you like that?"

"Very much."

Her eyebrows rose in an expression of agreement. She was a
rather tall woman. Andrew himself felt ungainly and coarse and
suddenly dirty. His hands felt dirty; perhaps he had touched the
railing outside. "Would you like to sit down or something?" she
said. She was probably as tall as Frank had been. Her hair was a
bright chestnut color, puffed up on the crown of her head so that
she looked even taller than she was. She looked as if she had half-
prepared to go somewhere, doing her face and her hair and then

losing interest, slipping into a shapeless dress, slipping into worn-out shoes. She said shyly, "I'm sorry it's so messy in here—"

With a gesture of his hand he dispelled the clutter. He smiled and sat and the girl wavered above him. She said, "Would you like some coffee or something? Or maybe some beer? What time is it?"

"About five-thirty."

"Well—would you like anything?"

"Thank you, no. I won't be staying long."

She hadn't the shrewdness to disguise her relief at these words. She sat facing him on a footstool, the sort of odd piece of furniture Andrew remembered as a *hassock*—how strange that such things had disappeared forever from his life! In the living room of his parents' tiny home and in the homes of his friends' parents there had been big, squat, shiny hassocks, usually red, often ripped, and they were a symbol of something, but he had no idea what. He wanted to laugh. This hassock was a gay orange-brown.

He did not laugh, but a pain shot up into his head. He said apologetically, "I wouldn't mind a glass of water. . . ."

She jumped up, eager to serve him. He was accustomed to this mechanical jumping-up and running-out from women. Service like that was a way of not quite seeing him as a priest, not listening to him or dealing with him; he supposed that he understood. The sight of a clerical collar had often disheartened even him himself. The girl went to the kitchen and, in his range of vision, selected an especially clean glass from the cupboard and let the water run to get cold and filled the glass and returned to him, like a handmaiden. She had a very light, lithe step, probably exaggerated.

"I sometimes get headaches when I travel. I carry a few aspirin," he said, explaining as he took out a small folded tissue and opened it and finished off the three aspirins left. The girl watched seriously. "Thank you," he said, returning the glass.

"You got a headache?"

"It's nothing serious."

She set the glass absent-mindedly on a coffee table between them. Andrew wanted to protest that it would stain the table, thinking of the expensive furniture at his seminary. He did not want to look at the table to see if there were other stains on it, and he did not want to look at the girl's rather distraught face. The jazzy music rose from the other room and he thought wildly that he had to get out of this place.

The girl jumped up. "I better turn that off, that's just junk," she said, explaining, and she snapped off the radio. He could see the radio above the sink—red plastic. It occupied a position of importance in the kitchen. The girl returned to him again, and his eyesight blurred, the repetition of her going out, coming back, unnerving him. He was not accustomed to women in such informal situations. There was something naturally jerky and alarming about women, particularly this kind of woman; his college students were rather different. This woman leaned over him and said, "You're sure your headache's all right? You feel all right?"

"Yes, thank you. Your name is Toni, isn't it?"

"Yes, it's kind of a silly name, I don't know where I got it from," she said, pleased and embarrassed.

"I'm Andrew Rollins."

She nodded eagerly and sat on the hassock and gripped her knees, watching him. He felt strange not to have shaken hands with her, but it would have confused her; better to sit still. Now it was too quiet between them, with the radio off. He said gently, "Your husband and I were very good friends at one time. I hope you don't mind talking about him."

"I don't know. I guess not," she said. "I talked about it an awful lot with my family and people and things like that; I mean, we talked about it but that didn't do any good. What good does it do?" This was a long speech for her but she spoke slowly and languidly, as if she were in a trance. Her earlier remarks had been abrupt and clumsy; now she lowered herself into a kind of dreamy sorrow. Her face was rather pretty. Then she did a strange thing: she yawned. It was a small surprising yawn that she tried to hide with her hand.

"How long were you married?" Andrew said.

"Oh, three years."

"I'm afraid that Frank and I lost touch in the last five or six years. I don't know why. I was always sorry about it."

"Oh, he showed me your letters, he saved them and was real proud of them," she said. "I've still got them. I used to read them, they were . . . interesting. . . . He didn't know what to write back to you but he liked your letters. Oh, I remember one letter," she said sadly, as if the letters of her husband's friend were the real sorrow in her life, "I remember you talking about Italy, describing someplace. . . ."

"Florence? The Vatican?"

"The Vatican, yes," she said, repeating the word exactly as he had given it, blinking, "that was very interesting, it was like we were there ourselves. But didn't everybody there speak Italian?"

"Some speak English."

"They do, why?"

Andrew smiled a quick, annoyed smile. "Languages are important to Europeans; they study many languages."

She nodded, but her expression showed that he had not answered her question. "Well, it was a vivid letter. It was vivid. It was nice to read a letter like that, from a priest and everything. I told Frank he should write you back but he was afraid you'd laugh at his spelling or something. He thought a lot of you."

"Do you go over to the cathedral, or where?"

This was a priestly shaft and he used it deliberately, innocently. The girl said, a little nervously, "Sometimes I go to the cathedral, yes. But you know, it isn't safe there any more—a woman was attacked at the six-thirty mass last week, on her way to it. What do you think of that?"

"I'm sorry to hear about it."

"The priest himself says we should be careful. Someone else, a Negro, was stabbed not around church but a few blocks away. It's terrible to be alone down here."

She had an ordinary doll-like face and most of her lipstick had worn off. But this pronouncement was almost tragic; Andrew frowned and wondered when he would begin to pity her. He said softly, "Are you all alone here now?"

"Well, yeah, my family went back to West Virginia. They got fed up here."

"Oh, you're from West Virginia?"

"Sort of. I was born there. But I'm really from right here. I mean, I'm not a hillbilly."

"Where did you meet Frank?"

"I don't know, at a dance. A blind date or something."

"Was he in the Navy then?"

"Oh, no," she said, shaking her head emphatically to set him right. "No, he was out of that for a long time. He was twenty-nine when he got married, that's pretty old for a man."

He felt that she had somehow accused him of being old and unmarried; he was Frank's exact age. But the girl was looking blankly down at her ballerina-type shoes, flat black shoes with pointed toes and worn-down heels. How like the girls of his childhood! The same wistful plucked look, the same ballerina shoes, the same thin, sloping shoulders that were carried without grace and yet without any clumsiness, the way a bird hops from one branch to another.

"I'd be real pleased if you stayed for supper. It's stew that I got on the stove, there's enough for you," she said suddenly.

"I really should be leaving."

"Are you visiting your parents here?"

"No, my parents are dead." He paused. "They did live here though, a few blocks away. But I should be leaving anyway. . . ."

"But I wanted to ask you something. . . ."

"Please ask me anything. It's just that I don't want to bother you, and you probably have something to do. . . ."

"You're not bothering me," she said in a faintly accusing voice, as if he had said something preposterous. She moved the toe of one foot in a little circle on the rug. "It's sort of funny that you and Frank were friends. I mean, you're sort of different."

"What do you mean?"

"Oh, he quit school and everything, he didn't like books—"

"He shouldn't have quit school."

"That's what his mother said. She told me that," the girl said quickly. Between them the image of Frank seemed to rise, a muscular, dark, blunt-jawed man of about five feet eight, sometimes suspicious, sometimes quick to smile. . . . "She always said she tried to talk him out of it but I don't believe that. Was that the truth?"

"I think his parents wanted him to quit. They wanted him to work."

"Ah. Sure," the girl said, nodding.

"He didn't like reading but he liked math. He was good at math."

"Was he?"

"Yes."

She stared at him. Her face was so young and thin that he was distressed, seeing that look upon it. "You think he could have done better than he did, I mean, you think he was smart enough?"

"Yes. I do."

He wondered how old she was. He had been wrong in dismissing her as an ordinary girl; she was solemn, dazed, pathetic, and only the cheapness of her plucked eyebrows and dress were ordinary. Her sorrow was not ordinary.

"I should have given you notice before coming here," Andrew said. "I don't want to make you unhappy."

"Oh, no! Please, no, it's just wonderful that you came," she said, staring at him. A minute passed in silence. He was afraid that she would cry and that her tears, unlike those of other women who cried in his presence, would be inexhaustible. "You sure you don't want to stay to supper? I got this stew all ready, I start it on Monday and have it every other day. . . ."

"But I don't want to inconvenience you."

"No, please stay. It's no inconvenience."

So he agreed and had to wince as she jumped up again, set for the kitchen. She said breathlessly, "I have to make biscuits. I have to set the oven."

She talked to him from the tiny kitchen as if anxious to let him know what she was up to, anxious that he might sneak out. He glanced around the living room. The coffee table had a formica top and of course could not be stained; there was no question of damaging it. The same was true of the other furniture, which was made of synthetic materials that could be washed easily—an easy chair, the sofa on which he sat, the hassock, a table, a few lamps—all of it anonymous and sad. There was no hint of any man having lived here and he realized suddenly that Frank had never lived here. He felt a vague curiosity about the rest of the apartment.

"Why did you move here?" he said.

She turned to him at once, at his service. "After the accident I didn't want to stay in the other place. It cost too much. And anyway, you know our boy was killed too—"

"No, what? What boy?"

"Our boy. Our boy was killed with him, in the car. They were both killed together," she said in a flat, embarrassed voice. Behind her something was whirring. The refrigerator. Andrew could think of nothing to say and so he did nothing but stare at the girl's delicate face. She said, blundering, not looking at him, "His name was Robert, Robin. Sometimes we called him Robin. On the birth certificate it was Robert, of course. He was two. They were both killed in the crash, I thought you knew that."

"I didn't know you had a son."

"Oh, yes, a son, that was Robert," she said vaguely, as if listening for something behind her, "and so . . . so I didn't want to stay there, so I moved over here where a girl friend of mine is . . . We both work downtown."

"Oh, do you work?" he said. He was trembling. For her sake he wanted to get this conversation going in another direction. What sorrow this girl had had to bear! He felt like a coward, he felt shame for himself, his achievement, and his security and his adulthood—it was shameful that he sit here so divorced from her, unable to take any of her suffering onto himself. The girl smiled slowly. "Yes, I like to work. It's in Millicent's, a women's store. I always liked to work. . . ."

"I'm glad you like to work. . . ."

"Let me get something; I almost forgot," she muttered, and turned. He sat there with a foolish strained look, waiting for her to return. When she did return carrying two glasses and a bottle of wine he felt immense relief.

"I bought this yesterday, isn't that lucky? Do you like this kind of wine?"

She showed him the label and it, too, was familiar. Now he never drank anything so cheap. But he smiled with a sincere delight and said, "That's wonderful, thank you," and she poured them both some wine with a self-conscious, elegant movement. They drank. The girl stared down at her long, angular foot and moved uncomfortably. "It's just a regular stew, it's nothing special," she said.

"It smells good."

"Does it?"

She looked at him quickly and critically. It was a meaningless look. The girl seemed to be listening to another conversation, or perhaps to sounds or utterances that were beneath hearing, and her talk with him was a surface affair that sometimes distracted her. She said in her rather sleepy, sad voice, "I like this apartment because it has a side porch. Just a little porch and I can stand out there and let my hair dry or anything. It's funny that Frank never saw it, because now it's a place I go all the time and stand there and, you know, think about things. . . . Off to the side there's a bird's nest on the railing with some eggs in it. I didn't want to scare the mother bird away but for two days she's been gone. I felt sort of bad about that. . . ."

"That's nice, I mean about the porch."

"It is nice," she said, nodding. Her eyes were large. There were slight hollows about them and he wondered again how old she was—twenty-six?—because there was something tired and ageless and familiar about her, even the slope of her shoulders. He could see the faint vaccination scar on her upper arm and how familar, also, that seemed to him. . . . He drank the wine and thought of people of his childhood, packed in so closely in houses that were divided and subdivided into apartments, packed in at school, packed in at church, and he, a child of ten or eleven, distracting himself from the solemn business of the Holy Mass by staring at the uncovered upper arm of a girl, in warm weather, at the faint white vaccination scars that were like symbols of a secret he could not understand and did not want to understand; something frightening and treacherous.

The girl was speaking. She sounded sleepy, as if the wine had rushed to her head. "It's funny how the birds do that, I mean, they fly south and then they fly back north, and they never make a mistake. Did you ever think about that?"

"Yes."

"And they can't help it? And they make nests, like the one outside, and—and they can't help any of it?"

"It is strange, yes."

"I wouldn't want to be like that," she said seriously.

"But it's the same thing that makes them live."

"What?"

"It's the same thing."

"What is?"

He didn't want to get tangled in any foolish conversation but it was impossible to back out. So he said, as if speaking to an especially slow student, "I mean that the principle that makes them migrate also makes them live—it's the same principle, the life force itself. It's all the same instinct."

She stared at him and he seemed to hear, replayed, his own words in her brain.

"What I wanted least of all was to upset you," he said. With the bottle of wine safely between them he felt more at ease; perhaps he could handle a more personal and yet more impersonal attack. "But it was a great shock to hear of Frank's death, and a woman down the street—"

"Oh, Thelma," the girl said flatly, as if she didn't think much of Thelma.

"She said I should talk to you. I had no idea about the other—about the child."

"Yes," the girl said, finishing her glass of wine, "that was sad. That was very sad. I don't know what to say about it."

"Do you have any pictures of them?"

"No, I don't," she said arrogantly. "His mother wanted them all so she could cry over them, so I said take them, go ahead and take them, and she did. She wanted back some goddamn old dish she gave us for a wedding present. It was tarnished anyway. I gave that back and good riddance and I don't see any of them, I mean his family."

"That's too bad," Andrew said, alarmed.

"Oh, the hell with them."

"But it's too bad—"

"It was a big goddamn dish made of silver or something, with a vine in it. A design. You were supposed to put meat on it or fish, I don't know, whoever in hell uses stuff like that? I think she won it at a bingo game. I don't think she bought it with money. Or else she got it with yellow stamps. Every time she came over to see us she'd ask me about the dish and I had to show it to her and she always said, *Why don't you polish it?* For Christ's sake, why didn't I sit around night after night while he went out bowling or whatever he did and polish that goddamn bowl! Why didn't I!" She rose unsteadily. She said, "I'll be right back."

Andrew had the idea that she was going to get the dish to show him, but she went instead into another room. He was glad to be alone. He poured himself more wine, making a face. It was an intolerable situation but here he was; in an hour or two he would be free. He could bear it. And she needed someone to talk to, obviously, it was a shame for a woman like that to be alone; she was a fairly attractive woman. He heard water running in another room. It was an intimate sound, and the feeling of the apartment, now that it was twilight, was intimate and pleasant. It was strange to think that Frank knew nothing about it. Time had passed over Frank, who was as old as Andrew and yet dead, mysteriously dead. Did Frank dominate their thoughts in spite of being dead, or had they hardly thought of him at all? When the girl returned, Andrew saw that she looked prettier. Embarrassed, awkward, she stood in the doorway on thin stork's legs and said, "Nobody wants to hear me talk about him anymore, I don't blame them. It's a bore. That's why I was glad when you came but I don't want you to feel bad or anything. . . ."

She sat again and dawdled over her glass of wine. Noises began in the apartment next door but she did not hear them. Andrew was hungry; he wondered about supper. If they ate, it would be something to do with their mouths that did not involve words. Good. Why didn't they go into the kitchen? He finished his glass of wine and felt a stab of hunger.

The girl said sleepily, "You and Frank had some hobbies together, didn't you? You collected some stuff?"

"Stamps. Just cheap stamps, and sea shells."

"Oh, sea shells?" she said, pleased. "Where did you get them?"

He talked. His memory blossomed as the sound of the sea blossoms magically in a shell, and he recalled for her the gritty November days and the dark afternoons after school and the hopeless Saturday mornings, when for him even to go outside was a risk—no use explaining that to his parents—and he and Frank would spend hours with their collections and their spiritless rehearsals of what revenge they would get upon the older boys who bothered them. They had been bothered endlessly, for years. Endlessly. It was an amazing fact that they had been struck and tripped and chased for years, and now he, Father Rollins, sat and discussed it all objectively, fairly, and his colleague in such shame was dead and it was all over, the terrible arena of their boyhood through which they had passed and which, itself, had not changed. Did its horrors exist for other boys, still? The exhaust and smoke of the great city were still present, heavier than ever, heavy as the clouds that drifted languidly across the sky from the great lakes, clouds that looked as if they must reek with filth. Very strange.

"I was very fortunate to survive this neighborhood," he said solemnly.

"Tell me more about it, you and him. In high school," she said. She leaned toward him greedily, her large eyes fixed and commanding. And so he talked.

After a while she had to go and finish preparing supper, so he came to the doorway and watched and talked. She seemed anxious to hear everything. He talked about things he had not thought of for years, things he had nearly forgotten. Then he said, breaking off, "You know, it's strange that Frank was never here. I mean in this apartment."

"Yes, I think about that too."

"Do you have any plans for the future?"

"What plans?"

She gazed at him blankly. He could not decide if she were stupid, or only dazed from her grief. What if Frank were watching them through the window, listening? What if Frank some-

how wanted to return but could not, just as he, Andrew, sometimes wanted to wake from nightmares but could not wake,
although he understood he was sleeping and needed only to wake
himself in order to be free . . . ?

"No, no plans," she said.

They ate in the kitchen. He liked eating here; it was artless
and direct. At the residence hall, of course, he ate in a large dining room with the other Jesuits and the only artlessness was in
seeming not to avoid certain boring people; they could not always
be avoided. In the past he had always eaten in kitchens. He was
not one of those Jesuits who came from good families; he had
never disguised his background.

"It's funny," said the girl, "but I'd swear that Frank's mother
wrote to you. She said she was going to."

"No. I wish she had."

"I'm pretty sure she said so." It was not clear to Andrew
whether he, or the mother-in-law, was being accused. But the
girl went on, "That old bitch always wanted to make trouble. She
thought we had to get married but that wasn't true. She went
around telling everybody that."

"She must be a very unhappy woman."

"Yes, unhappy, she's a miserable bitch. That's true," the girl
said agreeably. She ate thoughtfully but Andrew ate quickly, as
if he had been waiting a long time for this. He hadn't remembered to have lunch. Distrustful of his appetite, of most physical
demands, he often forgot to eat, and then the power of hunger
was terrible in him, a kind of revenge for his having ignored it. It
was very strange. He felt both heavy and lightheaded from the
shock of Frank's death, from the wine, heavy from the meal and
the relentless conversation and lightheaded from the occasional
bursts of absurdity in their talk—the girl's offhand reference to
Frank's mother—and the two sensations, heavy and light, passed
back and forth dizzily in his mind. The stew was good. It was
thick with potatoes and carrots and the meat was scant, but of

course meat was expensive and where did this girl get money?
She worked at a poor-paying job. It was evil of him to take food
from her, mouthful after mouthful, and yet his hunger was prodigious.

"It's awful when somebody dies," she said, laying down her
fork, "it's like it was torn out of you—you know—like a bandage
ripped off with the skin in it—something like that—"

For an instant he imagined Frank in the doorway, watching
them.

"I'm very sorry that you're alone," he said.

"Well, I got some friends."

"You wouldn't want to join your family?"

"Back there? Hell, no. No, I don't have to do with them now."

"It's a comfort to be with somebody at certain times. . . ."

"I like it here on my own. Except for how things are, I mean
how dangerous it's getting. . . . I was coming back from work
once and a man followed me from the bus, a white man, he
walked right after me, he had a funny look . . . it was like he
was asleep and walking in his sleep. . . . Oh, that was awful,
that was awful," she said, and sucked in her breath and covered
her eyes with her hands. Andrew stared at her. Then, after a
moment, she lowered her hands again and sat dry-eyed, though
faintly astonished.

It was a peculiar moment.

They went back into the living room and she poured more
wine, and he thought of how he must leave soon and how he
would be leaving her alone, and how empty this apartment would
seem. He spoke to comfort her and was not sure of where his
words would lead: "Every one of us goes through periods of un-
happiness, sometimes of depression, and the only way we get
through is by holding onto some words. In order to be Catholic
you must understand that: hang onto the words even when you
don't believe and then the belief will return to you. It will return."

"Was Frank a good Catholic when you knew him?" she said curiously.

"When I knew him."

"He made me turn Catholic, you know. Then he sort of forgot about it."

"He was a good Catholic then, back then," Andrew said emphatically. "We both got scholarships to the Jesuit high school across town. It was a wonderful opportunity for boys like us and I went from the high school right into the seminary. It was terrible that Frank had to quit. . . ."

"He might have got fed up with it too. That's how I felt."

"But it was different with us. Our school. It was an excellent school. Frank should have continued. . . ."

"You really think he was smart?"

"Yes, certainly."

She let her head fall against the back of the easy chair. She looked listlessly at him. "Well, I don't know."

"What?"

"I don't know, how smart he was."

"Why do you say that?" Andrew said, startled.

She made a noncommittal gesture, turning her hand idly one way in a half-circle, then turning it back. Yes, an eloquent gesture. Andrew stared at her hand and saw in it an old gesture of Frank's that had always annoyed him.

"He was smart in some ways. Some certain ways," she said. "But in other ways, I don't know." She yawned and opened her eyes wide in a look of ingenuous sorrow. "You know, he couldn't get ahead at work, and he used to yell at the kid. . . . He used to go out every night and I went with him, I knew enough to tag along because there were some women who wouldn't mind him, I knew that, but he never figured out why I came with him. He thought it was because I loved him so much."

"But what do you mean?" Andrew said, his face suddenly warm.

"I don't know," she said groggily. She reached around and found some cigarettes on the floor by her chair. "I used to tell myself when I was a kid that people aren't much good to each other. They're really better apart, not together, like my mother and father were always fighting and out of them being together all us kids were born . . . what's the point of it?"

"Haven't you ever experienced any happiness in your life?"

"What?" she said. He felt a strange panic. His knees were weak. The girl watched him levelly and said, "You said that when you're unhappy or something you keep yourself going by some words. Why do you do that?"

"We have to keep ourselves going."

"But you're a priest, you believe all sorts of things. You don't have to worry about things, or work."

He laughed. "I teach school. It took me five years to get my Ph. D."

"Yes, I mean, but . . . but it isn't the same because you can't fail and can't fall out, the way Frank did. You know, he fell out of things and could never get ahead, he was sort of a bum. . . ." Seeing Andrew's look of alarm she said quickly, "Oh, he was a nice guy, I know that, but he couldn't catch onto things the way you do, a man like you, you know how to talk and be polite but he didn't. And a priest has things he doesn't have to think about, that he believes."

"Priests certainly think about their religion. Of all people priests experience doubt."

"But does it mean anything?"

"Why wouldn't it?"

"Because you're a priest," she said sleepily, "and it's all set, you . . . you have that black suit you wear and I'd like something like that, something I could hide in and wouldn't have to worry. It's like a big black bird; nuns always reminded me of birds. Penguins."

Andrew laughed in surprise. "You don't have the right idea. It isn't unbelievers who doubt, but believers. It's believers who doubt."

"I never doubt anything. I know how things are," the girl said simply. "But when I was Catholic I worried about things, yes, that's right, about sins and things. I doubted things and then I stopped believing and didn't have any doubt left, I was free. Now I know how things are and don't think about it but it's about the same. I mean, I feel about the same. Whether you're Catholic or not doesn't make much difference."

"That's true."

He felt that his body had become quite warm and heavy. He was perspiring, nervous before the girl's relentless impersonal sorrow, which was brittle and glib as the sorrow of medieval madonnas on museum canvases. Strange girl! The dazed look of her face, the way her skin seemed stretched tight across her girlish skull, made him feel uneasy.

"Loneliness is dangerous. It's bad for you to be alone, to be lonely, because if aloneness does not lead to God, it leads to the devil. It leads to the self. Thinking too much." He spoke hypnotically. The girl exhaled a cloud of smoke. "The aim of the religious life is not to be conscious of oneself as an individual but to experience the universe, to feel its fragments unifying in us. . . . That experience is God."

She frowned in thought. She balanced one foot atop the other and the shoe of the higher foot loosened and would have fallen off, but she caught it on her toe. Her toenails were painted pink like her fingernails.

"Sometimes, when I'm very lucky, I can achieve this feeling," he said. His voice was rising with something like passion. "I wish I could explain it to you, I wish I had time. . . ."

"You have time. You can stay all you want, nobody's coming over tonight."

". . . at these times I feel that by merely looking at a person I can reconstruct his past life, or her past life, I feel that I enter

into his life as a lover, someone who loves . . . and sometimes I
feel that just by glancing at a photograph, in a magazine perhaps,
a photograph of mountains or a foreign country . . . I somehow
enter into the mystical life of that world, into its reality, I can
imagine a gigantic world beyond it, its history, an entire civilization running up to that photograph that is presented to my
view. . . ."

She nodded vaguely. She put out the cigarette and folded her
arms across her stomach, staring at him.

"Did you always want to be a priest?" she said.

Something seemed to have gone out of her voice. He said,
"No, I didn't. I found my vocation through the guidance of a
priest at my school. There was nothing simple about it. And
Frank, too, Frank might have considered—"

"Oh, the hell with Frank," she said.

He stared at her and his heart began to pound.

"Why do you say that?"

"Look, you don't know him. Maybe you knew him once but it
wasn't the same guy I knew. Look, the reason he cracked up the
car, the reason it happened was he was drunk. He was always
drunk. He was a loser and he had to take the kid out for a ride,
and that's that. The hell with him."

"But why did that happen? Why did he choose that kind of
life?"

"Why, why what? Who chooses what?"

"Certainly people make choices—"

"Look, where are you staying tonight?"

"At a residence in town here."

"Why are you here?"

"I'm on my way to Cleveland. I wanted to see Frank."

"After so many years?"

"I've wanted to see him often, but my time isn't my own."

"You sure his mother didn't write to you?"

"Yes, of course," he said impatiently, "of course."

She got to her feet and stretched. She was wearing a yellow dress. "I guess I have to go to bed. I have to work tomorrow," she said.

He got to his feet at once, embarrassed. "I shouldn't have stayed so long. . . ."

"You want me to show you my porch? Here, it's over here."

She led him to the other room and he followed obediently. She opened a door and stepped out on a small porch; it was just as she had said. Across the way was another old apartment building, its many windows lit in the darkness, and down on the ground were uncertain shapes half in shadow and half in light. Andrew saw something move down there.

"What's that?"

"Where?"

He smelled something faintly lemony about her, probably her hair. He was not thinking about her at all. It was a deliberate avoidance of thought, which he had learned as a young seminarian, and it had never failed him. She went over to one side of the little porch and felt for something and laughed.

"What's wrong?" he said.

"Nothing." She led him back to the living room, and now the way seemed clearer. Once back it was obviously time for him to leave; there would be no awkwardness about it. The girl smiled up at him, pleased. He said a few final things, she said a few things, there is no telling what people about to part can discover to talk of!—once they are safely released from each other. She went with him to the door. Almost out, good. A few more words. He said, "I'd be very happy if you wanted to write to me, I mean, if you ever had any doubts. . . ."

"But I don't have any doubts," she pointed out. She smiled and he smiled with her. She was like a clever student who courts her teacher by insights and coquettish bursts of intellect. He stepped out into the dim corridor, she leaned in the doorway, slender and somehow pleased with something, and as he turned to leave she said, "Oh, Father, wait—here's a little present for you. It's just nothing. It's for you."

And she deposited in his palm a tiny blue egg, a robin's egg.

"But what is it?" he said, amazed.

"Oh, I don't know," she said, smiling shyly and cleverly at once, and moving back, "just something I thought of. I'm kind of crazy sometimes. I just thought of it for no reason."

He descended the stairs rapidly, his heart pounding. It was terrible not to know why his heart was pounding! Downstairs in the foyer he opened his hand again, dreading what he must see, and there the egg lay—a tiny, perfect egg, a lovely blue, a miracle achieved by some forlorn, enslaved robin. "What the hell is this?" he muttered. He closed his hand suddenly upon the egg and smashed it, and when he opened his hand again there was just a mess there, any kind of mess and not necessarily the mess of an egg. He took out his wad of tissue and cleaned it off and rolled all the tissue into a ball and, being neat, did not drop it in the foyer or out on the cluttered street but put it back neatly into his own pocket.

$\mathcal{A}$ccomplished Desires

There was a man she loved with a violent love, and she spent much of her time thinking about his wife.

No shame to it, she actually followed the wife. She followed her to Peabody's Market, which was a small, dark, crowded store, and she stood in silence on the pavement as the woman appeared again and got into her station wagon and drove off. The girl, Dorie, would stand as if paralyzed, and even her long fine blond hair seemed paralyzed with thought—her heart pounded as if it too was thinking, planning—and then she would turn abruptly as if executing one of the steps in her modern dance class and cross through Peabody's alley and out to the Elks' Club parking

lot and so up toward the campus, where the station wagon was
bound.

Hardly had the station wagon pulled into the driveway when
Dorie, out of breath, appeared a few houses down and watched.
How that woman got out of a car!—you could see the flabby
expanse of her upper leg, white flesh that should never be exposed, and then she turned and leaned in, probably with a grunt,
to get shopping bags out of the back seat. Two of her children
ran out to meet her, without coats or jackets. They had nervous,
darting bodies—Dorie felt sorry for them—and their mother
rose, straightening, a stout woman in a colorless coat, either scolding them or teasing them, one bag in either muscular arm—and
so—so the mother and children went into the house and Dorie
stood with nothing to stare at except the battered station wagon,
and the small snowy wilderness that was the Arbers' front yard,
and the house itself. It was a large, ugly, peeling Victorian home
in a block of similar homes, most of which had been fixed up by
the faculty members who rented them. Dorie, who had something of her own mother's shrewd eye for hopeless, cast-off
things, believed that the house could be remodeled and made
presentable—but as long as he remained married to *that woman*
it would be slovenly and peeling and ugly.

She loved that woman's husband with a fierce love that was
itself a little ugly. Always a rather stealthy girl, thought to be
simply quiet, she had entered his life by no accident—had not
appeared in his class by accident—but every step of her career,
like every outfit she wore and every expression on her face, was
planned and shrewd and desperate. Before her twenties she had
not thought much about herself; now she thought about herself
continuously. She was leggy, long-armed, slender, and had a startled look—but the look was stylized now, and attractive. Her face
was denuded of make-up and across her soft skin a galaxy of
freckles glowed with health. She looked like a girl about to
bound onto the tennis courts—and she did play tennis, though

awkwardly. She played tennis with *him*. But so confused with love was she that the game of tennis, the relentless slamming of the ball back and forth, had seemed to her a disguise for something else, the way everything in poetry or literature was a disguise for something else—for love?—and surely he must know, or didn't he know? Didn't he guess? There were many other girls he played tennis with, so that was nothing special, and her mind worked and worked while she should have slept, planning with the desperation of youth that has never actually been young— planning how to get him, how to get him, for it seemed to her that she would never be able to overcome her desire for this man.

The wife was as formidable as the husband. She wrote narrow volumes of poetry Dorie could not understand and he, the famous husband, wrote novels and critical pieces. The wife was a big, energetic, high-colored woman; the husband, Mark Arber, was about her size though not so high-colored—his complexion was rather putty-colored, rather melancholy. Dorie thought about the two of them all the time, awake or asleep, and she could feel the terrible sensation of blood flowing through her body, a flowing of desire that was not just for the man but somehow for the woman as well, a desire for her accomplishments, her fame, her children, her ugly house, her ugly body, her very life. She had light, frank blue eyes and people whispered that she drank; Dorie never spoke of her.

The college was a girls' college, exclusive and expensive, and every girl who remained there for more than a year understood a peculiar, even freakish kinship with the place—as if she had always been there and the other girls, so like herself with their sleepy unmade-up faces, the skis in winter and the bicycles in good weather, the excellent expensive professors, and the excellent air—everything, everything had always been there, had existed for centuries. They were stylish and liberal in their cashmere sweaters with soiled necks; their fingers were stained with ballpoint ink; and like them, Dorie understood that most of the world was wretched and would never come to this college, never, would be kept back from it by armies of helmeted men. She, Dorie Weinheimer, was not wretched but supremely fortunate, and she must be grateful always for her good luck, for there was no justification for her existence any more than there was any justification for the wretched lots of the world's poor. And there would flash to her mind's eye a confused picture of dark-faced starving mobs, or emaciated faces out of an old-fashioned Auschwitz photograph, or something—some dreary horror from the *New York Times'* one hundred neediest cases in the Christmas issue— She had, in the girls' soft, persistent manner, an idealism-turned-pragmatism under the influence of the college faculty, who had all been idealists at Harvard and Yale as undergraduates but who were now in their forties, and as impatient with normative values as they were with their students' occasional lockets-shaped-into-crosses; Mark Arber was the most disillusioned and the most eloquent of the Harvard men.

In class he sat at the head of the seminar table, leaning back in his leather-covered chair. He was a rather stout man. He had played football once in a past Dorie could not quite imagine, though she wanted to imagine it, and he had been in the war— one of the wars—she believed it had been World War II. He had an ugly, arrogant face and discolored teeth. He read poetry in a raspy, hissing, angry voice. "Like Marx, I believe that poetry has had enough of love; the hell with it. Poetry should now cultivate the whip," he would say grimly, and Dorie would stare at him to see if he was serious. There were four senior girls in this class and they sometimes asked him questions or made observations of their own, but there was no consistency in his reaction. Sometimes he seemed not to hear, sometimes he nodded enthusiastically and indifferently, sometimes he opened his eyes and looked at them, not distinguishing among them, and said: "A remark like that is quite characteristic." So she sat and stared at him and her heart seemed to turn to stone, wanting him, hating his wife

and envying her violently, and the being that had been Dorie
Weinheimer for twenty-one years changed gradually through the
winter into another being, obsessed with jealousy. She did not
know what she wanted most, this man or the victory over his
wife.

She was always bringing poems to him in his office. She borrowed books from him and puzzled over every annotation of his.
As he talked to her he picked at his fingernails, settled back in his
chair, and he talked on in his rushed, veering, sloppy manner, as
if Dorie did not exist or were a crowd, or a few intimate friends, it
hardly mattered, as he raved about frauds in contemporary poetry, naming names, "that bastard with his sonnets," "that cow
with her daughter-poems," and getting so angry that Dorie
wanted to protest, no, no, why are you angry? Be gentle. Love me
and be gentle.

When he failed to come to class six or seven times that winter
the girls were all understanding. "Do you think he really is a
genius?" they asked. His look of disintegrating, decomposing
recklessness, his shiny suit and bizarre loafer shoes, his flights of
language made him so different from their own fathers that it
was probable he was a genius; these were girls who believed seriously in the existence of geniuses. They had been trained by
their highly paid, verbose professors to be vaguely ashamed of
themselves, to be silent about any I.Q. rated under 160, to be
uncertain about their talents within the school and quite confident of them outside it—and Dorie, who had no talent and only
adequate intelligence, was always silent about herself. Her talent
perhaps lay in her faithfulness to an obsession, her cunning patience, her smile, her bared teeth that were a child's teeth and yet
quite sharp. . . .

One day Dorie had been waiting in Dr. Arber's office for an
hour, with some new poems for him. He was late but he strode
into the office as if he had been hurrying all along, sitting heavily
in the creaking swivel chair, panting; he looked a little mad. He

was the author of many reviews in New York magazines and papers and in particular the author of three short, frightening novels, and now he had a burned-out, bleached-out look. Like any of the girls at this college, Dorie would have sat politely if one of her professors set fire to himself, and so she ignored his peculiar stare and began her rehearsed speech about—but what did it matter what it was about? The poems of Emily Dickinson or the terrible yearning of Shelley or her own terrible lust, what did it matter?

He let his hand fall onto hers by accident. She stared at the hand, which was like a piece of meat—and she stared at him and was quite still. She was pert and long-haired, in the chair facing him, an anonymous student and a minor famous man, and every wrinkle of his sagging, impatient face was bared to her in the winter sunlight from the window—and every thread of blood in his eyes—and quite calmly and politely she said, "I guess I should tell you, Dr. Arber, that I'm in love with you. I've felt that way for some time."

"You what, you're what?" he said. He gripped her feeble hand as if clasping it in a handshake. "What did you say?" He spoke with an amazed, slightly irritated urgency, and so it began.

II

His wife wrote her poetry under an earlier name, Barbara Scott. Many years before she had had a third name, a maiden name—Barbara Cameron—but it belonged to another era about which she never thought except under examination from her analyst. She had a place cleared in the dirty attic of her house and she liked to sit up there, away from the children, and look out the small octagon of a window, and think. People she saw from her attic window looked bizarre and helpless to her. She herself was a hefty, perspiring woman, and all her dresses—especially her expensive ones—were stained under the arms with great lemon-colored half-moons no dry cleaner could remove. Because she was so large a woman, she was quick to see imperfections in others, as if she used a magnifying glass. Walking by her window on an ordinary morning were an aged tottering woman, an enormous Negro woman—probably someone's cleaning lady—and a girl from the college on aluminum crutches, poor brave thing, and the white-blond child from up the street who was precocious and demonic. Her own children were precocious and only slightly troublesome. Now two of them were safe in school and the youngest, the three-year-old, was asleep somewhere.

Barbara Scott had won the Pulitzer Prize not long before with an intricate sonnet series that dealt with the "voices" of many people; her energetic, coy line was much imitated. This morning she began a poem that her agent was to sell, after Barbara's death, to the *New Yorker:*

> *What awful wrath*
> *what terrible betrayal*
> *and these aluminum crutches, rubber-tipped. . . .*

She had such a natural talent that she let words take her anywhere. Her decade of psychoanalysis had trained her to hold nothing back; even when she had nothing to say, the very authority of her technique carried her on. So she sat that morning at her big, nicked desk—over the years the children had marred it with sharp toys—and stared out the window and waited for more inspiration. She felt the most intense kind of sympathy when she saw someone deformed—she was anxious, in a way, to see deformed people because it released such charity in her. But apart from the girl on the crutches she saw nothing much. Hours passed and she realized that her husband had not come home; already school was out and her two boys were running across the lawn.

When she descended the two flights of stairs to the kitchen, she saw that the three-year-old, Geoffrey, had opened a white plastic bottle of ammonia and had spilled it on the floor and on himself; the stench was sickening. The two older boys bounded in the back door as if spurred on by the argument that raged between them, and Barbara whirled upon them and began screaming. The ammonia had spilled onto her slacks. The boys ran into the front room and she remained in the kitchen, screaming. She sat down heavily on one of the kitchen chairs. After half a hour she came to herself and tried to analyze the situation. Did she hate these children, or did she hate herself? Did she hate Mark? Or was her hysteria a form of love, or was it both love and hate together . . . ? She put the ammonia away and made herself a drink.

When she went into the front room she saw that the boys were playing with their mechanical inventors' toys and had forgotten about her. Good. They were self-reliant. Slight, cunning children, all of them dark like Mark and prematurely aged, as if by the burden of their prodigious intelligences, they were not always predictable: they forgot things, lost things, lied about things, broke things, tripped over themselves and each other, mimicked classmates, teachers, and their parents, and often broke down into pointless tears. And yet sometimes they did not break down into tears when Barbara punished them, as if to challenge her. She did not always know what she had given birth to: they were so remote, even in their struggles and assaults, they were so fictional, as if she had imagined them herself. It had been she who'd imagined them, not Mark. Their father had no time. He was always in a hurry, he had three aged typewriters in his study and paper in each one, an article or a review or even a novel in progress in each of the machines, and he had no time for the children except to nod grimly at them or tell them to be quiet. He had been so precocious himself, Mark Arber, that after his first, successful novel at the age of twenty-four he had had to whip from place to place, from typewriter to typewriter, in a frantic attempt to keep up with—he called it keeping up with his "other self," his "real self," evidently a kind of alter ego who was always typing and creating, unlike the real Mark Arber. The real Mark Arber was now forty-five and he had made the transition from "promising" to "established" without anything in between, like most middle-aged critics of prominence.

Strachey, the five-year-old, had built a small machine that was both a man and an automobile, operated by the motor that came with the set of toys. "This is a modern centaur," he said wisely, and Barbara filed that away, thinking perhaps it would do well in a poem for a popular, slick magazine. . . . She sat, unbidden, and watched her boys' intense work with the girders and screws and bolts, and sluggishly she thought of making supper, or calling Mark at school to see what had happened . . . that morning he had left the house in a rage and when she went into his study, prim and frowning, she had discovered four or five crumpled papers in his wastebasket. It was all he had accomplished that week.

Mark had never won the Pulitzer Prize for anything. People who knew him spoke of his slump, familiarly and sadly; if they disliked Mark they praised Barbara, and if they disliked Barbara they praised Mark. They were "established" but it did not mean much, younger writers were being discovered all the time who had been born in the mid- or late forties, strangely young, terrifyingly young, and people the Arbers' age were being crowded out, hustled toward the exits. . . . Being "established" should have pleased them, but instead it led them to long spiteful bouts of eating and drinking in the perpetual New England winter.

She made another drink and fell asleep in the chair. Sometime later her children's fighting woke her and she said, "Shut up," and they obeyed at once. They were playing in the darkened living room, down at the other end by the big brick fireplace that was never used. Her head ached. She got to her feet and went out to make another drink.

Around one o'clock Mark came in the back door. He stumbled and put the light on. Barbara, in her plaid bathrobe, was sitting at the kitchen table. She had a smooth, shiny, bovine face, heavy with fatigue. Mark said, "What the hell are you doing here?"

She attempted a shrug of her shoulders. Mark stared at her. "I'm getting you a housekeeper," he said. "You need more time for yourself, for your work. For your work," he said, twisting his mouth at the word to show what he thought of it. "You shouldn't neglect your poetry so we're getting in a housekeeper, not to do any heavy work, just to sort of watch things—in other words—a kind of external consciousness. You should be freed from ordinary considerations."

He was not drunk but he had the appearance of having been drunk, hours before, and now his words were muddled and dignified with the air of words spoken too early in the morning. He wore a dirty tweed overcoat, the same coat he'd had when they were married, and his necktie had been pulled off and stuffed somewhere, and his puffy, red face looked mean. Barbara thought of how reality was too violent for poetry and how poetry, and the language itself, shimmered helplessly before the confrontation with living people and their demands. "The housekeeper is here. She's outside," Mark said. "I'll go get her."

He returned with a college girl who looked like a hundred other college girls. "This is Dorie, this is my wife Barbara, you've met no doubt at some school event, here you are," Mark said. He was carrying a suitcase that must have belonged to the girl. "Dorie has requested room and board with a faculty family. The Dean of Women arranged it. Dorie will babysit or something— we can put her in the spare room. Let's take her up."

Barbara had not yet moved. The girl was pale and distraught; she looked about sixteen. Her hair was disheveled. She stared at Barbara and seemed about to speak.

"Let's take her up, you want to sit there all night?" Mark snarled.

Barbara indicated with a motion of her hand that they should go up without her. Mark, breathing heavily, stomped up the back steps and the girl followed at once. There was no indication of her presence because her footsteps were far too light on the stairs. She said nothing, and only a slight change in the odor of the kitchen indicated something new—a scent of cologne, hair scrubbed clean, a scent of panic. Barbara sat listening to her heart thud heavily inside her and she recalled how, several years before, Mark had left her and had turned up at a friend's apartment in Chicago—he'd been beaten up by someone on the street, an accidental event—and how he had blackened her eye once in an argument over the worth of Samuel Richardson, and how—there were many other bitter memories—and of course there had been other women, some secret and some known—and now this—

So she sat thinking with a small smile of how she would have to dismiss this when she reported it to their friends: *Mark has had this terrible block for a year now, with his novel, and so . . .*

She sat for a while running through phrases and explanations, and when she climbed up the stairs to bed she was grimly surprised to see him in their bedroom, asleep, his mouth open and his breath raspy and exhausted. At the back of the house, in a small oddly shaped maid's room, slept the girl; in their big dormer room slept the three boys, or perhaps they only pretended to sleep; and only she, Barbara, stood in the dark and contemplated the bulk of her own body, wondering what to do and knowing that there was nothing she would do, no way for her to change the process of events any more than she could change the heavy fact of her body itself. There was no way to escape what the years had made her.

III

From that time on they lived together like a family. Or it was
as Mark put it: "Think of a babysitter here permanently. Like
the Lunt girl, staying on here permanently to help, only we won't
need that one any more." Barbara made breakfast for them all,
and then Mark and Dorie drove off to school and returned late,
between six and six-thirty, and in the evenings Mark worked
hard at his typewriters, going to sit at one and then the next and
then the next, and the girl, Dorie helped Barbara with the dishes
and odd chores and went up to her room, where she studied . . .
or did something, she must have done something.

Of the long afternoons he and the girl were away Mark said
nothing. He was evasive and jaunty; he looked younger. He explained carefully to Dorie that when he and Mrs. Arber were
invited somewhere she must stay home and watch the children,
that she was not included in these invitations; and the girl agreed
eagerly. She did so want to help around the house! She had inherited from her background a dislike for confusion—so the mess
of the Arber house upset her and she worked for hours picking
things up, polishing tarnished objects Barbara herself had forgotten were silver, cleaning, arranging, fixing. As soon as the snow
melted she was to be seen outside, raking shyly through the
flower beds. How to explain her to the neighbors? Barbara said
nothing.

"But I didn't think we lived in such a mess. I didn't think it
was so bad," Barbara would say to Mark in a quiet, hurt voice,
and he would pat her hand and say, "It isn't a mess, she just likes
to fool around. *I* don't think it's a mess."

It was fascinating to live so close to a young person. Barbara
had never been young in quite the way Doris was young. At
breakfast—they ate crowded around the table—everyone could

peer into everyone else's face, there were no secrets, stale mouths and bad moods were inexcusable, all the wrinkles of age or distress that showed on Barbara could never be hidden, and not to be hidden was Mark's guilty enthusiasm, his habit of saying, "*We* should go to . . . ," *We* are invited . . ." and the "we" meant either him and Barbara, or him and Dorie, but never all three; he had developed a new personality. But Dorie was fascinating. She awoke to the slow gray days of spring with a panting, wondrous expectation, her blond hair shining, her freckles clear as dabs of clever paint on her heartbreaking skin, her teeth very, very white and straight, her pert little lips innocent of lipstick and strangely sensual . . . yes, it was heartbreaking. She changed her clothes at least twice a day while Barbara wore the same outfit—baggy black slacks and a black sweater—for weeks straight. Dorie appeared downstairs in cashmere sweater sets that were the color of birds' eggs, or of birds' fragile legs, and white trim blouses that belonged on a genteel hockey field, and bulky pink sweaters big as jackets, and when she was dressed casually she wore stretch slacks that were neatly secured by stirrups around her long, narrow, white feet. Her eyes were frankly and emptily brown, as if giving themselves up to every observer. She was so anxious to help that it was oppressive; "No, I can manage, I've been making breakfast for eight years by myself," Barbara would say angrily, and Dorie, a chastised child, would glance around the table not only at Mark but at the children for sympathy. Mark had a blackboard set up in the kitchen so that he could test the children's progress in languages, and he barked out commands for them—French or Latin or Greek words—and they responded with nervous glee, clacking out letters on the board, showing off for the rapt, admiring girl who seemed not to know if they were right or wrong.

"Oh, how smart they are—how wonderful everything is," Dorie breathed.

Mark had to drive to Boston often because he needed his pre-

scription for tranquillizers refilled constantly, and his doctor
would not give him an automatic refill. But though Barbara had
always looked forward to these quick trips, he rarely took her
now. He went off with Dorie, now his "secretary," who took
along a notebook decorated with the college's insignia to record
his impressions in, and since he never gave his wife warning she
could not get ready in time, and it was such an obvious trick, so
crudely cruel, that Barbara stood in the kitchen and wept as they
drove out. . . . She called up friends in New York but never
exactly told them what was going on. It was so ludicrous, it made
her seem such a fool. Instead she chatted and barked with laughter; her conversations with these people were always so witty that
nothing, nothing seemed very real until she hung up the reciever
again; and then she became herself, in a drafty college-owned
house in New England, locked in this particular body.

She stared out the attic window for hours, not thinking. She
became a state of being, a creature. Downstairs the children
fought, or played peacefully, or rifled through their father's
study, which was forbidden, and after a certain amount of time
something would nudge Barbara to her feet and she would descend slowly, laboriously, as if returning to the real world where
any ugliness was possible. When she slapped the boys for being
bad, they stood in meek defiance and did not cry. "Mother, you're
out of your mind," they said. "Mother, you're losing control of
yourself."

"It's your father who's out of his mind!" she shouted.

She had the idea that everyone was talking about them, everyone. Anonymous, worthless people who had never published a
line gloated over her predicament; high-school baton twirlers
were better off than Barbara Scott, who had no dignity. Dorie,
riding with Mark Arber on the expressway to Boston, was at least
young and stupid, anonymous though she was, and probably she
too had a slim collection of poems that Mark would manage to
get published . . . and who knew what would follow, who

could tell? Dorie Weinheimer was like any one of five hundred or five thousand college girls and was no one, had no personality, and yet Mark Arber had somehow fallen in love with her, so perhaps everyone would eventually fall in love with her . . . ? Barbara imagined with panic the parties she knew nothing about to which Mark and his new girl went: Mark in his slovenly tweed suits, looking like his own father in the thirties, and Dorie chic as a Vogue model in her weightless bones and vacuous face.

"Is Dorie going to stay here long?" the boys kept asking.

"Why, don't you like her?"

"She's nice. She smells nice. Is she going to stay long?"

"Go ask your father that," Barbara said angrily.

The girl was officially boarding with them; it was no lie. Every year certain faculty families took in a student or two, out of generosity or charity, or because they themselves needed the money, and the Arbers themselves had always looked down upon such hearty liberalism. But now they had Dorie, and in Peabody's Market Barbara had to rush up and down the aisles with her shopping cart, trying to avoid the wives of other professors who were sure to ask her about the new boarder; and she had to buy special things for the girl, spinach and beets and artichokes, while Barbara and Mark liked starches and sweets and fat, foods that clogged up the blood vessels and strained the heart and puffed out the stomach. While Barbara ate and drank hungrily, Dorie sat chaste with her tiny forkfuls of food, and Barbara could eat three platefuls to Dorie's one; her appetite increased savagely just in the presence of the girl. (The girl was always asking politely, "Is it the boys who get the bathroom all dirty?" or "Could I take the vacuum cleaner down and have it fixed?" and these questions, polite as they were, made Barbara's appetite increase savagely.)

In April, after Dorie had been boarding with them three and a half months, Barbara was up at her desk when there was a rap on the plywood door. Unused to visitors, Barbara turned clumsily

and looked at Mark over the top of her glasses. "Can I come in?"
he said. "What are you working on?"

There was no paper in her typewriter. "Nothing," she said.

"You haven't shown me any poems lately. What's wrong?"

He sat on the window ledge and lit a cigarette. Barbara felt a
spiteful satisfaction to see how old he looked—he hadn't her fine,
fleshed-out skin, the smooth complexion of an overweight
woman; he had instead the bunched, baggy complexion of an
overweight man whose weight keeps shifting up and down.
Good. Even his fingers shook as he lit the cigarette.

"This is the best place in the house," he said.

"Do you want me to give it up to Dorie?"

He stared at her. "Give it up—why? Of course not."

"I thought you might be testing my generosity."

He shook his head, puzzled. Barbara wondered if she hated
this man or if she felt a writer's interest in him. Perhaps he was
insane. Or perhaps he had been drinking again; he had not gone
out to his classes this morning and she'd heard him arguing with
Dorie. "Barbara, how old are you?" he said.

"Forty-three. You know that."

He looked around at the boxes and other clutter as if coming to
an important decision. "Well, we have a little problem here."

Barbara stared at her blunt fingernails and waited.

"She got herself pregnant. It seems on purpose."

"She what?"

"Well," Mark said uncomfortably, "she did it on purpose."

They remained silent. After a while, in a different voice he
said, "She claims she loves children. She loves our children and
wants some of her own. It's a valid point, I can't deny her her
rights . . . but . . . I thought you should know about it in case
you agree to help."

"What do you mean?"

"Well, I have something arranged in Boston," he said, not
looking at her, "and Dorie has agreed to it . . . though reluc-

tantly . . . and unfortunately I don't think I can drive her myself . . . you know I have to go to Chicago. . . ."

Barbara did not look at him

"I'm on this panel at the University of Chicago, with John
Ciardi. You know, it's been set up for a year, it's on the state of
contemporary poetry—you know—I can't possibly withdraw
from it now—"

"And so?"

"If you could drive Dorie in—"

"If I could drive her in?"

"I don't see what alternative we have," he said slowly.

"Would you like a divorce so you can marry her?"

"I have never mentioned that," he said.

"Well, would you?"

"I don't know."

"Look at me. Do you want to marry her?"

A nerve began to twitch in his eye. It was a familiar twitch—it
had been with him for two decades. "No, I don't think so. I don't
know—you know how I feel about disruption."

"Don't you have any courage?"

"Courage?"

"If you want to marry her, go ahead. I won't stop you."

"Do you want a divorce yourself?"

"I'm asking you. It's up to you. Then Dorie can have her baby
and fulfill herself," Barbara said with a deathly smile. "She can
assert her rights as a woman twenty years younger than I. She
can become the third Mrs. Arber and become automatically envied. Don't you have the courage for it?"

"I had thought," Mark said with dignity, "that you and I had
an admirable marriage. It was different from the marriages
of other people we know—part of it is that we don't work in the
same area, yes, but the most important part lay in our understanding of each other. It has taken a tremendous generosity on
your part, Barbara, over the last three months and I appreciate

it," he said, nodding slowly, "I appreciate it and I can't help asking myself whether . . . whether I would have had the strength to do what you did, in your place. I mean, if you had brought in—"

"I know what you mean."

"It's been an extraordinary marriage. I don't want it to end on an impulse, anything reckless or emotional," he said vaguely. She thought that he did look a little mad, but quietly mad; his ears were very red. For the first time she began to feel pity for the girl who was, after all, nobody, and who had no personality, and who was waiting in the ugly maid's room for her fate to be decided.

"All right, I'll drive her to Boston," Barbara said.

IV

Mark had to leave the next morning for Chicago. He would be gone, he explained, about a week—there was not only the speaking appearance but other things as well. The three of them had a kind of farewell party the night before. Dorie sat with her frail hand on her flat, child's stomach and drank listlessly, while Barbara and Mark argued about the comparative merits of two English novelists—their literary arguments were always witty, superficial, rapid, and very enjoyable. At two o'clock Mark woke Dorie to say good-by and Barbara, thinking herself admirably discreet, went upstairs alone.

She drove Dorie to Boston the next day. Dorie was a mother's child, the kind of girl mothers admire—clean, bright, passive—and it was a shame for her to be so frightened. Barbara said roughly, "I've known lots of women who've had abortions. They lived."

"Did you ever have one?"

"No."

Dorie turned away as if in reproach.

"I've had children and that's harder, maybe. It's thought to be harder," Barbara said, as if offering the girl something.

"I would like children, maybe three of them," Dorie said.

"Three is a good number, yes."

"But I'd be afraid . . . I wouldn't know what to do. . . . I don't know what to do now. . . ."

She was just a child herself, Barbara thought with a rush of sympathy; of all of them it was Dorie who was most trapped. The girl sat with a scarf around her careless hair, staring out the window. She wore a camel's hair coat like all the girls and her fingernails were colorless and uneven, as if she had been chewing them.

"Stop thinking about it. Sit still."

"Yes," the girl said listlessly.

They drove on. Something began to weigh at Barbara's heart, as if her flesh were aging moment by moment. She had never liked her body. Dorie's body was so much more prim and chaste and stylish, and her own body belonged to another age, a hearty nineteenth century where fat had been a kind of virtue. Barbara thought of her poetry, which was light and sometimes quite clever, the poetry of a girl, glimmering with half-seen visions and echoing with peculiar off-rhymes—and truly it ought to have been Dorie's poetry and not hers. She was not equal to her own writing. And, on the highway like this, speeding toward some tawdry destination, she had the sudden terrible conviction that language itself did not matter and that nothing mattered ultimately except the body, the human body and the bodies of other creatures and objects: what else existed?

Her own body was the only real fact about her. Dorie, huddled over in her corner, was another real fact and they were going to do something about it, defeat it. She thought of Mark already in Chicago, at a cocktail party, the words growing like weeds in his brain and his wit moving so rapidly through the brains of others that it was, itself, a kind of lie. It seemed strange to her that the

two of them should move against Dorie, who suffered because
she was totally real and helpless and gave up nothing of herself to
words.

They arrived in Boston and began looking for the street. Barbara felt clumsy and guilty and did not dare to glance over at the
girl. She muttered aloud as they drove for half an hour, without
luck. Then she found the address. It was a small private hospital
with a blank gray front. Barbara drove past it and circled the
block and approached it again. "Come on, get hold of yourself,"
she said to Dorie's stiff profile, "this is no picnic for me either."

She stopped the car and she and Dorie stared out at the hospital, which looked deserted. The neighborhood itself seemed deserted. Finally Barbara said, with a heaviness she did not yet understand, "Let's find a place to stay tonight first. Let's get that
settled." She took the silent girl to a motel on a boulevard and
told her to wait in the room, she'd be back shortly. Dorie stared in
a drugged silence at Barbara, who could have been her mother—
there flashed between them the kind of camaraderie possible only
between mother and daughter—and then Barbara left the room.
Dorie remained sitting in a very light chair of imitation wood and
leather. She sat so that she was staring at the edge of the bureau;
occasionally her eye was attracted by the framed picture over the
bed, of a woman in a red evening gown and a man in a tuxedo
observing a waterfall by moonlight. She sat like this for quite a
while, in her coat. A nerve kept twitching in her thigh but it did
not bother her; it was a most energetic, thumping twitch, as if her
very flesh were doing a dance. But it did not bother her. She
remained there for a while, waking to the morning light, and it
took her several panicked moments to remember where she was
and who had brought her here. She had the immediate thought
that she must be safe—if it was morning she must be safe—and
someone had taken care of her, had seen what was best for her
and had carried it out.

V

And so she became the third Mrs. Arber, a month after the second one's death. Barbara had been found dead in an elegant motel across the city, the Paradise Inn, which Mark thought was a brave, cynical joke; he took Barbara's death with an alarming, rhetorical melodrama, an alcoholic melancholy Dorie did not like. Barbara's "infinite courage" made Dorie resentful. The second Mrs. Arber had taken a large dose of sleeping pills and had died easily, because of the strain her body had made upon her heart; so that was that. But somehow it wasn't—because Mark kept talking about it, speculating on it, wondering: "She did it for the baby, to preserve life. It's astonishing, it's exactly like something in a novel," he said. He spoke with a perpetual guilty astonishment.

She married him and became Mrs. Arber, which surprised everyone. It surprised even Mark. Dorie herself was not very surprised, because a daydreamer is prepared for most things and in a way she had planned even this, though she had not guessed how it would come about. Surely she had rehearsed the second Mrs. Arber's suicide and funeral already a year before, when she'd known nothing, could have guessed nothing, and it did not really surprise her. Events lost their jagged edges and became hard and opaque and routine, drawing her into them. She was still a daydreamer, though she was Mrs. Arber. She sat at the old desk up in the attic and leaned forward on her bony elbows to stare out the window, contemplating the hopeless front yard and the people who strolled by, some of them who—she thought— glanced toward the house with a kind of amused contempt, as if aware of her inside. She was almost always home.

The new baby was a girl, Carolyn. Dorie took care of her endlessly and she took care of the boys; she hadn't been able to finish

school. In the evening when all the children were at last asleep
Mark would come out of his study and read to her in his rapid,
impatient voice snatches of his new novel, or occasionally poems
of his late wife's, and Dorie would stare at him and try to understand. She was transfixed with love for him and yet—and yet she
was unable to locate this love in this particular man, unable to
comprehend it. Mark was invited everywhere that spring; he flew
all the way out to California to take part in a highly publicized
symposium with George Steiner and James Baldwin, and Dorie
stayed home. Geoffrey was seeing a psychiatrist in Boston and
she had to drive him in every other day, and there was her own
baby, and Mark's frequent visitors who arrived often without notice and stayed a week—sleeping late, staying up late, drinking,
eating, arguing—it was exactly the kind of life she had known
would be hers, and yet she could not adjust to it. Her baby was
somehow mixed up in her mind with the other wife, as if it had
been that woman's and only left to her, Dorie, for safekeeping.
She was grateful that her baby was a girl because wasn't there
always a kind of pact or understanding between women?

In June two men arrived at the house to spend a week, and
Dorie had to cook for them. They were long, lean, gray-haired
young men who were undefinable, sometimes very fussy, sometimes reckless and hysterical with wit, always rather insulting in
a light, veiled manner Dorie could not catch. They were both
vegetarians and could not tolerate anyone eating meat in their
presence. One evening at a late dinner Dorie began to cry and
had to leave the room, and the two guests and Mark and even the
children were displeased with her. She went up to the attic and
sat mechanically at the desk. It did no good to read Barbara Scott's
poetry because she did not understand it. Her understanding had
dropped to tending the baby and the boys, fixing meals, cleaning
up and shopping, and taking the station wagon to the garage perpetually . . . and she had no time to go with the others to the
tennis courts, or to accompany Mark to New York . . . and

around her were human beings whose lives consisted of language, the grace of language, and she could no longer understand them. She felt strangely cheated, a part of her murdered, as if the abortion had taken place that day after all and something had been cut permanently out of her.

In a while Mark climbed the stairs to her. She heard him coming, she heard his labored breathing. "Here you are," he said, and slid his big beefy arms around her and breathed his liquory love into her face, calling her his darling, his beauty. After all, he did love her, it was real and his arms were real, and she still loved him although she had lost the meaning of that word. "Now will you come downstairs and apologize, please?" he said gently. "You've disturbed them and it can't be left like this. You know how I hate disruption."

She began weeping again, helplessly, to think that she had disturbed anyone, that she was this girl sitting at a battered desk in someone's attic, and no one else, no other person who might confidently take upon herself the meaning of this man's words—she was herself and that was a fact, a final fact she would never overcome.

Wild Saturday

Good-by to the white frame house with its rooms heavy with the odor of new paint, that awful smell; good-by to his mother and his grandmother—the child is restrained in his joy, being an intelligent and polite child. "Be sure to eat well. Be sure to ask for milk. Don't stuff yourself with candy," his mother says, as if he will be gone a year instead of a few hours. Her fingers arrange his clothing, pat his hair. Moving quickly over his face, they assert *possession*; he knows.

His mother peers out over his head to the end of the walk, where his father is waiting for him. Good-by, good-by!—until tonight he is off with his father, the whole week has exploded white-hot on Saturday morning, and not even his mother's worried angry kiss can distract him. Out there his father is waiting with his hands on his hips, a man. Yes, he is coming!

He runs from one parent to the other. It is only a few yards but the distance is great, the gravitational tug of one lessens and the other begins, most powerfully. He runs down the walk to Dad. With one eye shut in a conspirator's grimace, his father picks him up and cries, "Hey! Where're you going so fast?" The boy thinks that he is too heavy to be up like this—one time his father hurt his back moving furniture—and so he struggles to get down. There's no resistance. Off they jog to the car, his father's car. Very familiar, streaked with rust. A black Volkswagen with one fender dented in and another half torn off, from Sonya's crazy driving. On the windshield is a sticker in red and white that says *Faculty Parking;* under that sticker there are several others, all covered over. Year after year his father puts a new sticker on top of all the others.

"Well, Buchanan-boy," his father says in the fast good-humored voice with which he always begins his visits, "what's up for today? What have you got in mind?"

The child, Buchanan, last month ten years old, considers this question as if it were a serious one. He is small for his age; he has developed a squint, as if in defense against his father's cheerful sunny face or his mother's ridged forehead. Sullenly he says, "Last time you promised about the zoo—"

"The zoo! Absolutely, the zoo!" Dad cries, snapping his fingers. "And would you believe me, that's what I had in mind all along?"

Buchanan doesn't let on whether he believes it or not, not wanting to be found out. He glances over his shoulder into the back seat of the car where a battered tennis racket and some soiled shirts are lying.

"Is *she* coming along too?" he asks, not looking at his father.

"My little friend, it is Sonya who has prepared our lunch. Who else but Sonya? And your brother-in-spirit little Peter, don't you feel any big-brotherliness toward him, that lovely child?

Think what a model you can be for poor Peter!" Dad starts the
car in excellent spirits. The Volkswagen jerks a little as it is put
into each gear; Buchanan thinks it is a good little car, a faithful
car, to have withstood so much. Before the Separation of fifteen
months ago, Dad took Buchanan for a trip out West that, it
turned out, Buchanan's mother had thought would be a trip to a
Natural Science museum twenty miles away—but anyway the
car had taken them far, all the way to Arizona, before it broke
down.

Slowly Buchanan allows his expression to relax. He is with his
father now and everything is fine. Minute will pass by minute.
In that terrible instant between mother and father, just released
from his mother's tense arms and about to be grappled manfully
in his father's, he always runs on air itself—very precarious, very
frightening. Now Dad is busy talking. He chatters away. Buchanan, wise for his years, knows that the chatter will keep on for
a certain amount of time and then it will stop . . . of course,
Buchanan knows that everything, no matter how energetic and
promising, will stop after a certain amount of time.

But there's no thinking of that now. Here we are!—here is
Sonya on a corner, waiting, with a box cradled in her arms that
must hold their lunch, all sorts of food. Though Buchanan has
had a big breakfast, he is hungry at once. Little Peter is seated on
the curbstone at the corner, waiting. Dad stops the car and they
get in. "Everybody say hello! Hello, hello!" Dad cries. Sonya and
her little boy sit in the back seat. Sonya is a marvelous long-
legged girl, or woman . . . Buchanan finds himself squinting in
her presence too, as if her bright challenging face were too strong
for his eyes. His eyes are often watery. Everyone has a weak spot,
Dad is fond of saying, and Buchanan's weak spot is probably his
eyes—sometimes little nerves twitch in them, both on and beneath the eyelid.

"How the hell are you, Buchanan?" Sonya says, rubbing her

knuckles against his head. "You look sort of pale. Has she been feeding you oatmeal again?"

"What we need is lots of sunlight and a day in the open air," says Dad.

"And animals, we need to look at animals!" Sonya says. She has long floppy red hair and large, dark eyes, and her mouth is like Dad's—ready to twist itself up at any second, open and quick. Little Peter, sorry to say, is a dopey child, no denying it. He is about three years old and mopes around, whimpering against his mother's tight yellow slacks, or sucking his thumb, or sleeping. Buchanan feels sorry for him. He knows that he, Buchanan, is more interesting than Peter; the grownups like him better.

"Tell me everything you did since I saw you last. Everything," Sonya says, rubbing her nervous knuckles against the back of Dad's head now, leaning forward against the seat.

"In that terrible ten minutes I drove down Hechtman Street, from which we have just come, to the house at twenty-four forty where my unfortunate wife—ex-wife—lives with her bizarre mother. I parked the car neatly in front of the house. *She* was already on the porch with her little Bucky, dressed up as you see him for us to soil and her to lament, and we glanced at each other across the space of that innocuous sidewalk—"

"What does she look like?"

"You've seen pictures of her. You saw one picture of her."

"A little woman standing by a car, with her hair all curly? You were married to her?"

"That's a picture we took up in Maine. No, that doesn't look like her, not much, it's misleading. Actually, she looks like hell."

"Has she aged much?"

"Terribly. We glanced at each other and then glanced away, with a kind of modest hostility, like people in American movies. Whereupon *she* descended with her little Bucky, named for his

great-uncle who, by the way, did die recently and left no one
anything because his wealth was only a rumor, heh heh, and she
gave him one long final furious hug to keep him safe from his
father's deadly being, and then the child broke loose and ran to
him, gasping for breath—"

Buchanan has to laugh at this, it's so fanciful.

"Did the two of you speak?"

"My little boy and I? I should hope so."

"No, you and *her*. Did you speak?"

"Never."

Sonya laughs at this, content. She leans against Buchanan's
seat and lets her long narrow fingers play with his hair. He likes
this but will not show it. She smells like flowers, or sweet food, or
wine. . . . His own mother has no particular smell, he recalls
nothing. His grandmother smells like Dutch Cleanser, which she
uses often; she likes to clean things bright. But the whole house
has stunk for days with paint, because the rooms upstairs and
downstairs are being painted, gradually, and Buchanan is glad to
be out of it. Yes, it's true, maybe it is true that he was gasping for
air when he ran into his father's arms.

"That woman should be exposed in all her unimaginative cal-
lousness," Sonya says. The way she smiles at Buchanan, you
wouldn't think it was his mother she was talking about. Through
her ears are two enormous red hoops of plastic, with smaller black
hoops inside them. They all turn and move by themselves. She
has clear, radiant skin, this Sonya, and her eyes are rather large
and protruding as if with perpetual excitement. In some ways she
looks younger than the little boy Peter, that poor kid, who is sitting back with his knees up to his chest, moping over something,
very pale. He is jealous of Buchanan, of course. . . . Who was
Peter? Buchanan asked Dad one day. Why did *he* always have to
come along? Dad explained that Peter was Sonya's little boy, but
that Peter, unlike Buchanan, did not have a Dad to pick him up
on Saturdays and take him for rides and treats; so Peter was wel-

come to come with them. "You wouldn't want a poor little boy like that to be off on his own, would you?" Dad said.

"But he should find a father of his own," Buchanan pointed out.

He was an evil child sometimes, and he knew it.

Very fast they drive down the avenue, Dad's elbows pumping in imitation of a crazy driver chased by the police—both Buchanan and Sonya laugh. Sonya has a high rapid giggle that sometimes gets out of control. "We're off! Another week come and gone! Month in, month out! Even, odd—black, white—life, death—father, son— The cycles continue! And how is the good dedicated father?" Dad says, showing his teeth in a crazy grin. "He is high already, don't deny it, at ten o'clock high already in order to get through the glorious day—a day he anticipates all week long with gurgling innards and aching brains—"

Sonya giggles and pinches the back of his neck.

"He is a strong, brave man, he nibbles silently at the inside of his lip—drawing blood—what is there about his own blood that tastes so good?"

Sonya slaps the back of his neck. "You stop that," she says.

"At the age of thirty-six he is ready for retirement, this good man, this wreck, and therefore he drives faster and faster before they yank his car away from him. *Lewd and lascivious behavior* they may have to pin on him yet, they may stoop to that if they don't find any incriminating evidence on the premises—"

"Oh, nobody's going to raid you, nobody cares," Sonya said.

"Hey, is Arty waiting for us?"

"Oh, God yes. Arty's waiting, yes," Sonya says. Buchanan's heart sinks.

So Dad makes a U-turn on the avenue and chugs up a hill, straining the little car and straining Buchanan's heart, until on either side are old buildings that look ugly even in this pleasant autumn sunlight; going to get Arty. "How was your week, kid?" Dad says.

"All right. In school there was this man—"

"Is that Arty out like that? What's he wearing?"

But it isn't Arty, it's a stranger, a drunken man standing in the street in his underwear; he looks angry. Just when you would expect Sonya to giggle she is very serious. She says, "That poor tragic man, should we ask him what's wrong? Maybe he wants a ride or something . . . ?"

"And then what happened, kid, in school?"

"This man was for our special assembly. He was a magician. He did lots of tricks, he made a sword disappear down his throat. . . ."

"Hell, anybody can do that," Dad says.

"He had it on fire too."

"That explains it! Fire explains it all. . . . Now *that* is certainly Arty, over there." And sure enough it is Arty, their friend Arty, a tall loose-jointed man of about thirty who is wearing on this warm day a long grimy khaki coat. He waves at them as they approach, but without smiling. Arty is unshaven, bleary-eyed; Buchanan can already smell his stale goat's breath . . . and he joins shyly in with the others to cry hello, hello! as Arty crawls in the back seat of the car.

Arty is a *potter;* one day Dad took Buchanan to visit his studio, which is in one of these buildings, and showed Buchanan all his jars. Pots. Buchanan could not think of anything to say. He ended the visit by breaking a pot accidentally, and even then he could not think of anything to say except that he was sorry. Arty hadn't believed him. Between Arty and Buchanan there has been, since that day, a sense of dislike and mistrust, like the shrewd sense that arises between two children in the restraining presence of adults.

"Well, Arty, my friend," Dad says in his welcoming sunny voice, "how did you manage this week?"

"My father died."

"What, your father died?"

"The old man died," Arty said flatly.

They are baffled and silent for a moment. Sonya wipes her mouth with the back of her hand. Then she says, "I can't . . . I can't feel anything for you, I mean not yet, I don't . . . I don't really feel sorry. . . . How did he die?"

"I don't want to talk about it."

"Shouldn't you be with them then? For the funeral?"

"I don't believe in funerals. It's enough that he's dead." Arty crosses his legs angrily and jolts the back of Buchanan's seat. "My father was quite a brilliant man, far superior to me. He broke me when I was a child. I hated him, but he was a brilliant man."

"What was he?" Sonya says.

"A specialist in kidney disorders. An amateur botanist. A poet. He'd been working on his autobiography for thirty years when he died. . . ."

Then silence returns. Dad whistles thinly through his teeth. Sonya lights a cigarette nervously and throws the match out the window.

"I admit that I hate him, but he was also a brilliant man," Arty says.

No one takes him up on this. Dad says, "Don't bring death to my party, you son of a bitch, no pale horse is going to trot along on my outing! Ah-hah! Sonya, sweetheart, are you sure this is the way to the zoo?"

"Isn't it the way?"

"That is a factory over there; if I'm not mistaken it is a *button factory*. Why is there so much smoke? Surely we are in the wrong dimension, the wrong political zone. . . . Surely no animals can survive here? . . . Answer me, for Christ's sake!"

"I didn't know you were talking to me," Sonya says angrily. "I thought you were talking to yourself."

"I'm not that high yet," Dad says.

So it happens that they drive around for half an hour, aimlessly, back and forth through the low-lying clouds of orange-

tinted smoke along the river, and Buchanan sighs to himself a
centuries-old sigh, knowing it's best to sit back the way Peter
does and to take everything as it comes. At any rate, he is with
them. Good. Happy Saturday. Out of that dour house and its
stench of paint and suffering and good, worrying, righteous
women, his mother and his grandmother both marked by severe
lines running from nose to corner of mouth, lines of *censure,* out
of the house, free, riding in the car . . . good. Out of their embraces, their knowledge, away from the kitchen and the back
door he must always use when he enters the house . . . all this
is good.

They decide to go to Sonya's house.

"And if Petrie shows we'll kick him the hell out, right?" Dad
says. "I'm fed up with him and his little boys. Because my son,
you know, is of a malleable age; his mother insists that he be kept
out in the relative innocence of zoos and factories, and not in a
slutty flat where something interesting might be going on."

"Petrie owes me five dollars," Arty says.

"Look, I can't say who might turn up," Sonya says. "I can't
promise anything."

So off they go to Sonya's, which is where they usually go anyway. . . . Buchanan knows this, knows everything. He is a
small, eager child, with a puzzled expression. He is wearing a
clean new shirt of blue and green plaid, and new trousers that are
dark green. His mother dresses him up for these Saturdays in a
certain way—his clothes are stiff, starchy. They are to remind
him of something. He is a cautious child, a listening child. Having listened for so many years he is equipped with vivid fragments of knowledge, facts that would surprise both his parents,
but of a whole, coherent view he is dubious . . . are there such
things as whole, coherent views? He knows that his father is a
teacher, for instance. Not a grammar or high school teacher but a
college teacher. But what does he teach, exactly? And where does
he teach? Years ago he taught at a small, quiet college and Bu-

chanan is sure he remembers that clearly, but then everything was
lifted up and dropped down and he awoke to an apartment in a
city with buses and trucks making noise outside the window
. . . and now his father taught at a *university* . . . and then
for some months his father taught far away, driving sixty miles
each day, teaching Buchanan had no idea what . . . and now,
this year, according to Buchanan's mother, he is teaching at a
community college in a suburb. Last year there was trouble at his
job, always trouble, so he quit angrily and walked out. He told
Buchanan: "The ways of this world are rotten, kid, and you'd
better learn that now. This little girl came into my office, this
little bitch, and hiked her skirt up her leg and said to me, 'Mr.
Jarret, I believe I should warn you that I and some other students
have been writing down *every*thing you've told us this year.
. . .'" And Dad made a squawking noise that was in imitation of
a rooster with its head cut off maybe, but that frightened Buchanan because at first he couldn't think what it was . . . a joke
or part of his father's anger? There was so much joking, and so
much anger, and it was hard sometimes to tell where one left off
and the other began.

And he remembers a consultation with his mother's lawyer, at
home. His mother said, "Then if that's the case, if we know all
these things, then why can't the visits be revoked?" And Buchanan had held his breath, waiting.

He spent some sleepless nights trying to piece it all together, to
get it clear. If, between the two of them, he could make things
peaceful and calm, then maybe they would draw together again
and there wouldn't be this war of weekdays vs. Saturdays. Before
the Divorce his mother's nervous interest had been drawn exclu-
sively to his father, and the two of them could quarrel for hours
—what energy his mother had had in those days! Now she was
changed, the zest had gone out of her complaints, even, everything was limp and resigned about her very posture; while his
father seemed to have grown leaner and younger . . . not ex-

actly younger, maybe, but louder, faster, shrewder. He wore his
lank blond hair combed back from his forehead, and there were
patchy sideburns on his cheeks, and his clothes were likely to be
anything; still, he had that slightly whining, cultured voice of
his, a mark of his own past in the New York apartment filled with
paintings and musical instruments in which his parents had
lived. Buchanan had seen them only once or twice before they
died. His grandfather had been a fairly good violinist. Out of that
expensive but rather shabby apartment had stepped Buchanan's
own father, himself a boy, and he had let himself go across the
entire United States—so he liked to say, often—settling down
first in the gray middle-class with the daughter of an automotive
factory foreman, and now breaking loose once again before it was
too late and the end came for him. Thirteen years (the length of
this marriage, which was called now *experimental*) had been
enough. Now he was loose once again, trying to define himself
and to connect with the . . . with the *time* itself, with the *continent*. Buchanan did not really understand this, though the
words were familiar enough. At times it was difficult for him to
understand that this man was really his father. Sometimes, out
by himself, he had to hold his breath when he saw a teen-aged
boy come loping down the street with his hands stuck in his
pockets and his hair dangling—Buchanan had the uneasy feeling
that any boy, however wild, might metamorphose into his father
as they drew nearer.

Dad stops the car in the middle of the street before a drugstore
so that Sonya can run in for something. "Look at that," Dad says,
but Buchanan sees nothing but Sonya. She is a pale girl and that
head of heavy red hair is almost too much for her. She wears a
black sleeveless sweater and yellow slacks and boots that are imitation something—fur or leather—fake cowboy boots with tiny
spike heels. Lovely Sonya! When she laughs, sometimes there is
a strange moment when the whites of her eyes seem to be taking
over, and her large pale mouth grins too wide, and Buchanan has

the crazy idea that she will not be able to breathe in enough air to live—he worries about Sonya, he worries about them all. And the car, what if it breaks down as it did in Arizona?

Dad orders: "Tell me about your week in school."

Buchanan tells him, every week. He is dutiful and tedious. The very tedium of his story means that it is true, everyone believes him, they are relieved that he is doing so well because then they needn't hear much more of it. If something bad happens, Buchanan forgets it. The school doctor called him in one day and said that his teacher thought he, Buchanan, was restless and overexcited; what was wrong, did he have the flu? did he need vitamins? glasses? a hot lunch? Buchanan does not tell his father this.

"All those years, those years of childhood, are fake," Arty says suddenly.

Buchanan stares at him. Is his enemy winning? Arty has an angular, unsymmetrical head. One side is broader or perhaps puffier than the other. His eyebrows are tufted and messy, as if he has been rubbing them violently, and his lips are thin. Again and again they part in a malicious little smile to show Buchanan that he sees right through him. "You kids think you're so important because you're in your *formative years*. The hell with that. Children are not important because they are not interesting. They are bores, like dogs."

"Lay off Buchanan, that's my son," Dad says, watching for Sonya to reappear.

"In this country there is the illusion that kids are important. But they're nothing. They don't exist," Arty says.

"What are you jealous of Bucky-boy for? Are you jealous of Peter Pounce too?"

Peter is lying back in a corner with his thumb half in and half out of his mouth. He has drooled down over his blue T-shirt, which is decorated with a high-stepping horse on a mountainside, a little faded. Arty makes a snickering, uneasy noise.

In a minute or two Sonya appears again on the run, with a bag under her arm. She shakes her mane of hair. Getting in the car she cries, "I met the most extraordinary man in there! Ninety-two years old, a wonderful old gentleman; he cornered me and wanted to talk about his great-grandson who's an astronaut, what do you think of that!"

"You meet such people," Dad chuckles.

"Isn't that wonderful? He was such a character!"

Off they drive on the energy of such a happy encounter, up and down bumpy, hilly streets, through the ring of boarding-houses and tenement buildings that surround the famous university that is north of the city. Sonya's flat is on the top floor of one of these houses. She is not a student exactly, though Buchanan thinks she was a student once . . . or had intended to be one, or is going to be one in the future. The house has been painted green recently, putting Buchanan in mind of popsicles, exotic birds, exotic islands. The green is too bright for a house and makes people nervous. "Ah, what a color! A crucifixion of a color!" Dad sighs.

It's a steep climb up the sidewalk steps to the house—everything is hilly here—and once inside the house there is another long climb of three flights of stairs. Buchanan begins to pant. Sonya runs ahead with her box and her drugstore bag, and Dad follows, thumping on the steps with Peter under one arm like a rag doll. Buchanan wonders what is in Sonya's picnic box . . . sandwiches? pickles? He follows them upstairs, panting. A warm, dusty, dreamy odor rises about them as they ascend. What kind of crazy people live in this house? Buchanan passes an open door and inside some black men are jabbering at one another in a strange language, and on the landing stands a girl of about fifteen with a white powdered face and eyes eerily outlined in black and her hair in long pigtails—she puts out her hand to Dad as he passes, and he gestures her away—and the time before, Buchanan met a very old man in overalls who, Sonya said, worked as a janitor for a church and was a tragic person. He was so tragic that even Sonya thought he should be put away. . . . Up on the third floor Buchanan passes by another open door, and inside a bearded student stares out suspiciously at him.

Sonya's door is open when they get there. Jessie, a big-boned girl in her mid-thirties, is lying on Sonya's unmade bed. She is wearing a dirty pink bathrobe and her bare feet are dirty. She says, "I'm sick, I got the Asian flu or something."

Sonya tosses her things down on the kitchen table. "We couldn't find the zoo anywhere," she says. "They moved the zoo. They closed it down and slaughtered the animals."

Dad carries Peter straight into the back room, which is Peter's room. When Buchanan visits here he sometimes takes a nap in this back room; this is the kids' room. It is very small. The roof slopes down sharply on one side so that even Buchanan would have to crouch if he wanted to stand against the wall. Underfoot are towels and clothes and bed sheets. "Peter Pounce, is it your naptime?" Dad says. "Peter wants his nap now?"

Peter is too befuddled to say no.

Out in the other room an argument has begun. Arty says nastily, "I just don't want her bugging me today, that's all."

"I'm not going to bug anybody," Jessie says.

"You came here to contaminate me with your germs. You want to kill me," Arty says.

"Oh, is Peter in bed? Did you put him to bed?" Sonya says to Dad.

She sits up on the kitchen counter and swings her legs. She is very girlish but her forehead is ridged, like Buchanan's mother's; he is surprised at this. "Why do you always put him to bed, is that fair? He doesn't bother anyone," Sonya says.

Dad says, "Open the box and let's have lunch!"

They open the box with a flourish and Buchanan is disappointed to see only a bag of potato chips, three candy bars, and several loose cookies inside. Such a big box? She carried such a big box only for that? Dad puts on a record and at first there is no sound at all, then the volume is deafening, so that Buchanan cannot even hear the music. He is the only one who feels like eating. Jessie bites into a candy bar and declares, "I can't taste a thing. Is this candy or wax?" Sonya pouts, sitting on the counter. She turns one of the faucets on. She turns it off. She says something to Dad that Buchanan can't hear, then Dad says: "He said he wanted to nap, forget it!" Arty says, squatting on the floor, "That kid looks pretty dopey to me. Is he retarded? Does he get shock treatments?" Sonya stares at him. Blankly, she begins to pile hair on top of her head, rust-red hair, lovely hair, so that they all must watch her pretty pale hands. There is something fascinating and frightening about her. "She feeds him pills to keep him quiet," Jessie says loudly. Between her and Arty there is an angry unrest, as if they are involved in a contest. "Why not? It makes him more thoughtful. He listens more, he doesn't run around and break things like other kids. . . . I'd do the same thing if he was mine, so mind your own business, shut up."

Buchanan has gobbled down three candy bars in a row and now he feels a little sick.

A stranger comes to the door. He is shy, a handsome, dark-skinned young man with a white turban wrapped around his head. Very small-boned, like a girl. He talks with Dad and Sonya. Buchanan has nothing to do and the afternoon opens up before him like a chasm, something terrifying, but he shows no alarm; he tries to hear what they are saying through the din of the phonograph. What if he is sick to his stomach? Someone else comes to the doorway, the boy with the beard, and Buchanan finds himself pressed up against Jessie. He sits very still, keeping his stomach quiet. Jessie is telling them in a loud voice about the flu. "Asian flu. It's going to be an epidemic. It's a metaphysical disease, partly. It makes you doubt reality. It induces symptoms

of paranoia. I know. I have it now . . . in a way it's very interesting. . . ."

"Paranoia?"

"Little things seize your attention and are exaggerated. They
become terrifying. Part of the brain is inflamed, I think. . . ."

"The little boy, he should not be exposed to it," the dark-
skinned young man says, smiling courteously over toward Buchanan.

"That's my son," says Dad.

Buchanan is troubled but pleased at the same time, because
here he is; he is with his father. Everything is settled. Saturday
will be spent like this and Saturdays are always a problem. He
sits for a while in the midst of the music and talk, not hearing
anything, and finally goes over to the kitchen window. He looks
down into the rumpled back yard that ends in a clutter of lilac
bushes and brambles; next door is an abandoned house, boarded
up. Buchanan can see right over into its attic, where pigeons are
strutting. A dead house. Boarded up. No one lives there. He
thinks he would like to hide out there, secretly, making a nest for
himself, so that he could spy on Sonya and his father all the
time.

People come and go during the afternoon. Hours pass. Buchanan tries to play by himself, looking through magazines and
newspapers that lie around. He reads the comics in some old
newspapers, comics he has already read months ago at home, in
his mother's kitchen, but now he pretends they are new and reads
them slowly. His father makes eggs for him but the eggs are
burned in the frying pan. There is a sharp odor of burning
grease; the grease and the burned eggs are scraped into a paper
bag under the sink. Buchanan wanders around, out onto the
landing. . . . He wanders back inside the crowded flat and the
smoke bothers him. He is getting a sore throat. Sonya fusses over
him, kisses his lips, takes him into Peter's room. Peter Pounce is a
good boy, sleeping. He sleeps in a crib with a giant rubber doll, a

naked doll with many nicks and scratches on its body. Buchanan, suddenly tired, kicks some things together in a corner and lies down to sleep. He puts his hands over his ears.

From the other room come strands of music that make Buchanan think a nuclear attack has just begun. It would come like that, he thinks. In school they have drills "in case of nuclear attack." They march through the halls in two columns and go downstairs to the "shelter." At home, Buchanan's mother and grandmother would go into the cellar; the other day they received a pamphlet with a picture of the President of the United States on the inside page, instructing them about what to do "in case of nuclear attack." Buchanan's mother read it aloud. "Lie down flat on the floor in the best corner of your basement, or sit with your back against the wall," she read. "Do not leave this spot until you are told to. . . ." Buchanan loves his mother and grandmother but wishes, vaguely, that he will be in school when the attack comes. He would rather march in two excited columns down to the "shelter," which is the same thing as the locker room. A pleasant, stale odor lingers there. On Tuesday mornings this room is the boys' locker room, and on Thursday mornings it is the girls' locker room. The boys were all surprised to learn that. It was strange, to think of it being the boys' room on one day and the girls' room on another, because of course if you went down there on the wrong day everyone would laugh like crazy, it would be the end of you at that school. . . .

When Buchanan awakes, it is much later. He has a sore throat and he knows with a shiver of dread that something has gone wrong. He should be home by now because it is dark. His mother will call the police and have his father arrested. . . . What woke him was someone talking hysterically in the other room, telling a story, and Buchanan's head aches with the desire to know what is going on. But he does not move. In the crib Peter Pounce sleeps, his breath dry and rasping. Occasionally he snores gently. "I wish it would stop snowing, stop *snowing*," Sonya cries in a voice of real horror, so urgent that Buchanan jumps up and stares out the window, looking for snow. . . .

No snow. "I don't have to stand for this," Sonya says. Someone speaks to her. Is that Dad's voice? Buchanan, frightened, sinks back down into his corner and tells himself that sooner or later everything will be over. A few weeks ago a Negro man with a gray goatee hit Dad in the face and bloodied his nose, but nothing came of it, it passed. He himself will not always be ten years old. He will grow taller and heavier. He will not need his father or even his mother, he will not need to talk to them, he will grow older and grow free. . . . The door is pushed open and Sonya comes in. She is partly undressed. She walks stiffly, one hand outstretched, and says, "Where is that baby . . . ? I want my baby." Stumbling, breathing heavily, she walks into the crib. Peter says, "Mommy?" She gropes around the edge of the crib and makes sure that it is there, then leans over to embrace Peter. Her hands pat him eagerly, as if she is blind. She embraces him and presses her cheek against Peter's cheek, bent over the crib, and for a long time stands like this. Peter begins to whimper. He pushes at her, he tries to hit her with his little fists. "A baby, a little baby," Sonya whispers. Her face is beautiful and vacuous with wonder. From the corner so close to her, Buchanan can see how beautiful she is and how frightening to him. She begins to jerk her head from side to side.

"What? What are you saying . . . ?" she asks Peter. Is Peter saying anything? Maybe he's saying that the bed is wet—Buchanan suspects as much, from the odor in the room—and Sonya cannot understand him. "What? What? What do you want, why can't you tell me? Why is your face so strange?" She feels his face with her hands. She touches his eye. Peter shrinks back. "Here, this is it. This is wrong. This needs to be changed," Sonya says. Peter whimpers and pushes himself from her. Sonya, as if in a trance, returns to the other room. Buchanan knows it is all crazy, most of this is probably just a joke, the way it is every

Saturday, but still he is frightened. He lifts Peter out of the crib. "Now, you stop bawling. We're going to play a game, you shut up, we're going to play hide-and-seek right down here," he says, and Peter is too dopey to stop whimpering. Yes, he has wet his pants. No point in being disgusted with him; that's just Peter. Will he grow up and escape like Buchanan? Buchanan doubts this child's capacity for escape.

"Peter—" Sonya hurries back in the room. She is carrying something: a spoon? She bumps into the crib again and seizes the rubber doll, talking to it in a serious murmur as if it were Peter, and with the spoon she is doing something to it . . . she pries out one of its eyes. . . . The plastic eye falls back into the bed without a sound. Sonya is talking to the doll, calling it *Peter Pounce*. From one ear she takes an earring and works it into the eye socket of the poor old doll, swaying over the crib, talking to Peter all along. . . . Then she draws the blanket up over the doll. When she leaves the room, Buchanan goes over to the crib to make sure, he wants to see with his own eyes, and there is the dirty rubber doll with one eye gone and in its place a red plastic earring with black plastic hoops inside.

Finally the police do come, three policemen. Buchanan remembers Dad trying to wake up and he remembers the policemen's ugly angry faces, but everything is confused, he himself starts crying like a baby—how awful, that Dad can't quite wake up! He tries so hard but can't quite wake up! Once home, Buchanan is told not to expect his father on the following Saturday. That was unfair, unfair, he thinks in savage misery, why should he be blamed for everything . . . ? His mother, weeping and red-eyed, questions him again and again. *What* did they do? Was that awful girl there? *What* kinds of things did they take, *what* did they do to themselves? *What* did he see with his own eyes? Buchanan says with his eyes shut, "We went to the zoo. Saw lions and tigers. Saw elephants. The lady made a lunch and we had sandwiches in the park."

"Why do you lie? Why are you lying to me?"

"We had hot dogs in the park!" Buchanan shouts.

When she is finished, he runs out of the room. This house still smells of new paint. "I am not going to be any Pontchis Pilot," he mutters aloud, and he lets himself into the back room, forbidden for this week because of the fresh paint. It is a back bedroom, painted white. White walls and ceiling. The floor is covered with canvas that is rumpled and uneven and filthy with specks of paint. Buchanan seats himself carefully in the very middle of the room. He smooths the canvas out around him. Hugging his knees to his chest, watchful and suspicious, he sits in the center of the canvas and can see all about him, how blank and open everything is, how much empty space surrounds him.

How I Contemplated the World from the Detroit House of Correction and Began My Life Over Again

NOTES FOR AN ESSAY FOR AN ENGLISH CLASS AT
BALDWIN COUNTRY DAY SCHOOL; POKING AROUND
IN DEBRIS; DISGUST AND CURIOSITY; A REVELATION
OF THE MEANING OF LIFE; A HAPPY ENDING . . .

I EVENTS

1. The girl (myself) is walking through Branden's, that excellent store. Suburb of a large famous city that is a symbol for large famous American cities. The event sneaks up on the girl, who believes she is herding it along with a small fixed smile, a girl of fifteen, innocently experienced. She dawdles in a certain style by a counter of costume jewelry. Rings, earrings, necklaces. Prices from $5 to $50, all within reach. All ugly. She eases over to the glove counter, where everything is ugly too. In her close-fitted coat with its black fur collar she contemplates the luxury of Branden's, which she has known for many years: its many mild pale lights, easy on the eye and the soul, its elaborate tinkly deco-

rations, its women shoppers with their excellent shoes and coats and hairdos, all dawdling gracefully, in no hurry.

Who was ever in a hurry here?

2. The girl seated at home. A small library, paneled walls of oak. Someone is talking to me. An earnest, husky, female voice drives itself against my ears, nervous, frightened, groping around my heart, saying, "If you wanted gloves, why didn't you say so? Why didn't you ask for them?" That store, Branden's, is owned by Raymond Forrest who lives on Du Maurier Drive. We live on Sioux Drive. Raymond Forrest. A handsome man? An ugly man? A man of fifty or sixty, with gray hair, or a man of forty with earnest, courteous eyes, a good golf game; who is Raymond Forrest, this man who is my salvation? Father has been talking to him. Father is not his physician; Dr. Berg is his physician. Father and Dr. Berg refer patients to each other. There is a connection. Mother plays bridge with . . . On Mondays and Wednesdays our maid Billie works at . . . The strings draw together in a cat's cradle, making a net to save you when you fall. . . .

3. *Harriet Arnold's.* A small shop, better than Branden's. Mother in her black coat, I in my close-fitted blue coat. Shopping. Now look at this, isn't this cute, do you want this, why don't you want this, try this on, take this with you to the fitting room, take this also, what's wrong with you, what can I do for you, why are you so strange . . . ? "I wanted to steal but not to buy," I don't tell her. The girl droops along in her coat and gloves and leather boots, her eyes scan the horizon, which is pastel pink and decorated like Branden's, tasteful walls and modern ceilings with graceful glimmering lights.

4. Weeks later, the girl at a bus stop. Two o'clock in the afternoon, a Tuesday; obviously she has walked out of school.

5. The girl stepping down from a bus. Afternoon, weather changing to colder. Detroit. Pavement and closed-up stores; grill-work over the windows of a pawnshop. What is a pawnshop, exactly?

II CHARACTERS

1. The girl stands five feet five inches tall. An ordinary height. Baldwin Country Day School draws them up to that height. She dreams along the corridors and presses her face against the Thermoplex glass. No frost or steam can ever form on that glass. A smudge of grease from her forehead . . . could she be boiled down to grease? She wears her hair loose and long and straight in suburban teen-age style, 1968. Eyes smudged with pencil, dark brown. Brown hair. Vague green eyes. A pretty girl? An ugly girl? She sings to herself under her breath, idling in the corridor, thinking of her many secrets (the thirty dollars she once took from the purse of a friend's mother, just for fun, the basement window she smashed in her own house just for fun) and thinking of her brother who is at Susquehanna Boys' Academy, an excellent preparatory school in Maine, remembering him unclearly . . . he has long manic hair and a squeaking voice and he looks like one of the popular teen-age singers of 1968, one of those in a group, *The Certain Forces, The Way Out, The Maniacs Responsible.* The girl in her turn looks like one of those fieldsful of girls who listen to the boys' singing, dreaming and mooning restlessly, breaking into high sullen laughter, innocently experienced.

2. The mother. A Midwestern woman of Detroit and suburbs. Belongs to the Detroit Athletic Club. Also the Detroit Golf Club. Also the Bloomfield Hills Country Club. The Village Women's Club at which lectures are given each winter on Genet and Sar-

tre and James Baldwin, by the Director of the Adult Education
Program at Wayne State University. . . . The Bloomfield Art
Association. Also the Founders Society of the Detroit Institute of
Arts. Also . . . Oh, she is in perpetual motion, this lady, hair
like blown-up gold and finer than gold, hair and fingers and body
of inestimable grace. Heavy weighs the gold on the back of her
hairbrush and hand mirror. Heavy heavy the candlesticks in the
dining room. Very heavy is the big car, a Lincoln, long and black,
that on one cool autumn day split a squirrel's body in two unequal
parts.

3. The father. Dr.   . He belongs to the same clubs as #2.
A player of squash and golf; he has a golfer's umbrella of stripes.
Candy stripes. In his mouth nothing turns to sugar, however;
saliva works no miracles here. His doctoring is of the slightly
sick. The sick are sent elsewhere (to Dr. Berg?), the deathly sick
are sent back for more tests and their bills are sent to their homes,
the unsick are sent to Dr. Coronet (Isabel, a lady), an excellent
psychiatrist for unsick people who angrily believe they are sick
and want to do something about it. If they demand a male psychiatrist, the unsick are sent by Dr.   (my father) to Dr.
Lowenstein, a male psychiatrist, excellent and expensive, with a
limited practice.

4. Clarita. She is twenty, twenty-five, she is thirty or more?
Pretty, ugly, what? She is a woman lounging by the side of a
road, in jeans and a sweater, hitchhiking, or she is slouched on a
stool at a counter in some roadside diner. A hard line of jaw.
Curious eyes. Amused eyes. Behind her eyes processions move,
funeral pageants, cartoons. She says, "I never can figure out why
girls like you bum around down here. What are you looking for
anyway?" An odor of tobacco about her. Unwashed underclothes, or no underclothes, unwashed skin, gritty toes, hair long
and falling into strands, not recently washed.

5. Simon. In this city the weather changes abruptly, so Simon's weather changes abruptly. He sleeps through the afternoon. He sleeps through the morning. Rising, he gropes around for something to get him going, for a cigarette or a pill to drive him out to the street, where the temperature is hovering around 35°. Why doesn't it drop? Why, why doesn't the cold clean air come down from Canada; will he have to go up into Canada to get it? will he have to leave the Country of his Birth and sink into Canada's frosty fields . . . ? Will the F.B.I. (which he dreams about constantly) chase him over the Canadian border on foot, hounded out in a blizzard of broken glass and horns . . . ?

"Once I was Huckleberry Finn," Simon says, "but now I am Roderick Usher." Beset by frenzies and fears, this man who makes my spine go cold, he takes green pills, yellow pills, pills of white and capsules of dark blue and green . . . he takes other things I may not mention, for what if Simon seeks me out and climbs into my girl's bedroom here in Bloomfield Hills and strangles me, what then . . . ? (As I write this I begin to shiver. Why do I shiver? I am now sixteen and sixteen is not an age for shivering.) It comes from Simon, who is always cold.

III WORLD EVENTS

Nothing.

IV PEOPLE & CIRCUMSTANCES
CONTRIBUTING TO THIS DELINQUENCY

Nothing.

V SIOUX DRIVE

George, Clyde G. 240 Sioux. A manufacturer's representative; children, a dog, a wife. Georgian with the usual columns. You think of the White House, then of Thomas Jefferson, then your mind goes blank on the white pillars and you think of nothing. Norris, Ralph W. 246 Sioux. Public relations. Colonial. Bay window, brick, stone, concrete, wood, green shutters, sidewalk, lantern, grass, trees, blacktop drive, two children, one of them my classmate Esther (Esther Norris) at Baldwin. Wife, cars. Ramsey, Michael D. 250 Sioux. Colonial. Big living room, thirty by twenty-five, fireplaces in living room, library, recreation room, paneled walls wet bar five bathrooms five bedrooms two lavatories central air conditioning automatic sprinkler automatic garage door three children one wife two cars a breakfast room a patio a large fenced lot fourteen trees a front door with a brass knocker never knocked. Next is our house. Classic contemporary. Traditional modern. Attached garage, attached Florida room, attached patio, attached pool and cabana, attached roof. A front door mail slot through which pour *Time Magazine, Fortune, Life, Business Week,* the *Wall Street Journal,* the *New York Times,* the *New Yorker,* the *Saturday Review, M.D., Modern Medicine, Disease of the Month* . . . and also. . . . And in addition to all this, a quiet sealed letter from Baldwin saying: *Your daughter is not doing work compatible with her performance on the Stanford-Binet.* . . . And your son is not doing well, not well at all, very sad. Where is your son anyway? Once he stole trick-and-treat candy from some six-year-old kids, he himself being a robust ten. The beginning. Now your daughter steals. In the Village Pharmacy she made off with, yes she did, don't deny it, she made off with a copy of *Pageant Magazine* for no reason, she swiped a roll of Life Savers in a green wrapper and was in no need of saving

her life or even in need of sucking candy; when she was no more
than eight years old she stole, don't blush, she stole a package of
Tums only because it was out on the counter and available, and
the nice lady behind the counter (now dead) said nothing. . . .
Sioux Drive. Maples, oaks, elms. Diseased elms cut down.
Sioux Drive runs into Roosevelt Drive. Slow, turning lanes, not
streets, all drives and lanes and ways and passes. A private police
force. Quiet private police, in unmarked cars. Cruising on Saturday evenings with paternal smiles for the residents who are
streaming in and out of houses, going to and from parties, a thousand parties, slightly staggering, the women in their furs alight-
ing from automobiles bought of Ford and General Motors and
Chrysler, very heavy automobiles. No foreign cars. Detroit. In
275 Sioux, down the block in that magnificent French-Nor-
mandy mansion, lives   himself, who has the
C   account itself, imagine that! Look at where he lives and
look at the enormous trees and chimneys, imagine his many fireplaces, imagine his wife and children, imagine his wife's hair,
imagine her fingernails, imagine her bathtub of smooth clean
glowing pink, imagine their embraces, his trouser pockets filled
with odd coins and keys and dust and peanuts, imagine their ec-
stasy on Sioux Drive, imagine their income tax returns, imagine
their little boy's pride in his experimental car, a scaled-down
C   , as he roars around the neighborhood on the sidewalks
frightening dogs and Negro maids, oh imagine all these things,
imagine everything, let your mind roar out all over Sioux Drive
and Du Maurier Drive and Roosevelt Drive and Ticonderoga
Pass and Burning Bush Way and Lincolnshire Pass and Lois
Lane.

When spring comes, its winds blow nothing to Sioux Drive, no
odors of hollyhocks or forsythia, nothing Sioux Drive doesn't already possess, everything is planted and performing. The
weather vanes, had they weather vanes, don't have to turn with

the wind, don't have to contend with the weather. There is no weather.

VI DETROIT

There is always weather in Detroit. Detroit's temperature is always 32°. Fast-falling temperatures. Slow-rising temperatures. Wind from the north-northeast four to forty miles an hour, small-craft warnings, partly cloudy today and Wednesday changing to partly sunny through Thursday . . . small warnings of frost, soot warnings, traffic warnings, hazardous lake conditions for small craft and swimmers, restless Negro gangs, restless cloud formations, restless temperatures aching to fall out the very bottom of the thermometer or shoot up over the top and boil everything over in red mercury.

Detroit's temperature is 32°. Fast-falling temperatures. Slow-rising temperatures. Wind from the north-northeast four to forty miles an hour. . . .

VII EVENTS

1. The girl's heart is pounding. In her pocket is a pair of gloves! In a plastic bag! Airproof breathproof plastic bag, gloves selling for twenty-five dollars on Branden's counter! In her pocket! Shoplifted! . . . In her purse is a blue comb, not very clean. In her purse is a leather billfold (a birthday present from her grandmother in Philadelphia) with snapshots of the family in clean plastic windows, in the billfold are bills, she doesn't know how many bills. . . . In her purse is an ominous note from her friend Tykie *What's this about Joe H. and the kids*

hanging around at Louise's Sat. night? You heard anything?
. . . passed in French class. In her purse is a lot of dirty yellow
Kleenex, her mother's heart would break to see such very dirty
Kleenex, and at the bottom of her purse are brown hairpins and
safty pins and a broken pencil and a ballpoint pen (blue) stolen
from somewhere forgotten and a purse-size compact of Cover
Girl Make-Up, Ivory Rose. . . . Her lipstick is Broken Heart, a
corrupt pink; her fingers are trembling like crazy; her teeth are
beginning to chatter; her insides are alive; her eyes glow in her
head; she is saying to her mother's astonished face *I want to steal
but not to buy.*

2. At Clarita's. Day or night? What room is this? A bed, a
regular bed, and a mattress on the floor nearby. Wallpaper hanging in strips. Clarita says she tore it like that with her teeth. She
was fighting a barbaric tribe that night, high from some pills; she
was battling for her life with men wearing helmets of heavy iron
and their faces no more than Christian crosses to breathe
through, every one of those bastards looking like her lover Simon,
who seems to breathe with great difficulty through the slits of
mouth and nostrils in his face. Clarita has never heard of Sioux
Drive. Raymond Forrest cuts no ice with her, nor does the
C   account and its millions; Harvard Business School
could be at the corner of Vernor and 12th Street for all she cares,
and Vietnam might have sunk by now into the Dead Sea under
its tons of debris, for all the amazement she could show . . . her
face is overworked, overwrought, at the age of twenty (thirty?) it
is already exhausted but fanciful and ready for a laugh. Clarita
says mournfully to me *Honey somebody is going to turn you out
let me give you warning.* In a movie shown on late television Clarita is not a mess like this but a nurse, with short neat hair and a
dedicated look, in love with her doctor and her doctor's patients
and their diseases, enamored of needles and sponges and rubbing

alcohol. . . . Or no: she is a private secretary. Robert Cummings is her boss. She helps him with fantastic plots, the canned audience laughs, no, the audience doesn't laugh because nothing is funny, instead her boss is Robert Taylor and they are not boss and secretary but husband and wife, she is threatened by a young starlet, she is grim, handsome, wifely, a good companion for a good man. . . . She is Claudette Colbert. Her sister too is Claudette Colbert. They are twins, identical. Her husband Charles Boyer is a very rich handsome man and her sister, Claudette Colbert, is plotting her death in order to take her place as the rich man's wife, no one will know because they are *twins.* . . . All these marvelous lives Clarita might have lived, but she fell out the bottom at the age of thirteen. At the age when I was packing my overnight case for a slumber party at Toni Deshield's she was tearing filthy sheets off a bed and scratching up a rash on her arms. . . . Thirteen is uncommonly young for a white girl in Detroit, Miss Brock of the Detroit House of Correction said in a sad newspaper interview for the *Detroit News;* fifteen and sixteen are more likely. Eleven, twelve, thirteen are not surprising in colored . . . they are more precocious. What can we do? Taxes are rising and the tax base is falling. The temperature rises slowly but falls rapidly. Everything is falling out the bottom, Woodward Avenue is filthy, Livernois Avenue is filthy! Scraps of paper flutter in the air like pigeons, dirt flies up and hits you right in the eye, oh Detroit is breaking up into dangerous bits of newspaper and dirt, watch out. . . .

Clarita's apartment is over a restaurant. Simon her lover emerges from the cracks at dark. Mrs. Olesko, a neighbor of Clarita's, an aged white wisp of a woman, doesn't complain but sniffs with contentment at Clarita's noisy life and doesn't tell the cops, hating cops, when the cops arrive. I should give more fake names, more blanks, instead of telling all these secrets. I myself am a secret; I am a minor.

3. My father reads a paper at a medical convention in Los
Angeles. There he is, on the edge of the North American continent, when the unmarked detective put his hand so gently on my
arm in the aisle of Branden's and said, "Miss, would you like to
step over here for a minute?"

And where was he when Clarita put her hand on my arm, that
wintry dark sulphurous aching day in Detroit, in the company
of closed-down barber shops, closed-down diners, closed-down
movie houses, homes, windows, basements, faces . . . she put
her hand on my arm and said, "Honey, are you looking for somebody down here?"

And was he home worrying about me, gone for two weeks
solid, when they carried me off . . . ? It took three of them to
get me in the police cruiser, so they said, and they put more than
their hands on my arm.

4. I work on this lesson. My English teacher is Mr. Forest,
who is from Michigan State. Not handsome, Mr. Forest, and his
name is plain, unlike Raymond Forrest's, but he is sweet and
rodentlike, he has conferred with the principal and my parents,
and everything is fixed . . . treat her as if nothing has happened, a new start, begin again, only sixteen years old, what a
shame, how did it happen?—nothing happened, nothing could
have happened, a slight physiological modification known only to
a gynecologist or to Dr. Coronet. I work on my lesson. I sit in my
pink room. I look around the room with my sad pink eyes. I sigh,
I dawdle, I pause, I eat up time, I am limp and happy to be
home, I am sixteen years old suddenly, my head hangs heavy as a
pumpkin on my shoulders, and my hair has just been cut by Mr.
Faye at the Crystal Salon and is said to be very becoming.

(Simon too put his hand on my arm and said, "Honey, you
have got to come with me," and in his six-by-six room we got to
know each other. Would I go back to Simon again? Would I lie

down with him in all that filth and craziness? Over and over again.

a Clarita is being betrayed as in front of a Cunningham Drug Store she is nervously eying a colored man who may or may not have money, or a nervous white boy of twenty with sideburns and an Appalachian look, who may or may not have a knife hidden in his jacket pocket, or a husky red-faced man of friendly countenance who may or may not be a member of the Vice Squad out for an early twilight walk.)

I work on my lesson for Mr. Forest. I have filled up eleven pages. Words pour out of me and won't stop. I want to tell everything . . . what was the song Simon was always humming, and who was Simon's friend in a very new trench coat with an old high school graduation ring on his finger . . . ? Simon's bearded friend? When I was down too low for him, Simon kicked me out and gave me to him for three days, I think, on Fourteenth Street in Detroit, an airy room of cold cruel drafts with newspapers on the floor. . . . Do I really remember that or am I piecing it together from what they told me? Did they tell the truth? Did they know much of the truth?

VIII CHARACTERS

1. Wednesdays after school, at four; Saturday mornings at ten. Mother drives me to Dr. Coronet. Ferns in the office, plastic or real, they look the same. Dr. Coronet is queenly, an elegant nicotine-stained lady who would have studied with Freud had circumstances not prevented it, a bit of a Catholic, ready to offer

you some mystery if your teeth will ache too much without it. Highly recommended by Father! Forty dollars an hour, Father's forty dollars! Progress! Looking up! Looking better! That new haircut is so becoming, says Dr. Coronet herself, showing how normal she is for a woman with an I.Q. of 180 and many advanced degrees.

2. Mother. A lady in a brown suede coat. Boots of shiny black material, black gloves, a black fur hat. She would be humiliated could she know that of all the people in the world it is my ex-lover Simon who walks most like her . . . self-conscious and unreal, listening to distant music, a little bowlegged with craftiness. . . .

3. Father. Tying a necktie. In a hurry. On my first evening home he put his hand on my arm and said, "Honey, we're going to forget all about this."

4. Simon. Outside, a plane is crossing the sky, in here we're in a hurry. Morning. It must be morning. The girl is half out of her mind, whimpering and vague; Simon her dear friend is wretched this morning . . . he is wretched with morning itself . . . he forces her to give him an injection with that needle she knows is filthy, she has a dread of needles and surgical instruments and the odor of things that are to be sent into the blood, thinking somehow of her father. . . . This is a bad morning, Simon says that his mind is being twisted out of shape, and so he submits to the needle that he usually scorns and bites his lip with his yellowish teeth, his face going very pale. *Ah baby!* he says in his soft mocking voice, which with all women is a mockery of love, *do it like this—Slowly—*And the girl, terrified, almost drops the precious needle but manages to turn it up to the light from the window . . . is it an extension of herself then? She can give him this gift then? *I wish you wouldn't do this to me,* she says, wise in

her terror, because it seems to her that Simon's danger—in a few minutes he may be dead—is a way of pressing her against him that is more powerful than any other embrace. She has to work over his arm, the knotted corded veins of his arm, her forehead wet with perspiration as she pushes and releases the needle, staring at that mixture of liquid now stained with Simon's bright blood. . . . When the drug hits him she can feel it herself, she feels that magic that is more than any woman can give him, striking the back of his head and making his face stretch as if with the impact of a terrible sun. . . . She tries to embrace him but he pushes her aside and stumbles to his feet. *Jesus Christ,* he says. . . .

5. Princess, a Negro girl of eighteen. What is her charge? She is closed-mouthed about it, shrewd and silent, you know that no one had to wrestle her to the sidewalk to get her in here; she came with dignity. In the recreation room she sits reading *Nancy Drew and the Jewel Box Mystery,* which inspires in her face tiny wrinkles of alarm and interest: what a face! Light brown skin, heavy shaded eyes, heavy eyelashes, a serious sinister dark brow, graceful fingers, graceful wristbones, graceful legs, lips, tongue, a sugar-sweet voice, a leggy stride more masculine than Simon's and my mother's, decked out in a dirty white blouse and dirty white slacks; vaguely nautical is Princess' style. . . . At breakfast she is in charge of clearing the table and leans over me, saying, *Honey you sure you ate enough?*

6. The girl lies sleepless, wondering. Why here, why not there? Why Bloomfield Hills and not jail? Why jail and not her pink room? Why downtown Detroit and not Sioux Drive? What is the difference? Is Simon all the difference? The girl's head is a parade of wonders. She is nearly sixteen, her breath is marvelous with wonders, not long ago she was coloring with crayons and now she is smearing the landscape with paints that won't come

off and won't come off her fingers either. She says to the matron *I am not talking about anything,* not because everyone has warned her not to talk but because, because she will not talk; because she won't say anything about Simon, who is her secret. And she says to the matron, *I won't go home,* up until that night in the lavatory when everything was changed. . . . "No, I won't go home I want to stay here," she says, listening to her own words with amazement, thinking that weeds might climb everywhere over that marvelous $180,000 house and dinosaurs might return to muddy the beige carpeting, but never never will she reconcile four o'clock in the morning in Detroit with eight o'clock breakfasts in Bloomfield Hills. . . . oh, she aches still for Simon's hands and his caressing breath, though he gave her little pleasure, he took everything from her (five-dollar bills, ten-dollar bills, passed into her numb hands by men and taken out of her hands by Simon) until she herself was passed into the hands of other men, police, when Simon evidently got tired of her and her hysteria. . . . *No, I won't go home, I don't want to be bailed out.* The girl thinks as a *Stubborn and Wayward Child* (one of several charges lodged against her), and the matron understands her crazy white-rimmed eyes that are seeking out some new violence that will keep her in jail, should someone threaten to let her out. Such children try to strangle the matrons, the attendants, or one another . . . they want the locks locked forever, the doors nailed shut . . . and this girl is no different up until that night her mind is changed for her. . . .

IX THAT NIGHT

Princess and Dolly, a little white girl of maybe fifteen, hardy however as a sergeant and in the House of Correction for armed robbery, corner her in the lavatory at the farthest sink and the other girls look away and file out to bed, leaving her. God, how she is beaten up! Why is she beaten up? Why do they pound her, why such hatred? Princess vents all the hatred of a thousand silent Detroit winters on her body, this girl whose body belongs to me, fiercely she rides across the Midwestern plains on this girl's tender bruised body . . . revenge on the oppressed minorities of America! revenge on the slaughtered Indians! revenge on the female sex, on the male sex, revenge on Bloomfield Hills, revenge revenge. . . .

X DETROIT

In Detroit, weather weighs heavily upon everyone. The sky looms large. The horizon shimmers in smoke. Downtown the buildings are imprecise in the haze. Perpetual haze. Perpetual motion inside the haze. Across the choppy river is the city of Windsor, in Canada. Part of the continent has bunched up here and is bulging outward, at the tip of Detroit; a cold hard rain is forever falling on the expressways. . . . Shoppers shop grimly, their cars are not parked in safe places, their windshields may be smashed and graceful ebony hands may drag them out through their shatterproof smashed windshields, crying, *Revenge for the Indians!* Ah, they all fear leaving Hudson's and being dragged to the very tip of the city and thrown off the parking roof of Cobo Hall, that expensive tomb, into the river. . . .

XI CHARACTERS WE ARE
FOREVER ENTWINED WITH

1. Simon drew me into his tender rotting arms and breathed gravity into me. Then I came to earth, weighed down. He said, *You are such a little girl,* and he weighed me down with his delight. In the palms of his hands were teeth marks from his previous life experiences. He was thirty-five, they said. Imagine

Simon in this room, in my pink room: he is about six feet tall and
stoops slightly, in a feline cautious way, always thinking, always
on guard, with his scuffed light suede shoes and his clothes that
are anyone's clothes, slightly rumpled ordinary clothes that ordinary men might wear to not-bad jobs. Simon has fair long hair,
curly hair, spent languid curls that are like . . . exactly like the
curls of wood shavings to the touch, I am trying to be exact . . .
and he smells of unheated mornings and coffee and too many
pills coating his tongue with a faint green-white scum. . . .
Dear Simon, who would be panicked in this room and in this
house (right now Billie is vacuuming next door in my parents'
room; a vacuum cleaner's roar is a sign of all good things), Simon
who is said to have come from a home not much different from
this, years ago, fleeing all the carpeting and the polished banisters
. . . Simon has a deathly face, only desperate people fall in
love with it. His face is bony and cautious, the bones of his cheeks
prominent as if with the rigidity of his ceaseless thinking, plotting, for he has to make money out of girls to whom money
means nothing, they're so far gone they can hardly count it, and
in a sense money means nothing to him either except as a way of
keeping on with his life. *Each Day's Proud Struggle,* the title of a
novel we could read at jail. . . . Each day he needs a certain
amount of money. He devours it. It wasn't love he uncoiled in
me with his hollowed-out eyes and his courteous smile, that remnant of a prosperous past, but a dark terror that needed to press
itself flat against him, or against another man . . . but he was
the first, he came over to me and took my arm, a claim. We struggled on the stairs and I said, *Let me loose, you're hurting my
neck, my face,* it was such a surprise that my skin hurt where he
rubbed it, and afterward we lay face to face and he breathed
everything into me. In the end I think he turned me in.

2. Raymond Forrest. I just read this morning that Raymond
Forrest's father, the chairman of the board at   , died of a

heart attack on a plane bound for London. I would like to write Raymond Forrest a note of sympathy. I would like to thank him for not pressing charges against me one hundred years ago, saving me, being so generous . . . well, men like Raymond Forrest are generous men, not like Simon. I would like to write him a letter telling of my love, or of some other emotion that is positive and healthy. Not like Simon and his poetry, which he scrawled down when he was high and never changed a word . . . but when I try to think of something to say, it is Simon's language that comes back to me, caught in my head like a bad song, it is always Simon's language:

> *There is no reality only dreams*
> *Your neck may get snapped when you wake*
> *My love is drawn to some violent end*
> *She keeps wanting to get away*
> *My love is heading downward*
> *And I am heading upward*
> *She is going to crash on the sidewalk*
> *And I am going to dissolve into the clouds*

XII EVENTS

1. Out of the hospital, bruised and saddened and converted, with Princess' grunts still tangled in my hair . . . and Father in his overcoat looking like a prince himself, come to carry me off. Up the expressway and out north to home. Jesus Christ, but the air is thinner and cleaner here. Monumental houses. Heartbreaking sidewalks, so clean.

2. Weeping in the living room. The ceiling is two stories high and two chandeliers hang from it. Weeping, weeping, though Billie the maid is *probably listening*. I will never leave home

again. Never. Never leave home. Never leave this home again, never.

3. Sugar doughnuts for breakfast. The toaster is very shiny and my face is distorted in it. Is that my face?

4. The car is turning in the driveway. Father brings me home. Mother embraces me. Sunlight breaks in movieland patches on the roof of our traditional-contemporary home, which was designed for the famous automotive stylist whose identity, if I told you the name of the famous car he designed, you would all know, so I can't tell you because my teeth chatter at the thought of being sued . . . or having someone climb into my bedroom window with a rope to strangle me. . . . The car turns up the blacktop drive. The house opens to me like a doll's house, so lovely in the sunlight, the big living room beckons to me with its walls falling away in a delirium of joy at my return, Billie the maid is *no doubt* listening from the kitchen as I burst into tears and the hysteria Simon got so sick of. Convulsed in Father's arms, I say I will never leave again, never, why did I leave, where did I go, what happened, my mind is gone wrong, my body is one big bruise, my backbone was sucked dry, it wasn't the men who hurt me and Simon never hurt me but only those girls . . . my God, how they hurt me . . . I will never leave home again. . . . The car is perpetually turning up the drive and I am perpetually breaking down in the living room and we are perpetually taking the right exit from the expressway (Lahser Road) and the wall of the rest room is perpetually banging against my head and perpetually are Simon's hands moving across my body and adding everything up and so too are Father's hands on my shaking bruised back, far from the surface of my skin on the surface of my good blue cashmere coat (dry-cleaned for my release). . . . I weep for all the money here, for God in gold and beige carpeting, for the beauty of chandeliers and the miracle of a clean pol-

ished gleaming toaster and faucets that run both hot and cold water, and I tell them, *I will never leave home, this is my home, I love everything here, I am in love with everything here.* . . .

I am home.

The Wheel of Love

*Some must break
Upon the wheel of love, but not the strange,
The secret lords, whom only death can change.*

—*Stanley Kunitz, "Lovers Relentlessly"*

He and Nadia turned up the walk to their apartment building.

He and Nadia would go out to dinner that night.

He and Nadia could drive off any time they wanted, go anywhere: they were free.

David caught himself thinking this way, "He and Nadia," thinking about himself in the third person the way he had to think about Nadia, who was dead. She had been dead now for three months. But in his mind the sentences wound on, picking at the past and terrifying him with their hunger for the future. There was no longer any "He and Nadia could drive off any time they wanted. . . ." The fact was that while she had been alive they had not driven off like that; who was he trying to deceive?

So he thought clearly, "I have to be careful. I have to remember what has happened and, because of that, what can no longer happen."

That evening he was on his way to an ex-student's apartment for dinner. To a man so newly lonely, so newly alone, an invitation out meant an evening in other people's lives, and therefore freedom from his own, and it meant the possibility of laughter that would surprise him—how good it was to be alive and healthy, to have a body that had not given up in spite of everything. When he was with other people he realized that he had not really died along with Nadia after all.

The strange thing was that he hated to be invited out. He hated to play the game again, as one hates and fears returning to a childhood game that was once so easy. It was almost too much effort for him to show that he was alive when every cell in his body ached to die and have it over with. But he never turned down any invitations. He never said no because he was the sort of man, kindly and distracted, who would agree to anything; and what if he wanted to join the game again someday and he had no way to get in? He had parked his car down the block and was now walking quickly to his ex-student's apartment building. As he walked he listened to the curious lonely sound of his footsteps, a sound he had truly never heard before Nadia died, and he quelled the panic that rose in him by saying, "The hell with it. The hell with it," telling himself that he could stand anything, now that he had stood so much, that he could get through these few hours with a former student without breaking down.

The apartment building was shabby, and he felt his suit sympathize with the building and grow limp, wrinkled. Yes, he was shabby, he was tired. Why hide it? Everyone who saw him said, "that's the one whose wife killed herself," and made a moist clicking sound with their mouths; they would have wondered had he not been shabby. A young couple on their way out for Saturday night held the door open for him and he mumbled thanks and

ducked inside. He probably looked as if he lived here. All his life
David had melted into landscapes, just as Nadia had stood out
from them. Seen in the foyer of the expensive apartment house
where he lived, he looked as if he belonged there; seen in one of
the sleazy campus taverns, he looked as if he belonged there too.
Nadia had had the gift of eliminating all backgrounds. It had not
been her face, exactly, that angular, striking, nervous face that
always drew one's eye back to it, and not her long slender body
that looked always about to move on, to shift about restlessly
. . . but something in her manner, some indefinable impatience or intolerance in her voice. She blotted out landscapes and
other people, and she was beginning to blot out, for David, all of
the life he had led up to the time of her death.

Time led up a slight incline, like a cracked sidewalk, and at its
feeble peak was the top of his life: those several minutes when
they had explained to him that she was dead. Then time led
downward again, the same modest cracked sidewalk.

In the foyer he pressed the buzzer by Jerry Randolph's name
and was answered at once by another buzzer, which unlocked the
inner door. All this caution, David thought, in a neighborhood
like this? Why would anyone want to break in here? The buzzing had made him nervous and he tried to force the heavy door
shut behind him, but it was closing slowly of its own accord and
could not be hurried. He was standing there, no longer pushing
at it and not quite on his way again, when he heard: "Dr. Hutter? Hello."

Jerry stood on the landing, smiling nervously. "Hello," David
said. They both smiled. There was the awkward business of getting up the stairs with Jerry watching, but then they were on a
level and it was all right. "We live down here," Jerry said. They
walked along briskly. The corridor was gray and made David feel
nearsighted: something vague and fuzzy about the way it was
lighted. "We were lucky to get in here, so near school. . . .
Someone said he was moving out. . . ." David nodded to all

this, not really hearing it. He wished suddenly that he had stayed home. He wished that he had stayed safe in his own apartment, wearing out the hours until bedtime without bothering to turn on the lights, just sitting there in the living room that faced the park . . . . But Jerry was talking and David turned to him guiltily. He had always liked the boy and he forced himself to remember this.

"My wife Betty—"

This was a surprise: a wife. "Very pleased to meet you," he heard his voice say. She colored pleasantly, a pretty girl, ordinary and pretty and very young, like all the girls he noticed these days. They ushered him inside the apartment. They chattered together about the room, about Jerry's books and records, he had so many of them, and David gave the impression of listening. If he could get to the moment at which they offered him a drink he would be all right.

Jerry indicated the best chair. He sat. The little girl asked him about drinks and he said, "Yes, anything," and she disappeared. Good. Jerry sat and there was a moment of silence. But fortunately a record was playing and they listened to it carefully.

"Ah, Ives," David said.

"Isn't he wonderful?" said Jerry.

David could let the music answer for him. He sat back and relaxed. But he was such a fake these days, after Nadia had left him for the last time, that even his relaxing was just pretense. He had forgotten how to relax.

". . . eight more credit hours to go. It doesn't seem possible," Jerry was saying. David asked him about his plans for next year. The boy talked and now David had that drink. He smiled up at the girl, what-was-her-name, and accepted it. Because he needed it so much, he forced himself to sit and hear out one of Jerry's sentences to the end. Finally he said, "Here's to your new apartment. It's very nice."

They all drank. The girl smiled and then her smile weakened, became qualified. A tremor in his stomach told David when other people were thinking about Nadia; he looked away.

"What sort of work are you doing this semester?" he asked Jerry.

Jerry sat forward; he could talk for hours. He jumped from topic to topic as he had in class, his conversation a kind of free association of ideas and impressions, like the radical poetry published in the students' literary magazine. The girl was a little embarrassed. David caught something restless in her—she was blond and tanned, not the type David would have guessed for Jerry's kind of quibbling good nature, with a heavy gold bracelet weighing down one wrist. Too good for Jerry. Better background. In a minute Jerry would shift to the University and the class it represented, which had not been his class: his father had been unemployed for years and he, Jerry, was just now finishing up college though he was twenty-six.

". . . the trustees and the Establishment are identical," Jerry was saying.

They talked and the girl listened, fascinated by both husband and professor. When she excused herself and went out into the kitchen, David said, "Very lovely girl." The "very" made it sound insincere and this surprised him, since he had meant it.

"Yes," Jerry said, embarrassed. "She's the one I . . . I mentioned to you a few times. We finally got married in October. I'm afraid I was always bothering you, saying the most self-centered, self-conscious crap, wasting your time. . . ."

"No, not at all," David said vaguely.

"Your advice meant a lot to me. I might not have made it through school without it."

David took a drink, startled. He did not want anything frank or personal said to him this evening. He wanted nothing more than to play the game and hide behind drinks and dinner and ordinary, tedious conversation. Jesus Christ, he thought, does he mean it? He tried to think of what he could have said to this boy, while he himself had been carrying around with him daily the five-hundred-pound burden of a disintegrating marriage, a disintegrating wife. . . .

But Jerry was sensitive enough to switch onto another topic, racial discrimination at the University, which was so familiar that anyone could talk knowledgeably about it. And so on until dinner. They ate in the kitchen, but the overhead light had been turned off and there were candles on the table. David was touched by how hard the little girl was trying.

"More of this sauce?"

"No, thank you."

Eating was a pleasant distraction and he was able to relax a little. He wondered if it was true, what someone had said—that he looked tired, didn't he need a rest? A wave of self-pity swept upon him and he wanted to say, Yes, yes, I am tired, I am tired to death, someone please help me. But when he did speak his voice was as meaningless as the twang of a piece of metal.

". . . What do you think about that new law? Stopping and frisking men on the street?"

David tried to think what this was. He no longer read the newspapers; he had just forgotten about them. "Is it constitutional?" he said. This must have been a good answer, since it got Jerry going. He jiggled the table in his excitement, while David pushed food around on his plate. The girl said, "Oh, honey," and David was able to glance at his watch. It was still early. Jerry was talking about the police abusing a Negro woman, and how she had tried to cut her wrists in her cell. The girl said again, in a sharp surprised voice, "Honey." And all conversation stopped.

David kept on eating. He wanted to explain that it was all right. They need not be concerned. Please talk again. Talk. He ate to show them how composed he was after three months; he was not still thinking of his wife, who had taken every pill in the medicine cabinet, like a child playing a game, flooding her arteries with poisons that must have warred even on one another.

"Do you know Shapero's quartet? I want to play it for you,"
Jerry said, and when he got up he jiggled the table. The girl
steadied it and tried to smile at David, but her smile was unconvincing. From the other room Jerry called in: "Wait till you hear
the precision in this—it's stunning."

"Do you like music?" the girl said shyly.

Not really, David thought. Not any more. But he said yes,
because only those who are ugly and cruel and are never invited
anywhere admit they don't think about music at all—liking it or
not liking it.

They listened to the record. They had dessert. David thought,
eating, that food was a reality he had almost forgotten about. It
was real. Music and talk floated around and got lost, the hell with
them, but food was real and proved to him that he was alive.
There was always more of it. Music and talk and even people
could get lost, but food never.

Jerry got up and played the record again. They listened. The
girl pretended to listen and her frown of concentration seemed
to David lovely.

After dinner she remained out in the kitchen and he and Jerry
sat together, man to man. Jerry said, with the plodding sincerity
that had always made David like him, "I was sure sorry to hear
about it. I . . . I couldn't believe it at first. . . ." But if he had
known Nadia he would have believed it at once. ". . . all the
kids . . . I remember that one class, when you talked about
Keats. . . ." The class materialized in David's imagination, that
roomful of faces he had never realized cared so much about him,
were so sympathetic, so nosy. The girl returned, smiling shyly,
and Jerry brought that conversation to an undignified halt. He
was abrupt, graceless. The little girl stared down at her
feet—patent leather shoes, very pretty—and David wanted to
take their hands and bring them together, introduce them to each
other and leave, get out. What place had he, a forty-year-old
wreck still careening along with the force of forty years' momen-

tum, in this crowded happy little apartment? Tonight the girl would huddle in Jerry's arms and maybe even manage to weep, a few tears not for David but for the tragedy of it, how sad it was. . . .

Now they were talking about politics, and David could at least handle his side of the conversation. He felt aged, weary, a tennis player trapped in a game with someone twenty years younger, lunging to get shots no one expected him to get. He drank. Jerry drank and the little girl sat on the floor, her feet tucked primly under her skirt. This was the real thing, this kind of talk. Her eyes shone. She had heard so much about Dr. Hutter, the intellectual Dr. Hutter, and now David could not let her down. He had to perform, weary as he was. Every cell in his body ached but he kept on with the game.

"It really meant a lot—you coming here tonight," Jerry said. "Betty thought we maybe shouldn't bother you, but—" Jerry chattered on without noticing his wife's sharp, warning look. He had a thin, earnest, eager face, this boy who was no longer a boy but a man, growing into manhood and therefore forcing men like David on into middle age before they were ready for it. David felt a stab of sorrow to think that he was not equal to the boy's admiration. He was not equal to anyone's admiration. He wanted to explain this to them but his brain was clouded from the alcohol and the strain of keeping up talk, keeping his face sane and orderly. Jerry faltered, embarrassed and happy in that way only students can be happy, and his wife listened with a small worried smile, hoping he would not make another blunder.

Then it was time to leave. He would be carried along by the current of talk, right out the door and down the corridor into safety. Standing, they talked a little more easily than before. He had stayed late enough. The warm air of the room seemed to push drunkenly at him, pressing against his chest, and he felt as if he were on the brink of something terrible.

"I should—maybe I should explain—" he began.

They waited, but he did not go on. He stared past them and was silent.

Then the chorus of farewells again, and the open door, and the hall that made him feel nearsighted; and at last the night air.

Outside, he knew what he had wanted to tell them. It came to him suddenly, like a blow. They had to know—they shouldn't be fooled—that he was not mourning Nadia's death, but his own. He hated her for the selfishness of her death and for her having eclipsed him forever, obliterated him as if she had smashed an insect under her shoe. He would always be pointed out as the man whose wife had killed herself. That would be the only interesting fact about him, and how could he ever rise above it by anything in his own life?

"Like a slug. A filthy slug," he said aloud. His dead wife was a slug that had trailed its slime across the whiteness of his life, and this was what he had wanted to tell his student and that worried little girl. For a moment he thought about going back to tell them, running back and pounding on the door. "I want you to know the truth! The truth!" Then he recovered and went on home.

II

Three months before, on the day before Nadia died, they had been driving out to her mother's house. It was a Sunday and that day remained in David's mind always blank, blurred, pale, the sky not blue but not white either, overcast by a veil of haze.

She was driving and he didn't like the way she passed everyone, as if she really wanted to get where they were going. But she said, "I can handle the car. I'm fine." She wore a black and white checked coat, of a simple and expensive cut, like all her clothes. When David came home and found another of those packages on their bed, the long rectangular cardboard box with flimsy paper inside or lying half-crumpled on the bed, he always felt a mixture of anger and helplessness. The new suit or new dress would be in the closet and he could never tell which one it was, but the box was left out, accidentally, carelessly, as if she had forgotten about how he felt when her mother gave her money. She would say, her eyes large and restless in their deep sockets, "My mother wants to do it, why should I refuse her?"

She swung out into the left lane, preparing to pass another car. David said, "You should have let me drive." She said at once, "Don't talk to me like that. Don't make me angry." The car gathered power and rushed forward, leaving the other car behind. David lit a cigarette and saw how absurdly it trembled in his fingers.

"You keep at me all the time," she said.

"All right."

"You never let me alone." From the side, Nadia's face looked slender and anxious; she had a gambler's thin, suspicious nose. With her, words were just sounds to thrust out at David or at anyone—even her doctor, who had finally contacted David to ask his cooperation—to keep them at a distance, to distract them. She did not really listen to what she said and so it was a surprise when she remembered odd, stray little remarks of his, years old. She would smile at him with her dreamy calculating smile and recall observations he had made, years ago when he had been another person. It was the same power she had in her face, something he could not imagine until he experienced it, again and again: the power to turn her gaze upon him and excite him so that he felt shaken and helpless, as innocent as he had been when they had first met.

"Because of the way we came together, you can never respect me," she was saying. Their arguments made his head ache because he always gave in and, in giving in, he knew that the victory was nothing important to her; she was already thinking of something else.

"Look, please," he said. "It's a lovely day. It's Sunday. Why don't you relax?"

"In every car on this highway someone is telling someone else to relax," Nadia muttered. "What are you going to say to my mother? About my going to Toronto?"

"Nothing."

Nadia glanced at him. "Were you really so worried?"

He did not answer. His head was aching.

"David, look," she said. "I know how you feel. I know. But what about me? I keep thinking of going away, of going to strange places . . . can't you understand that? You've never tried to understand it. I think of dirty old buses, I think of walking, hitching rides . . . if you woke up one morning and ran outside and ran away from your life, wouldn't you come into a new one? What would it be? And if you had run away a day earlier, wouldn't you have gone to a different life still, a different world? When people know this, how can they stay in one place?"

"Nadia, we don't want to talk about this again. Not now."

"But you stay where you are and you're so permanent," she said, "you seem to me heavy and strange, like a statue. I can feel you behind me when I leave, I circle around you and feel you there, I don't know what happens. . . . He told me to call this Dr. Hack, but I'm not going to. I know very well what Dr. Hack is."

"We'll call him tomorrow."

"Everyone is like me! They want to have other lives, be other people. Don't tell me. If I have to be just one person I'll kill myself—"

"Don't talk like that, Nadia. Please."

"What day is today? Sunday?" She frowned and he saw sharp lines on her forehead, between her eyes. In a few years she would look like a witch, he thought. He was unmoved. The love he felt for this woman was a condition he existed in, the way he existed in a world of gases only accidentally fit to breathe. He needed this love for survival the way he needed air, but it would never have occurred to him to be grateful for it or to feel any affection for Nadia, beneath the surface of his passion. And what a famous passion it must be, he thought—married now for six years and still hollow-eyed with being so alert, with having to see in every stranger an object for Nadia's meticulous and always serious concern.

Right now it was a child on a bicycle, coming toward them. She rode on the muddy shoulder of the highway, a girl of about twelve. Hands firm on the handlebars, on red plastic guards that were probably soiled, body leaning forward, legs pumping . . . she wore sneakers and white socks.

"Wonder where she's going in such a hurry," Nadia said.

He saw her take the time to glance into the rear-view mirror, and he was bitter with jealousy. It was like a taste in his mouth. Her imagination sailed off backward with the child, to what ugly little farmhouse crouched on the edge of this highway, stunned by the road getting so wide and so busy over the years, to what drudge of a mother and what father resting all day from a week in the factory, now that these small old farms were no longer worked . . . ?

"I used to love riding a bicycle," Nadia said softly.

"We could get two bicycles. Keep them in the garage."

"I'm too old for it now. . . ."

"Everyone rides bicycles in the park. Grandfathers. Grandmothers."

"It wouldn't be the same thing," she said.

It was never the "same thing" with them. She was vague and exasperating. Why wouldn't it be the same thing? She was a woman who had abandoned her own life, her own body, and David felt shackled to a corpse.

She disappeared sometimes and when she returned to him, haggard and wistful, he always took her in. She had done nothing wrong, even when there had been other men involved, at

least nothing that should not have been done; and if she stayed
home for his sake in the apartment she had wanted so badly, she
could sit for four, five hours at a time in the bedroom, staring out
at the park. The building was expensive because its hundred or
so inhabitants could stare out their windows at the jumble of
leaves and branches that was the park, but there was a terror to
the silence of trees that could never be imagined by one living an
ordinary noisy life. He said to her, Call that girl you used to see,
what's-her-name, and go shopping. Have lunch. He said, Why
don't we have someone over? I can help you with dinner. He
bought tickets to plays and concerts, wooing her, luring her out,
but he got no happiness from her icy, beautiful face if that
drugged look was in it. Neutral to the touch as wax, neither cold
nor warm, having neither softness nor hardness—her skin lay on
the outermost limits of her body, and that was all. If she did not
run away on an impulse to Chicago or Toronto, she could be just
as far away lying beside him at night. She said, "I keep wanting
to go away but I need you here. I need you back here, waiting."

"Do you think that's healthy? Normal?"

"I don't know what that means, normal," she had said slowly.

He thought that if they went out driving more, went on sudden trips of their own, she would give in to him and become his
wife. A wife was a kind of possession and no husband thought
that way until something went wrong: there were things in life
you had to have, to possess, you had to be able to depend upon.
He tried to explain this to her. But his love was the anchor that
held her down and kept her safe, no matter how far away she
went. Without him, she would have had no one to encircle and
she would have kept going forever in one direction, lost.

Now she let her head fall back a little, in a girlish indication of
surprise. And chagrin. She said, "David, I don't think this is the
right Sunday."

"What?"

"I don't think she meant today. She meant next week."

"Are you sure?" David said.

"I think so. . . . Isn't this silly?"

If she questioned anything, David lost his capacity to be certain about it. She might have doubted his own past, the years before she came into his life, and he would have had to struggle to retain it. So he said, "Well, whatever you say. I'm not very anxious to keep going."

"I know."

"I like your mother, but. . . ."

"Mothers are all the same. Mothers, fathers," she said. "I hate your family and you hate mine, no, don't interrupt, I'm not complaining. Everyone knows these things. Well, what should we do?"

"What do you want to do? Keep on driving?"

"Please don't make fun of me."

"I wasn't. I'm just trying to understand you."

Nadia laughed. "But you're the one who's strange! How anyone can stay in one place, one room, for five years the way you did, the same job, the same life. . . . What should we do now?"

"We can turn around and go back home."

"But maybe it was today? I can't remember," she said. "Today or next Sunday? It's always a Sunday. . . . Why does she bother me, why can't she leave me alone?" she said angrily. "I have you now and I don't need her. I wish she could understand that."

"What did you mean just now?"

"What?"

"Not being able to understand me—"

"Christ, this car is hot," she said. The sun had broken through the haze. Nadia rolled down the window and the air blasted against her face, whipping her short dark hair back. "I can't stand driving, I hate being so hot and sweaty. Tell me what you want to do or I'll drive off the road. I'll turn the car into that field."

"Just slow down," he said. He spoke carefully, though his head was pounding with pain. "It's all right, Nadia. You can park on the edge."

She let the car roll to a stop. Now the sunlight pounded onto the hood of the car and through the windshield. "You don't want me to go anywhere again, so why should I? I'll stay in one place forever," she said. She snatched the keys out of the ignition and threw them out the window. They landed on the far side of the highway, with a thin metallic ting.

"It's all right, Nadia."

"Nothing's all right."

"We can just sit here and relax for a minute."

She was breathing hard. Always, confronted with the real woman and not just with the memory of her, David felt how inadequate he was—how little he knew, how little power he had. She was like a rich, complex gift bestowed upon him, one he had received without earning and so could not enjoy. "Please don't leave me again," he said. He took both her hands and turned her to him, he pressed her cold hands against his face. They sat like this for some time, both breathing hard, nervously. He thought, If I look up at her and she looks at me in that certain way, it will mean something.

He looked up and her eyes, in their dark, strained sockets, were fixed on him. She smiled hesitantly.

"Here we are, in this one life," she said.

A surge of love for her rose within him. He loved her and he was not going to let her go. For six years he had been strong enough always to draw her back, and he would be able to save her. Why not? Sunlight flooded the car and pounded on the side of his face, like the strength that coursed through his body and gave him such power.

III

About seven years before that day, in early October, David had been in his old room a few blocks from the University, waiting. He had waited part of a Monday and all day Tuesday, stepping out now and then onto the top of his landlady's back porch, which had been converted into a kind of balcony for anyone who rented the second floor. It looked out and down to a nondescript back yard, mainly crab grass and dandelions, and finally to a board fence; behind that a few yards was a railroad track, on a raised column of ground.

He would have to go out the next day, but Tuesday he could stay home, waiting for her, and at the thought of her coming to him he felt his heart pound violently. He was like a machine or a complicated toy whose parts have begun to speed up inside. In the medicine-cabinet mirror his face looked the same, his skin a little pale but cool, almost clammy. He had the look of a man who is waiting.

Every hour he turned up the radio volume and listened to the news. Listening to the news was like sliding downhill. At first there was confusion and pain, then you got numb, then you were at the bottom and could not remember how bad it had been. He listened, sweating, to the urgent details of crisis in China, Berlin, Cuba, and then to details of crisis in Washington, and finally to items about little children whose dogs had been found after two weeks, or children whose cats had been rescued from trees by the Fire Department. Then he turned down the volume again. He went out on his makeshift balcony and leaned on the railing, looking out into the rich golden air of early autumn and sometimes not even thinking about Nadia, not even thinking her name.

She did finally come, that evening. She had been breathless,

with her long hair disheveled about her face. David stared at her
hungrily to see what she was bringing him: and she looked back
at him and smiled. It was all right. He drew her into the room
and closed the door and they stood looking at each other, afraid to
let their excitement show. She said, "We've been talking about it
for two days nearly. All last night and today. I told him how I felt
and he understands, it's all over. He understands." She half-
closed her eyes, those languid bluish lids, in an adolescent expression of relief.

"Here, sit down," David said. They were furtive and bumbling, like children playing at being adults. "I bought this to celebrate. In case there was something to celebrate."

"Did you think I might not come?" she said shyly.

It took him a while to get the cork out and his face flushed. She
laughed with him, her own cheeks hectic and red. When she
held up her glass for him to fill, he noticed how it trembled in her
fingers.

"No, I knew you'd come," he said.

Even now, awkward as she was, this young girl knew the secret rhythm that women have for moments of intimacy; she was
awkward but not embarrassed. She sat back with a gesture of exhaustion that was only pretense, childish pretense, and smiled at
him over the rim of the glass, a lovely dazzling smile that meant
she had come a long way, a very long way to this room. "My God,
my God," she whispered. There was so much to say, so much to
ask, that David could not begin. He sat smiling as if enchanted,
staring into a light that was radiant but blinding.

She had first appeared to him as an indifferently ordinary
body, a girl in the company of other people. He could not truly say
when he had first seen her, but she remembered her first impression of him because of course he was someone special; even the
least of professors is a public personality. All this was teasing,
droll, but something in him hungered for it: her heavy antique
bracelets, her old-fashioned sapphire ring, and that air she had at

all times—even when sloppily dressed—of belonging strangely to both the present and a personal, private past. She was not a college student but instead the wife of a young instructor, and she explained rapidly and defensively that she had not graduated from college, no, she had dropped out in her second year. And then she would pause, as if only now did she recall why she had dropped out, and the recollection was unpleasant. "What I want is to get out of here. This city. I want to go back home, where my mother is," Nadia would say, gently and persistently, so that anyone who heard her knew she was demanding something. Of her husband she said little. "It was a mistake. I was too young. He'll be happy to stay here forever. And he listens to the opera on the radio, any opera, all day Sunday." She spoke in a rapid, clipped voice, flushed at her vulgarity but really not caring, carrying it all off whimsically and brusquely. She had decided to take a night course, not for credit, and so she had walked into David's life, idle and always perfectly dressed, with an odor or look about her of clear, sun-drenched days at the shore and a dark, studious gaze of utter frankness. She had always worn sleek, high-heeled shoes that made her long legs look even longer and more slender than they were, and made her shoulders arch slightly and the curve at the base of her spine show as if she were sucking in her breath. Her hair was loose on her shoulders and it did not make her look casual so much as it made her look impatient, restless.

And so she had run up his stairs and into his room, this elaborately furnished and cluttered room he had had for years all to himself, and changed both their lives. In his arms she was like treasure scooped up and flung upon him by the sea, overwhelming him, sweeping him along with its fragrant odor and its rich, heavy, entwining embrace, something that looked and felt soft but was strangely ornamental, even glittering. No one else existed in the world except them. There was no one.

David woke to hear a vague sputtering, some static: just the radio over on his desk. Its dial showed in the dark, a dim orange,

but he looked away and forgot it. She asked him something sleepily, and he answered, telling her nothing but giving her all she
wanted—the sound of his voice. The moment was sealed within
itself, David thought, and nothing could change it, as if he and
this girl were on an island together, able to read in each other's
eyes the opaque secret of life—huddling together, embracing,
loving, thwarted only at having at last to come apart and be two
people again. All of the world must be straining against his windows to get a glimpse at them, he thought fiercely; all of the
world must be sick with jealousy to know that it could never have
what they possessed together.

*F*our Summers

It is some kind of special day. "Where's Sissie?" Ma says. Her face gets sharp, she is frightened. When I run around her chair she laughs and hugs me. She is pretty when she laughs. Her hair is long and pretty.

We are sitting at the best table of all, out near the water. The sun is warm and the air smells nice. Daddy is coming back from the building with some glasses of beer, held in his arms. He makes a grunting noise when he sits down.

"Is the lake deep?" I ask them.

They don't hear me, they're talking. A woman and a man are sitting with us. The man marched in the parade we saw just awhile ago; he is a volunteer fireman and is wearing a uniform.

Now his shirt is pulled open because it is hot. I can see the dark curly hair way up by his throat; it looks hot and prickly.

A man in a soldier's uniform comes over to us. They are all friends, but I can't remember him. We used to live around here, Ma told me, and then we moved away. The men are laughing. The man in the uniform leans back against the railing, laughing, and I am afraid it will break and he will fall into the water.

"Can we go out in a boat, Dad?" says Jerry.

He and Frank keep running back and forth. I don't want to go with them, I want to stay by Ma. She smells nice. Frank's face is dirty with sweat. "Dad," he says, whining, "can't we go out in a boat? Them kids are going out."

A big lake is behind the building and the open part where we are sitting. Some people are rowing on it. This tavern is noisy and everyone is laughing; it is too noisy for Dad to think about what Frank said.

"Harry," says Ma, "the kids want a boat ride. Why don't you leave off drinking and take them?"

"What?" says Dad.

He looks up from laughing with the men. His face is damp with sweat and he is happy. "Yeah, sure, in a few minutes. Go over there and play and I'll take you out in a few minutes."

The boys run out back by the rowboats, and I run after them. I have a bag of potato chips.

An old man with a white hat pulled down over his forehead is sitting by the boats, smoking. "You kids be careful," he says.

Frank is leaning over and looking at one of the boats. "This here is the best one," he says.

"Why's this one got water in it?" says Jerry.

"You kids watch out. Where's your father?" the man says.

"He's gonna take us for a ride," says Frank.

"Where is he?"

The boys run along, looking at the boats that are tied up. They don't bother with me. The boats are all painted dark green, but the paint is peeling off some of them in little pieces. There is water inside some of them. We watch two people come in, a man and a woman. The woman is giggling. She has on a pink dress and she leans over to trail one finger in the water. "What's all this filthy stuff by the shore?" she says. There is some scum in the water. It is colored a light brown, and there are little seeds and twigs and leaves in it.

The man helps the woman out of the boat. They laugh together. Around their rowboat little waves are still moving; they make a churning noise that I like.

"Where's Dad?" Frank says.

"He ain't coming," says Jerry.

They are tossing pebbles out into the water. Frank throws his sideways, twisting his body. He is ten and very big. "I bet he ain't coming," Jerry says, wiping his nose with the back of his hand.

After awhile we go back to the table. Behind the table is the white railing, and then the water, and then the bank curves out so that the weeping willow trees droop over the water. More men in uniforms, from the parade, are walking by.

"Dad," says Frank, "can't we go out? Can't we? There's a real nice boat there—"

"For Christ's sake, get them off me," Dad says. He is angry with Ma. "Why don't you take them out?"

"Honey, I can't row."

"Should we take out a boat, us two?" the other woman says. She has very short, wet-looking hair. It is curled in tiny little curls close to her head and is very bright. "We'll show them, Lenore. Come on, let's give your kids a ride. Show these guys how strong we are."

"That's all you need, to sink a boat," her husband says.

They all laugh.

The table is filled with brown beer bottles and wrappers of things. I can feel how happy they all are together, drawn together by the round table. I lean against Ma's warm leg and she pats me without looking down. She lunges forward and I can tell even before she says something that she is going to be loud.

"You guys're just jealous! Afraid we'll meet some soldiers!" she says.

"Can't we go out, Dad? Please?" Frank says. "We won't fight. . . ."

"Go and play over there. What're those kids doing—over there?" Dad says, frowning. His face is damp and loose, the way it is sometimes when he drinks. "In a little while, okay? Ask your mother."

"She can't do it," Frank says.

"They're just jealous," Ma says to the other woman, giggling. "They're afraid we might meet somebody somewhere."

"Just who's gonna meet this one here?" the other man says, nodding with his head at his wife.

Frank and Jerry walk away. I stay by Ma. My eyes burn and I want to sleep, but they won't be leaving for a long time. It is still daylight. When we go home from places like this it is always dark and getting chilly and the grass by our house is wet.

"Duane Dorsey's in jail," Dad says. "You guys heard about that?"

"Duane? Yeah, really?"

"It was in the newspaper. His mother-in-law or somebody called the police, he was breaking windows in her house."

"That Duane was always a nut!"

"Is he out now, or what?"

"I don't know, I don't see him these days. We had a fight," Dad says.

The woman with the short hair looks at me. "She's a real cute little thing," she says, stretching her mouth. "She drink beer, Lenore?"

"I don't know."

"Want some of mine?"

She leans toward me and holds the glass by my mouth. I can

smell the beer and the warm stale smell of perfume. There are pink lipstick smudges on the glass.

"Hey, what the hell are you doing?" her husband says.

When he talks rough like that I remember him: we were with him once before.

"Are you swearing at me?" the woman says.

"Leave off the kid, you want to make her a drunk like yourself?"

"It don't hurt, one little sip. . . ."

"It's okay," Ma says. She puts her arm around my shoulders and pulls me closer to the table.

"Let's play cards. Who wants to?" Dad says.

"Sissie wants a little sip, don't you?" the woman says. She is smiling at me and I can see that her teeth are darkish, not nice like Ma's.

"Sure, go ahead," says Ma.

"I said leave off that, Sue, for Christ's sake," the man says. He jerks the table. He is a big man with a thick neck; he is bigger than Dad. His eyebrows are blond, lighter than his hair, and are thick and tufted. Dad is staring at something out on the lake without seeing it. "Harry, look, my goddam wife is trying to make your kid drink beer."

"Who's getting hurt?" Ma says angrily.

Pa looks at me all at once and smiles. "Do you want it, baby?"

I have to say yes. The woman grins and holds the glass down to me, and it clicks against my teeth. They laugh. I stop swallowing right away because it is ugly, and some of the beer drips down on me. "Honey, you're so clumsy," Ma says, wiping me with a napkin.

"She's a real cute girl," the woman says, sitting back in her chair. "I wish I had a nice little girl like that."

"Lay off of that," says her husband.

"Hey, did you bring any cards?" Dad says to the soldier.

"They got some inside."

"Look, I'm sick of cards," Ma says.

"Yeah, why don't we all go for a boat ride?" says the woman. "Be real nice, something new. Every time we get together we play cards. How's about a boat ride?"

"It better be a big boat, with you in it," her husband says. He is pleased when everyone laughs, even the woman. The soldier lights a cigarette and laughs. "How come your cousin here's so skinny and you're so fat?"

"She isn't fat," says Ma. "What the hell do you want? Look at yourself."

"Yes, the best days of my life are behind me," the man says. He wipes his face and then presses a beer bottle against it. "Harry, you're lucky you moved out. It's all going downhill, back in the neighborhood."

"You should talk, you let our house look like hell," the woman says. Her face is blotched now, some parts pale and some red. "Harry don't sit out in his back yard all weekend drinking. He gets something done."

"Harry's younger than me."

Ma reaches over and touches Dad's arm. "Harry, why don't you take the kids out? Before it gets dark."

Dad lifts his glass and finishes his beer. "Who else wants more?" he says.

"I'll get them, you went last time," the soldier says.

"Get a chair for yourself," says Dad. "We can play poker."

"I don't want to play poker, I want to play rummy," the woman says.

"At church this morning Father Reilly was real mad," says Ma. "He said some kids or somebody was out in the cemetery and left some beer bottles. Isn't that awful?"

"Duane Dorsey used to do worse than that," the man says, winking.

"Hey, who's that over there?"

"You mean that fat guy?"

"Isn't that the guy at the lumberyard that owes all that money?"

Dad turns around. His chair wobbles and he almost falls; he is angry.

"This goddamn place is too crowded," he says.

"This is a real nice place," the woman says. She is taking something out of her purse. "I always liked it, didn't you, Lenore?"

"Sue and me used to come here a lot," says Ma. "And not just with you two, either."

"Yeah, we're real jealous," the man says.

"You should be," says the woman.

The soldier comes back. Now I can see that he is really a boy. He runs to the table with the beer before he drops anything. He laughs.

"Jimmy, your ma wouldn't like to see you drinking!" the woman says happily.

"Well, she ain't here."

"Are they still living out in the country?" Ma says to the woman.

"Sure. No electricity, no running water, no bathroom—same old thing. What can you do with people like that?"

"She always talks about going back to the Old Country," the soldier says. "Thinks she can save up money and go back."

"Poor old bastards don't know there was a war," Dad says. He looks as if something tasted bad in his mouth. "My old man died thinking he could go back in a year or two. Stupid old bastards!"

"Your father was real nice. . . ." Ma says.

"Yeah, real nice," says Dad. "Better off dead."

Everybody is quiet.

"June Dieter's mother's got the same thing," the woman says in a low voice to Ma. "She's had it a year now and don't weigh a hundred pounds—you remember how big she used to be."

"She was big, all right," Ma says.

"Remember how she ran after June and slapped her? We were there—some guys were driving us home."

"Yeah. So she's got it too."

"Hey," says Dad, "why don't you get a chair, Jimmy? Sit down here."

The soldier looks around. His face is raw in spots, broken out. But his eyes are nice. He never looks at me.

"Get a chair from that table," Dad says.

"Those people might want it."

"Hell, just take it. Nobody's sitting on it."

"They might—"

Dad reaches around and yanks the chair over. The people look at him but don't say anything. Dad is breathing hard. "Here, sit here," he says. The soldier sits down.

Frank and Jerry come back. They stand by Dad, watching him. "Can we go out now?" Frank says.

"What?"

"Out for a boat ride."

"What? No, next week. Do it next week. We're going to play cards."

"You said—"

"Shut up, we'll do it next week." Dad looks up and shades his eyes. "The lake don't look right anyway."

"Lot's of people are out there—"

"I said shut up."

"Honey," Ma whispers, "let him alone. Go and play by yourselves."

"Can we sit in the car?"

"Okay, but don't honk the horn."

"Ma, can't we go for a ride?"

"Go and play by yourselves, stop bothering us," she says. "Hey, will you take Sissie?"

They look at me. They don't like me, I can see it, but they take me with them. We run through the crowd and somebody spills a drink—he yells at us. "Oops, got to watch it!" Frank giggles.

We run along the walk by the boat. A woman in a yellow dress is carrying a baby. She looks at us like she doesn't like us.

Down at the far end some kids are standing together.

"Hey, lookit that," Frank says.

A blackbird is caught in the scum, by one of the boats. It can't fly up. One of the kids, a long-legged girl in a dirty dress, is poking at it with a stick.

The bird's wings keep fluttering but it can't get out. If it could get free it would fly and be safe, but the scum holds it down.

One of the kids throws a stone at it. "Stupid old goddamn bird," somebody says. Frank throws a stone. They are all throwing stones. The bird doesn't know enough to turn away. Its feathers are all wet and dirty. One of the stones hits the bird's head.

"Take that!" Frank says, throwing a rock. The water splashes up and some of the girls scream.

I watch them throwing stones. I am standing at the side. If the bird dies, then everything can die, I think. Inside the tavern there is music from the jukebox.

II

We are at the boathouse tavern again. It is a mild day, a Sunday afternoon. Dad is talking with some men; Jerry and I are waiting by the boats. Mommy is at home with the new baby. Frank has gone off with some friends of his, to a stock-car race. There are some people here, sitting out at the tables, but they don't notice us.

"Why doesn't he hurry up?" Jerry says.

Jerry is twelve now. He has pimples on his forehead and chin. He pushes one of the rowboats with his foot. He is wearing sneakers that are dirty. I wish I could get in that boat and sit down, but I am afraid. A boy not much older than Jerry is squatting on the boardwalk, smoking. You can tell he is in charge of the boats.

"Daddy, come on. Come on," Jerry says, whining. Daddy can't hear him.

I have mosquito bites on my arms and legs. There are mosquitoes and flies around here; the flies crawl around the sticky mess left on tables. A car over in the parking lot has its radio on loud. You can hear the music all this way. "He's coming," I tell Jerry so he won't be mad. Jerry is like Dad, the way his eyes look.

"Oh, that fat guy keeps talking to him," Jerry says.

The fat man is one of the bartenders; he has on a dirty white apron. All these men are familiar. We have been seeing them for years. He punches Dad's arm, up by the shoulder, and Dad pushes him. They are laughing, though. Nobody is mad.

"I'd sooner let a nigger—" the bartender says. We can't hear anything more, but the men laugh again.

"All he does is drink," Jerry says. "I hate him."

At school, up on the sixth-grade floor, Jerry got in trouble last month. The principal slapped him. I am afraid to look at Jerry when he's mad.

"I hate him, I wish he'd die," Jerry says.

Dad is trying to come to us, but every time he takes a step backward and gets ready to turn, one of the men says something. There are three men beside him. Their stomachs are big, but Dad's isn't. He is wearing dark pants and a white shirt; his tie is in the car. He wears a tie to church, then takes it off. He has his shirt sleeves rolled up and you can see how strong his arms must be.

Two women cross over from the parking lot. They are wearing high-heeled shoes and hats and bright dresses—orange and yellow—and when they walk past the men look at them. They go into the tavern. The men laugh about something. The way they laugh makes my eyes focus on something away from them—a bird flying in the sky—and it is hard for me to look anywhere else. I feel as if I'm falling asleep.

"Here he comes!" Jerry says.

Dad walks over to us, with his big steps. He is smiling and carrying a bottle of beer. "Hey, kid," he says to the boy squatting on the walk, "how's about a boat?"

"This one is the best," Jerry says.

"The best, huh? Great." Dad grins at us. "Okay, Sissie, let's get you in. Be careful now." He picks me up even though I am too heavy for it, and sets me in the boat. It hurts a little where he held me, under the arms, but I don't care.

Jerry climbs in. Dad steps and something happens—he almost slips, but he catches himself. With the wet oar he pushes us off from the boardwalk.

Dad can row fast. The sunlight is gleaming on the water. I sit very still, facing him, afraid to move. The boat goes fast, and Dad is leaning back and forth and pulling on the oars, breathing hard, doing everything fast like he always does. He is always in a hurry to get things done. He has set the bottle of beer down by his leg, pressed against the side of the boat so it won't fall.

"There's the guys we saw go out before," Jerry says. Coming around the island is a boat with three boys in it, older than Jerry. "They went on the island. Can we go there too?"

"Sure," says Dad. His eyes squint in the sun. He is sun-tanned, and there are freckles on his forehead. I am sitting close to him, facing him, and it surprises me what he looks like—he is like a stranger, with his eyes narrowed. The water beneath the boat makes me feel funny. It keeps us up now, but if I fell over the side I would sink and drown.

"Nice out here, huh?" Dad says. He is breathing hard.

"We should go over that way to get on the island," Jerry says.

"This goddamn oar has splinters in it," Dad says. He hooks the oar up and lets us glide. He reaches down to get the bottle of beer. Though the lake and some trees and the buildings back on shore are in front of me, what makes me look at it is my father's throat, the way it bobs when he swallows. He wipes his forehead. "Want to row, Sissie?" he says.

"Can I?"

"Let me do it," says Jerry.

"Naw, I was just kidding," Dad says.

"I can do it. It ain't hard."

"Stay where you are," Dad says.

He starts rowing again, faster. Why does he go so fast? His face is getting red, the way it does at home when he has trouble with Frank. He clears his throat and spits over the side; I don't like to see that but I can't help but watch. The other boat glides past us, heading for shore. The boys don't look over at us.

Jerry and I look to see if anyone else is on the island, but no one is. The island is very small. You can see around it.

"Are you going to land on it, Dad?" Jerry says.

"Sure, okay." Dad's face is flushed and looks angry.

The boat scrapes bottom and bumps. "Jump out and pull it in," Dad says. Jerry jumps out. His shoes and socks are wet now, but Dad doesn't notice. The boat bumps; it hurts me. I am afraid. But then we're up on the land and Dad is out and lifting me. "Nice ride, sugar?" he says.

Jerry and I run around the island. It is different from what we thought, but we don't know why. There are some trees on it, some wild grass, and then bare caked mud that goes down to the water. The water looks dark and deep on the other side, but when we get there it's shallow. Lily pads grow there; everything is thick and tangled. Jerry wades in the water and gets his pants legs wet. "There might be money in the water," he says.

Some napkins and beer cans are nearby. There is part of a hot-dog bun, with flies buzzing around it.

When we go back by Dad, we see him squatting over the water doing something. His back jerks. Then I see that he is

being sick. He is throwing up in the water and making a noise
like coughing.

Jerry turns around right away and runs back. I follow him,
afraid. On the other side we can look back at the boathouse and
wish we were there.

III

Marian and Betty went to the show, but I couldn't. She made
me come along here with them. "And cut out that snippy face,"
Ma said, to let me know she's watching. I have to help her take
care of Linda—poor fat Linda, with her runny nose! So here we
are inside the tavern. There's too much smoke, I hate smoke. Dad
is smoking a cigar. I won't drink any more root beer, it's flat, and
I'm sick of potato chips. Inside me there is something that wants
to run away, that hates them. How loud they are, my parents!
My mother spilled something on the front of her dress, but does
she notice? And my aunt Lucy and uncle Joe, they're here. Try
to avoid them. Lucy has false teeth that make everyone stare at
her. I know that everyone is staring at us. I could hide my head
in my arms and turn away, I'm so tired and my legs hurt from
sunburn and I can't stand them any more.

"So did you ever hear from them? That letter you wrote?" Ma
says to Lucy.

"I'm still waiting. Somebody said you got to have connections
to get on the show. But I don't believe it. That Howie Masterson
that's the emcee, he's a real nice guy. I can tell."

"It's all crap," Dad says. "You women believe anything."

"I don't believe it," I say.

"Phony as hell," says my uncle.

"You do too believe it, Sissie," says my mother. "Sissie thinks
he's cute. I know she does."

"I hate that guy!" I tell her, but she and my aunt are laughing.
"I said I hate him! He's greasy."

"All that stuff is phony as hell," says my Uncle Joe. He is tired
all the time, and right now he sits with his head bowed. I hate his
bald head with the little fringe of gray hair on it. At least my
father is still handsome. His jaws sag and there are lines in his
neck—edged with dirt, I can see, embarrassed—and his stomach
is bulging a little against the table, but still he is a handsome
man. In a place like this women look at him. What's he see in
her? they think. My mother had her hair cut too short last time;
she looks queer. There is a photograph taken of her when she
was young, standing by someone's motorcycle, with her hair long.
In the photograph she was pretty, almost beautiful, but I don't
believe it. Not really. I can't believe it, and I hate her. Her forehead gathers itself up in little wrinkles whenever she glances
down at Linda, as if she can't remember who Linda is.

"Well, nobody wanted you, kid," she once said to Linda. Linda
was a baby then, one year old. Ma was furious, standing in the
kitchen where she was washing the floor, screaming: "Nobody
wanted you, it was a goddamn accident! An accident!" That surprised me so I didn't know what to think, and I didn't know if I
hated Ma or not; but I kept it all a secret . . . only my girl
friends know, and I won't tell the priest either. Nobody can make
me tell. I narrow my eyes and watch my mother leaning forward
to say something—it's like she's going to toss something out on
the table—and think that maybe she isn't my mother after all,
and she isn't that pretty girl in the photograph, but someone else.

"A woman was on the show last night that lost two kids in a
fire. Her house burned down," my aunt says loudly. "And she
answered the questions right off and got a lot of money and the
audience went wild. You could see she was a real lady. I love that
guy, Howie Masterson. He's real sweet."

"He's a bastard," Dad says.

"Harry, what the hell? You never even seen him," Ma says.

"I sure as hell never did. Got better things to do at night." Dad turns to my uncle and his voice changes. "I'm on the night shift, now."

"Yeah, I hate that, I—"

"I can sleep during the day. What's the difference?"

"I hate those night shifts."

"What's there to do during the day?" Dad says flatly. His eyes scan us at the table as if he doesn't see anything, then they seem to fall off me and go behind me, looking at nothing.

"Not much," says my uncle, and I can see his white scalp beneath his hair. Both men are silent.

Dad pours beer into his glass and spills some of it. I wish I could look away. I love him, I think, but I hate to be here. Where would I rather be? With Marian and Betty at the movies, or in my room, lying on the bed and staring at the photographs of movie stars on my walls—those beautiful people that never say anything—while out in the kitchen my mother is waiting for my father to come home so they can continue their quarrel. It never stops, that quarrel. Sometimes they laugh together, kid around, they kiss. Then the quarrel starts up again in a few minutes.

"Ma, can I go outside and wait in the car?" I say. "Linda's asleep."

"What's so hot about the car?" she says, looking at me.

"I'm tired. My sunburn hurts."

Linda is sleeping in Ma's lap, with her mouth open and drooling on the front of her dress. "Okay, go on," Ma says. "But we're not going to hurry just for you." When she has drunk too much there is a struggle in her between being angry and being affectionate; she fights both of them, as if standing with her legs apart and her hands on her hips, bracing a strong wind.

When I cross through the crowded tavern I'm conscious of people looking at me. My hair lost its curl because it was so humid today, my legs are too thin, my figure is flat and not nice like Marian's—I want to hide somewhere, hide my face from them. I hate this noisy place and these people. Even the music is ugly because it belongs to them. Then, when I'm outside, the music gets faint right away and it doesn't sound so bad. It's cooler out here. No one is around. Out back, the old rowboats are tied up. Nobody's on the lake. There's no moon, the sky is overcast, it was raining earlier.

When I turn around, a man is standing by the door watching me.

"What're you doing?" he says.

"Nothing."

He has dark hair and a tanned face, I think, but everything is confused because the light from the door is pinkish—there's a neon sign there. My heart starts to pound. The man leans forward to stare at me. "Oh, I thought you were somebody else," he says.

I want to show him I'm not afraid. "Yeah, really? Who did you think I was?" When we ride on the school bus we smile out the windows at strange men, just for fun. We do that all the time. I'm not afraid of any of them.

"You're not her," he says.

Some people come out the door and he has to step out of their way. I say to him, "Maybe you seen me around here before. We come here pretty often."

"Who do you come with?" He is smiling as if he thinks I'm funny. "Anybody I know?"

"That's my business."

It's a game. I'm not afraid. When I think of my mother and father inside, something makes me want to step closer to this man —why should I be afraid? I could be wild like some of the other girls. Nothing surprises me.

We keep on talking. At first I can tell he wants me to come inside the tavern with him, but then he forgets about it; he keeps talking. I don't know what we say, but we talk in drawling voices, smiling at each other but in a secret, knowing way,

as if each one of us knew more than the other. My cheeks start to
burn. I could be wild like Betty is sometimes—like some of the
other girls. Why not? Once before I talked with a man like this,
on the bus. We were both sitting in the back. I wasn't afraid.
This man and I keep talking and we talk about nothing, he wants
to know how old I am, but it makes my heart pound so hard that
I want to touch my chest to calm it. We are walking along the old
boardwalk and I say: "Somebody took me out rowing once here."

"Is that so?" he says. "You want me to take you out?"

He has a hard, handsome face. I like that face. Why is he
alone? When he smiles I know he's laughing at me, and this
makes me stand taller, walk with my shoulders raised.

"Hey, are you with somebody inside there?" he says.

"I left them."

"Have a fight?"

"A fight, yes."

He looks at me quickly. "How old are you anyway?"

"That's none of your business."

"Girls your age are all alike."

"We're not all alike!" I arch my back and look at him in a way
I must have learned somewhere—where?—with my lips not
smiling but ready to smile, and my eyes narrowed. One leg is
turned as if I'm ready to jump away from him. He sees all this.
He smiles.

"Say, you're real cute."

We're walking over by the parking lot now. He touches my
arm. Right away my heart trips, but I say nothing, I keep walking. High above us the tree branches are moving in the wind. It's
cold for June. It's late—after eleven. The man is wearing a
jacket, but I have on a sleeveless dress and there are goose-pim-
ples on my arms.

"Cold, huh?" he says.

He takes hold of my shoulders and leans toward me. This is to
show me he's no kid, he's grown-up, this is how they do things;

when he kisses me his grip on my shoulders gets tighter. "I better go back," I say to him. My voice is queer.

"What?" he says.

I am wearing a face like one of those faces pinned up in my room, and what if I lose it? This is not my face. I try to turn away from him.

He kisses me again. His breath smells like beer, maybe, it's like my father's breath, and my mind is empty; I can't think what to do. Why am I here? My legs feel numb, my fingers are cold. The man rubs my arms and says, "You should have a sweater or something. . . ."

He is waiting for me to say something, to keep on the way I was before. But I have forgotten how to do it. Before, I was Marian or one of the older girls; now I am just myself. I am fourteen. I think of Linda sleeping in my mother's lap, and something frightens me.

"Hey, what's wrong?" the man says.

He sees I'm afraid but pretends he doesn't. He comes to me again and embraces me, his mouth presses against my neck and shoulder, I feel as if I'm suffocating. "My car's over here," he says, trying to catch his breath. I can't move. Something dazzling and icy rises up in me, an awful fear, but I can't move and can't say anything. He is touching me with his hands. His mouth is soft but wants too much from me. I think, What is he doing? Do they all do this? Do I have to have it done to me too?

"You cut that out," I tell him.

He steps away. His chest is heaving and his eyes look like a dog's eyes, surprised and betrayed. The last thing I see of him is those eyes, before I turn and run back to the tavern.

IV

Jesse says, "Let's stop at this place. I been here a few times before."

It's the Lakeside Bar. That big old building with the grubby siding, and a big pink neon sign in front, and the cinder driveway that's so bumpy. Yes, everything the same. But different too—smaller, dirtier. There is a custard stand nearby with a glaring orange roof, and people are crowded around it. That's new. I haven't been here for years.

"I feel like a beer," he says.

He smiles at me and caresses my arm. He treats me as if I were something that might break; in my cheap linen maternity dress I feel ugly and heavy. My flesh is so soft and thick that nothing could hurt it.

"Sure, honey. Pa used to stop in here too."

We cross through the parking lot to the tavern. Wild grass grows along the sidewalk and in the cracks of the sidewalk. Why is this place so ugly to me? I feel as if a hand were pressing against my chest, shutting off my breath. Is there some secret here? Why am I afraid?

I catch sight of myself in a dusty window as we pass. My hair is long, down to my shoulders. I am pretty, but my secret is that I am pretty like everyone is. My husband loves me for this but doesn't know it. I have a pink mouth and plucked darkened eyebrows and soft bangs over my forehead; I know everything, I have no need to learn from anyone else now. I am one of those girls younger girls study closely, to learn from. On buses, in five-and-tens, thirteen-year-old girls must look at me solemnly, learning, memorizing.

"Pretty Sissie!" my mother likes to say when we visit, though I told her how I hate that name. She is proud of me for being pretty, but thinks I'm too thin. "You'll fill out nice, after the baby," she says. Herself, she is fat and veins have begun to darken on her legs; she scuffs around the house in bedroom slippers. Who is my mother? When I think of her I can't think of anything—do I love her or hate her, or is there nothing there?

Jesse forgets and walks ahead of me, I have to walk fast to catch up. I'm wearing pastel-blue high heels—that must be because I am proud of my legs. I have little else. Then he remembers and turns to put out his hand for me, smiling to show he is sorry. Jesse is the kind of young man thirteen-year-old girls stare at secretly; he is not a man, not old enough, but not a boy either. He is a year older than I am, twenty. When I met him he was wearing a navy uniform and he was with a girl friend of mine.

Just a few people sitting outside at the tables. They're afraid of rain—the sky doesn't look good. And how bumpy the ground is here, bare spots and little holes and patches of crab grass, and everywhere napkins and junk. Too many flies outside. Has this place changed hands? The screens at the windows don't fit right; you can see why flies get inside. Jesse opens the door for me and I go in. All bars smell alike. There is a damp, dark odor of beer and something indefinable—spilled soft drinks, pretzels getting stale? This bar is just like any other. Before we were married we went to places like this, Jesse and me and other couples. We had to spend a certain amount of time doing things like that—and going to movies, playing miniature golf, bowling, dancing, swimming— then we got married, now we're going to have a baby. I think of the baby all the time, because my life will be changed then; everything will be different. Four months from now. I should be frightened, but a calm laziness has come over me. It was so easy for my mother. . . . But it will be different with me because my life will be changed by it, and nothing ever changed my mother. You couldn't change her! Why should I think? Why should I be afraid? My body is filled with love for this baby, and I will never be the same again.

We sit down at a table near the bar. Jesse is in a good mood. My father would have liked him, I think; when he laughs Jesse reminds me of him. Why is a certain kind of simple, healthy, honest man always destined to lose everything? Their souls are as clean and smooth as the muscular line of their arms. At night I hold Jesse, thinking of my father and what happened to him—all that drinking, then the accident at the factory—and I pray that Jesse will be different. I hope that his quick, open, loud way of talking is just a disguise, that really he is someone else—slower and calculating. That kind of man grows old without jerks and spasms. Why did I marry Jesse?

Someone at the bar turns around, and it's a man I think I know—I have known. Yes. That man outside, the man I met outside. I stare at him, my heart pounding, and he doesn't see me. He is dark, his hair is neatly combed but is thinner than before; he is wearing a cheap gray suit. But is it the same man? He is standing with a friend and looking around, as if he doesn't like what he sees. He is tired too. He has grown years older.

Our eyes meet. He glances away. He doesn't remember—that frightened girl he held in his arms.

I am tempted to put my hand on Jesse's arm and tell him about that man, but how can I? Jesse is talking about trading in our car for a new one. . . . I can't move, my mind seems to be coming to a stop. Is that the man I kissed, or someone else? A feeling of angry loss comes over me. Why should I lose everything? Everything? Is it the same man, and would he remember? My heart bothers me, it's stupid to be like this: here I sit, powdered and sweet, a girl safely married, pregnant and secured to the earth, with my husband beside me. He still loves me. Our love keeps on. Like my parents' love, it will subside someday, but nothing surprises me because I have learned everything.

The man turns away, talking to his friend. They are weary, tired of something. He isn't married yet, I think, and that pleases me. Good. But why are these men always tired? Is it the jobs they

hold, the kind of men who stop in at this tavern? Why do they
flash their teeth when they smile, but stop smiling so quickly?
Why do their children cringe from them sometimes—an innocent upraised arm a frightening thing? Why do they grow old so
quickly, sitting at kitchen tables with bottles of beer? They are
everywhere, in every house. All the houses in this neighborhood
and all neighborhoods around here. Jesse is young, but the outline of what he will be is already in his face; do you think I can't
see it? Their lives are like hands dealt out to them in their innumerable card games. You pick up the sticky cards, and there it is:
there it is. Can't change anything, all you can do is switch some
cards around, stick one in here, one over here . . . pretend
there is some sense, a secret scheme.

The man at the bar tosses some coins down and turns to go. I
want to cry out to him, "Wait, wait!" But I cannot. I sit helplessly
and watch him leave. Is it the same man? If he leaves I will be
caught here, what can I do? I can almost hear my mother's shrill
laughter coming in from outside, and some drawling remark of
my father's—lifting for a moment above the music. Those little
explosions of laughter, the slap of someone's hand on the damp
table in anger, the clink of bottles accidentally touching—and
there, there, my drunken aunt's voice, what is she saying? I am
terrified at being left with them. I watch the man at the door and
think that I could have loved him. I know it.

He has left, he and his friend. He is nothing to me, but suddenly I feel tears in my eyes. What's wrong with me? I hate
everything that springs upon me and seems to draw itself down
and oppress me in a way I could never explain to anyone. . . . I
am crying because I am pregnant, but not with that man's child.
It could have been his child, I could have gone with him to his
car; but I did nothing, I ran away, I was afraid, and now I'm
sitting here with Jesse, who is picking the label off his beer bottle
with his thick squarish fingernails. I did nothing. I was afraid.
Now he has left me here and what can I do?

I let my hand fall onto my stomach to remind myself that I am in love: with this baby, with Jesse, with everything. I am in love with our house and our life and the future and even this moment —right now—that I am struggling to live through.

Demons

She came out the side door, with the dog tugging at his leash.
The worn leather grip jerked her hand and she said in a hushed,
embarrassed voice: "Stop that, you know better! Stop that!" The
dog was vain and partly bald. She never thought of him as an
animal, but as an extension of her father, whose dog he was;
indeed, the dog resembled his master. Both had vague mottled
skin, liverish and brown as if camouflaged, and their eyes were
watery with alertness. It seemed to Eileen that their ears, though
of different shapes and colors, had in common an unclear, intan-
gible quality of *intensity*—they both heard everything, heard
whispers not meant for their ears and words not spoken aloud,
heard even the echoes of words that should have faded away.

She took the long side walk to the street, holding back on the leash. The dog panted and yipped in a high womanish falsetto; there was a squirrel nearby. The dog wanted so badly to tear flesh with his jaws that Eileen stared at his flat, brutal skull and thought clearly that it would be better if this dog died so that they could have some peace. The dog belonged in the house the way Eileen's sister Marcey belonged: both were possessions of the old man and could get away with anything. The fact was that they never really did anything at all. They belonged to the old man. Eileen's mother was an invalid, or claimed to be, and she had nothing to do with the dog, which was not allowed above the landing—nor was the dog allowed in the parlor etc., etc.—these were the rules of the house that Eileen had grown up with and had supposed to be the laws of the city itself, each house on each street encumbered with balding vicious dogs and fathers and mothers and sisters, one sister good because she was "slow" and the other—Eileen herself—questionable because she was not slow.

"Stop that, you know better! Stop!"

Once on the sidewalk she could scold the dog more openly, since no one in the house could hear. But the dog paid no attention. He yanked at the leash and dipped his head as if he were trying to get free of the collar, a futile attempt. Eileen watched him with a passive hatred, nothing new. Then she saw him waddle to a tree and so she stopped watching and glanced back toward the house. She wanted no intimate relationship with the dog, and it was strange how perfectly respectable men and women, dignified and well-to-do, could walk dogs and think nothing of what they were involved in: it had no dignity, it was embarrassing, and yet there they were. Eileen noticed that their house needed painting. It was a large, rather formal house, set far back from the street, with empty spires and cupolas in a style that had always seemed to Eileen the only style for living. Living demanded restraint and a constant tugging back at the leash; you never gave in, never let the dog free. Never. The lace curtains at the front bay window moved a little. That meant her father was watching. She stared gloomily across the weedy front lawn and tried to make out his face, but saw nothing. Certainly he was watching her. And perhaps their eyes were meeting. But there was no acknowledgment, nothing. The old man stood safely back in the shadows, and back in the kitchen Marcey was making dinner—it was about five o'clock—and upstairs in the big bedroom with the silk wallpaper and the chandelier imported from—where?—Belgium?—her mother lay under a series of blankets that never warmed her, not even in this late June heat. Eileen's mother was a silent, peeved woman, dominated by the old man and yet, like the dog, relentless and cunning beneath that domination. There was a special kind of slyness that only grew out of being handled cruelly, but Eileen could not quite master it. At the age of twenty-seven she felt a comic absurdity in her own situation, her inability to master her life or even to sit down and think clearly about it. It seemed there was always static in her brain when she tried to think about such things, or someone in the house wanted something. Or the dog wanted to go out.

She walked along a little faster. This pleased the dog. The sidewalk they took every afternoon was strangely cracked, and parts of it looked as if they were heaved up by a swelling in the ground. Sometimes this was caused by the roots of great elms that lined the boulevard, and sometimes it was caused by sudden shifts in the ground. It gave a patchwork look to the neighborhood. All the houses were old, of varying styles. There were garages attached to them or nearby with rows of windows on their second floors, once servants' quarters but now just room for junk; Eileen's father was on the lookout for changes in the neighborhood and whenever he got word that someone wanted to take in boarders he wrote to the City Council and to the mayor and to several attorneys and judges. So the old servants' quarters remained empty and the neighborhood itself looked as if it were somehow withdrawing, emptying out secretly. Lawns were vast and, even when cared for, looked like deserts of silence. No children would run across these lawns, never again. It was strange, but there were no children. Dog, but not children. A few old people and a few servants and a few younger people like Eileen walked dogs daily in this neighborhood, but children never appeared, and even the dogs were not dogs that barked.

In summer everything took too long, Eileen thought. She liked better the harsh fast days of winter, when a late morning ran foggily into an early evening, and the afternoons were squeezed small. That was good. In summer windows were opened and one heard too much. And people strolling out on the sidewalk might hear too much from inside the house; certain peevish shrill remarks were just the kind to carry all the way out into the street.

She was crossing the street by the Norlan mansion when the dog jerked his leash again. He was after another squirrel. Eileen pulled him back and heard a low growling in his throat that frightened her absurdly. . . . For a moment they stood in a frozen tug of war, the girl with her heels firm on the sidewalk, leaning backward a little, her hand holding the leash down hard against her thigh, and the angry dog tottering on his hind legs in a small semicircle, his forelegs pawing the air and yearning outward, away from the leash and collar. Then something snapped. The collar gave way and the dog lunged forward and ran blindly across the street. Eileen looked around in surprise and saw a car bump the dog gently, as if this car had been lying in wait for months or years and only now had the opportunity to leap forward. But the bump was gentle. Yet, Eileen saw in horror, the dog lay like a sack and was silent.

The driver was out of the car before Eileen got there. The dog was dead, it seemed. Blood ran in small stringy rivulets out of its mouth. The driver's shoes were dusty and Eileen bent over the dog, stared at them, waiting for the dog to shake itself back to life, but groggily interested in the shoes. She did not seem to understand that a man was talking to her. After a minute or so, when it appeared that her father's dog was really dead and would not get up again, she brought her widened gaze slowly up the column of the man's body and saw that he was talking to her.

"What? Yes," she said in a vague, flat voice. "Yes, it was an accident. I know. It was the dog's fault."

"Would you like me to call the police?"

She stared at him. "I don't know. It's my father's dog, not mine. I don't think he would want the police, he doesn't like police . . . he doesn't approve of police in this neighborhood. . . . Except the private police. I don't know where they are. They're somewhere. . . ."

"Are you all right?"

He was a man of about thirty-five, a stranger. He wore a light summer suit and had a casual, anxious look about him; his concern for the dog was in a way too real, exaggerated. The dog was no longer real to Eileen except as it represented a problem she was to have in a few minutes with her father. But the dog itself was not real and was an embarrassment. She said slowly, "Yes, I'm all right. But it was the dog's fault, you saw it."

"I couldn't stop in time."

"He has tried to get away from me for years."

"I didn't think the car would hit him. . . ."

"It's my father's dog mainly," she said, straightening. The man's gaze was tawny and fair, rather like her own. He had a bridge of freckles across his nose and forehead, and she did not, but his light brown hair was the same color as hers. There was something tense and giddy in the air between them, some fragmentation of light or time. It was as if they had stepped into the shadow of an eclipse no one else knew about; as if, between the pompous peelings of a church's bells on Sunday, they had sought out each other for a secret look.

"Do you live nearby? I can drive you home and take the dog."

"I'd be very grateful. . . ."

He wrapped the dog in canvas from the trunk of his car and lay the body on the back seat. Eileen began to cry. She believed that she had always liked this dog, that it had not been an evil dog, but perhaps her father had come between them and made it impossible for her to feel affection . . . and at the same time she understood that this was an absurd idea.

"Sometimes I think, in this place, that I'm losing my mind."

It came out with a hoarse, alarmed little laugh, and the man turned to her in surprise.

"I'm sorry, I shouldn't have said that," Eileen said. "I've caused you enough trouble today. . . ."

"It was my fault, really."

"I think it was my fault. . . ."

"Did you say it was your father's dog? Is he an old man, I mean, will he be very upset?"

Eileen got in the car slowly, thinking. Was her father an old man? She often thought of him as *the old man;* but she was not sure that other people would think him old. Old men were usually quiet and somehow precarious, either in health or sanity, while her father got stronger year after year and the cords in his neck grew tougher.

"He's about sixty-eight, I think. Yes, he'll be upset."

"I'd like to pay you—"

"No, no. Father wouldn't hear of that. Please don't mention that."

"Are you sure you're all right? You seem a little upset."

He closed the door on her side and went around to get in. Eileen glanced around and saw that the dog was still dead, still dead. She had hoped it would shake itself back into life. The driver got in and looked at her. It was apparent that this man—with his air of having somewhere to get to, his intelligent, masculine worry—thought she was peculiar. Perhaps insane? She wanted to explain to him with a laugh that she was really not insane, though external evidence seemed to indicate that she was not quite normal. She would have liked to show him her diploma, her Master's Degree in Art Education; the few love letters a young man had once sent her; the snapshots of her and a girl friend in Maine, one happy summer a long time ago. These were proofs of her being normal, or at least of her having been normal, in those years before she gave up and returned home. But she had returned home. She had given up her job in New York, her friends, her own apartment, she had given up wearing lipstick because it annoyed her father, she had even given up thinking, except on long hot summer afternoons. So perhaps he was right in staring at her that way?

"You seem to be afraid of something," he said.

"Yes. My father," she said.

Her teeth had begun to chatter.

The next morning she sat in the kitchen, in a patch of sunlight, thinking. There was an air of silence around her that was the silence forced upon a guilty child, and her sister Marcey respected it. Yet Marcey also dared to talk to her; there was something girlish and sweet about her affection for Eileen.

"He won't be mad no more. Not today. You go see," Marcey whispered.

Eileen drew her hand wearily across her face. She was trying to think past yesterday's scene with her father, and past the scene in the garden where they'd buried the dog, past all this clutter, to that stranger's face. She was disturbed that she could not recall it. Her sister Marcey leaned down to look at her. "You crying?" she said.

"No, I'm not crying," Eileen said.

Marcey was finishing up the breakfast dishes. All the kitchenwork was her work, all the housework. She wanted to do it and would grow angry, even violent, if Eileen tried to help. But Eileen had not tried to help for twelve years. Marcey was a big, soft girl in a flowered house dress. She wore bedroom slippers most of the time because her feet ached in regular shoes. Her face was round like a pie but somehow out of focus, or, rather, the features were not quite balanced; perhaps one eye was slightly larger than the other, or one nostril larger than the other. She was a strong, pleasant girl when she got her way, and there was a constant air of heat surrounding her, as if she were always in a hurry.

"Poor Rob," Marcey sighed.

Rob was the dog's name. But when Marcey said that name it belonged to a person; just as it was a person's name in their father's mouth. Eileen sat and tried to think. She was waiting for her father to come back to the kitchen. He was reading the morning paper in his study. In a while he would come back here and ask for coffee and perhaps he would look at her in a certain way.
. . . She was waiting to be forgiven, though she knew it was foolish and degrading. Still, she sat waiting. Her former life, abandoned in a hysterical night when she had confessed to herself that nothing, nothing mattered to her so much as her family, had withdrawn to a few pieces of junk up in her room, souvenirs of another life that must have been rather festive. Certainly it had not been serious. She had taught art to fifth-grade students, how unreal. . . . That had been several years ago.

At last Eileen heard her father coming. She sat up and stared hard out the window, like a child. It was a bramble bush she stared into, a mess of what had once been a garden; there was a streaked gray statue somewhere in that clutter, of a boy riding a fish. The statue was in the center of a fountain, long since dried up. Wasps buzzed around it and had she ever wanted to explore, she would have been forbidden entry. She sat quietly and awaited her father.

He was a tall, handsome man with silver hair that was thinning. His liverish scalp was beginning to show. Eileen stared at him hungrily, her eyes darting to him. She was afraid and it was crazy. He ignored her. Marcey was his darling, Marcey was thirty-six years old and all of nine years old in the head, she was

her parents' darling and had been so for the last twenty-five years.
As soon as they had guessed at her problem they had baptized her
for their own, their special love. Eileen thought these thoughts
bitterly, but knew that they were true.

"Father, I hope you aren't still angry about the dog," Eileen
said.

"Fill up this cup. Where's the cream?" her father said to Marcey.

Marcey bobbed around and handed him the cream. She was a
good, good girl. The flesh on her upper arms bobbed with her.
Eileen stared at the two of them, her kin, the attractive cold man
with bluish veins streaking his forehead like cobwebs, and the
childish hulking woman in her yellow dress. Yes, indeed. Her
kin. She felt a pang of jealousy for Marcey, a renewal of the
jealousy she had felt for years but had nearly forgotten. "But it's
foolish to go on this way," she said intelligently, like a teacher.
"After all, we do have to live in the same house."

Her father dressed well every day, though he rarely bothered
to leave the house. Even in summer he wore a vest. His clothes
were excellent, expensive clothes, though certainly out of date
now; but what did that matter? He was an icy, shrewd, cruel man
whose vocation was money. When Eileen had left home she
often thought of her father as crazy, but that was too simple. It
was inaccurate. He was not crazy; he was himself. He had never
made an error in his life in any financial situation. Or perhaps
any other. No errors, nothing. His business day began at nine in
the morning and ended usually at about ten; he used the telephone.

"Marcey, bring me out some biscuits. And butter. And jam."

He went back to his study and left them, his daughters. Two
women! Marcey was the pleased, fluttery wife and Eileen the icy,
rejected bride. She stared at her sister's simple face and remembered the thoughts she'd had so often as a child, crying upstairs

in her bed or out behind the garage, when she had wanted nothing so much as Marcey's death so that she, Eileen, could take her place. Why not? She could take Marcey's place and no one would miss Marcey. . . . Now she sighed at the futile cruelty of such thoughts. For nothing had ever happened. It was she, Eileen, who had caught colds and chills; Marcey was always well. She was strong and healthy as the old man. Eileen took after her mother, the two of them being people who, when alone, have nothing better to do than listen nervously to their hearts. Such people! They do not take their pulses, but only because they are too squeamish. . . .

Eileen went out for a walk.

This was not, after all, good for her. She ought to be getting away as she had promised herself, breaking free as soon as it was clear that her mother was not really dying. (Eileen's mother had gone to bed, stricken, in order to get Eileen home.) But at the thought of packing her things and calling a taxi, at the thought of going to the decrepit railroad station . . . she grew vague and restless and glanced around as if waiting to be distracted. The morning sun was warm on her cheek. It was like the gaze of that strange man, which was returning to her now that she was away from home. She walked slowly and languorously. It surprised her to understand that she was still an attractive woman, a very young woman. Her hair was cut short so that the tips of her ears showed, and it was fluffed up carelessly around her head. She had a small, serious, childlike face, with clear blue eyes. Her face had always displeased her because it looked like a child's face. But Marcey was the child, the true child; Eileen herself was supposed to be rather intelligent. But what did you do with intelligence, how could you use it? And her body was useless, just a thin body. She had a dancer's body, but no dance. What pumped in her veins but the same cold blue ink that threaded up through her father's regal forehead?

She walked for a long time, back and forth along the winding streets. This neighborhood was an old, excellent neighborhood rather near the downtown of a large city, and fifty years ago millionaires had built their extravagant homes here, on huge lots. It was railroad money mostly. Now the houses were inhabited by a few old people with many servants, or a young family who had inherited, with distrust and daring, or no one at all. Ghosts. Dust. Vandals committed atrocities in secret, and though these were usually kept out of the newspaper, Eileen's father knew every detail. He knew everything. He had known on the night of the fire last year that it was the Archbishop's mansion and nothing else, and he had been right. A blaze in the west wing caused by a secretary careless of her smoking, he had even guessed that. Eileen remembered her childhood and it seemed to her that she honestly remembered more people in this neighborhood once: but perhaps she was imagining it. There would be a time when, like her mother, she would have to imagine everything.

Then she saw it—the car from yesterday. The stranger's car. It was parked in a driveway, the Heilmans' driveway. Eileen paused, wondering. She had not really noticed yesterday that the car was several years old. But the Heilmans' house was many years old, almost shabby. It needed repairwork. And the front lawn was a lost cause, burned out already in June, hopeless. The Heilmans' man, a Negro of more than seventy, was fooling around by the side porch, trying to wash out a word scrawled in white on the screen. Eileen did not want to see what the word was, but she supposed it was the same word she'd seen scrawled in white, or black, or red, quite frequently around the neighborhood. Little Negro boys, no kin to the Heilmans' Negro, were the criminals. It was hopeless.

She was standing there when the man appeared, her friend of yesterday. He descended the outside stairs of the servants' quarter, a rather tidy and pleasant brick building. Ah yes, Eileen thought shrewdly, they are making money illegally. They are renting. The man had seen her and was approaching her in his shirt sleeves. He came toward her as if he'd been waiting to see her and was quite pleased.

"Hello," he said, smiling. She smiled in return. They talked rather awkwardly. Eileen felt reckless and oddly angry; her lower lip felt greedy. She kept saying no, no, it had been the dog's fault. . . . Then they suddenly laughed together. Eileen remarked that it was unfortunate about the defacing of the Heilman's screened porch. But they laughed again, surprising themselves, and their laughter faded swiftly when they glanced at each other: they were so much alike—how strange! His hair was rather long for a man's, and if it were a few inches longer it would look like hers.

"What are you doing here, living here?" Eileen said.

He began to answer her, courteously and simply, and as she listened she had the idea suddenly that he was not telling the truth. He spoke too earnestly. In her girlhood she had loved boys, sometimes not at a distance, and always a certain giddiness began in the back of her head when she stood near them: this giddiness now began. It was girlish and pleasant, but, farther down, was a cold, hard seriousness that frightened her. She wanted to slide her arm through his and lean against him. She wanted to say, *Oh, I know what you want, and what all men want . . .* but she was surprised at herself for thinking this.

He asked her to walk and she agreed. Why not? She felt a lazy stirring in her, but it was not soft as it should be in a woman; it was hard. She felt that she was half a man in this conversation, half the man she walked with and half herself, the one nudging and guiding them, the other being nudged, being guided. Was this the way real women felt about men? Real women? Did they discover a man who broke open the stubborn little cells of their blood and did they at once give themselves to him? Did they force such men into love? She felt rather reckless; the obscenity on the Heilmans' front porch could have come to her lips, her own lips.

"I'm involved in a kind of crazy situation. My parents . . ." And she went on to tell him the whole story, which she'd told to friends at college and elsewhere, acting out for them with her doll's face all the nuances and failings of her life. See, she seemed to say, I know I am wasting myself, I know I'm chained to them, but I can't help it.

"Well, you could move out. I left my home," the man said.

She was disappointed at this and said nothing.

"Of course, if they're old and they need you . . ."

"They really do need me. It's serious," she said.

"And your sister must need you too."

"Yes, she needs me. They all need me really."

She waited for him to argue with her. They walked on in silence. Then she heard herself say bitterly, "It's my sister Marcey who should go away."

When she returned home that afternoon her father was waiting. Yes, he knew. He had not seen them talking idly, on the brink of love, but he knew. He knew everything. When Eileen turned up the walk she froze, seeing him behind the curtains. He was ghostly and yet quite hard, standing there behind the lace, visible and invisible.

He opened the door for her. "And where is Rob?" he said politely.

"Rob is not here, Father."

"What did you do with Rob?"

Her teeth began to chatter. The old man spoke in a loud actor's voice so that Marcey in the kitchen could hear and the old woman upstairs could hear, lying in bed or maybe crouched by the top of the stairs in secret. (Eileen believed that her mother could get out of bed, and did: how else to explain things on her bed-stand that had certainly been on her bureau the night before?)

"I asked you what you did with Rob. Where is his leash?"

"Father, you know what happened to Rob."

"Where is he?"

"You know what happened."

He stood there in his immaculate suit, contemptuous of her. She could not look at him. Something greater than tears overtook her and she felt herself shrinking rapidly into a child, as if she were being propelled backward along a road, seeing everything unraveling backward and getting smaller. She began to cry, de-fending herself. She said, *Father, Father!* She sank to her knees before the old man, half awake to the cleverness of this gesture and half deluded; she begged, "Please, Father, you're making yourself sick, you're losing your mind—" But it was she who was sick and demented. The old man was in control. He seized her by her hair, a fistful of hair, and shook her head from side to side.

"You let him get killed—you let him loose! Let him loose! You never liked him and so you let him loose!"

Her father's shouting awakened everyone in the house and out of the kitchen Marcey came, in a hurry. She stumbled against something but righted herself. Both Eileen and her father looked around, united, and saw Marcey's big, silent body hurtling itself along the corridor toward them. . . . Her father said, grabbing her, "Get inside here," and, suddenly docile, she scrambled to her feet and ran into the study. Just in time. The old man slammed the door and Marcey's yells began and Eileen, clever as a child, knew enough to lock the door. Marcey had gone mad, yes. Mad. Eileen had been waiting in terror for this for years. Mad with a butcher knife, with a scissors, with a burning hot iron? She had thought that her death might be a crazy death, over which she'd have no control. Now she went to the telephone and dialed the number of the police station with her clever, trembling fingers.

She had carried the number around in her head for years, since the first time Marcey had turned on her: she had been only five then, and Marcey had tried to drown her in the old fountain.

The next morning it was Eileen who made breakfast, and she made it well. She and her father went upstairs—her father carrying the tray like a gentleman—and they ate with her mother, who was sitting up in bed for the occasion. Their grief seemed to make their fingers longer and hungrier. "Yes, I saw it coming," Eileen's mother said sourly, and her father was polite enough not to contradict her. Despite their stricken bodies, their faces were set to enjoy a kind of ceremonial meal.

"A terrible thing, a scandal," Eileen's mother complained. "And what about my poor good girl here, what if she'd been hurt?"

Eileen felt a stab of pleasure. "Marcey couldn't help it, she was sick."

"Not sick. Sickness can be cured, but Marcey's trouble can never be cured. I always said that," said the mother.

"Maybe in a while—"

"I always said that."

Eileen's mother was a woman who was easy to forget. Her friends had forgotten her years ago, it was strange, and Eileen from time to time found herself thinking that her mother really had carried through her threat and died. But of course the old woman was quite alive and, despite her mysterious illnesses, she seemed quite strong. She dabbed powder on, and cologne, and her bedroom was an eyesore of expensive antiques.

They talked about Marcey. They talked about all the indications Marcey had given over the years, how they should have guessed this might happen finally. Despite the childish satisfaction she felt in being at her mother's bedside at last, as if she and her father were making a charity visit and were certainly going to leave together, Eileen felt a peculiar hollow sensation. It

was a sickish feeling. Something was not right, something was in-
complete.

That day she did not go out because she was much too busy.
She waited on her mother. Without Marcey, her mother needed
her all the time. "I suppose we should have a girl again," Eileen's
mother said. "I'll be too much trouble for you. . . ."

"No, not at all," Eileen said. But she spoke without enthusiasm. It was odd that her sister's disappearance should not mean
very much to her after all. After so many years. She had always
thought that her life would begin when Marcey was carried off,
but now she was not so certain.

That week was spent in work around the house. She made all
the meals and cleaned part of the house—only part of it was still
used—and she fixed herself up for their pleasure, like a child.
But it was a masquerade. She fooled them but could not fool
herself. Released from the slightly heady air of their meals together, and released for the day from her mother's demands, she
stared out her window at the great spotlight her father had
erected outside. She waited to see a figure moving down there, a
prowler. No one? Where was that man? He knew where she
lived, but he had not come near. A week had passed and he had
not come near.

It must have been the heat of July, because her body felt angry
and deprived. She kept thinking of that man. In close contact
with men some ten or twelve times in her life, she had really not
felt much: a kind of curiosity, part scientific. Little emotion. But,
away from men, she tended to think about them and to idealize
all maneuvers of physical love. She brooded upon this mysterious
man and wondered if he had told her the truth, wondered who he
was, why he had come out to talk with her, whether she would
ever see him again. . . . She felt a certain gratitude toward him
for having rid her life of that dog and of her sister. Yes, she was
grateful. And that night she dreamed of him, a dream of love; and
after she woke alarmed by this dream she slept again and dreamed

his dream of her, from his point of view. She was a pretty vase of a woman, delicate and costly and untouched. What could he do with her? What could a man do with such a woman?

She woke and walked angrily about her room. She looked out at the bluish spotlight, hating it because it might be keeping something from her. The spotlight lit up the ground with a weird graveyard festivity, but there was no festivity. It was a blank, moonlit, waiting for something to happen. She wanted that man and she was angry at anyone, anyone who kept him from her. She had never felt so dangerous and senseless. Imagine her father peering out the curtains at that man, should he ever come up to the front door!—what man would pass through the look of a skull's head in order to get to her?

The next day she woke early to her mother's thumping. She had to hurry to take care of her mother, who needed help getting to her bathroom. The old woman was a surprise out of bed, so small and brittle and clinging, like a baby. She kept crooning to Eileen, "That's my good girl, yes, my good girl," and Eileen tried to smile; after all, her mother could not help being an invalid. Eileen herself felt very tired.

After she finished with her morning work she slipped out the side door, stepping into a thick wall of heat. The air was oppressive, as if it were the air of another planet smothering the earth's air with its own languorous, perfumey air. At the front walk she tried to resist looking back, but she did turn and saw what she believed to be her father's figure behind the curtains. Yes, certainly it was he. Neither gave any sign of recognition and Eileen walked on as if she had somewhere to get to.

She kept thinking, *I will explain it to him* . . . but she could not complete the sentence because she didn't understand it. It was as if another voice were speaking in her brain, taking over. She walked fast, glad to be deprived of the dog, and her fingers sometimes jerked as if jerked by the tug of that dog's leash. She headed up toward the Heilmans' house. An accidental glance at her mother's limp, yellowish flesh that morning had frightened her: was that all that lay before her? What did it mean? Why were things so easily lost when, in one's keeping, they had seemed to have no value anyway?

She had begun to perspire, and a sense of recklessness overtook her. Truly this was the air of another planet, a jungle air. She believed she saw *that man* ahead of her, turning up a walk, but it was evidently someone who lived there—in a great English Tudor home that needed repairs. Still, her heart had given a lurch. Walking on, she believed she saw him again, on foot, this time strolling toward her on the other side of the street. When they grew nearer, however, she saw that it wasn't he but a young man in a pale, sporty outfit, something beige and white. She looked away. Then, as they were about to pass, she glanced over and saw that it was *that man* after all—he was looking at her too. She paused. He lifted one arm in a tentative gesture, motioning her over to his side of the street. He was on the walk by the Norlan estate.

Eileen did cross the street. She said nervously, "Something terrible happened at home—something terrible—" The man was smiling at her, as if pleased. He was wearing a beige pull-over shirt and white trousers, and light canvas shoes. She had the idea he had put on this outfit for her. "My sister had to be taken away. You know, my sister, I told you about her—"

He nodded and his smile withdrew politely. "How have you been?" he said.

She stared at him. His eyes were fixed upon her greedily; he seemed at any instant about to smile again. "It was terrible, the way she had to be taken out. They gave her a shot of something to quiet her and . . . and I guess she'll never be let out . . . I mean . . . it's up to us to agree to that . . ." But she saw that he was not interested in her sister and it occurred to her that she was no longer interested in that topic either.

"Let's walk through here. Inside here," he said.

He meant the Norlans' park, or what was left of their park. Eileen stared at him. "But someone might see us—"

"The house is empty. Just servants."

"They might see us still—"

"Come on. Let's get off the street," he said.

She hesitated, wondering if this were a joke. But he took hold of her arm and pulled her along. "I was out walking every day this week," he said. "Didn't you say you'd meet me?" Eileen could not remember having said that, but she was pleased to think that she might have said it. He led her on, into the heart of the old estate, which consisted of a city block of ragged trees and shrubs and ferns gone wild; behind the old house was a rose garden with the usual fountain and statues. The Norlan estate had a wild, decadent air about it, as if the jungle were encroaching upon it in the heart of a great city; it had a strangely private air. Eileen's man did not release her but pulled her on, and she forced herself to think of what might happen; was she ready for it? Had she wanted this? "We should go back. We shouldn't be in here," she said. "Now, don't talk like that," said the man with a grimace of impatience. She was staring at his pale lashes—very like her own—when the first rain drops began to fall.

Heedless of the rain, his face swung toward her, very serious and impersonal as a statue, and she felt her arms slide around him. His body was warm and damp. Eileen's heart began to beat violently and she thought, *I'm going to die,* and a part of her fled backward to the old house in which her parents awaited her, asking them for help. But still she embraced this man; for all her awkwardness, it was an affectionate embrace. He leaned back and smiled at her. There were pale, fair specks in the iris of his eyes. "I'm afraid," Eileen said, "please don't—" "We can be alone here," he said. But she was afraid, and she began to shiver with a fear that was part fear of this man and part fear of her father;

she slipped in the wet grass and would have fallen except for him. "I can't love you or anyone," she said bitterly, "it's because of *him*—I mean him back at the house—my father. I can't stay here with you—" "Not even to talk?" said the man. "Talk? Talk about what?" Eileen said in surprise.

They talked, and as time passed she drew back from him like a flat-footed dancer who has lost the rhythm of the dance. Seen from a distance, they had the lively, sullen look of statues in private gardens, arrested in the fulfillment of some intricate dance. He talked about himself, and then instructed her to talk about herself. And she talked, but the flood of truth she told him— meticulous and tedious—was no more convincing than what she supposed to be his lies.

Sometime later they emerged from the park, damp and criminal. "I'm sorry that I'm afraid of you. I can't help it," Eileen said. Her voice was a little hysterical and accusing. The man lit a cigarette, which was exactly the right gesture; it gave them both the healthy anonymity of movie actors. Even the rain was cinematic. They walked back toward Eileen's home and she kept saying, "No, I don't think I can see you again. I don't think so."

He said, "Tomorrow, the same time."

"No, I'm afraid."

"Tomorrow you won't be."

They approached her house, and she knew that the old man must be watching them. He must have been standing at the window all these hours. Her cheeks began to burn, and she said in a strange singsong voice, "He's watching us right now, right now."

"There's nobody there. At the window? Nobody."

They turned up the walk, bedraggled from the rain but also given over to a kind of reckless bravery. "We'll go right in and you can introduce us," the man said.

"That won't be possible," Eileen said with a terrified laugh.

His grip on her arm was firm and she returned it, her fingers turning rigid on his hand. She felt the strength of her body flow over into his, lose itself in his. There was a terrible urgency that they become lovers. She had never understood this urgency before, which was not physical but spiritual instead: it was a moral obligation upon her, and if she refused this man she would live out the rest of her life in shame.

"He won't allow you to come in," Eileen said.

"Yes, he'll allow it. I'll be inside in ten minutes. Five minutes."

Eileen said in a sudden terror, "I want to explain to you that I love them and I can't leave them—I love them both and I can't—"

He gave her a shake to quiet her. The front door was opening as if by itself. Eileen's father stood perfectly straight in his gray summer suit, in his vest, looking out at them. It was clear that his eyes had seen everything, what there was to see and what had not yet happened, took everything in and had converted it to a sublime fury.

"Come in here, Eileen," he said.

She would have obeyed except that all her strength had gone into this man. Her father's face was a little dark; one strand of his hair had fallen onto his forehead. Eileen felt a sudden rush of pity for him and started forward, but the man held her back.

"I said come in here."

"I'd like to introduce myself—" Eileen's friend said, but her father's look silenced him.

"I want Eileen in here. And I want you to get out of here."

Her father took one step out, about to come down to them. He was staring at them with a terrible hatred and groping with his foot, not looking down at the steps. He extended one hand like an old man, groping with that hand too through the rain, and Eileen did not come toward him or move away, but stood paralyzed.

"Sir—"

"You get out of here. Please get out."

Eileen's father came down to their level and took hold of Eileen's free arm. It was meant to be a symbolic gesture perhaps, but it turned out that he pulled at her and Eileen's friend pulled her back. She closed her eyes to this folly. When she opened them she saw her father rushing forward with a demented look, as if he were ready to strangle the man, and it was with a quick instinctive stroke of his fist that the man struck her father on the side of his head. He fell at once. He fell onto the flagstone walk and his face darkened.

She wanted to cry out, *Father!* but nothing came. It was as if he'd drawn out of her that very word, that she no longer had a right to use it. She knelt over him and wondered wildly if he were dead, if he had died so quickly. But his belling struggling cheeks showed that of course he was alive.

She seemed to come out of a trance, staring at the man's mud-splattered shoes and hearing his voice: "We've got to take him inside! Come on, help me. Please—"

Eileen woke and rose unsteadily. She helped the man lift her father, but bore hardly any of his weight; the man was really carrying him. He kept saying, "Open the door, please. Please open it," in a rapid, urgent voice that woke Eileen from the series of drugged little lapses she kept falling into; it was strange, she'd never had this happen before. When they finally got him inside the house, on the leather sofa of his study, he had died.

Eileen stood looking down at him, uncertain of his death. Her friend lit a cigarette shakily. "He was a pretty old man, you know. He lived a good life."

"Yes," Eileen said.

"It was the sidewalk that did it. He fell hard, he slipped in the rain," he said, as if instructing her.

"Yes, I think I saw that."

"Do you want to step out here?"

He led her out into the foyer and closed the study door. It was the same door Marcey had tried to break down, and Eileen could see the signs of her savage scratches and kicks; but they were fossils in an aging ruin. In a while those marks would have no meaning. The man was leading her down this familiar hall with his arm around her shoulders, whispering to her. "He led a full life, you know. This was bound to happen someday."

"Yes, I know that."

"You aren't too much upset?"

"I don't think so."

"We can call the doctor soon. Or should we call him now?"

"I don't know. I feel a little faint."

He led her to the end of the hall and then walked with her to the front again, comforting her. It seemed now that they had been together a long time, a lifetime. She knew that she belonged to him as a woman, her body and all the spontaneous womanly gestures of her soul, everything. She stood in his embrace and put her fists against his chest, weeping gently, like a woman. He led her into the drawing room, whose blinds had not been opened, and she was grateful for the dimness. Was this her room, her gift to this strange man, or was it somehow his gift to her? He whispered to her, and she wept and laughed nervously and clenched and unclenched her fists against his chest. Upstairs everything was silent. "Do you want me to leave now so you can call the doctor?" the man said.

"Do you think I should?"

"Whatever you want."

"Don't leave yet, not yet. I'm afraid. Not yet," she said. She seemed to blend into him, into the heat of his body. They stood for a while, swaying. Eileen closed her eyes and felt the galloping pace of her heart, a beating that was almost unbearable. She had to quench it. She slid her arms around the man and he moved her to the sofa, which neither saw. The sofa smelled of dust and caution. Eileen gave herself up to this man, and the mask of her face was stripped off between his hard white teeth, leaving a film of pinkish-red blood and membrane, the pulsing of minute and wild veins he might take between his teeth and gnaw.

Before he came to her he said, with a man's impractical practicality, "What about your mother?"

"Oh, let her die!" said Eileen in a voice of wonder.

B_odies_

She met him in the cafeteria of the Art Museum, on a Thursday. His name was Draier, Drayer—she couldn't quite make it out. "Please call me Anthony," he said, leaning forward against the wrought-iron table, jarring it, and his attempt at intimacy was blocked by the formality of that name also. Pauline's friend, their mutual friend, hadn't figured much in her life for several years, and she wondered where his loneliness was leading him—he had been reluctant to introduce Anthony to her, she could see that. Her friend's name was Martin. He had something to do with an art gallery; his art galleries were always failing, disappearing, and returning again with new names. Pauline wondered if Anthony was an artist.

"I'm not an artist. I'm not anything," he said. He smiled a sad, quick smile. She was startled by his frankness, distrusting it. He had a striking face, though he had not shaved for several days, his eyes set clearly beneath the strong, clear line of his eyebrows. Beside him, Martin was silent. Students from Pauline's art class were carrying their trays past this table with serious faces; their faces, like the work they did, were intense and prematurely aged.

"Pauline does beautiful work," Martin said. He seemed to be talking to no one in particular. "But it's very difficult to talk about art, or about anything. I can't explain her work."

"Why should you explain it?" Pauline said. She stood to leave; she never took much time for lunch. The noise of the cafeteria annoyed her. Formally, with a smile, she put out her hand to Anthony. "It was very nice to meet you," she said.

He looked surprised. "Yes, very nice. . . ."

She was out of the restaurant before he caught up with her. Before turning, she heard footsteps and it flashed through her mind, incredibly, that this man was following her—then she turned to face him, and her expression was curious rather than alarmed. "I thought—I thought I'd walk with you. Are you going to look at the pictures?" he said.

Look at the pictures. "No," she said. "I have a class at two."

His face, in the mottled light of the broad, marble-floored hall, looked sullen. She had thought he was fairly young, in his mid-twenties; now she supposed he was at least ten years older. His hair was curly, black but tinged with gray, and it fell down around the unclean neck of his sweater lazily, making her think of one of the heads she herself had done a few years ago . . . in imitation of a Greek youth, the head of a sweetly smiling child. This man stared at her rudely. She could not bear to face him.

"I have to teach a class at two . . ." she said.

They walked awkwardly together. Not far away were the stairs to the first floor, and once upstairs she could escape . . . the side of her face tingled from his look, she thought it foolish and degrading, she wondered what he thought of her face . . . was he thinking anything about her face?

"Do you live around here?" he said.

"No. Out along the lake."

"Out there?" His tone was suspicious, as if she had been deceiving him until now. This was her own fault—though she wore her pale blond hair in a kind of crown, braided tightly, and though her face was cool, slow to awaken to interest, held always in a kind of suspension, she wore the standard casual clothes of girls who were artists or wanted to be, living alone, freely, sometimes recklessly, down here in the center of the city. She wore dark stockings, leather shoes that had been ruined by this winter's icy, salted sidewalks, a dark, rather shapeless skirt, and a white blouse that had once been an expensive blouse but now looked as old as Anthony's sweater and blue jeans, its cuffs rolled up to her elbows, its first button hanging by a thread. Her hands were not stubby, but there was nothing elegant about them— short, colorless fingernails, slightly knobby knuckles, small wrists. She was anxious to get back to work, her fingers actually itched to return to work, and this man was a pull on the edge of her consciousness, like something invisible but deadly blown into her eye.

"I have to leave," she said abruptly.

"You don't have a place down here? In town?"

"I have a studio. But I live at home with my mother."

She faced him and yet was not facing him; her eyes were moving coldly behind his head. He had no interest for her, not even as someone whose head she might copy; she had done a head like his once, she had no desire to repeat herself. She felt very nervous beneath his frank, blunt scrutiny, but her face showed nothing. Like the head of an Amazon on a stand near the stairs—a reproduction of an Etruscan work—she was vacuous, smooth-skinned, patient. From art she had learned patience, centuries of patience. The man, Anthony, was humming nervously under his breath, sensing her desire to get away and yet reluctant to let her get away.

"Do you come around here often?" he said.

"No."

"Why are you so . . . unfriendly?" He smiled at her, his face grown suddenly shabby and appealing, his eyes dark with wonder. *Tell the truth,* he was pleading. It occurred to her that he was insane. But she laughed, looking from the inhuman composed face of that Amazon to his face, hearing him say again, *Are you going to look at the pictures?*

"Come over here. Can I show you something?" he said. He took her arm with a sudden childish familiarity that annoyed her. In the noisy confusion of this part of the museum, at noon, she had to give herself up to anything that might happen; it was part of coming here at all. When she had begun teaching at the Art Institute across the street, years ago, she had brought her own lunch and eaten in her studio, she had thrown herself into her work and that had been, maybe, the best idea. Meeting people down here was a waste of time. The people she spent time with socially were friends of her mother's, most of them older than she, a careful, genteel network of people who could never harm her. Down here, the city was open. Anything could happen. This stranger, whose name was Anthony Drayer, whose rumpled clothes told her everything she needed to know about him, now took her by the arm and led her over to a reproduction of another Etruscan work she had been looking at for years with no more than mild interest.

"Did you ever see this?" Anthony said. He was very excited. The piece was a tomb monument, showing a young man lying on a cushion with a winged woman at his side. The man's hair was bound up tightly, in a kind of band; his face was very strong, composed. Pauline had the idea that Anthony saw himself in that face, though his own was soft, sketchy, as if done with a charcoal pencil, not shaped vividly in stone. His smile moved from being gentle to being loose, almost out of control. "Who are these people?" he said, glancing at her.

She saw that his fingers were twitching. Her eye was too intimate, too quick to take in shameful details—it was a fault in her. She could not help noticing that the skin around his thumbnails was raw from his digging at it. "I moved down here a few months ago and almost every day I come to the museum," Anthony said. He spoke in a rapid, low murmur, as if sensing her coldness but unable to stop his words. He picked at his thumbnail. "I like to look at the pictures but especially the statues. You do statues? That must be expensive, isn't it, to buy the stone and all that . . . ? I could never do anything like this, my hands are too shaky, my judgment isn't right, I can't stand still long enough, but I love to look at these things, it makes me happy to know that they exist. . . . Are those two in love? Is that why she's reaching out toward him?"

"No, they're not in love," Pauline said, wondering if her tone could rid her of this man forever. "The man is dead. The woman is an angel of death, or a demon of death. You see how her hand is broken off?—she was holding out to him a scroll with his fate written on it. This is a monument to adorn a tomb. It isn't about life, it's about death. They're both dead."

Anthony stared at the figures.

"But they look alive . . . their faces look alive. . . ."

"Do you see how their bodies are twisted around? The demon's body is organically impossible, it's out of shape from the waist down, and the man's body is almost as unnatural. . . . That's a typical Etruscan characteristic."

"Why?"

"I don't know why," she said, avoiding his melancholy stare. "The artists weren't interested in that part of the body, evidently their interest was in the head, the face, the torso. . . ."

"Why is that?"

He scratched at his own head, at the dusky, graying curls. She could smell about him an odor of something stale, sad—cigarette smoke, unwashed flesh, the gritty deposit of decades in some walk-up room. Her own odor was clean and impersonal. Her hands smelled whitely of the clay in which she worked. Anthony looked sideways at her. His look was pleading, intense, threatening . . . for the first time in years she was afraid of another person.

"I have to leave," she said.

"Can I see you again?"

She was already walking away. Her heart was pounding. He was calling after her—she nearly collided with an elderly man making his way slowly down the stairs—she had the excuse of apologizing to this man, helping him, saying something about the danger of such wide stairs. "And outside it ain't no better, all that goddamn ice," the old man said angrily, as if blaming her for that too.

She escaped from them both.

It is a festival of some kind. Mules with muddy bellies and legs; a young man with a bare chest leading one of the mules. He is laughing. His head falls back with drunken laughter, as if loose on his shoulders. Another man is riding a mule, slipping off into the mud, laughing. Garlands of flowers are woven in the manes of these mules. What is happening? Women run by . . . their shouts are hilarious, drunken. I see what it is—someone is being pulled in a wagon. The wagon's railings are decorated with bruised white flowers, the man inside the wagon is speechless, his face dark with a look of terror, as if blood has settled heavily in his face and will never flow out again. Now a soldier appears on a

black horse, the horse's belly is splashed with
mud. The leather of his complicated saddle
creaks. . . .

She woke suddenly. Her head pounded. The dream was still
with her—the raucous laughter in the room with her, the whin-
nying of a horse. She looked around wildly, for a moment suspended of all personal existence, of thinking, not even afraid.
The wagon's wheels made a creaking noise and so perhaps it was
the wheels, not the soldier's gear, that was creaking. . . . Then
the dream faded and she felt only a dull, aching fear. For a while
she lay unthinking in bed and felt the cool, contented length of
her body beneath the covers, not thinking.

Twenty-nine years old, she had a sense of being much older, of
being ageless. So many years of patience, the shaping of clay and
stone, the necessity for patience had aged her magically; she was
content in her age. Her work was heads. She was interested only
in the human head. Out in the street she could not help but stare
at the heads of strangers, at their unique, mysterious, miraculous
shapes; sometimes their heads were a threat to her, unnerving
her. She couldn't explain. But most of the time she brought back
to her work a sense of excitement, as if her blood, in flowing out
at the instant of glimpsing some rare sight, had returned again to
her heart exhilarated and blessed. She felt at times an almost
uncontrollable excitement, and she would spend hours at her
work, feverish, unaware of time.

She and her mother had breakfast together every morning.
They ate in the dining room, enjoying its size, undiminished by
its high ceiling. The house was very large, very old, a house
meant to store collections—paintings, manuscripts, first editions,
antiques. Her father, now dead, had collected things. The house
had become a small museum, but polished and sprightly, ruled
by her mother's bustling efficiency. A woman with a firm place in
local society, her days filled with luncheons and committee meet-

ings and her weekends given over to entertaining or to being en-
tertained, Pauline's mother was that kind of middle-aged, generous, busy woman who becomes impersonal around the middle of
her life. She too collected things, antiques and jewels, and kept
up what she thought to be an enthusiastic interest in "culture"; it
was something to talk about with enthusiasm. "We're stopping at
the auction after lunch," she told Pauline. She chattered at
breakfast, her rich, rosy face ready for the day that would never
disappoint her, being a complicated day filled with women like
herself, the making out of checks, endless conversations. . . .-
"You look a little pale. Are you well? Did you sleep well?"

"I had a strange dream, but I slept well. I'm fine."

"I still think you should give up that job. . . . I wish the
weather would change. April is almost here and everything is still
frozen, it depresses me when winter lasts so long. . . ." she said
vaguely. She wore a dark dress, she wore pearls and pearl earrings; a slightly heavy woman, yet with a curious grace, a girlish
flutter at the wrists and ankles, which Pauline herself had never
had. She was in the mold of her father: tall, lean, composed, with
a patient, cool kind of grace, never hurried. Pauline had never
been able to accept the memory of her father in the hospital after
his stroke, suddenly an elderly man, trembling, with tiny broken
veins in his face. . . .

RITES TO BE HELD FOR PROMINENT
FINANCIER, PHILANTHROPIST

"Are you sure you're well?" her mother said suddenly.

"Yes. Please."

They parted for the day. Pauline's mother approved of her
"work," though she did not like her teaching down at the Art
Institute; she feared the city. She did not exactly approve of
Pauline's clothes and her tendency to wear the same outfit day
after day, but her daughter had a profession, a career, she was an

artist, unlike the daughters of her friends. Every few years the newspapers did stories on her when she won some new award or had a new show for the art page or the splashy women's page, the daughter of the late Francis Ressner, with large photographs that showed her standing beside one of her stark, white heads, her own head beautiful as a work of art. There was a certain stubbornness in both her and in her work. She had very light blond hair that fell past her shoulders, but she wore it braided around her head, giving her a stiff, studied look; she had worn it like that since the age of fifteen. Her cheekbones were a little prominent because her face was too thin, but she attended to her face with some of the respect for clarity and precision that she applied to her work—though she wore no make-up, she kept her eyebrows plucked to a delicate, arched thinness, and she saw that her face was smoothed by oils and creams, protected against the city's sooty wind. She was pleased to have a kind of beauty, pale and unemphatic; her father too had been a beautiful man. Her mother, florid and conversational, had been startlingly pretty until recent years, a perfumed and likable woman, but Pauline was another kind of woman altogether and pleased with herself. Sometimes, in the privacy of her studio, she sat on a stool before a mirror, her long legs stretched out before her, and contemplated herself as if contemplating a work of art. She could remain like this for an hour, without moving. It pleased her to be so complete; unlike other women, she did not want to turn into anyone else.

That morning, entering the Institute, she saw one of her girl students talking to the man she had met the day before, Anthony —they were standing just inside the door, and both looked around at her. She smiled and said hello, not waiting for any reply. Her heart had jumped absurdly at the sight of him and she had no desire to hear his voice . . . she was afraid he would hurry after her, take hold of her arm. . . . Safe in her class, she put on a shapeless, soiled smock. She directed eight students in their own work with clay. She was efficient with them, not friendly, not unfriendly, never called anything except *Miss Ressner*. She felt no interest in her students' lives, no jealousy for the girls with their engagement rings and wedding bands. The girl who had been talking with Anthony had long black hair and an annoying eagerness. She had a small, minimal talent, but she was one of those students who want to be told, at once, whether they will succeed or not, whether their talent is great enough to justify work, as if the future could be handed to them on a scroll, everything figured out by a superior mind, determined permanently. . . . And she felt no interest in the men, who were both older and younger than she; their pretensions, their sincerity, their private, feverish plans did not interest her.

After class the girl said to her, "Miss Ressner, that man was asking about you. Out there. Did you notice him?"

Pauline showed no curiosity. "I saw you talking to someone."

"He asked a lot of questions about you. . . . I know him a little, not well, he hangs around down here in the bars and places. . . ." Then, embarrassed, she said quickly, "But of course I didn't tell him anything."

Pauline felt tension rising in her. She dropped her paper cup into a wastebasket, conscious of spilling coffee in the basket, onto napkins . . . coarse paper napkins that soaked up the liquid at once. . . . It was ugly, a mess. She went out into the drafty corridor. That dream was still with her. . . . She was tempted suddenly to go over to the museum to see if anything there could explain it, surely it had an origin in something she had seen and forgotten. . . . *Why a procession of mules, why garlands of flowers, why a bare-chested victim in a wagon?*

Later that day she saw Anthony again. He was standing in front of a restaurant, doing nothing, as if waiting for her. . . . She had left her studio, restless, wanting to get away from students who dropped in to talk with her. She was too polite to discourage visits. Why did people waste her time talking to her?

Why did they ask her vulgar, personal questions, about where
she got her ideas, about whose work she admired most . . . ?
Why did people talk to one another, drawn together mysteriously, fatally, helpless to break the spell? She had sensed, in certain men and in a few women, a strange attraction for her—
something she had never understood or encouraged. Gentle,
withdrawing, but withdrawing permanently, she backed out of
people's lives, turning aside from offers of friendship, from urgency, intensity, the admiration of men who did not know her at
all. She liked all these people well enough, she just did not want
to be close to them. And now this Anthony, whom she would not
have liked anyway, was hanging around her, a dragging tug at
the corner of her eye, a threat. Her mother's first command
would be to call the police, but Pauline, being more sensible,
knew that was not necessary.

It would have been a mistake to ignore him. She said, "Hello,
how are you?" Her smile was guarded and narrow in the cold
sunlight.

"Hello," he said. His voice sounded uneven, as if he was so
surprised by her attention that he could not control it. "Where
are you going? Would you like some coffee?"

"I don't have time," she said, side-stepping him. She felt her
face shape itself into a polite smile of dismissal. Anthony smiled
back at her, mistaking the smile . . . or was he pretending to
mistake it? Was he really very arrogant? She felt again a sense of
fear, a suffocating pounding of her heart.

He rubbed his hands together suddenly, warmly, as if pleased
by her. Today he looked more robust; he had shaved, his black
curls fell more neatly down onto his collar; he wore a short,
sporty coat that was imitation camel's hair, only a little soiled; he
wore leather boots, cracked and marred like her own shoes.

"I'd like to talk with you," he said. "It's very important."

"Not today—"

"But I won't hurt you. I only want to talk." He smiled a dazzling smile at her—he was about to move toward her, about to take her arm again. She jumped back, frightened. But he only said, "I want to talk about different kinds of living, I want to know you . . . how it is for you, your life, a woman who looks like you. . . . I spend my time watching things, or listening to things, music, in a bar or in somebody's apartment, listening to records. . . ."

"I have to leave," she said thinly, bowing her head. She could not look up at him.

"Yesterday, when I saw you, I thought . . . I thought that I would like to meet you. . . . Why does that offend you?"

She said nothing.

"I asked him, what's-his-name, to introduce us. He didn't want to. It was very important to me, something gave me a feeling about you, meeting you, I was very nervous . . . last night I couldn't sleep. . . ." She stared at his boots. Strong lines and faint lines, a pattern made by the salted ice in leather, ruining it. The pattern was interesting. One of her own shoes was coming apart. . . . What if friends of her mother's saw her standing here, one Second Avenue, talking to this man? His long, shabby curls, his striking face, the slouch of his shoulders and the urgent line of his leg, bent dancerlike from the hip, even the stupid cowboy boots, would upset and please them probably: looking like that, he must be an artist of some kind.

Stammering, embarrassed, she interrupted him, "I'm older than you think . . . I'm over thirty . . . I don't have time to talk to you, I don't go out with people, I'm not the way you think. . . ."

"How do you know what I think?" he said angrily.

His anger frightened her. She was silent. Why was she here quarreling with a man she didn't know? She never quarreled with anyone at all. She never quarreled.

"If you're so anxious to leave, leave," he said.

Released, she could not move. For a moment she had not even heard him.

"Don't run—I won't follow you!" he said angrily.

Back for her two-o'clock class, trying to control herself. She had another cup of coffee. Shaking inside. The coffee tasted bad. Everything down here was cheap, her students' talent was cheap, common, their faces had no interest for her, she could not use them in her work, why was she pretending to need a job? She should quit. Move her studio out. There were only two genuinely talented students in her class, both men, and she guessed from their nervousness and the frequency with which they cut class that they would never achieve anything, they would disintegrate . . . other talented students of hers had appeared and disappeared over the years, where did they all end up? And yet when former students did come back to visit, most of them art teachers in high school, she was unable to show more than a perfunctory interest in their careers; why did people surround her, clamor into her ears, what did they want from her? What secret?

"He's crazy," she thought.

During the next several days, aware of him at a distance out on the street, she sometimes felt terror, sometimes a kind of dizzy, abandoned excitement. It was necessary for her to be afraid; she knew the police should be notified, barriers raised, bars put into place; yet she wondered idly why she should be afraid, why . . . ? She could not believe that anything might happen to her. She was safe in her composure, her strength, she had been taking care of herself for years, and so why should she be afraid of that man, why should she even think about him . . . ?

Getting into her car one afternoon, late, she saw him at the edge of the faculty parking lot, watching her. She was tempted to raise her hand casually in a greeting. Would that dispel the danger or make it worse? She imagined him leaping over the low wire fence and galloping up to her. . . . She did not wave. She did not give any sign of seeing him. But when she drove by him she saw him take several quick steps, faltering steps, after the car, in the street . . . his action was ludicrous, sad, crazy. . . . She wondered if she herself had become a little crazy.

> Bodies in a field. The field is sandy, a wasteland, but great spiky weeds grow in it, needing no water. The end of winter, not yet spring. The bodies come to life: a man and a woman. The woman has long, ratty hair, the man's hair is mussed. It is confused with his face. Their bodies are twisted and their faces in shadow. They laugh loudly, waking, they embrace right on the sand, in the open field. . . . Near them is something dead. Is it a dog or a large rat? Let it be a large rat. Frozen hard from winter, not decayed. . . . In the presence of that thing the man and woman embrace violently, tearing at each other's skin, their laughter sharp and wild. . . . They make love right there in the open, among the spiky weeds and the dead rat, aware of nothing around them.

She woke with a headache again, unable to remember what had wakened her. A dream? It was still dark. Only six o'clock. She got out of bed, her body suddenly aching. She dragged herself to her closet, put on a warm robe, stood in a kind of perplexed slouch, wondering what to do next. . . . Her shoulders and thighs ached, her head ached. Her eyes in their sockets were raw and burning, as if someone had been sticking his thumbs in them. Nearby, on a handsome old table, was a head she had done recently, in white; the model had been an old man, but very clean, dignified. He had had a light fringe of hair, almost like

frost, but she had dismissed that and the head was bald, an exact-
ing skull. It interested her strangely. The head of an old man, a
dignified shape of bone, interlocking bone. Ingenious work of art,
the human skull. His forehead was solid, bony, broad. The nose
was rather flat, but broad at the bridge; a strong nose. The eyes
were stern, the eyebrows strong and clear, the mouth slightly surprised, but withdrawing from surprise. She had wanted to convey
a certain emotion—terror, really, but at the same time the refusal
to accept this terror, even to allow the surface of the skin to register it. She ran her hand over the top of the head, over the face.
Cold lead. Cold skin. She pressed her cheek against the top of the
head. A completed work.

In her bathroom the light was too strong. It was reflected from
the cream-colored porcelain of the skin. The house was old but
the bathrooms and the kitchen had been remodeled at great ex-
pense; Pauline had never liked the change. She had liked the old-
fashioned fixtures with their heavy, exaggerated handles, the
mirror beginning to show lead beneath it—like the gray bones
beneath a skull's skin, without shame—and the old, creaky
shower, the worn black and white tile. Now everything was new
and clean, as if in a motel. It had no history.

She peered at herself in the mirror. In a few weeks she would
be thirty years old, which seemed to her surprisingly young.
Surely she had lived more than three decades . . . ? Yet her
face looked very young. It was pale, untouched, soft and baffled
from sleep, as if with a child's apprehension. What had she
dreamed? She took a jar of night cream out of the cabinet and
smoothed it onto her face. It was necessary to lubricate her skin,
she had to take care of herself. It was a duty. One day, twenty
years ago, her father had told her bluntly that she was dirty—
disheveled hair, socks running down into her shoes. "I don't want
you to look ugly," he had said. It was a command she took seriously, because she had his face, a striking, beautiful face, and

that face brought with it a certain responsibility. There is a terrible weight in all kinds of beauty.

> Skin is an organ of the body. It consists of many layers of cells. No one could have invented it. Cells absorb moisture and lose moisture; they pulsate in their own secret rhythm, in their own private time. Invisible, elastic. Each human being has his own skin, unique to him. It is a mystery. Someday a dead woman will wear the skin that belonged to a living woman, and it is the same skin exactly. Then it decomposes. . . . The skin is the most impermeable barrier of the body. It is always thirsty. Its thirst is insatiable. Human thirsts are satisfied from time to time, but the thirst of the human skin is never satisfied so long as it lives.

She wandered aimlessly through the house. Downstairs, she looked out the window down the slope of their long front lawn, at car lights on the avenue, a distance away. Where were all those people going? It surprised her to see the cars out there, people driving all night, into the dawn, with secret, private destinations. . . . Something moved out on the lawn. She did not look at it. Then, feeling helpless, she looked at it . . . she saw nothing, only shadow . . . it was not possible that anything had been there.

If that man followed her home?

Years ago, a student in London, she had modeled for a class. They were sketching heads, torsos. The instructor had been a peculiar man—middle-aged, wheedling, argumentative, but enormously talented, a big man with hairy arms. He had always spilled coffee on the floor, knocked ashes everywhere. Pauline had sat there in the center of a circle, motionless. She had never been shy or self-conscious. Her face, protected by its film of impersonality, was invulnerable. . . . The instructor's name was Julius. She had sat on a stool, relaxed, and he had stood wrenching her into shape, turning her face one way, then another. "Remain like that. Don't complicate our lives," he had said. Somewhere on the other side of the silent, working students he had stood, smoking, staring at her. He had a large, ungainly, gracefully clumsy body. He never talked to anyone personally, he never bothered to look anyone in the eye. She loved him, with rushes of enthusiasm that did not last, imagining him kneeling before her, kissing her knees, in the pose of a certain decadent painting . . . and her staring down through mild, half-closed eyelids at him, uncomprehending. But nothing happened. One day she imagined he was about to embrace her—they were alone for some reason in the studio—she had an uncanny, terrifying moment when she was certain he was going to embrace her, pressing her face against his, his large hands wild in her hair. . . . But he only opened a drawer and some objects inside rattled around. She had gone out into the wet air relieved, ready to weep, feeling totally herself once more.

Since that time she had thought herself in love with two other men, one of them a painter who still lived in this city but whom she no longer bothered to see, another a lawyer, the son of a wealthy couple in her parents' set of friends. But nothing had happened. Nothing. She had approached them as if in a dance, she had noticed something in their faces, a certain intense yearning, and she had gracefully, shyly, permanently withdrawn, not even allowing the surface of her skin to register the excitement and dread she had felt. So it had ended. She was complete in herself, like the heads she made, and like them she felt her skin a perfect organ, covering her, a surface that was impregnable because it was so still and cold.

Statue of Mars. Brandishing a spear, attacking.
The muscular body is in contrast with the
graceful pose, almost a dancer's pose. One hand
holds the lance, the other probably holds a
libation bowl. Lips are inlaid in copper and eyes
in some colored material; helmet separate and
attached. Gently modeled eyes, strange
expression of mouth, almost a smile. Tension
of body: elegance of face. Small, tight, careful
curls descending around ear, down onto
cheek.

EMERGENCY NUMBERS:
FIRE   POLICE   SHERIFF   DOCTOR
STATE POLICE   COAST GUARD
or dial Operator in any emergency and say "I
want to report a fire at ———" or "I want a
policeman at ———"

She was walking with a friend of hers, another art instructor,
down a street of bookstores and bars and restaurants, student
hangouts. While the man talked, her eyes darted about franti-
cally. It was still cold. She had forgotten her gloves. Her fingers
ached with something more than cold, because it was not that
cold. Her friend—a married man with four children, a safe man
—was talking about something she couldn't concentrate on when
Anthony appeared in a doorway ahead of them. He looked out of
breath, as if he had just been running. Pauline had the strange
idea that he had run around the block just to head them off. He
was staring at them, but her friend noticed nothing, and as if this
were a scene carefully rehearsed, everyone between them—students in sloppy overcoats, a Negro woman with her children—
moved away, clearing the view. Pauline and her friend were going to pass Anthony by a few feet, pass right by him. There was

nothing she could do. She stared at him, unable to look away, catching the full angry glare of his eyes, the tension in his head. Cords in his neck were prominent. His coat was open, his hands thrust in his pockets. He glared at her, his glare surrounding her as if the coldness were forming a halo, magically, about her body. The line of his jaw was very hard, his mouth was slightly open as if he were breathing with great difficulty. . . .

He jumped out at them, grabbing her arm. She tried to break lose. In silence he swung a knife, the blade suddenly bright and decorative, and slashed at his own throat. Pauline screamed. Her friend yanked her away, but not before Anthony's blood had splashed onto her. "What are you doing? What—what is this?" the man cried. Anthony, staggering, caught her around the hips, the thighs, as he fell heavily, and she had not the power to break herself loose from him; she stared down at the top of his head, paralyzed.

In a few minutes it was over.

He was taken away; it was over. Her friend answered the policeman's questions. An ambulance had come with its lights and siren but now it was gone. "It's all over. Don't think about it," her friend said, as if speaking to one of his own children. Pauline was not thinking about anything. She walked woodenly, looking down at her blood-splattered shoes. Her coat was smeared with blood in front. Her stockings might have been bloody also, but she could not see; she walked stiffly, not bending at the waist, her shoulders rigid.

"You'd think they would catch people like that before they do something violent," her friend said.

Teen-aged girls, passing them on the sidewalk, stared in amazement at Pauline.

MAN SLASHES OWN THROAT IN UNIVERSITY AREA

Anthony Drayer, 35, of no fixed address, slashed his own throat with a butcher knife this noon on

Second Avenue. He is in critical condition at
Metropolitan Hospital. No motive was given for
the act.

<small>TEMPERATURE HOVERS AT 32°; WEATHERMEN
PREDICT FAIR AND WARMER THIS WEEKEND</small>

When she got home, she went right up to her bathroom, avoiding the maid. Safe. She tore off her coat, sobbing, she threw it
onto the floor, and stared at her legs—blood still wet on her
knees, on her legs, splattered onto her shoes. As if paralyzed, she
stared down at her legs; she could not think what this meant. She
kept seeing him in the doorway, his chest heaving, waiting, and
she kept reliving that last moment when she knew unmistakably
that she dare not pass near him, it could not be done; and yet she
had said nothing to the man she was with, had kept on walking
as if in a trance. Why? Why had she walked straight toward
him?

She was shivering. In horror, she raised her skirt slowly. More
blood on her stockings. On the inside of her thigh, smeared there.
It was a puzzle to her, she could not think. Why was that man's
blood on her, what had happened? Had he really stabbed himself
with a knife? How could a man bring himself to draw a blade
hard across his own throat, why wouldn't the muscles rebel at the
last instant, freezing?

She took off her stockings and threw them away. In a ball,
squeezed in her fist, they seemed harmless. Blood on her legs,
thighs. She stared. What must she do next?

She took a bath. She scrubbed herself.

She fell onto her bed and slept heavily, as if drugged.

On the table are four heads in a white material,
a ceramic material. It shines, gleams cheaply,
light glares out of the eyes of the heads. . . .
The first head is my own, the face is my own.

A blank white face. The next face is my own,
but smaller, pinched. Shocked. The next head,
also white, is my own head again . . . my own
face . . . the lips drawn back in a look of
hunger or revulsion, the eyes narrowed. Can
that be my face, so ugly a face? The fourth head
is also mine. White, stark white. A band tight
around the head has emphasized a vein on my
temple, a small wormlike vein in white, standing
out. The eyes are stern and empty, like the eyes
in Greek statues, gazing inward, fulfilled. That
head is in a trance-like sleep, like the sleep of a
pregnant woman. I walk around and around the
table as if choosing. My hands are itching for
work of my own. I can feel the white clay
beneath my fingernails, but when I look down
it is not clay but blood, hardening in the cracks
of my hands.

Driving to the Institute, she was overcome by a sudden attack
of nausea and had to pull her car over to the side. Now it was
April. She sat for a while behind the wheel, too faint to get out,
helpless. The nausea passed. Still she did not drive on for a while
but remained there, sitting, listening intently to the workings of
her body.

The doctor stands above me. I am lying on an
old-fashioned table, he is holding a large pair of
tweezers, his glasses are rimmed by metal, he is
bald, the formation of his forehead shines,
bumps shine in the light, I am ready to scream
but the straps that hold down my legs also hold
back my screams. . . . This happened centuries
ago. A slop pail is beneath the sink. The doctor

holds up his tweezers to the light and blows at a
curly dark hair that is stuck to them . . . the
hair falls slowly, without weight. . . .

While teaching her class, she felt a sudden urgency to get out
of the room. She went to the women's rest room. Safe. She stared
at herself in the mirror, seeing a tired, pale, angry face. Dull
splotches of the metal that backed the mirror showed through,
giving her a leprous look. She recalled a mirror like this in a
public rest room, herself a girl of thirteen, pale and scared and
very ignorant. She had thought she was pregnant. At that time
she had thought pregnancy could happen to any woman, like a
disease. Like cancer, it could happen.

For weeks she had imagined herself pregnant. Her periods had
been irregular and very painful. She struck at her stomach, weeping, she went without eating until she was faint. . . . One day,
kneeling with her forehead pressed against her old bathtub,
thinking for the five-thousandth time of the terrible secret she
held within her, she had felt the first painful tinge of cramps and
then a slight, reluctant flow of blood. . . . So she was not pregnant after all . . . ?

How did a woman get pregnant?

She lifted her skirt again to stare at the smooth white skin of
her leg. Blank. Blood had been smeared there, but now it was
clean; she showered every morning and took a hot bath every
night, anxious to be clean and soothed and free of his blood.

The living cells of the blood, insatiably hungry
for more life, flow upward. They rise anxiously,
viciously upward . . . in test tubes they may be
observed defying the well-known law of gravity.
Also, blood splashed onto bread mold will devour
it and be nourished by it. Also, blood on foreign
skin or fur will harden into a scab and work its

way into the new flesh, draining life from it.
Also, blood several days old, dropped into tubes
containing female reproductive cells, will unite
with these cells and form new life.

At a dinner party one Saturday in April. Her escort was a
bachelor, a lawyer. She rose suddenly from the table, trembling,
careful to pull back her chair without catching it in the rug, her
head bowed, demure, her diamond earrings brushing coldly
against her cheeks. Not all the candlelight of this room could
warm those earrings or those cheeks. She hurried to the bathroom, she clutched at her head, her face, she realized with a
stunning certainty that she was pregnant.

She was sick to her stomach, as if trying to vomit that foreign
life out of her.

On Monday, not wanting to worry her mother, she drove out
though she had no intention of teaching her class. She parked
around the university and walked for hours. She was looking for
him, for evidence of him. Her breasts felt sore, her thighs and
shoulders ached. She knew that she could not be pregnant and
yet she was certain she was pregnant. Her face burned. After
hours of walking, exhausted, she called a cab and went back
home, abandoning her car. She wept.

"I just found out about Drayer," Martin said, stammering.
"They said he cut himself and attacked a woman, and I knew it
would be you, I knew it. . . ." Pauline was silent, holding the
telephone to her ear without expression. "I knew something like
that would happen! He was very strange, he never appreciated
what I did for him, he was forgetful, like a child—he was always
forgetting my name and he had no gratitude—he was like a criminal— I would never have introduced you but he insisted upon it,
he said he couldn't take his eyes off your face—I knew I shouldn't

have done it, please, do you forgive me? Pauline? Do you forgive me?"

She hung up.

> A woman in a stiff brocade dress, wearing
> jewels. Evening. Candlelight. Her face is
> shadowed . . . is it my mother, my aunt? She
> opens the window, which is a door, and a large
> dog appears. It is a greyhound, elegant and
> spoiled and lean, with a comely head. The
> woman takes hold of the dog's head in both
> hands, staring into its eyes. The dog begins to
> shake its head . . . its teeth flash . . . foam
> appears on its mouth. . . . I turn away with a
> scream, slamming my hand flat on the keyboard
> of a piano: the notes crash and bring everything
> to a stop.

Her mother was packing the large suitcase with the blue silk lining. Weeping, her mother. Her back is shaking. A friend of her mother's talks patiently to Pauline, who lies hunched up in bed, rigid. "If you would try to relax. If you would let us dress you," the woman says. Her own son, at the age of seventeen, once tried to kill her: so she has had experience with this sort of thing. No doubt why Pauline's mother called upon her.

"You understand that you cannot be pregnant and that you are not pregnant," the doctor says. He shapes his words for her to read, as if she might be deaf. She feels the foreign life inside her, hard as stone.

Bleeding from the loins, she aches with cramps, coils of cramps. The blood seeps through the embryonic sack, not washing it free. How to get it free? She has a sudden vision, though she is not sleeping, of a tweezers catching hold of that blood-swollen little sack and dragging it free. . . .

Dr. Silverman, a friend of her father's, visits her in this expensive hospital. He talks to her kindly, lovingly, holding her stone fingers. He is a very cultured man who, having lost most of his own family in a Nazi death camp, is especially suited to talk to her, arguing her out of madness and death. No doubt why her mother called upon him.

Her hair has been cut off short. She cannot hear him.

The nurse says sourly, "You'll get over it." She is lying in warm water, frightened by a terrible floating sensation, as if her organs are floating free inside her, buoyed up by the water. Only the embryo is hard, hard as stone, fixed stubbornly to her arteries. She tries to scream but cannot scream. Anyway, it is dangerous to open her mouth: they feed her that way, tearing open her mouth and inserting a tube.

> . . . He is an ancient Chinese, his face unclear.
> He stands fishing in a delicate stream, his heavy,
> coarse robe pulled up and tucked in his belt. He
> catches a fish and pulls it out of the water, pulls
> it off the hook with one jerk of his hand . . . he
> tosses the fish onto the bank where the other
> fish lay, bleeding at the mouth, unable to close
> their eyes. . . .

Her mother brings a box of candy. Cheeks haggard, spring coat not very festive. She is a widow, and now it is beginning to show. She sits by the bedside weeping, weeping. . . . "Do you hear me? Why don't you talk to me? Do you hate me unconsciously? Why do you hate me?" Her mother weeps, words are all she knows, she turns them over and over again in her mind. "That man . . . you know . . . the one who stabbed himself, well, it was in the paper that he finally killed himself, in the hospital where he was being kept. . . . Why don't you hear me, Pauline? I said that man did away with himself. He won't bother you any more, he can't bother you. Are you listening? Why aren't you listening?"

She lies listening.

It is a monument in dark stone. A body is being cremated. Birds in the air, crows. It is finally spring and everything is loose. Children are running around the base of the monument, with no eye for it. What do children care about the monuments of the world! They throw flowers at one another. . . . Atop the monument is a statue, two figures. One is a youth with curly hair, a thick torso, protruding blank eyes. The set of his mouth shows him both angry and frightened. The other figure is an angel of death, a beautiful woman with outspread wings, though her body is shaped unnaturally from the waist down. She holds out her hand to the young man.

I am standing before him. He sinks to his knees and embraces me, he presses his face against me. Leaning over him, with lust and tenderness that is violent, like pain, I clutch him to me, I feel the tight muscles of his shoulders, I press my face against the top of his head. . . .

We kneel together. We press our faces together, our tears slick and warm. . . .

Boy and Girl

The boy was loose and gangling and looked about fifteen instead of eighteen; it was embarrassing that his father was so handsome. The girl was slight and had the frail powdery look of a moth, a colorless fluttering insect of some sort. It was embarrassing that her mother was so solid and horsey; in fact the girl, Doris, called her mother "the horse" behind her back with a kind of smirking, satisfied affection. The boy, Alexander Jr., spoke of his father as "my father" and to his father's face he said, "Father. . . ."

They kept meeting all their lives, in and around Lakeshore Point. He went to a boys' school and she to a girls' school and their friends overlapped, though neither of them really had "friends"; they had new and old acquaintances. It was an achievement that they had both lived for so long in Lakeshore Point, because it was a suburb people moved in and out of constantly; it was a surprise, in April, how all the "For Sale" signs went up before houses, in time for a quick deft selling in a day or two, a few weeks of arrangements, and the move to the next city and the next suburb as soon as school ended. So, in the midst of all this coming and going, the loading and unloading of great Allied Vans that proudly conquered the continent, sooner or later Doris and Alex would have fixed upon each other, at least for a while. As Doris grew older—she was now sixteen—it occurred to her that the atmosphere of a typical school dance was the atmosphere of life itself. Partners went out to dance, the music changed, partners came back, switched around, danced again, and the gymnasium would be filled beneath its fluttering strips of crepe paper with the shuffling of legs and feet and the movements of arms: so many bodies. It was like this in Lakeshore Point itself, with strangers always moving in and strangers moving out.

They were different types: Doris was popular and had a nervous irritating laugh, the laugh of girls in crowds who are sure of being overheard. Alex was faintly stereotyped, liking chess and astronomy and complicated crossword puzzles his mother could not understand. Prepared for Harvard, he had been deeply wounded in his senior year at Lakepoint Boys' Academy when his application at Harvard had been rejected. He had the usual extraordinary grades, and his hobbies—chess and astronomy and, at an adviser's suggestion, ice hockey—had seemed good enough. It was a mystery, his rejection. So he would be going to the University of Michigan in the fall, and he walked about with his stoop more pronounced than usual, muttering in reply to greetings, casting away imagined slurs with a nervous wave of his hand. When the other boys bothered to think about him, they thought he was rather queer. Everyone had an opinion of Doris Moss, even at distant high schools, but Alex wasn't up on any recent news; he and Doris had gone to the same orthodontist several

years before and he remembered her as a slight, shy child, perpetually twelve.

Alex had decided firmly to become a doctor and to go into medical research, and somehow his rejection from Harvard was not
believable. He carried this rejection about with him everywhere,
anxious to drag it out and admit it, humble, questioning, nervous
in the hope that it had all been a mistake and he was accepted
after all. He was the kind of boy adults believed they could talk to,
until they talked to him. His parents' friends approached him
with stiff, helpful smiles.

He had decided to go into medical research because his father,
a doctor, was in a kind of medical research himself. One evening
when his parents were having a dinner party Alex had heard
something that impressed him strangely and changed his life. He
had come in from a movie—he always went alone—and used the
downstairs guest bathroom, in the back of the house. There was
something about this bathroom he liked. It was done in black and
gold, with decanters of scented soap and lovely scented tissue and
toilet paper, also gold, and small exquisite guest towels that were
white linen with gold embroidering. On the dressing table was a
delicate mirror, balanced for the fine-lashed eyes of his parents'
lady guests; underfoot was a black, black rug. Alex liked to use
this bathroom because he felt very special in it. He felt like one
of his parents' guests. Before parties he cautiously checked this
bathroom, by himself, since the maid was always harassed and
could not be trusted to see whether the soap was clean or not.
The special soap in this bathroom was ball-shaped, gold and
white, and it gave off a lovely sweet scent. But sometimes the
soap balls grew dusty because they were never used.

This feeling for the bathroom was important, because it might
have had to do with Alex's decision. He was in there when he
heard his father and another man come into the kitchen, and his
father's grave words were somehow mixed in with the scent of

the toilet paper and the soap. His father was saying, "It's a hell of a complex operation. You don't have a neat laboratory situation, of course. You must consider the environmental factors—the humidity, the wind, the area, the particle size, the amount of saturation, the method of ejaculation. You can imagine the variability there." The other man, unknown to Alex, said something about computers. "Yes, computers are certainly helpful," Alex's father said in his kind, serious voice, "but beyond a certain point only the existential fact is real. Nothing else is real. An event happens only once and that's the difficult thing about life—it isn't a laboratory experiment."

Alex was strangely agitated. He admired his father and feared him a little and it seemed that each of his father's words was valuable. His father worked for the government now on classified projects and it was sometimes necessary for him to be gone for weeks at a time. Perhaps these long trips or the isolation of the laboratory had made Alex's father rather remote about most things, as if holding them out at arm's length; so it was intimate, hearing his father talk like this. Above the clinking of ice cubes his father said, "The biological cloud agent is a totally new frontier. It's fascinating work. You have to think of it as disease control in reverse, breeding pathogenic organisms that we've usually thought of in rather negative terms. And then, apart from the physical reality, there is a totally unexplored area of psychological reaction—what the bonus effect in terms of enemy panic might be, we don't know. We have some ideas, that's all."

Alex remained in the bathroom after they left. He kept hearing his father talk about "reality." His father's other words rose and circled in Alex's brain, and he could not quite understand them, but again and again the word "reality" returned to him. What was real? What was real? "Beyond a certain point only the existential fact is real," his father had said solemnly, and Alex tried to understand that concept. It was strange that he could be so quick at school and so slow, even dense, around the house. It was as if his father gave off a kind of glimmering cloud that fogged up Alex's glasses and also fogged up his brain.

Inspired, he wrote a theme for his English teacher, Mr. Godwin, called "Precisely What is Real?" Mr. Godwin was very pleased with it and read it to the class, embarrassing Alex immensely. Mr. Godwin, though not so tall and handsome as Alex's father, was a minor, substantial hero in Alex's life. He was a raspy, enthusiastic man with nicotine-stained fingers.

Though Doris was younger, she was more experienced than Alex. For years she had been a child and she recalled those years with a kind of disbelief. Then, one summer, she had stayed with a girl friend at Cape Cod and met a boy who was supposed to be a television actor, or had hopes of being one. He told her about the television business and the people who ran it that you never saw and had no idea existed; they were the people who really counted, he said. He had a narrow, darkly handsome face and might have been fifteen or twenty-three. There was something indeterminate about him, as if he were waiting to be instructed about himself. "The people that run things are off to the side. Hidden. You don't see them, you stupid guys at home," he said with a sneer. When they were together on the beach it was like a television scene. He was always close to her, with the head-on, slightly myopic look of actors on television; he seemed also to be saying words he had used before. Doris had a fragile, freckled look and a rather thin body. He had forced her to take an icy cold shower with him on the first night they met, and since then her body felt faintly unreal, tingling and numb at the same time. Her body held this sensation for some time. She could not get over it, her mind wanted to break free but couldn't, her body retained this daze—it was nothing she could explain. She didn't talk about it. What she remembered about the boy was his face and body and hands and especially his words, which were strange. "On television there's all these people running around you never

see, and cameras and stuff. You stupid bastards at home don't
know anything. You don't know how things really are and even
the people on television, that work for it, they don't know either.
It's too big."

Though what he did to her was no different from what other
boys were to do to her when she returned to Lakeshore Point, she
could not get over his words. There was something forlorn and
angry in them, something violent. She kept hearing the violence
in them, replaying the words in her head, and her body had that
vague, suspended feeling about it, numb and excited at the same
time.

Doris' mother insisted upon a Saturday-morning ritual of shopping. Doris shrank from anyone seeing her with her mother, and
her small, closed, sleek face and her rather pigeon-toed, arrogant
step quite clearly distinguished her from her mother. Her mother
had a long, kindly face; it was unfortunate that her two front
teeth were prominent. Doris' parents were both rather homely
and sturdy; Doris was lithe and quite a surprise. While her
mother chattered about nonsense in the stores, Doris dreamed of
what he would be doing that evening on her date, and about
whether she gave a damn if the boy called her again.

Alex's mother knew Doris' mother slightly. Both belonged to
the Village Women's Club. Doris' mother had inherited quite a
lot of money and seemed to apologize for it with her big, toothy,
hesitant smile; Alex's mother, coming from a less wealthy background, was therefore sharper and knew whom to befriend and
whom to slight; she always avoided Doris' mother. Sometimes she
saw the mother and daughter out shopping on Saturday—the
mother galloping along enthusiastically in short, squat, thick-
heeled shoes, and the girl dressed like a little slut in a short skirt.
At such times Alex's mother called out, "Why, hello, Edith!" and
breezed on by.

Yes, she thought with an involuntary satisfaction, that girl
what's-her-name did look like a slut.

She had her own problems with Alex. Though he was eighteen, his skin was still awful; it was a pity to look at him. Every Saturday she packed him in the car and drove him all the way into the city—and she hated the city—to a really superb dermatologist who played squash with her husband at the Athletic Club and who administered to poor Alex X-ray treatments, dried-ice treatments, a variety of pills and hormones, and numerous salves. Poor Alex had to wash his face with a white sponge and work the lather up and then rinse it away, using only lukewarm water. No hot water. Acne was caused by overexcitation of the oil glands, his mother had learned to her distaste, and so he must not make things worse. She thought the word *acne* was at least as ugly as the problem itself. It always startled her to see her own son—such a tall, gangling boy!—come out of the doctor's inner office and into the waiting room, with that apologetic stoop to his shoulders, that half-chagrined, half-challenging smirk, and that terrible bluish-violet acne all over his face— It fascinated her in a way. It was lumpy and flaky at once. Some pimples were very hard, like berries; others were ripe and soft and draining. Sometimes it was all she could do to keep her hands off his face, but no, no, one never squeezes these problems away; nothing so violent. After a good lathering and a good tepid rinsing, Alex applied a special ointment to his poor bumpy face, and it was also a shock to come upon him late in the evening—that tall, thin boy in his pajamas looking for food downstairs, his face covered with a ghostly white film of medicine that flaked off as he walked.

Poor Alex.

In the spring of his senior year in high school, something began to happen to him. He lost his appetite. He walked about mumbling to himself, arguing over something. His father was in Washington for most of April. His mother had a number of teas and luncheons; Alex felt vaguely protective, knowing that his mother dreaded to be alone and that loneliness was increased by this constant round of parties, and yet he was uneasy with such knowledge and did not know what to do with it. Should he have such an understanding of his own mother? Was it proper? Though he was forbidden by Dr. Lurch to eat chocolates, he ate them secretly, like a twelve-year-old. When his father called, every evening at eight, he made sure he was not around, though he would have liked nothing better than to talk to him. He felt dizzily as if he were becoming a child again. . . .

His mother began to plead with him. Wasn't he an intelligent boy, at the head of his class? Then what was wrong? Why was he so argumentative? Why did he so hate to change his clothes? His underwear? Ah, his mother pleaded with him! Alex knew that he was becoming strange but he did not understand it. He felt a peculiar resistance to taking showers or baths and he disliked brushing his teeth because . . . because in this way wasn't he stirring up germs . . . ? But he did not want to think about it.

"What will your father say about this?" his mother cried.

She was a pretty, dismayed woman. Every day she rose at seven-thirty and showered and put on excellent clothes, all the required paraphernalia of a woman, including high-heeled shoes; every day she went out at about noon or twelve-thirty to have luncheon somewhere or to play bridge or to do something, Alex wasn't sure what—she was tremendously and wonderfully busy. On the other days her friends visited her and she served luncheon—chicken or shrimp or crab in some kind of cream dish, usually, with a delicate icy fruit dessert—and Alex loved the very odor of such days, the rich promise of his mother's happy life. He did not want to disturb her. It would be a disgrace for any son to disturb so happy and busy a woman, and yet . . . he felt that there was indeed something wrong with him, some dissociation from his body, a fear and a distrust of his own skin.

For Mr. Godwin he wrote an unassigned essay called "The Limits of Reality." It was long, rambling, and feverish. He wrote it late at night and was quite proud of certain sentences: "The nature of disease may well be the ultimate reality, and the method of survival in adjustment. Isolation and adaptation. Living with disease. Nothing can be repeated. History comes and goes. There is nothing but the Existential Fact. My skin is a dense, swarming sea of maggots invisible to the eye. . . ."

He handed the essay in with great excitement on a Friday morning, and that evening he went to a party against his wishes, at his mother's wishes. She was concerned about his "social life." It was a party for high school kids at the big Payne house, and he was probably invited only because his mother played bridge with Mrs. Payne, no other reason. He spent most of his time eating, scooping up dip with his finger. He ate a lot of shrimp. In the recreation room—which was long, with a low, stucco ceiling and a great fireplace at one end, without a fire—couples were dancing in the darkness. Alex half-knew everyone there and disdained them. Betty Payne had been rude to him, which meant she had been forced to invite him. So he stayed by himself and his face was fixed with a knowing, philosophical smirk as he ate shrimp.

There was a commotion in the recreation room. One girl, dressed in white, stamped on the floor and threw herself about in what was either a new dance or a tantrum. She thrashed her body, flung her arms around violently, let her long hair fly out about her face—from the way others were watching her, Alex decided it must be a tantrum. The girl had a thin, delicate body and her legs were quite thin; it was Doris Moss. She was associated with a crowd Alex had been aware of for years, without taking any real interest, having heard of their perpetual adventures and daring every Monday throughout high school. He had heard a number of things about them but did not exactly believe everything he heard. The girl Doris continued stamping the floor in her shiny white low-heeled shoes, exactly like a child, and a boy shouted something in her face.

She whirled around and stalked out of the room and came right to Alex. "Hi, Alex, how are you," she said in a taunting voice. "Let's go for a ride and get out of here. Do you have a car?"

"I walked over."

"I've got a car. Come on."

Her face was wet with perspiration and strands of hair stuck to it. A few kids were watching her, but Alex ignored them. "Come on, come on," she said in a husky, flirtatious voice, tugging at Alex's hands. "Let's get out of this place before I suffocate."

He followed along with her, both surprised and pleased. She kept touching him with her small, darting, nervous hands and he wondered if perhaps a new self might rise out of him, a new Alex, popular and assured. But she said as they left the house, "Why don't you have a girl friend?" This hurt him a little and he did not reply. "Are you queer?" she said with a happy stamp of her foot. She leaned around and laughed up into his face. "There's my car. It's boxed in," she said, pulling at him. "No, don't look in that car, leave them alone! You really are queer, aren't you?"

They got into her car and she managed to get out by driving over the lawn. She had to back up and drive forward a few times, impatiently turning the wheel, and she finally managed to get out. Alex watched the doorway of the house for someone to appear and shout at them, but no one came.

"Why don't you have a car? Why don't you have a girl friend?"

"I don't know. Don't want them."

Her brisk, brassy manner was good because it expected nothing of him. She talked so fast and so loudly that she hardly listened to him. "No, really, tell the truth for once," she said, poking him in the ribs, "is it some religious thing or something? The way you act?"

He had been drinking at the party, but it had not released a freer, bolder Alex. Instead he felt hot and nervous. As Doris drove along the boulevard, she kept laughing in a strange, mocking way. "Alexander Junior!" she said with a snicker. Then her mockery changed to a kind of fake sugary concern. "Your father's kind of cute though. I like your father. Why didn't your father come to this lousy party tonight?"

She drove carelessly and kept jabbing at him and teasing him, and Alex wondered if this was the usual way for girls to behave with boys; he didn't know if he liked it or resented it. "Tell me what you're doing these days," Doris commanded. "Are the braces off your teeth? What's wrong with your skin? Tell me about your father. Tell me something, say something," she laughed. She let her head fall back and her mouth opened blankly. On her delicate ears tiny earrings glinted; Alex liked them. He was glad he had found something about her to like.

"My boy friend pierced my ears for me. This was someone you don't know, some bastard. I don't go out with him any more. First you get it clean and then you put a piece of cotton behind the ear, you know, to protect that—you know—that vein or artery or something that's there—but anyway it bled a lot— My mother gave me these earrings for Christmas."

"They're very nice."

She reached over and seized his hand. "Do you like me, do you think I'm beautiful? What are you thinking right now?"

"I have sort of a headache. . . ."

"I've got this crazy idea, it's a great idea, there's this little kid I'm going to take for a ride. Let's take him for a ride. On Sundays people drive up and down the lake shore with kids on rides, looking at the lake, so let's go get him, all right?" There were flecks of saliva around her mouth. Alex, staring at her, felt his head begin to ache seriously and wondered how he would get out of this situation. She was driving fast and carelessly. She turned off onto a darker street and raced along it, not stopping at intersections, and after a while she braked the car to a fast stop before a ranch house. Alex sat in the car, bewildered, and she ran out.

A few minutes later she appeared at the door of the house, backing out, and then she turned and ran down the walk with something in her arms. It was a baby. "Look. This is my brother Dorsey's baby. Look at it. It's my nephew. What do you think, I'm an aunt. No, let me drive, I want to drive," she said rudely, though he had only slid over to look out at what she held. It was a baby, yes.

"What's that?"

"What's it look like?" she laughed. "I told the kid inside, she's in seventh grade at Cooley, I told her we'd be right back, we wanted to take the baby for a ride. It's sort of a nice baby. Here."

Alex did not want to hold the baby, thinking he was not good enough for it, wouldn't know how to hold it, would frighten it. But she thrust it at him and started the car again.

"But maybe we shouldn't—"

"Oh, shut up," she said. The baby began to whimper and Doris snapped on the radio. "This is a lousy car. This isn't my car. This is Fred's car, Fred Smith, do you know him? Of course you don't."

"Fred Smith?"

"You don't know him and you don't know anybody. Can't you stop that baby crying? What kind of a father are you?"

Alex rocked the baby experimentally and it did stop. He felt a kind of numbness move over him, as if he were indeed a father, and the frantic perspiring Doris who sat beside him were his wife, a mother. He stared down at the baby in awe. "Fred's this guy I have kind of a thing with, he's real wild. He's real strange, he's from Olcott. He doesn't hang around with any bunch. This is Fred's car that he lent me for tonight, I was at his place and drove it over, my mother thought I was at Toni Sargant's. There's a slumber party there tonight. She thinks I'm going there but I'm not."

"Where are you going, then?" Alex asked suspiciously.

He held the baby as if in accusation of her, rocking it gently.

The girl cast a sideways glance at him. He could not figure out her wild chatter, and then he remembered suddenly talk at school about certain kids who took pills; Doris had been mentioned. He saw at once that of course she was high. She had a strange waxen look beneath the perspiration, a dummy's look. Seen in ordinary light, she would have been a girl of about sixteen with a slightly snubbed nose; in the changing, disruptive lights from the drive-in restaurants and gas stations they were passing she looked as if her skin had been painfully tightened around the blunt hollows and ridges of her face. "We'd better go back," Alex said.

"This Fred is awfully strange. He lives by himself," Doris went on. A car approaching them flicked its lights and finally blew its horn to urge her back onto her own side of the street. "I said I'd be back around twelve but I got hung up with someone, that Tommy, but he made me mad . . . and Fred will get mad, but . . . but I don't know if I'll go back to his place. . . . I don't know. I should get his car back or he'll be mad. I took a bus over to his place but that was during the day . . . but if I go back he'll make me stay . . . he's sort of strange. . . . He's twenty-four."

"Doris, we'd better go back. Let's take the baby back."

He felt a little sick. Doris had driven out quite far and was in a dark, dinky suburb now, rushing along the main street. "I want to get to the country," she said angrily. "I'm so sick of all this, I could puke. We've got a cottage up north we could go to, nobody'd know. My brother Dorsey, he's a goddamn show-off, he's really my stepbrother and he's an awful lot older than I am. I don't remember him, really. That might not have been his house. I think it was. I told the babysitter my sister-in-law wanted the baby and she believed me, and I'm pretty sure it's the right baby, my nephew. His name should be Walter. . . . Isn't that a stupid name for a baby?" she said angrily.

The baby began to cry again, as if startled by her remark. Alex stared helplessly down at it and felt, once again, a magical sensation of being its father: the two of them besieged by the cruel, crazy words of its mother. He wondered suddenly if there might not be some danger of their infecting the baby. His hands were very large, holding it; his skin looked dangerous and flaky in the mottled light.

"I know what, let's play a trick on Dorsey. Let's fix him," Doris whispered.

"What?"

"Let's kill it."

"What?"

"The baby here," Doris said. "Isn't that a wild idea? Huh? What do you think?"

She stopped the car. She leaned over to Alex and stared down at the baby's face; Alex leaned away from her. "We could let it drop out of the car by accident. We could say it got out by itself. Some other car would hit it, not us. We could watch. . . . We could stuff that blanket in its mouth, what do you think, isn't that wild? What do you think?"

Alex's head was pounding violently. "You're crazy," he said.

"Who's crazy?"

"You, you're crazy. Why do you want to do a thing like that?"

Doris laughed and laughed at him. Oh, he was absurdly intelligent; he'd never get over it any more than he'd get over his acne. Doris lay back against the seat laughing until she began to sob angrily. Alex stared at her. "You want me to drive back?" he said cautiously.

"Stupid bastard like you don't know how to drive," she muttered.

She said nothing more. Her stare was fixed upon something before her, on the dashboard, maybe. Or on nothing. Her mouth opened upon rapid, jagged gasps. Once in a while she giggled convulsively and Alex waited, frightened, but she did not speak. He said shyly, "I'll drive back," and Doris made no resistance when he squeezed over her and got behind the wheel.

He drove back to the Payne's house and parked in the circle driveway and walked home by himself, terribly frightened. His fear was a kind of intoxication, and he could not think straight. Later he was to hear that the police had been called, that the baby did belong to Doris' brother, and that Doris had been found unconscious in the car; the baby was crying on the seat beside her.

And who was to know that Alex had been involved?

He told no one about it, no one. His father returned from Washington and had a talk with him. He was a serious, handsome, busy man and it was a serious matter that he take time to talk so lengthily with Alex. He talked about being normal. "Do you think it's normal," he said, "to hoard your dirty clothes? Not to change your socks, to wear them in bed?"

"I'm not bothering anybody," Alex muttered.

"Your mother says this is getting worse. It's getting worse. And what about this essay you wrote?"

Mr. Godwin had called Alex's father about the essay. It was no surprise; Alex should have known better than to write such a thing. *What is reality? Reality is germs and microbes and infectious scum. . . .*

As he listened to his father read these strange, angry words, he was torn between a knowledge of their insanity and a hope, a terrible hope, that his father would glance up at him with respect. But his father held the paper at some distance, reading, his mouth working the peculiar words as if they themselves were infectious. Finally he said, "Do you think this is the work of a *normal mind?*"

Alex broke down at that point. He confessed to his father about the terrible odor of his skin, the infection of his skin, the sensation of crawling and gnawing and fluttering. . . . Oh, it was terrible, it was terrible, and his voice rose to hysteria; he began to claw himself. "It's all over me, I tried to keep it secret but it got worse. I don't want it to fly off or anything . . . the X-ray treatments help, it isn't on my face . . . it needs to be burned off, not stirred up, that's the danger if I fool around, I don't want it to get stirred up and go off on other people. . . ."

"What's wrong with you? What are you talking about?" his father demanded. His father showed no fear; he was calm and logical, and Alex tried to imitate him, though his skin became cancerous with germs as he spoke; so active, so restless! His very skin crept upon his bones and his scalp moved of its own accord. "I think it could be treated but I don't want to miss school," he said sorrowfully. "I know something's wrong with me, I know it isn't normal, and I'm sorry. I'm sorry. Please don't tell Mother or she'll worry about it. . . ."

So he was taken by his father to Dr. Mate, a friend of his father's from Harvard Medical School. Dr. Mate was a psychiatrist whose practice consisted entirely of disturbed adolescent boys. Alex's problem was judged not a serious one because it did not threaten violence, and it was not even an uncommon one: a neurosis induced by feelings of Oedipal aggression further stimulated by a sense of inferiority and frustration. He clawed at himself, in the opinion of Dr. Mate, because he could not claw at his father. Still his "problem" did not go away. After many sessions with this doctor, who reminded Alex of his own father, Alex was made to understand that it was his mind that was sick and not his skin. They arranged for him to spend some time in a hospital called Oakridge Manor, about twenty miles from home, and he was cautioned not to tell the other patients his secret about his skin being infected and seething with germs. Oakridge Manor cost sixty dollars a day but was worth it, everyone said. After a while Alex's father transferred him to another private hospital, Foxridge Manor. He was allowed to come home on weekends. He liked these visits home but he was unable to relax; he carried himself about cautiously and stiffly through the familiar rooms, his own former room, the lovely guest bathroom downstairs, and when he spoke, it was in a cautious, stiff voice. His mother talked to him about the way the living room was going to look when it was painted and the drapes changed.

"But why are you sitting like that? You can let your arms rest on the table, please, Alex, don't sit there like that—you know you're perfectly all right, please," his mother said.

"Yes, I know. That's right," Alex said.

"Then why are you sitting like that? You look so strange."

"I'm sorry. I know there's nothing wrong with me."

She rushed on to talk about the painters' union and the terrible fight a friend of hers had had with a painter. First he had painted her friend's dining-room walls white, and then apparently he had leaned on them with his dirty hands—and so the walls were blotched and smudged—and what did he think? What did Alex think happened next?

Alex said vaguely, "Out at the hospital the other day there was a girl I thought I knew. She was sitting in the reading room. She was leafing through magazines very fast. There were little scabs on her fingers, it looked like, as if she bit her fingernails, but . . . but maybe there weren't scabs, I didn't get that close. . . . I thought it might be Doris Moss."

"Was it?"

"I don't know."

His mother said slowly, avoiding his eyes, "Well, it was awfully sad about Doris. Of course I don't know anything about it. But some boy beat her up. Some man. He beat her up very badly a few weeks ago in some awful place downtown. It was such a shock."

"Then what happened?"

"To her, you mean? I don't know." She was staring at Alex with her blank, flattened-out look, a pretty, dismayed mother who had seen too much and thought about too much, who had been destined for a life of luncheons and dinners and the fulfillment of a good marriage and the enjoyment of a successful son . . . and instead, this had happened. She stared at him.

"She didn't die or anything?" Alex said.

"I don't think so, no, she didn't die. I don't know what happened to her," his mother said. The telephone began ringing in the next room. "That's the contractor with the estimate," she said apologetically and with a rush of mild enthusiasm; after a decent moment she rose and went to answer it and Alex heard her in the next room talking about the living-room walls. They were to be painted either white or oyster. That was the conclusion of their talk about Doris Moss, and the subject never came up again.

*T*he Assailant

There are those strange, ugly times when your body seems transparent, your skin drawn too tight, something, so that the heightened beat of the heart and the minute hissing of blood through veins seems a concern not just of yourself but of everyone watching you. I knew this once but had forgotten it; sitting in the hospital waiting room, I am reminded. Outside the hospital, past its bright green lawn and immaculate swept sidewalks, people are walking without this knowledge. It is spring, May. Why should they bother with this knowledge? If they glance at the hospital, it is a glance that does not sharpen, but scatters their thoughts; for why should they be reminded of the transparency of their bodies under their handsome clothes?

And this is a weekday too; I am conscious, among the other people who wait, of being truant from something. Years ago I would have felt guilty at being out of school. Now, what am I absent from? At this time of day—ten-thirty in the morning—everyone belongs somewhere. We are those who have been selected out of ordinary routines because something has gone wrong. We are conscious of a mistake somewhere. Those we have come to visit are being propped up with pillows, tubes are being adjusted in them, blood pumped into their indifferent arteries: who knows what magic is being performed? The nurses are young and healthy and professionally impersonal. They know secrets of the kind we out here cannot be trusted with. Our bodies would refuse such knowledge. It is kept from us behind walls. When we leave the hospital and hurry out into sweeter air, they will tend our secrets for us and keep us from thinking. And, later, when our loved ones are dead, or recovered and free like us, we too can walk past the hospital without seeing it.

My friend sits beside me knocking ashes into the stained ash tray. It has a floor stand and is made of metal with markings to suggest wood; its early, flashy brilliance is marred by rust spots. Bargain basement. A wad of pink gum with tiny tooth marks in it lies in the ash tray; fortunately, it is the kind of gimmicky ash tray you can manipulate into opening, so that the gum falls through and disappears.

My friend glances at me after he does this, but I have looked away. Impossible to keep up the strain of love if we share such things. . . . When I look back at him the gum is gone, he has recrossed his long legs, he smiles tentatively at me.

Time for the visit. My friend remains seated. He avoids the nurse's gaze, and the unlegal, unofficial nature of our relationship is advertised. He and I are nothing to each other, nothing that can be filed away. At the extremes of life and death we will part company. I follow the nurse along the corridor. The foyer must be a recent addition, for the floors and walls there are handsome. As soon as you leave the foyer, the dingy, rather damp hospital itself begins . . . they have no dignity, disease and death. There is here the paid-for anonymity of county buildings with their clerks and counters, the anonymity of certain police stations and public libraries at the very centers of huge American cities. Dying must be easier in these gray impersonal surroundings, for their dimly white walls and chipped bedposts and noiseless wheeled carts have nothing in them to suggest a world to be envied. Or do I say this to myself to keep from feeling terror? The nurse walks ahead, in rubber-soled white shoes. All the money he pays, and what is so good about this . . . ? I try to be grim and practical; my father could admire no qualities in me except these.

And here, suddenly, he is. Propped up by pillows as I had imagined, and yet not the man I had imagined. He is still stunned and baffled. He is old. We think of our fathers not as they are but as they appeared to us one day—when we were ten, maybe, and everything was vivid and uncomplicated. We have no heart to think of them as they are, as if that were a betrayal.

"He likes the sunlight. He was sitting up for breakfast," the nurse says. She is pretty, with brown hair. In spite of her white uniform and the sure, practiced look of those hands accustomed to death I think of her not as a function of the hospital but as a woman—someone my friend, waiting back there with the old rumpled *Time* Magazine, might find pleasing to look at. "Please don't tire him," she says, as if he is her father and not mine.

I sit by the window, in a wicker-backed chair painted pale green. The hospital room is smaller than I remembered. So much money for this? But it is expensive, this death and dying, there is suddenly no room for the economical eye that charted us for so many years. The old man in bed watches me attentively, as if I might make a sudden movement. His eyes are still intelligent, though his face and body are wasted. Or are they intelligent? That is the sort of thing one carries back from the hospital, a little half-whispered remark to be made to friends who want to hear it. I sit and talk to him, leaning forward. I am aware again of my body as if it were transparent, and of the urgent set of my spine. What is that on his table? Something made of rubber, red-brown rubber? Everything frightens me. I talk on and on, about relatives, about the lawn at home, about the squirrels that dig holes in the lawn, about the man down the street with the annoying dog. . . . If some of these topics are familiar, good. My father wants to be told only what he already knows. This devastating stroke that has paralyzed his body and ruined his speech has done no more than point up what he has always been—but I am not allowed to think that. Something hurts my throat. I am not allowed to think such things of the dying.

I talk on. I am bright as the sunshine coming through the curtainless window, bright as the cheap handles of the drawers in the metal night stand. It occurs to me that I have blundered into the wrong room and am talking to someone else's father. Good, good. Someone then is in my own father's room, chatting away as if no one ever lived or died or suffered, but as if the horizons of human life were cleanly circumscribed by neighbors, relatives, dogs, the latest news from . . . friends thought forgotten, or friends of friends never really remembered.

"Aunt Thelma's neighbor, that one, you know, that won the car in the raffle, well, they went down to Florida with it and guess what . . . they had an accident down there." I am dutiful and pleased with myself, to report such a thing. If only I had more misfortune to lay quietly on his bed! But his stroke was brought on by someone beating him—an unidentified assailant. "Unidentified assailant." They are not sure if he remembers this or not, so I should not make any reference to violence. Automobile accidents happen only to those who deserve them: he always felt that, obscurely. So I can talk about automobile accidents. But anything else may be bad for him: flowerpots falling accidentally

out of windows onto innocent heads, children accidentally
drowned in ditches, "man accidentally electrocuted while working with television set. . . ."

That unidentified assailant! I wonder, while I talk cheerfully to
my father's wrinkled, mute face, what that assailant is doing now.

My father breathes quietly. Does he resent my body, transparent as it is? Marked for an assailant as it is? He cannot help
but narrow his eyes at my talking mouth, wondering how it happened that he somehow brought that mouth into existence. He
must begrudge the life he gave me; perhaps he is even bored with
me. I am bored with the self he inspires in me. And as I fall into
guilty silence, with a faint strained smile on my lips, I think of the
more desirable self others inspire in me and of how that has always determined my love for them. As soon as I hurry back into
the foyer and my friend glances up at me, another self will appear; this talkative self, this daughterly-maternal self, will be left
behind with the antiseptic odor of the hospital. Another self! Of
all absurd things, I catch myself trying to see my reflection in the
hard shiny surface of the metal stand.

And yet I do love this man sitting motionless in bed. I love him,
but we are paralyzed with each other. He is dying and I am living,
and customarily, like people speaking different languages, we are
fearful and bored in each other's presence. I can translate nothing
of his into my own language. Painfully, he tries to speak—he
cannot speak. Nonsensical sounds come from him. I listen with
my spine urged forward in that foolish way, a way I have just
learned. Never have I sat like that before coming into this room. I
listen; I frown; I stare at the floor. Nothing. I love him but cannot
tell him so, for as soon as I said the word "love," that word would
have no meaning. What little trinkets and souvenirs can we give
to people on their way to die? At the end they must toss everything contemptuously aside, the way we clean out attics and
drawers of things that belong to other people.

Afterward, my friend and I drive out toward the country, away from the hospital. It is nearing noon, evidently. People are out for lunch. At a school crossing my friend has to wait impatiently while a woman with a white band around her waist and chest holds up a sign that says STOP. Children run across the intersection; we watch them without interest. Negro and white children. They are energetic and vicious in the spring air; careless of color, they mingle, and their blows are delivered brightly, without discrimination. The woman lets her arm fall wearily. My friend— whose face in profile is hard and has the illusion of being chipped, so deep is the cleft between the lips and chin—drives on.

We stop before reaching the country at a park I've been in a few times: a grade-school picnic once, I think. A fairly large park for the city. People are playing tennis on the courts as we stroll across the ragged grass. My friend is smoking a cigarette as if this were an offering to me—some normal distraction, something for him to do instead of talk. Like all men who are conscious of their bodies, the breakdown of someone else's body is an obscure embarrassment. He has never met my father and never will—my father would have hated him and he my father—yet he senses an alliance. Out of deference to that unknown man's suffering, he frowns and pushes his sunglasses up, unnecessarily, on his nose. We watch the tennis players. An Oriental boy dressed in white shorts, his chest bare and tanned. Marvelous, graceful strokes; a flash of triumphant teeth. His opponent wears dark slacks and looks uneasy, though he plays well.

"I used to play tennis all the time," my friend says. "I won second place in a tournament once—just a city tournament."

But this saddens me, because though he is a young man, his tone refers to something far in the past.

We walk on. On another court two girls are playing. Two women. They are poor players, but happy; we hear one call out to the other. My friend's teeth must be bared in an angry smile, for he hates the display of anything graceless. Once when I pulled my

skirt up a little and side-stepped a newspaper fluttering down the
street at me, he stared and said how graceful I was—like some
kind of bird; like a swan? Only in flashes does he reveal himself.

As if we are following a map, we pass the tennis courts and
some disorderly picnic tables and go into the woods. Here the
paths are wide and rutted with bicycle tire tracks. The woods is
thin; we can see traffic moving through it, out on the other street.
Because we are very new to each other, everything is dreamy and
tentative. He puts his arms around me and kisses me. I feel something against my back—the rough bark of a tree—and we say
nothing, for we do not know each other well enough yet to be
friends. We have nothing to say. In silence, like this, we are acting out a frayed drama that will be repeated this evening, right
here, and the knowledge of our impersonality excites me. I love
him, I think, though with my eyes closed I cannot remember what
he looks like exactly. He is here, he is touching me, there is more
reality in his embrace than in the mysterious, abstract relation-
ships between fathers and children, fathers and daughters. . . .

Then I understand: here is the assailant. "Unidentified assailant!" He is in my arms, and out of a mechanical urgency I caress
his back, for isn't this what is always done? My father's assailant,
with his rigid, critical profile and his mouth that is too soft and
demanding, both at once, and his unidentifiable body pressed
against me. He is the only honest person I have met. He is imitating nothing. Before the honesty of his passion everything lacks
substance: the wearying sympathy, the hospital corridors that
only seem to lead in one direction, the rooms with television sets
droning inside, the nurses, the father enthroned in his last shrine,
mysterious and vague with his appliances on the table or in the
drawer, hidden, or in some nurse's care, ready to be switched on
and switched off. If my friend is a liar sometimes—I know he is,
he must be, for he so insists upon his truth—he is not a liar now.
Only at this time men do not lie and are immortal.

I want to say, "What did you do to him? Why? Why did you

jump out of that doorway and beat him? What did you use—a hammer? An iron bar? Why did you pick him, that particular old man?"

He draws back from me. His face is enough for me to love. My anxiety is not for him or for any nuances between us, but only to get everything over as quickly as possible—we will drive over to his apartment. We will drive over there at once. How tired I am of this transparency, and how I want to take on the innocence of passion and hide myself!

"What about *him?*" he says, for as he shakes aside the violence of passion some forlorn human memory touches him; he will become a liar again. He lifts one hand and the fingers part in a gesture of quaint, offered freedom. His eyebrows rise. "I mean, you're not going to . . . get upset, are you?" he says. "You're not going to get upset?"

The Heavy Sorrow of the Body

FOR GENE MCNAMARA

It was nearly noon and for hours they had been carrying boxes and bundles up to the apartment. There was a kind of chaos about them, a gaiety in their words and caresses, and only when the moving was finished and things lay all about them, on the floor and on the bed, did they sense the completeness of their action. Here they were. They were together.

With so much junk on the floor, the rooms looked smaller than they had. There were two rooms and a bathroom, at the back of a large Victorian house that had been partitioned off into apartments. A casual, half-pleasant disorder lay about the place, an air of the domestic and tolerant. The kitchen window looked out upon a wild, scrubby back yard in which two clothes poles had been set up, with a drooping clothesline between them. The clothesline was empty. Across the back way was a factory with soot-darkened windows, and behind that were other factories, great ugly buildings inside wire fences. Smoke of various hues poured out of the smokestacks and rose sluggishly into the air. . . . Nina and Conrad stood at the window, looking out. They were silent, now that the exertion of the moving was over, and they were settled, the two of them, in these rooms. Nina believed she could smell the poisoned air seeping in to them.

But Conrad said, "Don't be silly, you can't escape it. Why try to escape it? Everything is poisoned, everything is polluted . . . live with it, forget it."

They turned to each other out of habit. The habit turned to joy, it was automatic; they loved each other very much, and their love was bright and sharp, it took them by surprise. Nina was always surprised. When she was with Conrad she gave herself up to him entirely, and when she was apart from him she thought about him . . . about his meaning to her, about his body, for it was his body she loved and his body that possessed his soul. She loved his soul, she loved him passionately, as if under a kind of enchantment. Yet, in his embrace, entangled together and very warm, accustomed to the clumsiness that always came with love, Nina could sense the still, silent chaos of this apartment they had for some reason chosen, which was waiting to be straightened out and made normal. A normal apartment, normal people. And she sensed the larger, more silent chaos of the vacant lot outside the window and the factories that ringed the city, a heavy poison not to be escaped.

"Yes, live with it. Transcend it," Conrad said.

They got up and began to put things away. Conrad's books, ten boxes of books. The boxes were from a neighborhood grocery store and had once contained Sweetheart Soap and Kleenex tissue. Now Conrad's battered books were stacked in them, fallen over, ripped, watermarked, broken-backed. . . . Nina had a

sudden presentiment, in looking at this mess, of how he would
treat her. She sat back on the bed and lit a cigarette. Conrad
continued with the books, impatiently. He had blond hair that
fell in jagged streaks across his forehead, and his neck was strong
and rather muscular. Did he look thirty-five? But he was thirty-
five. In this context—the cheap apartment and the avalanche of
books, the torn cardboard boxes, the clothes still on hangers
thrown hastily across other things—he had a sharp, squinting,
youthful look: he looked maybe twenty-five. And Nina . . .
Nina was not his age, she was slightly younger. And she looked
younger. There was a lazy, ironic, calculating expression about
her, even her hands shared this expression; she was very thoughtful. Yet her thoughtfulness often broke into laughter.

"Don't laugh, how can you laugh?" Conrad said. "All this crap
represents my life. It's an accumulation of my life. It's myself, you
might say, it's *me*."

Nina talked nonsense to him while he worked. She liked to lie
back on beds and sofas, stretch her long lovely legs, and smoke
and talk. She smoked and talked all the time. Did he understand
how she loved him? She wanted to know. Did he understand
what it meant to her, to give up Peter in that manner, to make
Peter unhappy? Never, never had she wanted to make Peter unhappy. . . .

"The hell with Peter," Conrad said.

He wiped his hands on his thighs. He wore only trousers, no
shirt. No shoes or socks. She looked with amused interest at his
filthy feet. With Conrad in her life, everything became dirty.
She herself was a little dirty. She was no longer really a girl, she
was a woman, and yet she lived in dirt with a dirty careless man
and did not mind it.

Did he know how she loved him?

"You do have a certain weakness," he admitted.

He had a self-assured, strong face. Yet he himself was not

strong. His life was confused and energetic and without purpose.
Now he was studying history, and his intention was to be a *histo-rian*. He believed that historians had always lived in the past; he
had his own theories about history. In his lifetime, which seemed
to belong partly to other people, he had at one time wanted to be
a musician and he had wanted once to be something ordinary: a
businessman, a lawyer. He had wanted to lead people. A leader
of minor causes, dedicated, arrested, marked for execution by his
own men. . . . People told Nina about him, warning her, but
she wouldn't listen; she said, *So what?* She had fallen in love with
him at a party. She loved to talk, and it turned out that Conrad
loved to talk. So they had talked at each other for hours, sharp,
bright, hilarious, sarcastic. . . . Nina had sensed that they
would become lovers and her excitement made her mean, brought
her lazy deadly sarcasm to the surface; later, when they were
lovers, he would understand. It was a duet, a duel. They had been
loving each other already in this way.

When his books were stacked on the shelves, in no particular
order, Nina rose to help him with the other things. She picked
up several hangers with clothing on them. It shamed her a little,
to have Conrad see her dresses hanging like this, as if they were
disguises, costumes, colorful skins of herself. "Ah, look at this,
look at this," Conrad said in disgust. He held up an old suit of
his, royal blue, very rumpled. "My life is a wreck," he said. It was
true that his clothes were bad, they had no style, nothing, so that
one looked at Conrad himself and saw nothing else. His face had
hard, rather prominent bones at the cheeks and forehead. He
looked military and Teutonic, with blond eyebrows and blue,
ironic eyes. His body was a little muscular, or had been muscular
once. On his chest and stomach were curly blond hairs with a
glint of red to them, and over most of his body was a light, soft
fuzz or down. Nina had never loved a man the way she loved
him. Each man had raised her higher, buoyed her higher in love,

and at the very highest point Conrad had turned to her and said,
"You're Nina. I've heard all about you, Nina. I know all about
you."

He hadn't known all about her but he wanted to know. He
wanted to know everything. Walking along the street for that
first week, curious and eager and a little impatient, he had asked
her about her life. She was a beautiful girl and he hadn't known
beautiful girls, he'd always avoided them; what was it like to be
beautiful? And Nina shrugged. "You feel no hostility from other
women? It doesn't bother you?" Conrad asked. But Nina said no,
why should she care about other women? She didn't care about
other people at all. Being beautiful was all she had known for
years, it was just an accident of her skin and nothing more, she
accepted it. "But you take care of yourself, you fix things up, eh?
It isn't all nature, is it?" Conrad wanted to know. Nina said that
no beautiful woman lets her face go, it's just habit to keep it up.
Cold cream, astringent, certain medications. . . . Why not?
"The kind of men who make love to faces would pay you a lot,"
Conrad said. "You're worth money. But me, I'm different, it's the
soul I make love to. . . . Is your soul shaped like your face, sweetheart, would I recognize you?" And she felt him already moving
upon her body, claiming her. It was joyous to walk with him. For
a week she held him off, she talked about nonsense in her
amused, ironic, lazy voice, making him stare at her, making him
fall in love. She felt his desire for her. There was a strange, nervous happiness between them on these walks before they were
lovers, with the thought of her dear friend Peter somewhere behind them, betrayed, and who knows what friends of Conrad's?
—for that heavy, hearty face and that muscular body must have
had a cosmic experience behind them.

Nina hadn't been beautiful all her life; the miracle began
when she was about twenty. She had a healthy, vexing beauty.
Her hair was brown and she wore it pulled back in a large, loose
knot; her eyes were steady and clear, always a little ironic, and

her lips were rather small, rather sweet. Out of those lips anything at all might come—but still they looked sweet. She had a
long-legged stride on the street and she wore striking clothes,
often slacks, so that people stared at her without really seeing her
as a person. They stared at the effortlessness of her, at her look of
freedom. Conrad himself like to stare at her, assessing her. He
had the cool, transfiguring look of a sculptor, eying material. She
complained that he was always looking at her and thinking about
her as an object, and she wanted nothing more than their union
—a continual closeness, a magical intimacy. They argued in an
off-again, on-again manner; their arguing was a series of hard caresses. "But beneath it we understand each other," Conrad liked
to say. They drank beer in one of the neighborhood bars, or
lounged around with friends in someone's apartment, drinking,
or they strolled hand in hand through the dreary city park. "I
don't want a woman who's always pushing at me, putting her ear
against my chest to hear what's going on. I want someone like you,
you're like a man yourself, though of course you're very womanly
—but still you have that quality of being yourself—your own
person—that these other bitches don't have."

But she was immune to the flattery of words, it meant nothing
to her. When she was in love, she needed no words. She didn't
need assessments, mythologizing. She liked to lie in bed with
Conrad until late in the morning, the two of them lethargic with
love and affection, two good friends. She wanted to be his best
friend, not just his lover. She demanded it. Was she his best
friend? "I don't know you that well," Conrad said with his usual
frankness. On certain days she got up early to report for her job
—she was a substitute teacher in the city's public school system. It
wasn't much of a job and she was a woman designed for the
domesticity of love and men, but still, returning from one of
those exhausting days, she would talk on and on to Conrad in a
voice that sometimes rose with lyricism and then sank with despair, mock despair, telling him about that day's classroom and its

peeling walls, its dirty windows, its heat or its cold, its thirty-five
or forty Negro children in such colors, like a flower bed: red
sweaters, blue shirts, pink dresses, polka-dot slacks . . . everything. Conrad would sit and listen, staring at her. Perhaps he was
trying to envision her life as a teacher, at a job, apart from him
and independent as a man. "No, start over," he would say. "Be
more precise. What did they ask you? What time did you get in?
What happened?" And she would lie back and smoke, and tell
him about the teacher in the next room, a battered old man-
woman, identity unknown, who cautioned her about catching
something . . . lice, maybe? An infectious disease? She told him
about the window that was boarded up permanently, or, in another school, about the pipes that went crazy and started a dance,
bucking and jumping six inches at a time, so that all the kids
laughed and she, Nina, gave up and laughed too, though she
knew well enough that the pipes might explode and send jets of
scalding water over them all. And what else . . . ? The crazy lessons. What a crazy place it was, what a crazy system, Nina
laughed. In one class the kids told her that she was number three
that week. It was a fifth-grade class held in one dingy corner of a
very old gymnasium, whose other corners were occupied by other
classes, and she was number three that week. "Christ, you mean
the third substitute they had in a week? The *third?*" Conrad said.
Teachers came and went, recruited out of anywhere, they wised
up or were frightened out, or, in sheer muscular reaction, fled
after a half day. Oh, Nina had to laugh at it, it was so sad and so
crazy, some of the kids swore they had been studying Mesopotamia the day before, other kids swore they'd been reading about
the American Indians, still others were scared and blank and malicious. Totally lost. A bobbing class of Negro kids, a long-legged
white teacher, a woman, bemused and ready to have them read
about anything from the big soiled "history" book the system
forced upon them, something like a catalogue of photographs advertising other parts of the world. The other parts all looked bet-

ter than this part. China's exports, China's rivers. Trade routes. Latitude and longitude. Wars, enemies. Allies. Great religions. If they mixed it all up with long division and the Iroquois and the Pledge of Allegiance and Mesopotamia she was sorry, she was really sorry, but what could she do? Let them read out loud from the big book. Let them take turns. Time would pass. The day would pass.

"I really think you feel guilty about this, Nina," Conrad would say seriously. "All your chatter isn't convincing. But look: it isn't your fault that it's all shit."

She agreed with him. She didn't want to feel guilty, she didn't believe in guilt. Anyway, she hadn't time for it. When she and Conrad had met, she was trying to break off a relationship with an earnest, dour, intelligent young man of Slavic descent—oblong headed, with glasses, unsparing in his criticism of all failures except his own, really a nice person. She couldn't stand him. At first she had drifted into loving him, in that mild maternal way women love men when they are really "between" men but need someone around, need to keep in practice, and Conrad was the end of that. Peter was going to be a success as a professor, give him time, he had just received his Ph. D. and was off to teach at a small Catholic college—he said he needed Nina, but Nina couldn't understand how anyone could need anyone, let alone her. "If you have marriage in mind ultimately," Conrad said, "maybe you should stick with him." He was being frank. Nina listened to him frankly. "You know how my life is," he said. "I can't even think of marriage, the first time was enough . . . . I'll be paying her off the rest of my life and I don't have anything to pay her, it's hell. So if you want marriage and a house and all that, it isn't too late to get Peter back." Oh, the hell with Peter, Nina said, the hell with respectability and security and dull, deadly niceness; what she wanted was Conrad with his dirty feet and his profanity, even if he was a bastard. She gave them a year together, one good year. Conrad showed surprise at this. "I can't imagine anything that temporary," he said. "I'm really monogamous, I have a monogamous soul. It's just that marriage repels me, the papers and the blood test, and it does nothing for love, and. . . . But a year, Nina? Only a year? Surely you give us more than a year together?"

They took an apartment together a few blocks from Nina's old place, in a Victorian horror given over to mysterious tenants—bachelors of various ages and sizes, working girls with bright blotched faces, a lady who wore gauzy white gloves every day. Peace, a desperate privacy. Even the odor of gas from downriver was peaceful. It took them all morning to move and all afternoon to put away their things, scolding and teasing each other. There was something very pleasant about working together. Nina felt quite gay; she picked up one of Conrad's books, *The Magic Mountain,* and asked him about it. Was it about magic really? Was it about a mountain? Conrad said, "It's a beautiful novel about the decadence of Western civilization. Lovely! Monstrous! What is man, tell me, what is man?—*man is water, mostly, and cellulose.* Are you made of water and cellulose, my dear Nina?"

This offended Nina. She tossed the book onto the floor and turned away from him. She was really offended, it was unlike her. "What's wrong? What is it now?" Conrad cried, trying to embrace her. They struggled. In his bare feet, Conrad danced around her, clowning, though he was thirty-five years old and would soon be thirty-six, indeed he would soon be forty-six, and still he was Conrad and still he lived in such rooms. "Dear Nina, beautiful Nina, I didn't mean anything insulting . . . if you're water and cellulose, such cellulose has never been seen before, it's enchanted, I could write a book about it!"

Slowly, out of habit, their bodies twined together. They embraced. They were friends, though perhaps not best friends, they were in love. When they made love Nina thought, *There, that's accomplished, if we die now we're that much to the good. . . .*

Danger was all about her. She was thirty now and lazily she knew that something ought to shape her life, some form should arise, she should get a permanent job and take up with permanent people, good citizens, stop this sluttishness, get her eyes examined for glasses. . . . *We're that much to the good,* she thought. If they remained together for a single year, it would overcome her brain to assess all the love that would pass between them, all the energy used up, prized. She liked to lie beside Conrad, the two of them in a pleasant, heavy stupor, and with her curious hand touch his face, his neck, his chest, all the parts of his body, examining him gently, as if trying to re-create him for the inner, blind Nina who saw nothing but felt everything. When their passion spent itself out, she still returned to him, as if looking for an answer to the mystery of their love: it was so intense, surely they were more than water and cellulose. How could water and cellulose perform such miracles? She touched the hard strong muscles of his thighs, wondering why he had muscles there, why, since he never did any work? The mystery of his being was not explained in his body, but it lay deep inside his body, in himself. It was not in his private keeping, not in his knowledge. She felt that, as a woman, there was no mystery in her, but everything was simple and opened simply as a flower; it was in Conrad the mystery lay, in his strength. She loved him. Her love for him ran round and round in a circle as she touched him, not quite caressing him but only touching him, examining him with her fingertips.

"Ah, Nina," he said, "you're not like those other bitches. . . ."

That evening someone knocked at their door. Their first visitor. Nina resented the intrusion but Conrad only said, annoyed, "Who's out there?" It was a girl, a friend of Nina's from her old apartment building. She was embarrassed and, to explain everything fast, held out an envelope to Nina. "It just came special delivery and the man knocked at my door. It must be important, so . . . so I came over, I'm sorry to barge in here like this."

Nina took the envelope, staring at it. Conrad said, "No, that's all right, how do you like what we've done . . . ? Tomorrow night we'll have everybody over. . . . Where's that letter from?" Nina had turned away and was reading the letter, a single sheet of white paper.

"I don't think it's from Peter, otherwise I wouldn't have brought it over," the girl said. "It's from out of town."

They stared at Nina's back as she read the letter and then read it again.

"It isn't bad news . . . ?" Conrad said.

The girl left. Conrad tried to put his arms around Nina, awkwardly. "What is it? Something from home?"

She handed him the letter angrily. It read:

Dear Nina,
    I am writing this letter for your father. He is very sick and would like you to come see him. I am sending this letter to the address he has here and I hope it reaches you, since your father is very badly sick and would like to see his daughter.

The signature was a stranger's signature, very clear and feminine. Conrad said, "What the hell, is it a nurse? You said your father lived alone, didn't you?"

Yes, he lived alone. Nina was very angry. She went to the door and opened it to look down the stairs, as if wanting to call her friend back, and then she went to the back window. . . . She was trembling. He lived alone, yes, he was a strange man and had never cared much for her, and she hadn't cared for him, and now . . . now he was dying and what the hell did he want with her?

"How do you know he's dying?" Conrad said.

But she wasn't going to go. She began to walk wildly about the apartment, pulling away from Conrad. No, she wasn't going to go. She raved angrily about that letter, the summons to her father and his death, which was a stranger's death and had nothing to do with her. She hated him, she refused to remember him. At the age of seventeen she had left home, glad to get out, and for two years she had lived with a bitch of an aunt and she'd made her own way, everything in her life was her own and she needed no one else. She did not remember her father. She hated him, his sickness and dying, and there was something particularly repulsive about the thought of an old man dying. He was a stranger to her, he was nothing. They were all strangers to her, and she could not even remember them.

II

She drove Conrad's car up north, a bruised, dented old Buick that looked like a small boat, with fins made for an element thicker than air. She resented the long drive, her body already querulous with being alone, apart from Conrad. Her body, by itself, was a little nervous and did strange things—she kept wanting to stop at a gas station and use the rest room, she was anxious and jumpy as a child, and yet these stops were not really necessary; her body was just playing tricks on her. The absence of Conrad was very real. It was oppressive, frustrating. She did not think about her father, waiting ahead.

Unlike her friends, Nina never bothered to talk about her parents. She had forgotten them, she'd gone beyond them. She was really free and not deluded like many of her friends, who believed themselves free but were really not. Her mother had died years ago, freeing Nina, and her father had receded with his queer life of handyman, town gossip, everyone's friend, an embarrassment. She recalled him as a fairly young man, with a head of thick brown hair, wearing overalls, telling jokes. Her father? He could have been anyone's father.

For the last six or seven years he had lived alone in a cabin on a lake. The lake was an adequate lake, not one of the more famous ones in the northern part of the state, but there was a fairly good tourist trade. The cabins around the lake were rented or owned by city people to whom her father was a handyman, a watchman, a protector. He lived all year round on the lake and watched over everyone's cabins for a fee. In the summer he fixed things. He had such a "mechanical touch"! So her father had turned out to be a handyman, Nina thought, and what did that mean? Nothing. It didn't embarrass her because it meant nothing. Driving up to Lake Fredonia, she saw with distaste the roadside archery outfits and miniature golf courses and drive-in movies and restaurants— all of this new since she'd lived with her parents in a small city nearby. She disliked the sleaziness, as if it somehow degraded her father's illness. And she resented this illness, drawing her so far north, away from Conrad and the warm easy intimacy of their life together. She began to see the cabins that lined Lake Fredonia, pressed close together. Cheap, standard, bringing an urban look to the country, marked off by narrow driveways and mailboxes out of Sears, Roebuck. Which one was her father's . . . ? She knew with an instinctive revulsion that his would be the ugliest, the worst of all, a wreck. It was early May now and no one was up here, but out of one cabin chimney smoke was rising thinly—her father lived there.

The name on the mailbox was Julius Weber: and Weber was also her name.

She drove up the bumpy, muddy driveway and stopped. Another car was parked nearby, a junker, probably her father's. The lake was very bright and drew her eye to it at once. Slashes of sunlight bobbed on its surface, it was uncanny in its beauty, and she stared toward it until her eyes began to narrow, as if such beauty was another kind of degrading, an insult to her father's suffering. The shore was pebbly and not very clean. The land sloping down to the lake was untended, just scrubland, and the cabin was not too bad—bad enough, but not exactly a horror— made of nondescript wood and propped up on blocks. Next door was a sleazy cabin with yellow siding and a stretch of beach that was pebbly and strewn with unidentifiable junk. And, on the other side of her father's property, was a newer, larger cabin painted bright pink. Pink, in this setting? The color was coy and mewing; Nina turned angrily away from it. Pink! Lake Fredonia! As a child she'd come out here with other kids and swum off the rough beach, ignoring the No Trespassing signs. She and her friends were always being chased away down the beach. Get home, get out of here, didn't they know this was private property . . . ? And now her father had sold or maybe lost the old house in town and had moved out here, a handyman, a keeper, and he had his own forlorn stretch of beach that kids from the town probably invaded. Nina was home.

A woman was coming out to meet her. Yes, this was a nurse. Nina stared at her, at the woman's set, tidy face. She got out of the car and introduced herself. They shook hands. In spite of herself, Nina felt her eyes searching this woman's face, leaping to her eyes. She had to know, suddenly she was desperate to know the truth. "Well, your father is very sick. The operation is set for day after tomorrow," the woman said. "And I thought . . . that is, he wanted . . . he wanted to see you before . . ." Nina stood flat-footed in the mud. She listened to the woman's drawling, dutiful voice and tried to attach herself to it. Was this really happening? What did it mean? An old man was going to be operated on, and Nina was his daughter? For the first time in years she felt a dull stirring of fear. She was suddenly vulnerable. The nurse apologized for not being well herself. A cold. She indicated her reddened nostrils, pink rabbit's nostrils. The nurse's manner was becoming more deferential as Nina stood without speaking, with the power of silence. Nina's beauty awed her. That was something Nina took for granted, and while people stared at her uneasily she was free to think, figure a way out, a solution . . . she'd gotten through bad times that way in the past, her first few teaching assignments in miserable classrooms, her first few good-byes to men. She could count on her beauty to impress people as brains.

They went inside. Nina was not prepared for the odor of the cabin. Was it her father, that odor? Or the odor of his sickness? He was lying propped up in bed, with a heavy quilt over him— the quilt looked maternal, warm, domestic, crisscrossed with black and red stitching, very nice. Nina was glad for that quilt. Then father and daughter looked at each other. Nina, ashamed of herself, came to him and took his hand. What could she say to him? Desperate, her mind raced. But her father said, "Nina. Thank you for coming. Thank you," and his feebleness was dignified; still her mind raced.

She chose her words as if from a distance, listening to them: "Hello, Daddy. I got your letter. . . . How do you feel? I drove right up. . . ."

Their talk was peculiar and stilted. They might have been talking across a dangerous distance, a chasm. Her father's mouth worked slowly and as he spoke she did not look at him, not yet. She hadn't yet looked at him closely. Her mind was in a daze, captivated by the quilt and its look of suffocating warmth.

"I was worried and I drove right up. . . ."

The nurse said something to Nina about a coat. She remembered that her coat was still on, buttoned up, and she took it off and lay it over a chair. At home now. Dressed in a black sweater and plaid slacks a little tight, with a hard knowing deftness about her that did not settle into the eyes of her father and the tired nurse. Nina at home. With her father, transformed into an old man in bed . . . an odor of flesh and mustiness about him . . . and he insisted upon talking slowly and painfully up into her frightened face.

"Had a long drive up, eh?"

"No, it was all right."

"Got your own car now?"

"I borrowed a friend's."

"Sort of lost touch. . . . You seen this place before though?"

"I don't think so."

"Yes, sure."

"Maybe I did. . . ."

"This was Meyer's place. Meyer. He went to Florida. I bought it from him. Been here ever since, taking care of things . . . real nice here, private all winter. Nobody around. In the summer there's lots of work. All that wood outside is firewood. . . ."

She still hadn't looked at him. His talking mouth took up all her attention. Was he in pain? What was wrong? The illness that had brought her hundreds of miles to him was a secret, something not to be mentioned. Yet it was real. Her father talked about Nina's relatives, dead and distant, about people whose names she half-remembered, someone's hardware store, someone's farm, and on and on, and she answered him with short rushes of her life, maybe lies and maybe not, she hardly knew, and none of this was as real as the sickness in his body and yet they could not acknowledge it.

"In the winter there's not a sound. Nowhere. Not a sound," he said.

Later, when her father slept, she walked outside with the nurse, Mrs. Stocker, and the banal secret was told. "It's a tumor he's got, you know that, it's one of them down here," the nurse said with a clumsy embarrassed gesture, halting the gesture at once so that Nina didn't really have to look. But she knew, she supposed she knew. They walked on the planks that led out along the driveway, protecting their shoes from mud. They were very much together, Nina and Mrs. Stocker, mulling over the old man's sickness and his dying, trying to think *what to do next* in the way that women think, automatically. Nina wasn't a woman with much memory, no interest in memory, and yet she began to wonder automatically about death, arrangements, a funeral, a burial plot. . . . and would the grief be much? Already she feared the grief. It was crazy, all this happening, her standing up here in a cold May drizzle with a registered nurse, Mrs. Stocker. A stranger. They had stopped talking. Mrs. Stocker was waiting for her husband to pick her up. Having nothing else to do, Nina waited with her.

The cabin was cozy and dirty. She didn't mind dirt. She was even relieved to see it because it meant time, years, days gotten past—grime on the walls, on the refrigerator door, grease spots on the ceiling, food stains, smoke stains. An accumulation of a life's dirt. While her father slept, she looked around. There was a storeroom off the main room, into which a beaten-up sofa had been shoved. She would sleep there. Everywhere there were newspapers and magazines on the floor; in one corner were rusty hunting traps with chains tangled around them. Everything abandoned, forgotten. She came back to her father to watch him sleep. He had become a small man. His hair was no longer thick and brown but very thin, ratty, and his strangely elongated skull shone through it. But his skull wasn't really elongated. It was an ordinary skull, an ordinary head. Nina sat and watched him sleep, her mind jammed and yet strangely at peace. He would sleep. And they would operate on him. And then, whatever happened, she would leave.

Mrs. Stocker came back early, before seven. Nina made coffee. Her father's best time was in the morning, obviously. He tried to sit up and he made unnecessary, slightly bullying demands— Mrs. Stocker made a clicking sound with her tongue and teeth, but Nina said, *Yes, why not?*—hunting around in the back room for a map of the lake region he wanted her to see. It took her half an hour to find a map, but it wasn't the right map. Her father wanted to talk about the lake. "Real estate is high as hell here," he said. "You got any extra cash, invest it here. Right here. This place I bought, it was seven years ago, you know what it cost?"

Nina had no idea.

"Two thousand. Now its worth three, four thousand. I bet you."

He was a small tidy vessel, contracting in upon itself with pain at certain unguarded moments. Easing back, trying to relax, Nina began to see him. His face was lined and slightly pitted. His eyes were dull, as if covered with a film of intense concentration; he had to talk. Nina realized that everyone had to talk.

The ambulance was coming for him that afternoon. Knowing this, they circled the topic, alluding to it, united by their helplessness and pressed onward toward more talk. When her father closed his eyes, exhausted, Nina took up the burden of their conversation and began to tell him about her life. She was a substitute teacher. It was hard work, but very exciting . . . once there was a colored boy of twelve who had drawn a picture of her . . . a strange, filmy, but rather beautiful picture, drawn in crayon by a retarded Negro boy . . . and she had been very pleased. . . . "Do you live near the colored?" Mrs. Stocker asked politely. "No. Yes," Nina said. Then Nina's father had to go to the bathroom and he tried to lift himself out of bed, using the strength of his arms and shoulders. Mrs. Stocker hurried over. "No, no," she said loudly, as if speaking to a deaf baby, "don't you strain yourself, Mr. Weber." Nina stared at the porcelain bedpan Mrs. Stocker took out of somewhere. It was strange that she was not repulsed by it. But she remained at the bedside, waiting, carried along by the eerie relentlessness of the moment, ready to begin again the slow offering of talk that was her only gift. . . .

She recalled having gone with this man, her father, somewhere in a truck. In those days they lived in town. The truck had been a pickup truck and she had gone along with him to the lumberyard—she must have been about eight—and her father was at that time a solid, muscular man with a permanent tan and permanent stains of nicotine and grease on his fingers. He liked to joke, he had a loud, hearty voice. At the lumberyard he had begun talking with someone, and time passed while Nina wandered around alone, peering into the hot, sunlight-striped depths of the buildings, smelling the sharp odor of lumber. Time passed. She went to sit in the truck, dangling her legs out the door. She wanted to go home, she had to go to the bathroom, she felt a sudden pang of fear that her father had forgotten her. He was in the building, talking. Talking. She sat in the truck, right out in the sun, feeling the heat swell about her, miserable, waiting, too proud to run to the door and say, *Daddy I have to go home.* . . .

Perspiration had broken out on her father's face. He must have been suffering, but the pain was held inside him, a secret. She felt a reluctant admiration for him. Then, when he lay back, relaxed, his face drained white with pain or terror, she lit a cigarette and began to talk quietly again. She slipped back beyond the stories of her life in the city, her teaching, her years at college, and began to root around in the memories of her childhood: he had shared those memories with her, as an adult. And yet he did not seem to remember. He listened, his face serious and frail, and he nodded, but clearly their pasts did not quite coincide. She might have been making up stories for him. What had happened to Rose Smith, she asked, what had happened to the Latham boys, the twins . . . ? It seemed very important to her now. But her father could not recall those people.

By the time he was taken to the hospital, Nina was herself exhausted. He was brought up to his room in a wheelchair. Another man, another old man, was in this room and his bed was near the window. Nina stared at him bitterly. She did not want him in this room with her father. Stubborn and frightened, knowing she was wrong, she tried to find the doctor. Where was he? What kind of a place was this? She talked to the nurses, complaining. She wore lemon-colored slacks and a bright silk blouse, and her hair was pulled back loosely from her face. The energy of her body and the authority of her face seemed to be failing her here. She understood that she was not properly dressed.

"What are you going to do to him next? What's the next thing?" she demanded.

"He'll be given an injection at four."

"And what else? Anything else?"

"I'm going to wash him a little. . . ."

"No, I'll do that. I'll do that myself." Nina's teeth were nearly chattering, she was so nervous. She was frightened. In the hospital room, with its deafening white walls and its basiny white odor, her father looked forgotten already. "I want to do that myself," she insisted.

They set up a screen around the bed, of white gauze through which one might look. But no one would look. Nina's father was humble in this new setting. From time to time he stared at the length of his body beneath the thin covers, his eyes protruding slightly, a habit of the old that means . . . that perhaps means *I am emphasizing this moment, for no reason.* Nina took the sponge from the nurse and began to wash her father. Her hands were trembling, but her face was set, determined. She had an angry look. Her father's body was uncovered and it was a man's body, but there was something half real about it, as if it were the body of an unformed man, a child. The washing took some time. Nina drew the large white sponge over her father's body slowly, as if she were moving it across him, blind, seeing with her fingertips. She had the idea that his skin was painful to him. Even air would hurt it. But she was proud to see that her father wasn't dirty, as she had feared—Mrs. Stocker had probably seen to that. He was clean. There was a soiled, shabby look about him, brought in from that untidy bachelor's cabin, but really he was clean in the blank, empty way of the body that is a vessel at rest, emptying. Nina bent over him in silence. She washed him and patted him dry with a large white towel of that rough, gritty material of institutional towels. Her yellow slacks were damp with water stains.

Finally the nurse said, "That's good. That's a good job."

As if under a kind of enchantment, Nina did not want to stop. She stared down at her father. His eyes were closed upon his thin, pale, flabby flesh, pale as wax . . . the look of flesh with its fat eaten away, dissolved. The pouches and pockets of its swellings remained behind, empty. "I . . . I want . . ." Nina began.

"That's a good enough job," the nurse said.

Nina waited downstairs. She had nowhere to go. She sat in the small empty lobby in her bright outfit, staring into space. Behind the counter, a lady watched her with disapproval. Nina tried to think, she had to think of what came next . . . and she kept remembering instead her father's body, remembering the long, patient washing of it, the strong odor of the soap, the odor of the bedsheets, the odor of her father. She must have sat there for two hours, in a daze. Then, abruptly, she went outside into a dreary May afternoon and walked down the street to a restaurant, where she ordered coffee. The restaurant was new, it had a shiny black front. But when she looked around, slowly, waiting to be served, she remembered the place: it wasn't new, it was an old restaurant with a new front. That was all. Nearby, a man was looking at her. It was the brightness of her outfit, the jaunty colors, her face. . . . She was disgusted with herself suddenly. She hated herself.

She got Conrad's car from the hospital parking lot and drove slowly out to Lake Fredonia. There was no telephone at the cabin. Should she call the hospital? When should she call? . . . She knew nothing about the procedures of ordinary life. She had been outside life and had had no interest in it, and now she was like a child, helpless. In the cabin, she made her father's bed and sat at one of the kitchen chairs, thinking. The cabin was small, oppressive. It pushed upon her. Fake wood paneling gave it a sly look, the curtains at the windows were of red and white plastic, tacked to the window frames. Piles of newspapers and magazines. A spider ran out of one and disappeared in a hole somewhere. . . . Nina thought she might read a magazine or two, for something to do, but it was too much trouble for her to bend down and pick one up.

. . . She was thinking of Conrad, remembering Conrad. On one of their walks, that first week, striding along with a volley of jokes between them . . . and suddenly Conrad had taken hold of her wrist and said, "Now, that's enough," and his face had gone hard, he was very serious. Nina tried to pull away. But he did not release her and his grip began to hurt. "Enough, enough! Enough crap!" he said. And, under the pressure of his fingers and his dead-end voice, Nina gave in as she always gave in to men when they arrived at this point—if they arrived at it—thinking that she did indeed belong to him now, it was inevitable that they should be lovers, it was dishonest to resist. She gave up pretending. Her irony vanished, her darting eyes became docile, she gave herself to Conrad and fell in love with him. . . .

. . . And she was thinking of her father, or perhaps of his body and not of him, for she had never really known him. She remembered him as a presence at the supper table, years ago. Her mother was another body, another presence. He wobbled the table, sometimes, crossing his legs. Smoked during supper. He'd had long, careless legs, he'd worn overalls most of the time. From walking out in the fields or fooling around with lumber he had burrs and dust and hayseed on his clothes, especially his trouser legs. How much they must have talked together, her mother and father! All the words they had used up, the avalanche of meanings they had summoned!—and now it was silent, the house was sold to someone else and Nina hadn't even thought of driving past it, all that was forgotten. She wondered how this had happened. She herself was thirty. Until now she had not thought about the heavy gravitation of her body that was pulling at her in such silence. She had never thought about it. From time to time she had talked with her friends about "life." They all had plans. *I'll give up being a slut and get serious,* Nina said, using a word that

was a parody of what respectable people might think about them.
They used the language of respectable people from time to time,
to test it, stretching their mouths upon it, showing distaste and
hilarity. But she was too lazy to give up being a slut. She was
herself, Nina, she couldn't be serious, she had no interest in the
security of marriage and a home in a suburban development, one
or two children, shopping at supermarkets, being good, voting,
wearing stockings. . . .

She did not go to bed, but pulled the quilt up around her and
remained sitting. She did not move. From the shock of seeing her
father's exposed body, her own body felt vague and dazzled. She
had no appetite, she could not remember what eating was. It was
not revolting to her but was instead meaningless. Sitting there,
with a single light on, she had time to look around the cabin at its
shadows, memorizing them. Her thighs stretched the fake-silk
material of her slacks tight. Sitting, she seemed heavier than she
was. She felt heavy. Her hands lay heavy and motionless on the
quilt. The nails were colorless and blunt. There were several
large ghostly half-moons on her nails; they looked like something
peeking out from under her skin, peeking out at her. She stared
down at them and could not move.

The next day she returned to the hospital. The operation was
over. She walked upstairs in a daze, very weak. Walking beside
her, the young doctor talked—he was about her own age yet
seemed younger—he was in such control that she felt her head
begin to ache in envy of him. She was desperate with envy. Her
father was very sick, he said. It had spread, the operation was
stopped after half an hour, it was hopeless, she had to understand. . . . Yes, yes, Nina said angrily, she had understood all
along. She wanted to see her father.

It seemed that he had changed from the day before, that
quickly. So a person can change that quickly. There was a soft,
bloated look about his wasted flesh. His eyes were rimmed with

red, as if he had been sleeping for years. He was doped up. He tried to ask her something but the words were crazy, so Nina said loudly, "They don't know yet. Tomorrow. Tomorrow they'll know." She stared at him. He seemed to be dozing. He was really a small man, what was left of him was small, old. Not very substantial. Was this, then, her father? She looked over at the other man, whose bed was in a more favorable position by the window. Another old man. A body beneath the thin white blanket. He too might be a father, he might be her father . . . he too lay asleep or pretending sleep. In the end, one lies asleep or pretending sleep. The important thing is silence.

III

After her father died she worked around the cabin, cleaning it up. She burned the piles of newspapers and magazines slowly. It took some time because she had to open them so that they could burn. They were damp, musty, and the smoke that rose from them seemed unclean. She burned other things too—hip boots, oily rags, pieces of junk. Some of it would not burn, but lay charred and smoking in the rubble. Nina took her time. It was now early June.

She began to go for long walks out along the beach. She was at peace, walking slowly. The early June air was cold, so far north, so she found an old pair of trousers back in the cabin and put them on. They were loose, a little soiled, very comfortable. She felt at peace. Out on the beach at dawn, with the mist rising frigidly from the water, she stood with her hands in her pockets and stared out at nothing.

She wrote Conrad: *My father should be getting better soon. I'll be back soon but he needs me now.*

When Conrad's letters came, she did not bother to read them.

She burned them in the rubble heap. She threw them in with other things, not wanting to make a ritual of burning them, not wanting to emphasize anything.

The beach was deserted, and the cabins were deserted. Out on the highway cars passed often, so she did not go out there. She was running out of money but she did not think about it. She ate little, she had forgotten about eating. She sat for hours in her soiled, baggy clothes, men's trousers and men's shirts, thinking. She felt strangely quiet, fulfilled, as if under a final spell. Inside these clothes, protected by them, she remembered many things clearly. She remembered her father, and Conrad, and other men . . . they had been presences, certain substances. They had cast shadows. They had passed. Her own body went about its functions, not to be stopped. She paid attention to it, curious, feeling no shame but only curiosity. She was a woman and she had a woman's body, she was a woman because she had a woman's body, and the processes that belong to such a body. The processes could not be stopped. But she was at a distance from them, observing them as a man might observe them, without comment or shame.

One day, out back of the cabin, she saw some women down on the beach. They belonged to the ugly pink cabin. They had driven up from the city and were wearing dresses, city clothes; they were talking in light, animated voices. Nina stared at them. She felt that they were ugly in their bare legs, storks' legs, with their high, shrill voices. . . . Men had a kind of anonymity she desired; they were negations, most of them. Their clothing negated them. They belonged in a vast sea of faces and bodies and were not anxious to emphasize themselves, to be bodies *with names*. Women, she noticed, were always shrieking their names.

So she was no longer a woman: she withdrew.

She stopped going out to the mailbox because there was nothing to interest her. For hours she sat in the cabin, thinking, wondering how everything had let her down, why it had happened

like this, why no one had told her. Her delusion was finished.
She wanted to draw into herself the terrible experiences of her
life—the violence of her love for men, the violence of her fear of
them—and, in herself, bring them to nothing. She would force
them to nothing.

Conrad came up finally, by bus. He stormed around, arguing.
He'd been drinking on the bus and he had a pint of liquor with
him. "What the hell is this? What's going on?" he shouted. His
face was flushed, he was amazed, incredulous. "Why did you lie
to me, Nina? So he's dead, he's buried, it's all over with?" He was
not the kind of man she wanted to be. He bumped into things, he
was loud, impatient, he emphasized things, he tried to argue with
her. Nina, no longer lazy in the old way, but still, alert, and silent
in a new way, stared at him from her distance. She wore men's
clothing, but not the kind of clothing Conrad wore. They weren't
the same kind of man. She explained to him that she was not
coming back. He told her she was crazy; what the hell? She told
him she would stay here, she'd make a living . . . maybe she
could rent out the cabin and make money that way. . . . No,
she wasn't going back. She was finished with that.

Conrad stayed for two days, going out to get more liquor and
coming back to the cabin as if it were his. But it was not his. He
understood that her power was stronger than his, or his body understood, for he did not try to make love to her, he used only
words in his bitter argument with her. And finally he said, on
his way out, "Stay here! good-by! So if you're crazy, I at least got
back my car!"

Matter and Energy

1956

I am coming home from school; I see myself with
books, an old, wrinkled, soft paper bag that must have
. . . my gym clothes in it, my soiled gym clothes
. . . and a towel. . . . I am carrying the books and
the bag and my purse up against my chest, so that my
shoulders are a little hunched. Sharon is with me, she
and I are talking. She laughs at something I am saying.
I clown around. I imitate a teacher at school, Miss
Strong, who is very thin and cries sometimes. . . .
But the Fear is beginning: there it is. At the end of

this block, and when we turn onto the next block . . . at the end of that block it will be waiting for me. It has a shimmering shape, no shape to it.

I am sick inside.

I am twelve years old on this afternoon. Sharon chatters with me. In front of our old house we are standing, two girls with books and things hugged up against our chests. We make faces. We roll our eyes. Behind me, inside the house, behind the pulled shades, the Fear is waiting.

"See you tomorrow," Sharon says.

She leaves me to it.

Inside the house, silence. The living room is too empty. Nothing is out of place, nothing knocked over or torn up. . . . I stand in the doorway thinking, *What if somebody has broken in and has killed her, and now he's waiting for me with a knife?*

Nothing.

The living room empty. Kitchen empty. "Ma . . . ?"

There are two of us now, since my father left. I call out, "Ma? Ma?" Yesterday she was in bed at this time. I go back to her room, "their" room . . . the bed isn't made. A smell of cigarettes, closed-in air. "Ma? Where are you?" The shower I took after gym class was too hot, then it was too cold. My body is filmed over with a fuzz of perspiration grown cold, terrified. I put my books down on the kitchen table. There is weeping in the air, but silent. Out in the back yard, nothing. The clothesline is empty.

The basement?

Down here the silence is heavier. The weeping heavier, but still silent. Dark air. "Ma, are you down here?" I am angry. There she is, squatting behind the furnace. No, she is sitting on something "What are you doing? Why are you hiding?" I ask her. I can smell her sweat. She says nothing.

I can feel the weight in her, her body. She is panting. She hugs herself. She is making a funny noise— her teeth are chattering. "Why are you down here? Why are you down here hiding?" I scream.

1969

It is my job to outline precisely the lives of others. Here is Elizabeth A. Price. Coordinator of Urban Humanities League. Born Philadelphia, 1921 Wellesley B.A., Michigan M.A. and Ph.D., Psychology. Married to Norman Price, lawyer. Active for fifteen years in Humanities League. Civil rights marches. Committees . . . city, state, federal. . . . Cover story, *Look*, 1967. . . . A big blossomy woman with rouged cheeks, very energetic. She sits waiting to be interviewed on our show. You can almost see the energy in her, in her plump upper arms and the tension of her throat! The star of the show is Vince Ellman, famous here in Detroit. He smokes quickly, helplessly, with his rogue's smile. A boy. A boyish boy of forty-five. We have ten seconds to go. Eight seconds. Vince is fooling around. Everyone in the studio laughs. Mrs. Price laughs. She is wearing a nondescript suit and her laughter booms out, ruddy and delighted.

We are on the air.

"This morning we have with us Mrs. Elizabeth Price, known to all of you for . . ." Vince begins. His voice is abrupt and smooth, a little sly. He is a handsome man and he wears his hair long, in the style of the day, with sideburns. Boyish and a little sinister, he smiles into one camera and then another, he reaches over to pat Mrs. Price's hand. . . .

Watching the monitor, I go blank: I think of myself watching the monitor. I am behind the cameras, out of sight. I am sitting in a chair that is in a row of chairs, clipboard on my lap, my mind blank. . . .

Vince chats seriously with Mrs. Price. The terror of Detroit!—the tragedy of Detroit!—all put into words here this morning on the Vince Ellman show, so that people watching it can forget what is behind the words. If it can be talked about like this, a handsome man and a motherly woman, chatting, smiling seriously, if it can be televised and talked about, it cannot be real and nothing will happen. "It's certainly a pleasure to meet someone with a positive outlook," Vince says, glancing significantly at the television camera. I can feel his audience nodding, grateful and pleased. Vince smiles. To smile like that you must slit the corners of your mouth carefully, with a razor blade. When the bleeding stops, you will be able to smile like Vince.

1956

I am downtown alone, in a movie house. I have run away for a day. My head aches because I haven't eaten. I have run away, I have slowed down, I am sitting through a double feature, picking at my nails. There is a sudden impulse in me to lean forward and knock my head against the seat in front of me, I don't know why. . . . At home my mother sits sometimes and hits her head against the wall, gently. I think she is trying to remember something. She sits clumsily facing the wall, as close as she can get, and then leans forward and bumps her head. Between the two of us there is a certain space, a certain kind of air. We are mother and daughter. When she knocks her head against the wall, something jumps in me, like a memory of my own, I don't know what it could be . . . there is a force inside me that wants to be let out, to get out of me, but I don't know what it is.

This movie is about soldiers. Technicolor. A strange force makes the men run around—they are shooting guns, they are jumping across ditches, they are writhing on the ground, dying, coming to life again, shouting, they are not like my mother and me but I don't understand the difference between us—why are some of us bodies, sitting in the dark, and some of us running around, our arms and legs so energetic? But now something has happened: the sound track goes dead. The actors continue to move their mouths. Silly. A man in the audience giggles. I hate this silence. There is too much of it in the movie house. I am afraid the Fear will shape itself out of this silence.

1969

Vince leaning forward in the lovely fading light. Snow in heaps about us, cars passing slowly. . . . The sky is overcast, the sky is a few inches over our heads. Vince says, "What are you always thinking about? Why are you so mysterious?" He teases me, he is a little annoyed by me. Doesn't he know there is a heaviness in me, a center of gravity deeper than his own? He takes my hand between his hands and rubs it, briskly, though we are out in public, on the sidewalk in front of Topinka's. "My little girl has cold hands!" he says, frankly and sweetly. He is like this on the show, often. It is his truest self. I fell in love with him, I think I fell in love with him, seeing him on the monitor that first day on the job. When I met him I saw a man of only moderate size, perky and talkative, with a strangely smooth, innocent, even bald face . . . when I saw him on the monitor my heart contracted, a face stark and handsome and in control, words coming from it with such magic. . . . "You are on an island and I'm coming to rescue you!" he says, joking and not joking.

1957

Three months of health! Aunt Thelma comes over all the time. Father tried to come over—she wouldn't see him. (He is drinking a lot, they say, he misses work all the time.) But still she is healthy, she is changed, she goes to the beauty parlor and has her hair done like all the other women at our church, a permanent wave; ugly. She smiles beneath the ugly hair. She makes breakfast and dinner for us, she makes real dinners, she goes out shopping by herself, and for three months she is healthy. . . . Then, one day, the shakes are upon her . . . I can feel the floor of our battered old house vibrate . . I scream at her, "You're doing it on purpose! You hate me! You're doing it on purpose!" The spell begins. She lies in bed, dressed. Her fingernails are dirty. She is staring, her face is pasty and bulbous, something is straining to get out. She reminds me of a tree, a dumpy tree, lying capsized, chopped down. Her fingers could turn to

twigs, they are so silent. She mutters to herself: "If
that was all I had to do . . . bitches strutting down
the street . . . I don't have to slave for them, I can
tell them to go to hell. . . . I won't put up with his
stinking. He comes over here, that bastard sets a foot
in the door, I'll call the police and they can have him.
. . . I don't have to put up with anything. . . ."

1969

    The television studio has no shadowy corners, no
smudges. Everything glares with light. I wake up at
five every morning, I can't sleep. I think. I go to work.
I carry my papers up to the studio in a big leather
purse. There is light everywhere up here, light in the
corners, clarity. I make precise outlines of the lives of
real people: Nicholas Bruno, Guitarist. Born Brook-
lyn, 1934. Recordings on Capitol label. His latest release is . . . Feature role in the new Paramount movie
. . . Vince takes the papers from me, reads them
greedily in a few seconds. I watch his eyes dart along
the lines. In those few seconds he takes over everything
I have researched, he knows everything, he sits down
to face his guest of the morning. Today a lively show?
Controversy? Vince has a pleased, sinister smile, he
will lead his guest into dangerous territory if he can.
. . . The other day he got a Unitarian minister to
state his disbelief in God . . . at least the minister
seemed to be saying that . . . a hundred telephone
calls followed, angry women, ready to fight! Vince
lights one cigarette after another. I watch him on the
monitor, lighting a cigarette. It is thought that television is unreal, that the people whose faces appear on it

are actors, not real people, saying words that are rehearsed and not real. In houses people lean forward,
trying to peer into the world of Vince Ellman, curious
about the real Vince Ellman . . . but I am here a
few yards from him and I prefer the image on the
television screen: more vivid, more handsome, without
distractions, winking intimately to the housewives and
to me, only to me. . . . After lunch, Vince takes me
to lunch. He kisses my hand. He has a wife and four
children, he looks younger than his wife, I love him
and my heart pounds stupidly in his presence, I want
to shake myself free of the fear that weighs my body
down. But I can't. He says, "Where are you going
now?" "To see my mother. It's Wednesday," I tell him.
"You want me to drop you off?" he says. I tell him no,
the hospital is too far away. No.

1958

Is that blood on the floor? Blood splotches on the
wall, the bathroom door . . . ? She must be in the
bathroom. I am standing in the hall. Silence. Waiting.
Inertia. I feel her silence on the other side of the door,
her body, like my body, inert, waiting. The silence
grows heavier. Last night she came in late, out drinking, she slipped in the kitchen and said I'd spilled
water on the floor, she scraped her knuckles somehow,
she screamed at me. "You want me to die! You're always wanting me to die! Don't you know I can hear
what you're thinking?" She threw the flour canister at
me, it didn't hurt. It hit me in the chest and fell to the
floor and broke, flour exploded everywhere, all over.
. . . Now she is in the bathroom. I wait. In a few min-

utes I will open the door: there, in the tub. Her body.
Heavy, collapsed, the breasts bluish-white and collapsed, her body a strange luminous color, all its energy gone and yet still alive, still alive. . . . Smears,
streaks of blood. The knife on the floor. Oh, the ugliness of blood, its smell! The ugliness of a face that
has no consciousness! I begin to scream. I scream at
her to wake up. I am still screaming.

1969

Split-second timing, a magician's timing: my love!
He clowns, he rolls his eyes, the camera turns upon
him and he is "normal," he begins to speak. I lean forward, entranced by his words. He is not speaking of
the silence of a house or of the sky at night . . . he
is not speaking of the terror of empty spaces, parking
lots, deserts, city libraries at closing time . . . the
look of a knife in a kitchen drawer . . . flour that
won't come out of a plaid skirt. . . . No, he is speaking of a furniture sale, a March sale . . . half-priced
sofas, love seats, chairs, lamps, dinettes. . . . He
knows exactly what he is saying, the words say themselves and are finished, nothing to worry about. I
love this man but I am afraid of him. Inside myself I
am sweating with fear, but outside myself I am a
pretty young woman, always on time. A high school
teacher told me, a spinster who gave advice to girls,
Your talent can be to always be dependable. That is
my talent.

1958

The ambulance arrives. She is carried out on a stretcher, not dead. So much blood! The bathroom door is closed. I mold my face out of my hands, still seeing her. Why did she do it? Why not my aunt, why not the woman next door? Why not my friend Sharon's mother? I am sick with hating, hating, hating. My Aunt Thelma moves in now and I hate her, I want to go down behind the furnace and lie on the dirty floor, press myself against the floor, try to get through it. My mother used to lie on the floor, trying to get through. . . . She has a face someone has clawed at, her hair is wild, streaked with blood; oh, her hands are the roots of trees torn out of the earth, and she longs to get back into that dark, dark air and that silence. Though she is gone now, to the hospital, I can still see her. My aunt opens a can of beef noodle soup for me.

1969

Slumped over, a woman in a baggy blue dress. A regulation dress. My mother has a scattered, shrill, queenly face—her cheeks are flushed, without rouge; her eyes are sharp, very sharp. She stares at me rudely. She knows very well who I am but will not say hello, won't kiss me. I don't want her to kiss me anyway! What can I bring to this witch, what good is the bag of fruit, what good for her yellow complexion, her angry skin? "I'm the same, don't look for happy signs,"

she says, moving her mouth. Our eyes meet as if by
accident. "Go away. Don't stare at me. You think I'm
in a freak show?" she says. "I'll leave if you want me
to," I say. "What did you come for?" she says. "Just
to talk . . . to say hello . . ." I say. "You're spying
for them," she says listlessly. "No," I say. "They use
you without your knowing it, you're so stupid," she
says. "They can hear what you're thinking . . .
you're too stupid to shut it off! You don't know how!"
Other women sat around us, yawning and blinking.
Drugs keep them at the bottom of the ocean. My
mother's eyes are feverish with the fight she makes
against falling asleep, against surrendering. If she
surrenders, something will happen to her, she thinks.
. . . "They do things to the brain," she says. "They
operate on it. First they stick a needle in you and
press your knees down on the table and you fall
asleep, then they do anything they want . . . they
scoop out your insides . . . they pick around in your
brain. I know." Sudden silence.

"Ma, you're looking much better . . ." I tell her.
Gravity. Silence. Eternalness. The lounge is formica
and plastic, a pleasant beige color, the other women
are shapeless and contented, sleeping and smiling,
probably all mothers. Here we sit, mother and daughter. We have come to rest. I fight the urge to lie
down at my mother's feet and press my body against
the floor, the linoleum floor, to make everything outside me stop moving. I am sweating inside. Globs of
sweat form in my stomach.

1960

The second hospital. The third hospital. She stuffs herself and gets fat—her stomach swells. Her stomach then shrinks. Now I am sixteen years old and the house is sold. My father leaves for California. I sleep: I dream of the blood-splattered hallway, the door, the woman inside, bleeding. In my sleep I follow the trail of bloodstains.

1969

In my sleep I follow the trail of bloodstains. It leads to my future! I run along a hallway following those little starlike explosions of blood, I am being led into my life, into my future. . . . I grab at the door-knob and open the door. . . .

I rouse myself and on the monitor I see a "distinguished" Negro face. Judge Wright. He speaks fast, faster than Vince, he is smarter than Vince, he is even beginning to finish Vince's sentences for him . . . tension rises between them. . . . Vince has an ironic eye for the camera that Judge Wright can't see.

1963

The ornamental quality of the light: golden splotches. The half-drawn, cracked shades. His face, his shadowy eyes. We whisper to each other, "I love you. . . ." I hear myself saying these words clearly

enough. Am I drugged? Am I like my mother in the
home, drugged and heavy-lidded and lying? But my
lover whispers these words and he is not drugged. Our
bodies, wound together, are heavy and very warm. I
love this boy. I don't love this boy. I am loved by him
. . . ? I can't believe that I am loved by him, I am
not loved, I am not even in this secret room, I am not
even alive.

Lying here, I imagine her lying on the floor somewhere, the way she lay on the basement floor. I press
myself against this boy. His warm, damp chest. His
forehead. Warm, damp hair.

1969

> Sunday. A sunny day. She is fatter, her cheeks
> fatter. A book on her lap. "What are you reading, Ma?"
> I ask, feeling happy. "It's just from the library . . . a
> silly book . . ." she says, embarrassed. Now she is
> easily embarrassed by herself. She sits clumsily, her
> cheeks flushed.

1967

Hospitals. Six months out, eight months in. Fat,
baggy stomach. Shrunken stomach. She stuffs herself
with food, then she starves herself . . . she screams
at the nurses and at me, she sits in silence, in sorrow.
A plump, fresh face. A haggard face. The months
come and go, the pendulum swings back and forth, she
is "making a new beginning," and now she is breaking out into a freezing sweat. . . . The years are all

mixed up. My head spins with the years and months,
mixed up, the real hallway and the hallway in my
dream, the real blood and the blood in my dream. . . .

1969

The novel she is reading is *Glory of Dawn*. Her
hands are plump and look healthy. I want suddenly
to bump my head against hers, gently, trying to understand something, to remember something. There
are secrets in her she must tell me someday. I want
to ask her, *Why did you go crazy?* I want to ask her,
Why did you marry my father? I want to ask her,
Why don't you let me go? Inside her skull, with its
patchy gray hair, are all these secrets. I want to bump
my head against hers, seizing her, screaming into her.

Afterward, I must see Dr. van Geel.

Dr. van Geel: Are you aware that she fears you?
She says you threaten her.

How could I threaten her?

Dr. van Geel: In spite of her appearance, she is
really very disturbed. We don't understand. She gets
confused easily and claims to hear what people are
thinking. . . .

*Doesn't she hear me think of love? how loudly must
I think of love? I am twenty-five years old, sitting in
this hospital office, thinking of love and trembling.*

Dr. van Geel: No, if you stop your visits she'll become depressed. You must continue seeing her. It's all
she has to live for, really. . . . When she fights with
the other women, it's always about their daughters,
you and the other woman's daughter, first they talk
together in a very friendly way, then your mother

starts to get excited, then the fighting begins. . . .
Now, the first part of this week your mother was ex-
tremely well-behaved, she did her assigned work, she
kept herself very clean. Then, on Thursday, it began.
She kept talking about you. She became very confused. She pressed her hands against her head and
told us she was trying to get in contact with you, to
find out if you were in danger. . . .

*Once she tried to kill me, I won't forget that.
Smashed crockery, flour everywhere in the kitchen,
suffocating dry taste of death, white flour everywhere,
everywhere, in my eyebrows in my mouth my
lungs. . . .*

Dr. van Geel: I wish we could figure out why she
says you threaten her on these visits. You haven't any
idea yourself? You don't say anything to upset her?
From Thursday till Sunday she becomes increasingly
nervous, waiting for you, preparing for your visit . . .
no, you must continue to see her . . . she would have
nothing left if you stopped.

1968

I am introduced to Vince Ellman. A brisk handshake. The television studio: lights, cameras, thick
glass, rubber cords heavy on the floor. Jokes, banter.
This man is a handsome man. It was rumored he was
going to divorce his wife to marry someone, a young
girl, whatever happened to her . . . ? The divorce
apparently did not take place. He was "in love" with
two women, his pals said. He fell out of love with them
both.

I think about him constantly.

Sunday visit at the hospital: the flowerpots, the other visitors, the ceramic saints, the fluorescent-red bows, the pay telephone booths, the smell of the lounge, the smell of permanent sickness. My mother's voice emerges out of the confusion. "I was very sick," she says. "Now I am getting well."

"Yes. You're looking wonderful."

"I'm awful ashamed of how I acted."

"Oh, Ma. . . ."

"What is it like at home? Is it all right?"

You know very well the house was sold.

"Everything is all right."

She stares at me. Silence.

"I am getting well," she says slowly. "I am going to leave here pretty soon. . . ."

Why do you tell such lies?

"On Easter, did I tell you, some real nice girls came in from a high school to sing to us . . . they were about thirteen or fourteen, the cutest nicest girls. . . ."

And you loved them! You loved them, but when I was that age you tried to kill me!

"Then all this week I worked in the laundry . . . I worked real hard . . . I didn't do anything wrong, not once. . . ."

Yes, you tried to kill me. I won't forget that.

1969

Monroe W. Mason, Civil Liberties Union, degrees from Columbia and Harvard, lawyer, married, three children, tufts of sandy hair, perfect teeth, long nicotine-stained fingers. He and Vince are earnest, intense, interrupting each other. I watch them on the

monitor. A man is a man: a woman falls in love with
the idea of a man, but in place of this man another
may be put, a substitute. There is a space in the air
that needs filling. A man steps in to fill it. It is not
Monroe E. Mason, the man on the right, whom I
love. It is the man on the left I love, Vince Ellman.
Watching them on the television screen, looking carefully from one to the other, I cannot judge them. I
cannot say why it is that I love one man and not the
other. I don't know either of them. There is nothing
in their faces that is personal. There is nothing in
anyone's face that is personal. What can you get from a
face? Too many smiles wear out a face, that's true,
but my mother, who almost never smiles, has a worn-
out face. My own face feels worn, but not from smiling. I sit here while the minutes of the program flash
by, second after second—time rushes when you are
on the air—and I feel the old, dull, sickening trance
begin in me, a crystallization of the Fear. Why? I
will be sensible about this. The Fear did not exist,
ever. It was a lie. Never, behind the drawn blinds of
a house on Dougal Street . . . never behind the
bathroom door . . . never, never shaping itself in
the darkness of the basement, never . . . all a lie,
all of it. A sick woman, that is all. My mother, aged
thirty-four, became sick, and off and on for years she
was sick, she was well, she is sick, she is well. . . .
Nothing else. There is no Fear, there was never any
Fear, only sickness.

1969

"I want you to be married. I want you to be happy."

—That is my mother speaking. She speaks in a "logical," slightly singsong voice, as if imitating Dr. van Geel. He, being Dutch (I think), speaks in a very logical singsong voice, as if always speaking to children.

Confused, I nod at my mother. I agree.

She is telling me what to do with my life. I feel the contraction of her muscles seeking to expel me from her forever. She wants to squeeze my head down out of her body—she wants me to leave her, to be born, to walk out of the hospital lounge, to wrap my arms and legs around a man, a stranger. I begin to cry. Oh, she is hateful, she wants me dead! The secret of mothers and daughters: that daughters should be "married," that they should be "happy." Just what does that mean?

"Why are you crying?" she says, alarmed.

She is embarrassed. What if one of the other patients sees us? (They are all spying on us. They know.) What if one of the nurses hurries over and seizes me, claims that I am just as crazy as my mother . . . ? My mother wants it all for herself. She wants to be sick herself, but she won't let me be sick. She wants me to walk out of here. A woman in a blue dress, her feet in ugly support shoes, she is safe in her fifteen-year sickness and she is too selfish to share it with anyone else.

Why do you lie to them about me? You tell them I threaten you!

"Why are you crying?" she says.

"I thought you could read people's thoughts. If you could read them, you'd know," I tell her flatly.

This is the day Mrs. Price was on the show. Watching her and Vince that morning, I felt a terrible pang of sorrow, or desire . . . the two of them, a man I loved and a woman who might have been my mother, two people I might have loved, on that small screen . . . talking earnestly about the "children" of the slums. Who are these children? Why are they more valuable than we other children, who are living alone, grown up, whose heads ring with the terrors of childhood?

"I can't read thoughts. That was part of my sickness," my mother says carefully. They have taught her to say this. I smile, to show that I see through it all—her lies. Of course she can read my thoughts! Mothers can read their daughters' thoughts, as if listening in on a telephone line, but they don't want to admit it. My mother is pretending to be well now and she won't admit it. She tells lies.

"I was sick then . . . when I said that," she explains.

I say nothing. Let her keep hearing her own lying words, echoing in our heads. Lies. She tells lies. Let her keep hearing them. We can sit here together for the next ten years, staring at each other, both knowing the truth. This will never come to an end! There is no way out for us, we must sit here forever! We are two bodies, weighed down, and inside us our spirits have died, nothing is left but our two bodies and everything they remember.

"Yes, I want you to get married. It's time," she says. "I want you to be married and happy."

"You were married and you weren't happy," I tell her.

"We're talking about you and not about me," she says.

"It's the same thing," I tell her.

1969

At last the seconds run out—the show is over. Smiles. Congratulations. Monroe Mason shakes hands with Vince. He shakes hands with me. In a man's handshake there is a certain pressure, a question, that a woman senses but does not acknowledge, if the space in her that needs love is filled. I do not acknowledge this pressure. Vince is on the telephone, I go to the women's lounge, I wonder if I should leave the studio without saying good-by to him. . . . Too much chatter up here. The restraint of being on the air, of extreme tension, makes everyone chatter afterward. Words. We caress each other, we fight each other, with words. In the years of my mother's silence I think I became mute, because she could not hear me. My words went nowhere. I had no secrets left, I owned nothing—what did I have in my life that was my own? Even the Fear became public. I told my girl friends about it, I joked about it, I laughed at myself. The Fear. Inside me, where the Fear once was, there is nothing—a scooped-out womb.

Vince catches up with me and helps me on with my coat. My heart pounds at his nearness. I am afraid of him. I really don't want him. While he chatters, I think of my mother in the hospital . . . I want to see her this evening, I want to make her confess . . .

confess something. . . . I don't want love from this man! I want love from her. I don't know why women love men. What is there about their grins, their sweat, their big hands, that women must love? and must lie down to love? Years ago I had a lover, a boy, and what passed between us was like a movie I had seen years before, nothing more. I know he was my lover. I remember his room, the sunlight through the cracked shades . . . it must have happened . . . I remember his face, even. But it is no more real to me than a story in a movie. It is less real, because the movie could be seen again, sharply remembered upon a second viewing, but the act of love is gone forever and cannot be remembered.

Vince walks with me to the elevator. Someday I will make up a report on him for myself: Vincent Ellman, WWT-TV, television personality. Born Waco, Texas, 1924, worked with twenty-two radio and/or television stations in the United States, England, and Canada, came to Detroit in 1963, married, four children, not quite my lover. What more can I find out about him? What is his interest in me? Is it my slightness, my pretty face, my turned-away face, my fear of him? Is he interested in my stillness, Vince who is so busy with mouth and hands? I am twenty-five years old but I have not accumulated twenty-five years. . . . There is nothing in me. No years. My life is like a story being told by a camera, on a screen, with my face in the center, a story that keeps renewing itself in episodes, but that does not add up. There is no story line, no progress. And the heroine does not get older. She never changes because, inside her, there is nothing—it has been scooped out to prepare her

for a sickness of her own, yet even that sickness eludes
her.

1969

I come to visit her, out of breath—the visiting hour
on Wednesday evening—it is already seven-thirty! I
am going to demand tonight that she tell me the truth.
Earlier today Vince walked with me around the Fisher
Center, around the parking lots, past the General Motors Building and the expensive restaurants, the two
of us walking, him bent toward me to explain the
world as he must explain it to people, again and again.
Does he hate his wife now because he has finished his
explanation of the world to her? She knows everything
about him. She is forty-three years old, a good-looking
woman, no fool. But she knows all his jokes. She
could finish his sentences for him, his mannerisms
are as familiar to her as her own . . . perhaps they are
her own. She is almost old enough to be my mother,
that woman! Her husband is attracted to something in
me, some stillness. He took me to Topinka's for a
drink. Some people from the studio were there. He is
best in such settings, against a background of other
busy people, of tablecloths and silverware and drinks;
at these times it hardly matters what he says. I stare at
him, in love. "You are on an island. You live alone on
an island," he says. "Do you want me to rescue you?"

I drive all the way out to the hospital to see her, out
of breath and angry. I am so angry! But I don't know
why, exactly. My mother detaches herself from a small
group, it's clear to me that she would rather talk with

these other women, these crazy old women, than with me. My face shows this. I won't lie.

Neither of us speaks. It is she who is "sick" and she resents speaking first, I suppose. Finally she gives in. She says, "I didn't think you'd come here to-night. . . ."

My face is flushed with anger. A nurse is standing not far away, sent by Dr. van Geel to spy on us. Her uniform is too tight across the hips, the thighs—she is a sluttish woman in her forties. I wonder about the nurses. I wonder about the intimacy of nurses and their patients, all those hours, the dreary overcast days, the baths, the massages, the routine matters of these secret days in hospitals. . . .

My mother and I sit facing each other in silence. We will never be free of each other. She can stare at me all she wants and she will never make me leave. "I want to ask you something," I say after a while, my voice low so that the nurse won't hear, My mother looks tired. At her age women look tired unless they smile, and it is too difficult to smile.

"What?" she says.

"When are you coming home?"

She stares at me.

We have no home.

"The doctor doesn't think I can leave yet . . . not right now. . . ."

"How long do you intend to stay here?"

She looks frightened. She will tell the doctor how her daughter frightens her, how I bring the noisy broken-up world in here, into her safety, and threaten her with it! She wants to lie in bed all day, I know her. She wants to chatter and gossip with those other women. She will do laundry work here, and wait on tables here, and slave away in the kitchen here, but when she had a "home" with me she wouldn't do anything, she hid down in the basement and cried. I could smell the panic on her then. She didn't want to be my mother! Now she pretends to be my mother and she says to me, *You should get married, you should be happy.*

"You can't hide in here forever," I tell my mother. I am speaking quickly. "They won't let you stay, it's the law. Dr. van Geel told me himself."

The muscles in her face begin to clench.

"No, you want me to leave you alone, you want me to disappear," I tell her, whispering. I lean toward her. We are so close, my mother and I, that I can feel the gentle pores of my skin breathing as if in memory of their breathing twenty-five years ago, inside her body, the seeping of her blood into me and out again, the two of us one body, the same matter. She knows this. I can hear her thinking it, but she will not admit it.

"You want me to disappear! You want me to leave you. . . . When you tried to kill me that time, when you did all those crazy things for years, did you think I would forget them? How can I forget them?"

A television set in a corner. Applause. Squeals.

"You're dirty and hateful," I whisper. Suddenly I remember all that blood. Blood on the floor, on the white tub, splashed onto the wall—the pig! "You sit there proud of working in the laundry, doing other people's filthy laundry, and you wouldn't do mine— you hid down in the filthy cellar crying down there! Didn't you? Didn't you? How can I forget that?"

My mother begins to cry. She covers her face with her hands.

The nurse comes over. "Is something wrong?" she

asks me. I must look frightened, she feels sorry for
me, she looks from my mother to me and back again.
I take my mother's hands away from her face. Yes, it
is there, the ugliness, the hate. The nurse and I stare
at it.

"Ma, please don't. Please don't cry. I have to leave
in a few minutes," I tell her.

"Would you like something? Some tea?" says the
nurse gently to my mother.

1969

Spring. Vince drives me out to the country. Everything is rising, rising in sunlight, but I feel myself
drawn downward. The Fear is somewhere outside
me, waiting for me. Vince turns the radio on, switches
stations restlessly as he drives. And he talks. Chatter
about news at the studio, about friends of his, anec-
dotes—he knows so many people! Once he was going
to divorce his wife to marry some girl, whom I have
never met, and now I think . . . I think he would
divorce that same wife to marry me, but I can't concentrate upon this fact. While he talks, my mind
wanders. He talks, he talks, I make my face glow with
health and youth and a certain kind of petite, sinister
prettiness, and so he talks into me forever, trying to
fill me up . . . but no one can fill me up. He
knows about my mother. He is sympathetic. It makes
me weak in his eyes, like a cripple, a handicapped
child—I should be grateful for him, always, for his
interest. That is why I appear to listen so carefully
to him. I am almost young enough to be his daughter.

I am young enough to be his daughter. But his daughter does nothing but keep away from him, right now she is bumming around Europe and hasn't written or telephoned for weeks, she wants to be free of her parents, but I am obedient and stupid beside him in the car, listening. Yes, I think he would marry me. He sees in me no life of my own, no distractions. Women are always after him—beautiful women, actresses, models, the wives of his wealthy friends—but they are too healthy for him, too solid, their beauty is too sure of itself, they don't need him to fill them up. So he turns to me. I will never alarm him with my own life. I will never turn weeping to him, confessing the death inside me, the death of my childhood, the trail of splattered blood leading to my future. . . . I will say nothing about the constant silence. Nothing about the wall of craziness she hid behind. Always outside, out there in the world, is the other side of that wall and I will never get to it. I am trapped. I keep following the trail of bloodstains in my sleep or when I am awake, and I am trapped in that hallway, I can't escape. I really am dead, though I sit here listening to this man, smiling. But I will never tell him about it. I will tell him nothing.

And so nothing will change. Nothing is expected to change.

"What did the doctor say?" Vince asks.

"The usual thing."

"That you're accusing her . . . ? Threatening her?"

"Yes. I don't want to talk about it."

Vince shakes his head. "Jesus, that must be tough on you. Why should she turn against you? You visit her all the time, you bring her things . . . she should be grateful as hell. But I suppose that's part of her sickness, the things she says about you."

I accept this in silence. He is right.

Out in the country, we go for a walk. The earth is spongy. My body is drawn downward. I want to press myself against the earth, straining against it, to get everything silent again, truly silent. I understand why the earth absorbs our bodies when we die. It is our bodies straining downward, suffocating the earth, wanting to get back inside it. Should I lie down here? Should I press my face against the earth, claw at the earth, scream into it? . . . Vince embraces me lightly. I am frightened of him but I don't move away. Today? This afternoon? I will give into him, I will love him? He kisses me and I don't step away, though I feel panic. I feel myself small and rather sinister, ratlike, very sly, very graceful in this man's arms. If I lie on the ground and allow him to love me, then. . . .

Not today.

We walk together. The Fear withdraws. Vince is boyish, very cheerful. In his heart he feels certain of me, for I am like a daughter, emptied of everything except obedience; you can tell that by my face. My hair is long, to my shoulders, sleek and brown and obedient. My eyes are brown and obedient. He does not love me, but he loves his reflection in me, as if I were a screen in which he can view himself end-lessly, admire himself, his words, his language, the magic of his manliness, his immortality. He loves me. And yet, as he talks, I am thinking of the schoolbooks and the bag of gym clothes and my purse held up against my chest, I am thinking of the walk home from school, the front steps, the advertisements stuck in the mailbox, the silence of the house . . . I am thinking of the trail of bloodstains. . . . Vince bends to pick a weed. It has little green buds where flowers would have been. The buds are very small, not even green; they are white. They are bloodless, tiny, tight, turned in upon themselves as if in an agony of dreaming. Vince makes a bow, he presents me with the "flower." "Do you love me a little?" he says as a joke. I take the flower from him. It is not a flower, and it will never be a flower now. "Yes. I think so," I tell him.

He seems satisfied.

Y*ou*

You are leaving the airplane—stuffed into something white, your earrings swinging like tiny meathooks, your outlandish shoes with their stacked heels and buckles and square toes, shoes costing seventy dollars or one hundred dollars, who knows, dragging down your sweating feet, too heavy for you to manage with all the glare in your eyes. Sunlight. A morning. Where the hell are your sunglasses? You hate mornings—anger rises in you, bubbling like something sour in your throat—but you grin into the morning because someone is approaching you, shouting a magic word. Your name.

You are welcomed to the West Coast.

"Madeline, love! You're beautiful! Look, she's beautiful!" a man is crying.

A few photographers to take your picture. No, they are not important photographers; those men are somewhere else, snapping the pictures of better-known murderers and celebrities. You are alone in the sunlight and the flashbulbs make you turn to them, involuntarily, smiling. You smile in spite of the rotten taste in your mouth. How you hate sunshine! How you hate morning! How you hate this man who is embracing you, making a fuss over you, a bastard you know only too well!—but there's nothing to do but walk along with him into the terminal, managing your heavy stylish shoes and your short white skirt eight or ten inches above your knees, managing your face in the glare, smiling angrily, listening while your agent rattles off a list of engagements into your ear.

You, forty years old. You, an outrageous figure in white, with hair bleached bone-white, a face without lines or any sign of thought, only that empty, angry grin, fighting down nausea. Too much to drink last night. Too much yelling last night. Your agent's breath is sticky and close to you—how you hate men, really!

"Where the hell is my luggage?" you say suddenly, to get him away from you.

Everyone is too slow. The world moves too slowly.

"Luggage! Luggage!" A boyish friend of your agent's appears and claps his hands, bustling around. They will get your luggage for you. Don't worry. Scuffed white suitcases, very expensive, dragged around as if they had no value, and indeed they have no value.

You, what are you doing out in California?

A ride in the taxi. Your agent touching your silky knee—all right, his touch means nothing, you sit back and stare out the window and try to ignore it. Really, you despise men. You've said so and luckily you were not overheard by the wrong people. "My dear, my love, you look beautiful! Why did you scare me over the phone? What the hell was that business about breaking up— cracking up—eh? You, of all people, never sick a day in your life!" And he squeezes your hand.

Your hand is constructed of clever, metallic, very hard little bones, padded with soft, perfumed, pale flesh, a lady's flesh, lovable.

Madeline Randall.

"What do you think of the script? The lady doctor?"

The script. Stains on the blue cover. Pages you turned over and over on the plane, trying to read, trying to memorize. You hate Xeroxed scripts.

You shrug your shoulders.

"But that part is exactly you. The new you. It could have been written exactly for you!"

You, Madeline, being checked into the motel. The odor of chlorine and bug spray. Deep white carpets in the lobby. You nod vaguely as someone passes you and grins hello, *Are you Madeline Randall?* You, you, standing so that enormous, outrageous, crazy bosom of yours is outlined against something (what the hell is it? a glass wall with palms trees behind it?)—your legs exposed, silky and perfect and forty years old, or maybe forty-one years old, slim ankles, heavy fashionable shoes that may have cost two hundred dollars, who can remember? Your luggage is being wheeled around. Stuffed in the suitcases are dresses that presumably are worth two or three or four hundred dollars, since that is what you paid for them, now stuffed together, wrinkled, bunched together under mounds of shoes and other junk. When you open your smallest suitcases in five minutes, you will cry out in rage— a bottle of greenish-blue mouthwash has leaked!

"Goddamn it! Jesus Christ, goddamn it! Why is everything so loused up!"

You stomp around the room. In the mirror your angry blond

head looms, the head of a minor celebrity. But the mouthwash is spilled in spite of your beauty and your money and all the people who envy you—you stand screaming at your agent and his boy friend, telling them to shut up, to get out and leave you alone, you've got to make a telephone call—you've got to go back to New York—

"No, no, no, Maddy! Please!"

"It's my daughter—"

"You can't disappoint everyone, Maddy! Look how my hands are shaking!"

Jerry shows his trembling hands; you stare at them, wanting real proof of his anguish. Yes, he is trembling. He has not been a well man for the last twelve years.

"But there's trouble with one of my daughters," you say blankly.

It strikes you that this is an important scene, an emotional scene. People are watching you anxiously. You might be in a play. Not one of those crappy television plays like the kind you have flown out here to film (you'll do five tapes and make thousands of dollars, thousands!) but a real play, like Chekhov, like . . . like Chekhov, where people do cry out at each other and hold up their shaking hands, pleading.

Yes, this is a scene in an important life, your own.

"Relax, please," you tell Jerry.

You hate men because of their weaknesses; then you love them because they are so weak. You take Jerry's hands in yours. You are half a head taller than he, but you are not old enough to be his mother. You can't be everyone's mother! He smiles at you, grins shakily at you, while the boy who has accompanied the two of you up here stares, admiring you both. You understand how in this elegant mirrored room you are the most elegant object, the most expensive object, a beautiful woman. You are an outrageous, beautiful woman and who can help but stare at you? They need you. They need you to be good to them.

"My hands never tremble. Look."

Your lovely white hands with their diamonds. Steady after all these years.

"I touch my toes one hundred times a day," you tell Jerry. Someone knocks on the door and the boy opens it with a flourish. A girl with dyed curlicue hair, orange-red, wearing a smock. You don't bother with her but continue your proud recitation—Believe it or not, I exercise an hour a day! Wouldn't miss it! I can do push-ups even. I tried jogging in the park but the goddamn dogs got too excited, so I run at home—you know—I run in place, standing still."

They all stare at you, in awe.

"Madeline," Jerry says, "you're wonderful! But now—"

"You want to see me do twenty-five push-ups right now?"

"Maddy—"

You get down on the floor, the carpet. Kick off your shoes. You sink down on your firm muscular forty-year-old stomach and on your great breasts, and with your arms you push yourself up off the floor—once, twice, three times! "This is nothing," you gasp. "I can do them all morning."

"Madeline, my God, you're so athletic, so beautiful and—and athletic—Isn't she something?" Jerry cries.

Now hurry, hurry into the next scene, the next room—change your clothes, grunting, tugging at a zipper—and the girl will fluff out your hair and spray it with a sticky perfumed spray, just right for this windy edge of the continent. Your fingernails are painted platinum. Your toenails are painted platinum. Your legs are smoooth and shaved, perfect legs, you don't bother even to look at them—you hardly bother, these years, to stare at your face, it seems immortal. Yet there is a strange look to you—I noticed it once, when you were going in a restaurant—a look of strain, of craziness, as if your lovely blue eyes were about to cross, out of anger. Your crazy anger.

You like to smash things. Push them over. You used to like to set traps for waiters—while important people chattered around you, you would set waiter traps and laugh when five or six dishes spilled their hidden contents on the floor or on someone's lap, how funny! How funny to see a mound of peas breaking into separate peas, rolling across the table and into everyone's laps, how funny to see the faces! Oh, you like to set traps but you don't like to clean up after them. As a matter of fact, you never clean up after anything. Your room is a sty. You never clean up. You like to smash things, you like to burn things (theatrically, in ash trays and in wastepaper baskets, letters that could just as easily be crumpled up and thrown away with no fuss, their contents being insignificant), and you like to rip telegrams into careful bits, while other people stand by and stare, worried, but afraid to ask you what is wrong.

Now they are herding you to the elevator and now I am walking through the rooms of our apartment in New York, my head pounding—now they are herding you out to a taxi, fussing over you, admiring you, and now I am dialing the telephone again. You, our mother, are now telling a joke—"It seems that Ted Kennedy was sailing in his sailboat and what floated by but . . ."—and I, your daughter Marion, the less striking of your twin girls, but cute enough, honey-haired, seventeen years old, blue-eyed like you but less youthful than you—I am listening to the phone ring at the other end, ringing and ringing in Peter's apartment.

You are being seated. A menu. You slap it down. "One martini on the rocks." A bird sings somewhere—a caged bird singing in the air-conditioned cave of a restaurant, singing just for you. Someone is staring at your neckline. Someone hands you an ash tray. Now you launch into a joke you heard in London the other week. "It seems this Catholic nun is in the Congo, and the whole convent but her is wiped out, and—how does it go?—and a chieftain says to her . . ." You laugh loudly and angrily at your own joke, while I dial the number again, standing at the window and looking down at Central Park. The eleven rooms of this apartment are very empty. A multiplication of emptiness. Without you here, without your impatient footsteps and that sugary brassy voice of yours, it is paradise but too empty, it is not quite real.

I dial another number, one scribbled down on a notepad. The ringing at the other end is patient and relentless, as if the same telephone were ringing in the same apartment, with no hope of being answered. Where are all Miranda's friends? Where is everyone? A sound behind me . . . no, it is the absence of sound, nothing. I imagined I heard you slamming a door shut, Mother, with your typical grace, not having found what you wanted. This apartment, this city, is filled with your absence, peaceful and dismal without you. Still the telephone rings. I put down the receiver gently. Now . . . ? Now I must dial another number. I must keep dialing. You are not here to bully me—"Stop scowling! Stop slouching! Walk like I do, walk like you're *proud* of your body!"—and so I must keep moving, thinking. From the twelfth floor of our building I can see the pattern of trees and drives and lakes in the park, deathly familiar to me, mixed up with all our lives together. "This marvelous building! And your view!" people are always cooing to you, and you smile eagerly, Mother, though nothing can keep the winter wind out of these ungainly old-fashioned windows, and the landlord will not fix the leaky plumbing or the stains in the ceiling, and Miranda and I have been freezing all our lives in the back bedrooms, never mind, it is your apartment and you can't live anywhere else.

You can't live here either, but never mind about that.

I dial another number from Miranda's notepad and this time the telephone is answered at once. "Hello?" says a girl.

"Is Miranda there?"

"Who is this?"

"Marion. Her sister."

"Marion who?"

"Her sister Marion—is Miranda there? Do you know where she is?"

"Why would I know where she is?"

Foggy, dull is the girl's voice—somewhere down in the East Village, just waking up for the day—one of Miranda's newer friends, a wreck.

"You haven't seen her?"

"But why me, why ask me? I don't know everything. I don't know her, really. People don't get to know Miranda. . . . She is very mysterious, quite the opposite of her mother, whom I admire for being exactly what she is. Miranda is not a very sincere person . . . she tells lies to everyone. . . ."

"When did you see her last?"

A pause. A yawn. "Are we talking about the same person?"

"She left home last night and —"

"No, I don't remember anything."

She hangs up and the conversation is over. It is a shock, how quickly a conversation can end.

You are having another martini. You eat the olives hungrily. Someone is kissing your hand, the fingers of your lovely lady's hand, shapely and white. Ah, to be kissed with such impersonal devotion!—they all love you, impersonally, they love your hands and your face and your incredible body, but without personal complications, without liking you. You butter rolls. You are shelling lobster and eating, eating—it looks like a giant cockroach on your plate, Mother, boiled red! Still, you eat with great appetite. It is a joy to watch you eat. The producer, that youngish old man with his tinted hair and his trim red-flecked eyes, watches you over his plate of fruit and cottage cheese, envying you your jaws, your muscles, your excellent stomach. *What a woman, Madeline Randall! She's just what everyone says!*

There you sit now—a change of scene—a mirror, lights. Someone is working on you. Someone in a white smock, like a nurse, rubbing lotion into your skin, loving you. The manicurist is a young girl who will never grow up into *you;* pity her. Behind you, grinning bouncily into the mirror, is the hairdresser, a man of middle age, short, curly-haired, possibly Spanish. His breath is light on the back of your neck. He brushes your hair energetically, lovingly. A workout. It is like a gym, you think, all this activity! Years ago, when you were hardly a woman, you were driven crazy by the activity that centered around your body. You were driven permanently crazy, don't deny it. So much activity, attention, so many hours of being photographed, so many reels of film, so many rehearsals, so much money, so many people, their faces looming toward you—recognizing you—demanding vigor from you—it's a wonder you didn't turn into a man, Mother, needing so much energy! The little hairdresser chatters away as if his bright flow of words is part of his salary, and you stare at yourself unsurprised in the mirror, hanging onto *that,* that reflection, that face. Very real. Your face in very real. Your body is even more real. It is not possible to believe that you will ever lose these things, that your arms will rot off; no, don't think of it; it is not possible that you will lose anything that belongs to you, like one of your darling twin daughters, whom people are always cooing over and you respond by smiling eagerly, falsely, as if thinking, "What? Do I have twin daughters? *Twin* daughters? When did I have them? Was it in the newspapers? Do I love them? Where are they? How old are they?"

You are a woman of beauty and everyone else is ugly. Ugly, overweight, scowling. Just look at them in the street, in airline terminals, in your audiences! They are ugly, their faces are blanks or smears, it is quite fitting that they buy tickets to see you in noisy Broadway shows said to be comedies, occasionally "musical" comedies, and that they watch you on television, hypnotized not by your perfect teeth and nose but by the humming surface of the television screen, which tells them that all is well, they are behaving like normal, proper, ugly people, not you or your kind. Not *you* or your kind.

The cleaning lady arrives; it is ten o'clock. Down on the street people are walking dogs, heading into the park. It is eight hours since you and Miranda walked out of here, but not together, rushing out of each other's lives and out of my life, or so you said—eight hours since Miranda jumped up on this window sill (which is about to rot off, did you notice?), threatening to throw herself out the window. Eight hours since you abandoned ship. Now, staring at yourself in the mirror, feeling hysteria work itself up gently in your muscles because you *hate*, you *despise* these people working on you, you can't stand to be touched by all these strangers, now you make yourself rethink . . . rethink the script, which you have memorized in patches . . . thinking of the personality you will become, a certain kind of woman not yourself and therefore inferior to you, but a new personality, a challenge. You don't think of the dialogue of the night before and of all the nights before, the whining, the unoriginal bickering, the corny hate—nobody wrote that dialogue for you, you didn't sign a contract to act it out, and so you can forget about it.

Last night, Miranda and I saw the madness in you. You gave it away by the break in your voice, which was not rehearsed. Listen:

"I have renounced that man! I have discarded him! If you *persist* in seeing him I will discard you! If you *persist* in refusing to see the doctor I am finished, finished, finished with you! Finished with you! You can go to hell!"

You walked angrily around this room, this "study" lined with unread books and decorated with that tawdry, laughable, glamorous painting of you, all pink flowers and red lips, which passed through the hands of two husbands and is still chaste, as if mythical. Walking, stomping angrily, stomping your bare heels into the rug. "You will not listen to the common sense of your mother and your sister, no, you will not listen to anyone, you look like hell, your face is wearing out, your hair is a *mistake*—" (Miranda had dyed her hair jet black, Indian black, in order not to look like me) "but you will not make demands upon me, no, not me, not Madeline Randall, I do not fear ugly publicity and I do not fear a seventeen-year-old brat, not me! Not me!"

You began to cry, so angry. The violence is in you, Mother, we saw it last night and we've been guessing at it for years. Looking from your face—where the water-clear tears ran lightly—to Miranda's face, where the tears were ugly, wearing rivulets into her skin, looking from you to my sister and back again, listening to this noisy argument, I had the feeling that we were all in a scene we hadn't known was coming up, let alone a scene we might have had a hand in choosing. So I said suddenly, "Don't decide anything tonight. Wait until the morning."

You both looked at me.

"She's been overdue now for how long, how long?—four weeks?" you cried. "Every week that goes by, the risk is greater! Do you know anything about life, about reality?"

"What makes you think I'll have an abortion?" Miranda said.

"Listen to her! Look at her ugly face, and that damn ugly hair —a squaw, she looks like a squaw, camping out in my life!" Except for Miranda's drawn-up legs—she lay back on the sofa as if to protect herself—you might have rushed at her and grabbed hold of that long hateful hair and yanked it in handfuls out of her head.

"I am not ugly. I was ugly but I'm not ugly now. I don't look like you or like anyone in the family. I'm not ugly now," Miranda said quietly.

Miranda, my twin sister, the companion of my childhood—a child not much like me, except for her sweet little pearlish face and her small body—there she lay, rejecting me, hating me because, like her, I came out of *you*. But she felt no personal hatred for me. No anger. You have taken all our anger from us. You have taken our energy from us, leaving us with these schoolgirlish bodies, flat chests, thin legs. Yes, we are pretty enough, but pretty in a honeyed, gentle, unimportant way. We walk onstage but the center of the stage is always elsewhere; it is spotlighted on you, your flailing arms and white white smile and blue eyes that always look as if they are about to cross. . . .

Once, outside a midtown restaurant, I overheard some men on the sidewalk on their way from lunch while *you* and your wacky friends were on your way in—I overheard them saying, "Jesus Christ! Look at her! Is that all real?" You were ten pounds overweight then, spilling out of a tight red dress, your hair a kind of pyramid on top of your head in the style of that year, your legs knock-kneed because of the tight skirt, your feet squashed into tiny pointed shoes balanced on thin spikes. "Ugh," one of these men groaned, but it was not really a groan of disgust; it was a sound jerked out of him.

"Ugh, that's Madeline Randall, you know—Madeline Randall."

We know. Madeline Randall.

You shot around at these men a look of utter pride and loathing—your face too white with make-up so that it looked like a highway reflector sign, your lips far too red, outlined with a purplish color—seizing them and releasing them, a woman far too magnificent for any man, giving them your contempt and flirting with them crudely, laughably. You are so crude and so laughable, Mother, why is it more people don't laugh at the sight of you? But they don't. The men stared at you, as if frightened, and you and your friends swept into the restaurant, noisy and happy. I thought you must be insane then. To dress like that out on the street, to look at people like that, twisting your mouth into a parody of a smile, twisting your body in front of them, a taunt.

You are always taunting us.

Now you are leafing through the script—cigarette ashes fall onto it—someone is adjusting your dress. Heavy rubber cables underfoot. Cameras, which you never bother looking at. Your chest is a little damp with perspiration. You are very excited suddenly. You are about to become another person.

Back in New York I am still Marion Randall, one half of a set
of twins, but out in Hollywood you are no longer my mother but
someone else—a lady doctor, is that what the script demands?
Oh, what a laugh! A lady doctor, *you!* Singlehandedly you will
save an entire Mexican town from the plague! No, you are not
Madeline now, you are someone else, and everyone who stares at
you, admiring you, loving and envying you, gives you the power
to be this new outlandish person, this female doctor—your audience gives you the power of complete nonbeing, nonexistence as
yourself. You come alive in another personality. You are excited,
overjoyed, you have forgotten about everything else, your veins
flow with the blood of a new personality! The critics never recognized how good you were, really.

—"Your mother is so absurd. How can she exist as such an
absurd human being?" a girl at school once asked Miranda and
me.

—"Your mother has no talent. Your mother is a criminal type,"
one of your ex-lovers told us, right in this apartment at a big
party; I think it was that Swede who came between Niles-the-
plastic-surgeon and Peter himself.

—"Your mother is a marvelous comedienne, but only when
she's playing serious roles," another actress told us, flying high
from alcohol or pills or both.

—"Your mother is not really a woman," said Father.

But they didn't see, just as the professional critics didn't see,
the genius you had for turning yourself inside out, woman or not-
woman, whatever you are. I always saw it. Miranda saw it. It
explains your professional success, your talent right now—right
at this moment—for escaping into someone else while your own
life is about to fall around you in ruins.

I find myself over at Peter's office, out of breath. Peter seems
fairly good this morning—his tan looks unpermanent, as if
rubbed into his skin too dryly, his smile is jagged, yet he is all
right, he seems all right. "No, I haven't seen Miranda. You know

I haven't seen her for two weeks," he says. "What's happened?"

"She walked out last night. Mother left too, she's in Hollywood—they had a terrible fight, the worst one yet—I thought she might have come to you."

Silence. Peter's agitation. Behind him a small air conditioner rumbles in a window, as if sharing his agitation.

"But you know that your sister and I . . . we broke it off. . . ."

"She didn't call you?"

"No."

"I don't know what to do. I don't know where to look for her."

"What did they fight over? Me?"

"Yes, you, but more than that . . . something more. . . . I think you know."

Silence again. Peter walks slowly around his office. He bumps into the edge of his desk.

"I don't . . . I don't know what you mean," he says.

"She won't see the doctor. She won't take a test."

"A test?"

"You know."

I have begun to tremble a little, alarmed and ashamed. It is as if I am a stand-in for my sister, confessing all this.

"Is she pregnant?" Peter whispers.

"She won't see the doctor to make sure."

He stares at me. He doesn't know what to do. Yet he is probably thinking of you, Mother, fearful of your wrath—thinking of you and not of Miranda—what revenge will Madeline take now? Peter was the most intelligent of your lovers, Mother, and no one will ever know why you kicked him out as you did, that morning in Aspen. At breakfast. On a whim. Like Niles and like Tony Hunt, he came back to haunt us, having lost you but still loving you, latching onto Miranda and me. Your ardent ex-lovers, bruised from you, are always attracted to Miranda and me, in no special order. Sometimes Miranda first, sometimes me.

"Does she really think she's pregnant?" Peter says.

"She won't talk about it. She doesn't seem to care; it's Mother who cares."

"Jesus. . . ."

We are both terribly embarrassed. Peter once took me aside, pressed my hands between his, told me that he loved me and wanted someday to marry me. I was sixteen at the time. Still in school. The next week he was telephoning Miranda. For half a year he went out with her, the two of them had a crude half-serious secret from you, Mother, though certainly you knew about them . . . ? Didn't you know about them, really . . . ? It seems impossible that no one told you. And then one day you found out or pretended to find out, you expressed surprise or pretended to express it—how furious you were, that two people in your life, orbiting around you, should defy you!

"Then you don't know where she is?"

"I'm afraid not. Was she very upset?"

"Yes. I think I should call the police."

"And Madeline is in Hollywood?"

"She'll be back Monday."

"You don't think there's a chance Miranda is just kidding?"

"Kidding how? What do you mean?"

Peter is very agitated suddenly. His tan deepens.

"Well . . . I assume . . . I assume she threatened suicide. . . ."

"Yes, she did."

We stare at each other in embarrassment. The air conditioner rumbles. I feel sick, I feel off-balance. I think suddenly, *Men are weak, there is nothing to them.*

"Did she talk about that with you? About killing herself?" I ask him.

"Once or twice, but it was nothing serious. She was just being emotional. . . ."

"What did she say?"

"I don't remember."

"You mean she . . . she talked about *that?* What did she say?"

"Marion, I don't remember. When is Madeline coming back?"

"Monday."

"Has she called you yet?"

"No."

"She left this morning?"

"Yes."

"Do you think I could . . . would you give me her number?"

Still he's in love with you, Mother! Listen to him! You kicked him out, you forgot about him, he has impregnated my sister and half of his life is spent with his wife and his three little boys in Connecticut, he is a decent, intelligent, serious, good-humored man of forty-two, and yet, and yet he is in love with you, still in love with you! I am seized with the conviction that there is nothing to men, really, they are to be pitied or despised, the men who make up nothing more than an audience for women like you. . . .

"I can't give you her number. You know that."

We stare at each other in anguish. We are ashamed.

"I'm sorry," he says, "but what can I do? About Miranda . . . ? You know I love her, I would do anything in my power for her and your mother and you—believe me—but what can I do? I don't know her friends. The people she's been hanging around with now, those freaks, those acidheads—they made fun of me, I never got to know them. They cut me off from them and she preferred them to me."

I am looking around for something—my purse. Time to leave. But I don't have my purse with me, I must have run out without it. I keep looking around on the floor, on the beige carpet, around the legs of chairs, wondering what it is I am missing.

"Where are you going now?"

"I have a music lesson at two. . . ."

"But what are you going to do? About Miranda?"

"I don't know."

"Are you going to call the police?"

"I don't know."

"Why don't you wait awhile? Until tomorrow?"

"Yes, Peter. All right. I'll wait."

He walks with me to the door. On the other side of this door his secretary is sitting—when we cross over into her office everything between us must change. He knows this and so, now, at the very last moment, he takes my hands between his . . . a father, a lover, an ex-lover? "Marion, take care of yourself, please. You look so distraught. I'm sure that everything will turn out well."

"We won't tell your wife anything, Peter," I assure him.

He is not shocked by this. I thought it would shock him, but it doesn't; he nods slowly, gravely. A little ashamed. After all, he is forty-two and Miranda is seventeen.

"Call me as soon as you have any news," he says.

You might think this is the end of Peter, but it won't be. I know better. People enter one another's lives and fight and break up but they come back again; people born in the same family never even leave. They are always pressing their bodies together, bumping their heads together, clawing at one another. Families. Mothers, fathers. Twin sisters. The family is the deepest mystery, deeper than love or death. I have not seen my father for six years but I think of him every day, just as he thinks of Miranda and me—every day. He lives in Minneapolis and we live in New York. We live permanently apart. Even when we are not thinking of each other, we are in the presence of the other, that inescapable Other. A daughter, a father. Father was no more to you, Mother, than any other man, a stray acquaintance, a marriage finished in four months. You admired him for his restraint and his good manners and then you laughed at him with your friends because of his restraint and his good manners. He became a joke. All the love in your life, talked of loudly enough, forced into anecdotal form, becomes a joke. It is your peculiar power, Mother, to transform everything into a joke.

You, Mother, should be the biggest joke of all. We tried to laugh you off. We fed ourselves daydreams of running away from you, slamming doors in your face, abandoning ship. Yet we will never leave you, you will never leave us, the relationship is permanent. Miranda and I, hating you and hating each other, are bound together as surely as if we still lay in that same blood-warmed sac, our veins and skulls only gradually, reluctantly separating . . . a tiny smear of life, a hardening object, two objects, two fish, two mammals, two daughters, the daughters of Madeline Randall.

Now you are launched into your rehearsal—now you are at the top of your power, the peak of your life. The world has just become marvelous. Now I wander by the fountain near the Plaza, a girl without a purse, half of a set of twins, with nowhere to go for another hour. The fountain interests me, draws my eye to it. The tiny holes from which water rushes. I would like to climb into the fountain and wash all this dread from me, all this thinking. If I could cross over into another personality, like you, Mother, or if I could cross over into forgetfulness by taking pills, like Miranda, I would not have to remember so much. The water sparkles in the sunlight—the sunlight is a little strange today, almost oily from the impure air. A rainbow might break from it at any second. . . . Looking at the fountain, I think a thought not to be recorded. Yet I will record it because I want to tell you everything—

If Miranda kills herself, then only I will be your daughter.

You are treading a river of words. People watch you, amazed by you. Your energy, your bouncy face, your tireless voice. You will be recorded on tape for a television show you won't even bother to watch. Miranda and I used to watch all your shows, icy with dread at the fool you might make of yourself. But you never did. Not quite. We went to your big hit, twelve-year-old twins in leopard-skin coats and caps, photographed on either side of you for *Harper's Bazaar* . . . your hit, "Tea for Three," something that had to do with a millionaire-spy's impetuous mistress, an Arabic playboy, a Russian diplomat, etc. We remember only you stomping around onstage, throwing your body around, getting in everyone's line of vision, an insult to ordinary bodies. Miranda and I looked exactly alike then, our bodies interchangeable, the same weight. . . .

While I am at my music lesson, hunched painfully over the keys, you are still in the television studio. What a professional you are! Everything about you is professional, for sale. You make few mistakes. I struggle with this piece by Mozart, which I have practiced five hundred times and which I can play faultlessly back in the apartment . . . but here, under the eye of my middle-aged Hungarian teacher, a refugee with an ornate past, I struggle along, my fingers are numb and cold, everything falls apart. A desire for failure must be deep in me; I am a permanent daughter. Miranda too is a failure. She took art lessons for years —no luck. I took violin lessons—no luck. We both took ballet lessons. We both took "drama" lessons. Now I am back with the piano, and Miranda, before her trouble, was fooling around with pottery and jewelry down in the Village, a way of passing time. We should go to college but that would put off our "success" for four years. I still dream of the notices of my first recital, my quiet but splended debut . . . but here, in this uncooled, humid apartment, here in reality I am making mistakes and I can't remember how the piece goes. The notes of music are not like the words you can memorize so easily, Mother. I cannot memorize anything. I cannot stride along these notes the way you stride along words, as if walking on water, like a goddess.

"Stop. Begin that again."

I stop. I begin again.

"What is that *scurrying?*—is that your word, to *scurry?* You are like a mouse, all that fast business—it is not right—it is nervous to hear."

The hour comes to an end. Release. I am free and it is only three o'clock. Jonnie, the maid, is still at the apartment. And, yes, I put out your stained velvet suit for the cleaner's—you forgot all about it. I wander back toward home. Now I am passing that restaurant you entered . . . now I am going around some construction work, the sound of an air hammer makes my breastbone vibrate, it is misery to me, all this noise, these strangers. . . . My reflection in the window of an antique shop shows a soft, pale face, soft as something hiding inside a shell. Ugh, the things you might find in shells, hiding! I should telephone you, Mother, and bring you back home. I should telephone the police. I should track down those people Miranda hung out with lately . . . but their names, if I ever knew them, pass out of my mind and there is nothing I can do. I am helpless.

Smells from an expensive restaurant's ventilator—garlic, grease. I have forgotten to eat today, our chop suey of the night before (delivered in a leaky package) was enough for me, enough food for me. The mothers of our friends were always urging food on us, not liking our flat chests and skinny legs. The mothers of our friends were always urging food upon *them,* their daughters. It is normal, evidently, for mothers to feed their daughters. But with you there were rarely meals at home. No time. A bowl of stale Rice Krispies in our ugly drafty kitchen, milk always a little sour, burned toast scraped into our sink. With your million dollars, we could never afford a good toaster. There was never time for a new refrigerator, a new stove, everything remained old and drafty and ugly in our prestigious building, so that we could trade dour sympathetic remarks with the millionaires' wives who rode with us in the jerking elevator, complaining about the landlord, shaking our heads. Helpless New Yorkers, in the grip of eternal landlords . . . helpless in our mink and leopard coats, our heads bowed by sooty skies, ringing with the noise of sirens on cross streets. . . . "I could never live anywhere else," you were always saying of our apartment, in your ringing, challenging voice. No one opposed you.

I wander back home. Fifteen blocks. It is a very hot, damp day. I am a little nauseated by the smells of the city—the drifting odors of food and fumes. Across from the park a vendor is selling hot dogs. Boxes of popcorn. Chocolate-covered ice cream cones. The sight of a sprinkling of peanuts on one of these cones makes me go sharp with hunger and with nausea, and I think angrily, *Why don't you feed me? Why have you gone away without feeding me?* I remember suddenly that morning in Aspen, breakfast in the sunny, airy, space-intoxicated restaurant high in the mountains, Peter with us, a holiday. The four of us flew out for a weekend of skiing. That morning I saw how you were as a woman, a *female.* You were scooping up wet patches of egg yolk with your toast and getting rid of Peter at the same time, cleaning the plate, kicking out Peter. Did you plan it, or did it just flash into your mind? It happened. Miranda and I had hoped that Peter would be the one, the next husband, the permanent husband. We adored him. And yet:

"I don't think I'll go skiing after all. I want to do crossword puzzles. I don't want to go outside. Take the girls, Peter, and please don't lean on me like that . . . I can't stand to be touched. . . ." And suddenly, to our surprise, that rim of madness showed in your eyes and you began whispering to Peter, in front of us, "I can't stand you! I'm finished! Please don't interrupt, please go back home. Go back to your wife. I want to work on crossword puzzles today. I want to get my mind straight. I can't talk to you, I don't have time, I have to make a telephone call in ten minutes. . . . Look, I'll tell you everything! I can't feel anything with you. You know. I don't respond to you. I've tried and I've failed, it's a failure, let's forget about it . . . actually, I don't care about men very much, that's a secret of mine, a secret failing . . . I don't understand why women fall in love with men, not really. I suppose it's a cultural thing. A cultural determinism. I read that women are always determined by their culture and their heredity. But I can't help it—I don't feel anything much with men. I never did. Maybe I don't try hard enough, I suppose a woman has to concentrate. But when I make love I don't have time. I have too many other things to think about. Maybe that sort of thing is for women without careers, you know, careers to think of, appointments, maybe they can lie down flat for an hour and go blank, I don't know, but I have other things to think of and I don't intend to apologize for what I am. . . ."

That was one morning, at breakfast.

Now you are finished with the day's work. It was hard work. You are ready for a bath, ready for cocktails and food; the scene changes, the background music changes, you zip yourself up into a tight dress of yellow silk. Barefoot in your room. Alone for a few minutes. You turn on the television set—and here in our apartment I turn on our television set—and we wait for the news, a little nervous. The advertisement you are staring at is for a new automobile called the Scorpion, which is photographed careening madly over sand dunes, driven by a beautiful long-haired blond girl; the advertisement I am staring at is for a hair shampoo that makes the model's head look like Medusa's, all soapy and sparkling and deadly. We wait for the news to come on. Earthquake tremors in Southern California. Here, trouble in Harlem. An emergency session of the United Nations. The kidnaping of the three-year-old daughter of a governor in the Midwest. You turn off the television set, suddenly frightened. Why are you frightened? I am hypnotized by this television set and cannot move, staring at the film clips of terrified people being led out of the subways this afternoon after a power failure. There is something wise in their faces: the dawning of horror, knowledge of the city in which they live.

In this city, the loss of Miranda will not be so terrible.

You were like Medusa, charming us. You walked naked through the rooms of this apartment, memorizing lines, soaping your crazy fake-blond hair, dialing the telephone, naked. Should daughters look upon their naked mothers? Miranda and I always looked away, ashamed and frightened. No, we were not going to be women like you. It was pointless to look at you; we would learn nothing about ourselves. The time you came out with a towel around your head and a wet, soiled slip and your eyebrows shaved off, and Miranda burst into tears, I knew we could learn nothing from you. . . . "She's a freak! A freak!" Miranda screamed.

The telephone rings in your hotel room. Important people. The telephone rings here—people after you, cooing after you. "She won't be back until Monday," I tell them. You are ready now for the evening—breasts stuffed in place, heavy crystal earrings, turquoise eyelids, two rows of fake-gold eyelashes on your upper lids and one row on your lower lids, bursting like stars, metallic-looking, wonderfully unreal. Lips outlined in pink but filled in with a very light, pale peach, almost bronze, a gloss. Wonderful. You look dead, but death becomes you. The telephone rings as you leave your room, chattering with the people who've come to get you, and you don't bother to go back and answer it. Here, the telephone rings and when I pick it up I know it is news of Miranda—that respectful silence, the pause of someone's breathing, the careful clinical question, "Is this the residence of Madeline Randall?"

You have difficulty fastening your seatbelt. Too much gin. The plane veers, you think hopefully of death, a blinding crash and a photograph in the papers—but no luck, the plane is safe, everyone safe. Perfect landing. You gather yourself up like an ungainly balloon, feeling bloated. Have you been crying? Your face, leaking tears, shows no signs of grief—but then, you are not acting the part of a grieving mother, you are the mother yourself, there is no need to fake.

I am waiting for you. Marion, alone. Petite Marion, grim-browed, oddly loose as a mirror's image without its object, a twin without her twin. People push me around. There is an air of nervousness here at the airport. Do people expect the airplanes to crash down upon them? In the newspapers there are headlines of bizarre events—an attempted assassination of the President, mysterious nuclear explosions in the Pacific. Seeing so many headlines in the terminal, propped up on all the newsstands, has an unsettling effect on us; we are at a loss to say what we want, milling around here in this great city of a terminal, waiting to be flown to other cities or to welcome passengers home, all of us unsettled. But your plane lands safely. People around me express relief. Was there danger? Is there always danger? The plane taxis to a stop . . . the steps are wheeled out . . . I am still a little sick from last night's visit to Miranda at the hospital, but the old excitement rises in me, the wonder, *Will people recognize her? Will she kiss me? Will they guess that I am her daughter?*

The door is swung open and the first passengers appear. I press forward, watching anxiously. I must see everything. Where are you? The first three passengers are men, the next are a child and her mother. Another woman, not you. And then . . . then you appear. . . . Yes, it is you. Madeline Randall. But you look so different, you are hardly yourself . . . you stand in the doorway of the plane as if afraid of getting out. . . .

Your shoulders are a little stooped. You stare out at us, at the waiting crowd. I wave at you but you don't notice. The sunlight

must be dazzling to you, you are staring into it without sunglasses, squinting. . . . At this distance I can see the pain in
your face as you squint. Too pale, that face. Too much make-up.
Your blond hair is not very neat; it has been mashed out of shape.
Your body is the body of an aging woman. I can see that now.
Everyone in this crowd can see it. You hesitate for another moment, then step down . . . you descend the steps with your
hand on the railing, as if fearful of falling. If you do fall, you will
fall into the perfunctory waiting arms of a man in uniform below
who does not seem to recognize you. No one seems to recognize
you.

I press forward in the crowd, eager to get to you. I want to take
your arm. But someone steps in front of me and when I can see
again you are nowhere in sight . . . where are you? You are
nowhere in sight! A blonde woman is walking briskly toward the
gate, but it is not you. She is not you after all. She is a stranger,
a blonde with a pale, overdone, attractive face, not your face! Not
you! I stare blankly at her as if reluctant to give her up. But no,
no, she is not you, someone else is meeting her, taking her arm,
kissing her powdered cheek. . . .

There you are, in the doorway of the plane. It frames you perfectly. This time I see that it is you, exactly you, in a gray outfit
suited for a not-quite-mourning mother, shirt very short, wearing
oversized sunglasses. There is a kind of turban, silvery-gray,
wrapped around your head. *Here* is Madeline Randall. You don't
look the way I imagined you. . . . You may or may not be
looking at me. Nevertheless you come straight toward me, walking fast, carrying a small white suitcase, and people glance at you
and part for you, half-recognizing you, admiring you, irritated at
your air of hurry, bustle, importance, grief. The grief in your face
is like a beacon, like a sign too bright for us. It will be too bright
for Miranda, in the hospital, speechless and imbecilic after all the
pills she crammed into herself. . . . Before you stride over to

me, in this last moment, I put my hands to my face and begin to cry. No, you are too strong for me!—your face is too bright!

You seize my wrist with your strong, gloveless hand. "Marion!" you say. It is an absolute claim. You are back.

I Was in Love

I was in love with a man I couldn't marry, so one of us had to die—I lay awake, my eyes twitching in the dark, trying to understand which one of us should die. He lived alone in a big drafty house and ruined himself with people, giving himself to people, letting them devour him in the anonymous disinterested manner of maggots, without passion. I lived with my husband and my son, and no one else came near me. He had no family. I had my parents and my husband's parents. Was I of more worth? I lay awake trying to understand which one of us should die, he or I. A future of love with him was a skeleton with quivering skin stretched on it, skin twitching in fear. The fear had to stop.

The months and years ahead were shaped as if by bones, in the shape of a skeleton. I felt this.

In the morning my eyes were dry. After my husband left, I sat at the table and I reached over to touch the dry crumbs on his plate. Toast crumbs. Someone came to the doorway behind me and stood there, watching. The silence was a shout. I needn't look around. After a few minutes I heard him saying something —my son Bobby saying something—so I looked around. The bones in my neck seemed to function oddly. There was a mechanical movement in them. Bobby was saying something in anger, pointing to his shirt. He is eight years old, my only child. Is it my fault that he is slight in the body, small, that he looks out of proportion? Or is it a trick of the eye? I worry about this. But the doctor says his development is normal. I accept this with relief, nodding, a grateful mother. "Yes, he is a good eater, yes . . . " I tell the doctor with gratitude, pulling the words out of another mother's mouth—a woman I heard chattering in the waiting room about her own small, slight, out-of-proportion son. As a child I stole things from drugstores and five-and-tens and the desks of friends, I stole things and became terrified and threw them all away; now I steal words from other people. There is a silence in me that needs filling up. "Yes, a good eater. He even eats vegetables," I always tell the doctor.

"This is ripped. This is rotten," Bobby said angrily.

He flapped his arm to show that the shirt was ripped under his arm

"How did you do that?"

"It's rotten!"

"It isn't rotten, what do you mean? Don't say that!"

I found some things in a closet rotten with damp once, children's clothes that didn't belong to us. It was in a place we rented in Maine. I lifted up the pajamas of a strange child, the pajama bottoms, and for some curious reason pulled at them, experimentally, drawing my hands apart. The material ripped.

Why had this made an impression on my son?

"Don't be silly, your shirt can't be rotten. Come here. Our things aren't rotten." He came to me, staring down at the floor, pretending to be disgusted. His face shows disgust well. I put my arms around him. On Monday mornings he is never ready to go to school. I don't know why: our Sundays are tedious enough. Sometimes I drive out to "get some things" and see my lover, a ten- or fifteen-minute visit, and rushed and desperate I drive home again, and for that period of time Sundays are not tedious for me. For normal people, Sundays are tedious. Bobby leaned heavily against me, then jerked away. This is a habit of his. When he jerks out of my arms—as if having just thought of something urgent—I feel the ghostly pain of a baby jerking in my body, wanting to get away. I feel also this child's small urgent strength.

"I put an orange in your lunch, honey."

He said nothing.

"Are you eating them or throwing them away?"

He shrugged his shoulders.

His head seems large for his body. The back of it looks precarious. His fawnish brown hair is not enough to protect that delicate skull; I am terrified of his perpetual danger. At his school this past year, children have had strange accidents. A girl stuck her head through a small opening and couldn't get it back out— she butted her head through. Another girl was hit in the head by a swing seat, flying backward through the air and catching her right between the eyes. She must have been standing watching it. A boy was kidnaped, or abducted, but was found a few hours later walking around downtown—he couldn't remember much about the men who had picked him up. White men, he said. Unharmed and unworried.

I was in love with a man and could not think about these things. I had to think four hours each day of him, only of him. I was condemned to him. When the telephone rang I did not dare to answer it, for fear that it would be someone else. When the telephone rang I listened to it very carefully but did not answer. The ringing of a telephone is always louder in an empty house.

On that morning Bobby went to school as usual. A few complaints. No tears. I helped him on with a new shirt and the two of us threw the old shirt in a wastebasket, as if this were an important ceremony, a way of beginning the week. He seemed anxious to get rid of it and to make sure it was really thrown out. Yet it wasn't an old shirt—it was older than the shirt he consented to wear, but not an old shirt. Obviously he had ripped it on purpose. Why? I thought about asking him but decided against it; this was as good a way as any of beginning the week.

After he left, I drove out to get away from the house. I feared the telephone. I decided to have my hair cut—a first step. If I were to die, my hair should look right. I was not thinking of the open casket—a beautiful waxen face, peace, etc.—I was thinking of those shocking minutes when I would be found, in a motel room, in a fourth dimension. It was easy to imagine myself dead. I tried to park on the street but my rear right tire kept hitting the curb, bouncing up and falling back down again. My body was jolted. As I hit the curb, slowly, again and again, I kept thinking of the distance between my lover and me; I thought of him out in his house, not eating enough. I thought of bringing him some raw vegetables and watching while he ate. It is not true that my son is a good eater, not as mothers understand good eaters. I sometimes can't remember if he has eaten at all. I take the plates from the table, scrape them off into the garbage dreamily, and without passion, having rid myself of passion earlier that day, I can't distinguish between my husband's plate and my son's plate and my own. The garbage disposal grinds everything up like a good stomach. The food disappears. After I had my hair cut I would go to a farmer's market and buy some raw vegetables.

I like to plan the future down to its most minute parts—finger-nails and toenails.

I parked the car and locked it. I walked to a hairdresser's salon but they wouldn't take me; "There's only one girl in today," they said. I thought this must mean something. I walked down the street and looked into windows, looking for another sign. It was true that one of us had to die: which one? My heart pounded with the urgency of my hatred for our love, our condemnation of love; I was sick of it, I was fed up, I was looking for a sign. . . . In the looking glass of a window I saw myself, a strangely eager woman. My face is a hateful face, too sharp. There is this perpet-ually alert, eager, intense look about it—overlarge eyes, a Semitic look, vaguely hunted. In my early twenties it seemed to me that men were hunting me down, several men, hounding and bully-ing me. One of them was later killed in a plane crash in the Atlantic, the plane dropping mysteriously out of the sky. His body was one of the few recovered, but it was only a body. An-other was the man I did marry, finally.

In a drugstore I leafed through magazines, not buying any-thing. I have the look of a woman who always buys things; peo-ple trust me. My heart began to beat faster, as if I were approach-ing a revelation. To have our lives decided, his and mine, to have everything finished! I looked through a woman's magazine and was fascinated by several full-page, colored photographs of food. I would drive out to that old house and heap food upon my lover, make him eat. Why didn't he eat right? Was his indifference to food a kind of suicide, a way of eluding me? What did he think about when he was alone? He has a small, sweet, still smile . . . he is an indefinite person, hardly defined. For years he has been on the move, packing up and driving across the country in his Volkswagen alone, leaving behind books, magazines, cracked plates, worn-out rotten clothing, wornout friendships. . . . A photograph of broccoli amandine. Melted butter, almonds, lemon

juice. . . . My stomach was an empty sack, useless, but I remembered the uses of other stomachs, grinding up food to pro-
vide life. It was my responsibility to feed several people and keep
them living.

Walking along the street I saw how people, approaching me,
did not remain in focus. My own skin is pale as potatoes cut
swiftly with a knife, that surprised look of potatoes cut in half.
My hair is dark with streaks of red and, lately, streaks of gray.
My face is sharp and smoothly innocent, like the faces of drivers
who run over animals but never know until they feel the impact
that they have hit something; they may even see the animal on
the road, watching them, but nothing is in focus until they feel
with their thighs and buttocks the small shock of an animal being
crushed by a heavy automobile. Once, at my in-laws', Bobby was
playing in the driveway and my father-in-law nearly backed over
him.

My car was parked strangely. The back left tire was turned
out, as if flirting with traffic on the street. I got in and drove
slowly out toward the country. The house my lover is renting is
drafty and ugly, not good for his health. There is no one to take
care of him. My own husband weighs two hundred pounds,
dresses well and warmly, eats well, is loved as a second self is
always loved, without commotion. It is not necessary for me to
look at him often. The two of us are permanently together, no
worry. I feed him, give him warmth at night, pull up the blanket
around his shoulders. He shudders and stumbles in his sleep,
climbing small treacherous slopes. I keep him warm on these
climbs. I don't have to think about it; it is like pulling a blanket
up to keep myself warm. My thinking turns upon the other man.
Each day I must think about him for a number of hours, and
when I am not thinking about him, yet I am still thinking about
him, aware of him, like an actor aware of someone approaching
him onstage and yet not aware, communicating to the audience

this double dimension. My head aches, the nerves in my eyes twitch with this doubleness. The relief of one of us dying will be felt everywhere.

Before falling in love, I was defined. Now I am undefined, weeds are growing between my ribs. The chore of thinking about a man for hours every day is worse than memorizing Bible verses or dates in history. The calendar is always set in his favor: days in a new month already crossed out, blotted out, lost. . . . I stopped at a big modern supermarket, not the small grocery store I had wanted, and bought some vegetables—tomatoes, carrots, spinach. My heart was pounding with the sudden desire to make this man eat. He was too tall, too thin. His ribs showed. When he moved, they showed painfully, as if dancing beneath his skin, but to him it was only a joke, inconsequential bones. I lay on his bed and wept those effortless tears we weep in cold weather. He laughed gently, I wept gently, making the same sounds.

. . . He clutches his head, as if my tears are destroying him. "You have either got to stay here or leave," he says, clutching at his head.

He lived outside town but not in a suburb. Certain areas are zoned for suburban houses and neat colonial-style plazas with dry-cleaning stores and drugstores and small meat markets, all beneath the same white trim, in one long neat Williamsburg row. He lived in an unzoned country, in too much space and too little. There were vacant lots that would not remain vacant. WILL BUILD TO SUIT TENANT, signs said. The highway was cracked and pitted with mysterious holes, as if the land beneath it were surging at night, shrugging its shoulders. There was an airport nearby for small private planes, weedy and nearly deserted. There were hot-dog stands and bowling alleys and taverns out on the highway, all of them third-rate, marked for extinction. There were bungalows strung side by side, crowded strangely, though this was the "country" and the factory workers and mill-workers who lived in them were proud of living in the "country" and not in the "city." Only a few farmhouses remained, big old homes on land that had retreated to one or two acres, their barns knocked down. My lover rented one of these houses. He thought it was attractive. There were cracks in the floor people might whisper through, blowing cold air up my legs. He spent most of his time in the kitchen. The house was not his, he rented it. He never owned anything. He only rented things.

My heart had been pounding dangerously and then it was relieved: yes, his car was in the driveway.

I began to hate him for my own fear of his not being home. I hated fearing him, fearing his absence. *Before I met you I must have been very happy,* I would tell him.

For instance, I worked on a committee to preserve standards in the city's public schools. We argued about the falling tax base and the rising tax assessments, we drank coffee and smoked and argued about the families (white) that were moving out and the familes (Negro) that were moving in, the teachers who were leaving for better jobs, the "unprepared" (Negro) students who were holding classes back, and my face would grow white, deadly white, as I denounced the white, nervous families with money who were moving out, moving out!—constantly, steadily, daily moving out of our city! Bobby went to the neighborhood school where, every year, more little Negro children were showing up, prepared or unprepared, and it did not truly seem to me a matter of great importance whether he learned as much as he should have learned, or whether the school's best teachers were leaving. *I was very happy* on that committee, drinking coffee and smoking cigarettes and arguing violently, lengthily, happily, a mother and a wife and a citizen. . . .

His car was home, he was home. I knocked at his back door. He came to open it, pushing his chair back from the kitchen table, blundering toward me, already smiling.

We embraced nervously. We kissed.

"How long can you stay?" he said, surprised.

He smelled of mildewy, damp, rotted mornings, a gentle odor. His face had a faint Slavic broadness and innocence to it, eyes without much color, hair dark brown and very thick. He was working on a book. He had been given a grant to write a book and to use the excellent library of an excellent university forty miles away. His book was going to explain the theory of space-time relativity in nineteenth-century poetry, with an emphasis on Shelley, I think . . . I never listened when he explained it to me. Though the real future had no shape to him, though he never planned his life, each day to him had a shape tight and dry as the skeleton of a small animal, small enough to hold in the palm of one's hand.

I began to weep dry tears. He comforted me. I stood in his arms for a while and then jerked away, jerking out of his arms. "Is he still here?" I whispered.

He tried to smile. I had sensed this guilt, that was why I had jerked out of his arms.

"Didn't you tell him to leave . . . ?"

"I did."

"But he's still here? Where is he?"

"Upstairs, sleeping. He's sick, how can I kick him out if he's sick?"

A friend from the East, bumming his way to California, had been in this house for four days. Currents of electricity were jerking through me. My eyes twitched.

"Don't cry, please, you look so upset," he said.

I pushed him away.

I had been thinking of his death, but now, to punish him, I saw that I was the one who would have to die. Then he could never look in the mirror at himself and say those words he said after we made love, *I am perfected.*

"Let's drive out somewhere," he said. "Can we go to your house?"

"No."

"Can we go somewhere? For a drive?"

I went to the table where his books and papers were. He wrote in a small, neat hand, an accountant's handwriting. This always seemed to me his true self.

His "true self" popped up at me from the dust jackets of his books, snapshots of a younger, more serious man, a "promising" young man. His "true self" flashed to me one evening in New York when a cousin of his said to me, of him: "We always loved each other. We're the same age. But there was this emptiness in him that was a sin—he got filled up with anyone who came along. People filled him up. Then he left them, frightened, and then he met someone else and was filled up again, like gas. He was always being inhabited by the spirit of someone else, so that when I met him I could tell, in the first five minutes, what kind of person it was now—hopeful or hopeless." This man, the same age as my lover, was Slavic in the face and his hair was thinner; therefore his skull more vulnerable. A married man, separated. My lover had never married and therefore could never be separated from other loves.

They wrote to him, they telephoned him, they showed up in his rented rooms and flats and houses. They begged to stay with him and, out of kindness and cowardice, he sometimes consented. "She slept beside me for the night," he would tell me, tears in his eyes, "she slept on the outside of the covers, like a child . . . in the morning we wept together and she left." He told me everything.

I had wanted him to die when he told me that. Now I'm not so sure.

I snatched up his schedule for the day; it embarrassed him when I looked through his things. Every day he rose at six in the morning, believe it or not, he rose and wound his watch, came downstairs, made coffee, and wrote out his schedule for the day. Then he followed it, every detail.

"*Turner*—what's that?" I said.

"A book I need. I'm going to drive to the library."

"When?"

"I thought around noon."

My heart pounded viciously.

"What if I had come to see you . . . ?"

"I was going to call you first. . . ."

"What if I hadn't been home, what if I had been on my way out here, all the way out here?"

"I was going to wait . . . you don't usually come after noon. . . ."

We stared at each other. It was plain that we were not in love.

"I'd better leave."

"What?"

He had not shaved that morning, which meant that truly he had not expected me. On Friday we had spent several hours together, strolling around the art center. I delighted in wasting his time, wrenching his perfect schedule out of shape. I always waited for him to say, "But I can't take the whole afternoon off. . . ." He never said it. Yet I felt that he wanted to say it. On Friday I had said I couldn't meet him for several days, he had had a headache, we went to a Cunningham's Drugstore and sat at the counter, he took several aspirin. A curiosity was stirred in me: I could make a man sick.

"Do you feel better? You didn't feel well on Friday."

"On Friday?"

"Did the headache go away?"

"I guess it went away."

He took my hands and stared at me. *This is nothing,* I wanted to say contemptuously, *my husband holds my hands also!* He was almost forty years old but looked twenty-five; there was a sham innocence about him. I wondered if he would age after my death. Would his fingernails and toenails continue to grow? Dead, I would be unavailable to him. Parting of the ways. My husband, my family, my in-laws, my friends would take care of me. Not him. On the morning of the funeral he would rise at six, wind his watch, make coffee, write out his schedule for the day. . . .

"I'd like to get out of here. I need to talk to you," he said.

"I should be leaving. . . ."

"Why are you angry?"

"I'm not angry."

"You look upset."

We stood staring past each other. There was a kind of glow about us, not of love. I said finally, "I want to die."

He glanced down at his worktable, as if death might be a notation on a piece of paper, something I had read and stolen from him. His hands moved oddly, one of them rising as if to cover his face, the other tapping at his chest. Silence. I was always stealing jokes and small references from him; I played back to him his special loves, as if feeding him. (He had a complex jazzy vocabu lary of slang and allusions based on popular music and left-wing corny slogans, farmers' and workers' movements certain liberals pretend to cherish, decades out of date. And there was a slightly gangsterish, adolescent flair to him, born of Saturday matinees when he was a skinny underfed kid in New York.) Alone, when I remembered these jokes, I could never remember that they were meant to be funny. It sickened me to think that I was playing a role with this man when he was not worth it.

"There is something empty in you—there's nothing in you," I said bitterly. "I can't fill it up. Let someone else fill it up. What's inside you . . . what's empty inside you . . . you yourself—" I stammered, out of breath. I could not look at him. He was wearing a familiar dark-green shirt buttoned all the way up to his neck, with the collar turned up, which meant that he imagined he was catching a sore throat. The shirt was not tucked in his pants. I hated that look, it reminded me of Bobby and his friends.

"Please, please . . ." he said.

I closed my fist and hit the table.

"Why is he still upstairs?" I whispered.

He made a gesture that showed pain.

He sat shakily on the edge of the table and drew me to him. He stroked my hair. "Don't cry, don't make both of us cry, don't be so evil . . ." he said in a murmur. I suspect him of being a father: there is always a lullaby in his voice, eager to show itself. His talent is for putting people to sleep. When we sleep together, really sleep, he draws the covers up over my bare shoulders lovingly, but with a father's love. I understand then that this is the way he has drawn up covers over other people's shoulders, just so, like this, with the same love. . . . He is not a defined human being.

I drew back to look at him. His face was not quite made up, like a mind not made up. Something was held back, guarded. He might have thought I would close my fist and strike him.

If, in love, your lover puts up with evil from you, then you are loved. You must always test him. "If one of us died, really died . . . ?" I whispered. He nodded. "You've thought of it?" I said. He nodded again. His eyes were colorless. I felt the impact of my words sink in them, neutralizing them, making them colorless. I wanted suddenly, thirstily, to drain the blood out of this man and be finished with him; then I could drive back home.

"Walk with me. Let me walk you out of it," he said.

He put his arm around me and walked me into the other room, as if walking a sick woman. A woman who has taken too many pills, to call attention to her pettiness.

"I feel sick all the time. I can't work," he said. "You don't want to stay here with me and you don't want to go for a drive, you won't let me come to your house any longer. . . . On Friday you kept looking around as if you were expecting someone better to show up. Why did you do that?"

"Did I do that?" I said, alarmed.

"Why can't we go to your house?"

I hated him for one thing, mainly: his failure to admire my house. He must have noticed the good furniture, the curtains, the gold and silver and white, the heavy shaggy black rugs, but he said nothing.

"I'll go away," I said.

"What will that solve?"

If he were dead, the telephone would ring with a different sound. I would always hurry to it, ready for an adventure. Walking in the park, I would answer the greeting of a strange man, I would take his extended hand, I would follow him into the bushes, into the trees!—I would be generous to everyone!

"I have to pick up Bobby from school this afternoon . . . he has to go from school right to the doctor. . . ."

This sentence began as a lie but ended as the truth. Bobby did have a doctor's appointment that day.

"But so what? That's this afternoon, that's hours from now."

"I don't want to be upset when I get him."

"Do I make you upset?"

"If one of us died, if we could decide something . . ." I said with a smile.

"Do you want me to die?"

Holding my husband in my arms at night, I shed tears for the man I was not holding; I held the one man tighter, to imagine the other.

My mother had said wisely, "After you're married, you'll discover that the best thing is to take care of your children and have parties. Do things for people, feed them and talk to them and keep them warm. Forget about the rest of it." She meant love, forget about love, she was bullying me out of my anguish at the thought of marriage. It was time for me to marry; she had talked to me about what I should think about and what I should forget.

"I'll see you in a day or two," I said wildly. I felt that I had to get away from him.

"But if you have until this afternoon . . . ?"

"The appointment is for earlier. I have to pick him up earlier."

"That's a lie."

We walked back into the kitchen. The stove was large and blackened, ugly as a locomotive engine. It was nearly that size. The table was a workbench, littered with papers and books. For a few minutes we stood together, holding hands, in silence. We could think of nothing to say. Then my words slid uglily back onto something familiar: "These people hanging on you . . . I hate you for letting them . . . you are so empty inside, there's nothing there. . . . They're ruining you!"

He walked me to the door. We looked out at the foundation of a barn, what was left of a barn. On the far side of "his" pasture was a gas station, an unprospering place. I bought gas there sometimes, as if patronizing local businesses would show my lover that I was interested in him, in the welfare of his community.

He leaned his forehead against the cracked glass of the door.

"They crawl in bed with you. They eat your food. They clip stories out of newspapers and mail them to you. All the spit that dribbles out of their ugly mouths! Don't you know they hate you? They want you to fail, like them, they want you to get burned up in a fire from them smoking in bed. . . ." I began to cry again.

"Randolph doesn't smoke," he muttered.

Love is testing. You prick him with a small needle. You reach behind his eyes with your fingernails and give a tug to the optic nerve. You accuse his friends of wanting him to die when you are the only friend he has and you are the only person who wants him to die: the others want to borrow money from him.

Suddenly everything changes and I think, *Why, I have brought myself to this man, why am I crying? I have brought my body and my love to him, why is he pressing his forehead against the door?*

"Look, please. I love you." I touched his arm.

He seemed to be staring down from a dangerous summit. He did not trust me.

"I love you. Don't hate me." I brought his hand to my lips and kissed it. Pleased, he stared at me. A dizziness rose in us like the sun. Evidently we were in love.

"I brought you something in the car. You don't eat right," I said.

"Did you bring me something?" he said eagerly.

There was a dazed, futile look to him. We went out. He took the bag of vegetables out of the car, very pleased. It startled me to see how his face glowed.

"What is all this? Carrots? Spinach?"

"You don't eat right," I said shyly.

"Thank you, it's so kind of you . . . you are so wonderful. . . ."

He stared into the bag.

We are exposed, being outside. Anyone could see us.

When we went back inside, he set the vegetables down carefully. "You won't throw them away?" I said, teasing. "You'll eat them?"

"Oh, yes. Yes. I'm hungry right now."

We each ate a tomato. I fell in love with him, eating a tomato with him. My tongue prodded the flesh of the tomato; the seeds of tomatoes are very soft, a little slimy. They are more like human seeds than they are like the hard little pits of other fruits.

"I love you, I love you like this," he said. His face glowed. He was not a handsome man, but his face glowed with innocence and excitement, behind his skin, warming it. If he died, what remained of him would be misleading: those photographs on his books, his cousin's remarks.

I loved him with a strength that rose in my blood, in silence. He was a man of beauty. I licked the tomato juice from my fingers.

Upstairs someone was walking around.

"These people are hell to me, yes," my lover said, rolling his eyes skyward.

A confession.

"Why do you let them stay with you, then? Darling . . . ?"
He shrugged his shoulders.

"Too much love . . . you love too much . . . you're going
to wear out and die," I said, teasing. I loved him and I wanted to
slide my hand inside his buttoned-up shirt, slide my hand between his ribs, take in my fingers his wonderful pulsating heart!

"I'll get rid of him today," he said.

In his face was a glow for me, his love for me. I had wrenched
him from his schedule. If I wanted, I could go to his table and
turn it over, knock everything onto the floor. I had knocked some
books down once, wounding him with my hatred. I had done it
once, successfully, and had no interest in doing it again.

Randolph came downstairs noisily.

A short, rodentlike man, nervous, with a beard. A look of stale-
ness and sweetness. Very helpless. He always looked as if someone had released him from a machine of torture just minutes before. Gratitude for being released, but memory of pain . . . his
face was pale and ravaged and curious, like a rat's face. In the
distance there was the sound of jets. His eyelids fluttered, the
sound must have frightened him.

He said, "I'm going out for a walk."

We did not reply. He buttoned his shirt all the way up to his
chin and went out, as if to face danger.

"Tonight I'll tell him to leave. I will," my lover said.

It was a vow.

We went upstairs. There were three bedrooms in this old
house. The biggest one was my lover's, with a bed whose covers
were neatly pulled back, and some suitcases that had not yet been
totally unpacked, on the floor. The wallpaper was peeling. It
looked as if it were weeping. We sank against each other as if
trying to push past each other, speaking past each other. In the
distance was the sound of jets, growing louder and fainter. I
heard the voices of my family chattering at me, scolding me,
Why have you gone so far from us? my mother said indifferently,

Is your need for love really so great? I felt that she was relinquishing me, glad to be rid of me.

A woman spends time before mirrors, content to imagine herself always in a mirror, somewhere, her truest self, while her body walks around in the world. It is the mirror self that certain men love, and that loves them; the other self is busy scraping garbage off plates and emptying the drier of great hot coiled heaps of sheets and towels and underwear and socks. It is the mirror self that loves without exhaustion, loves with passion and violence, with tears; the other self puts the stained sheets in the washing machine and turns the dial.

I breathed from my stomach, from the muscles there. My breathing was painful. Pain shot up through my loins.

He cried out, "Oh, did I hurt you . . . ?"

I said no,

He lay in my arms. His back was wet. His hair was wet. I could not move under his weight.

I closed my eyes and I was in my first bedroom again, sick or pretending to be sick. A heavy weight lay upon me. It was not a man but a quilt. I wanted to kick it off, sweating under it. I hate weights on me. You must always think about a weight when it is on you; you are not free to think about other things.

"Do you love me?" he said.

He raised his head to stare anxiously at me. His eyes were dim with small despairing veins. The irises were a very faint blue, a very faint gray.

I kissed him. His weight turned into panic.

"Then don't answer," he said.

We were safe here, in his room. No one could spy on us. From the sky, this house was a weatherbeaten old wreck, not worth bombing.

I closed my eyes and saw small explosions of light. They reminded me of bees. I had seen bees in a line once, flying in a line. Like a whip. Since falling in love I had headaches, my eyes ached, my throat ached with the need to cry perpetually, my loins ached from the love of two men, I was the beloved of two healthy men. The bees were always present inside my eyes. I imagined them whipping across my body, stinging lightly and at random, giving off sparks.

When I was gone from him, my lover doodled pictures of me, heads and shoulders. He thinks I am beautiful and he loves me, therefore I lie with my arms aching beneath him, my belly slick with sweat. His pictures of me are not of me, but they show his love. I keep them in one of my bureau drawers where they will be found one day by my husband.

"Come see me tomorrow? Please?"

"You'll be alone here?"

"Yes. Oh, yes."

When I left I was very happy. I drove down the highway and passed Randolph, rushing past, no time even to flash him a sign of victory.

Nothing has been decided, I thought. Why was I happy?

It was two-thirty already. I hadn't eaten. I felt sick.

I drove around until quarter to three, then I drove to Bobby's school. My happiness made me dizzy. I couldn't handle the car right. I felt shame in taking my son to the doctor: he was too slight in the chest! Why did the doctor lie and say that he was normal? Waiting at the curb, I tried to get my happiness out of my face, to keep my mouth still. My mouth kept wanting to smile a slick small smile, an evil smile. This is the smile of adultery. I pulled at my lips and my fingers came away stained with lipstick.

When Bobby and the other children piled out the door, I made a show of waving for him. He caught sight of me at once and hurried my way, as if to quiet me. He was carrying a book and a large piece of paper, taped to cardboard.

"Oh, what's that, honey?" I said. My voice was too loud. Its joviality must have startled my son. "Did you draw that by your-self?"

A picture of a jet airplane.

"Are you hungry? Did you eat all of your lunch?"

He stared at me.

"What's wrong?" I said. "You're not afraid of the doc-tor . . . ?"

"No."

"Are you all right? Honey?"

He looked away. There was something in my face that fright-ened him.

I drove. Bobby began to kick at the floorboard. I chattered toward him, reaching out with one hand to touch his hair. He glanced sideways at me.

"You been crying?" he said finally.

"What? Crying? Of course not."

A strange tension rose in the car. The air between us grew hot. The men in my life are innocent and I am guilty, because they love me and I am loved by them. Beloved of too many men, I have given my body to too many men, my body is rebelling and wants to die. Bobby was leaning against the car door as if sick-ened by the odor of my body. *He can smell that other man,* a voice told me wisely.

"Sit up!" I said. "Sit still! Stop that kicking!"

"You shut up!" he shouted.

Years ago he had tried, experimentally, to tell me to shut up. It had passed.

I said nothing.

"You shut up," he whispered.

We looked at each other. In his face there was a glow of terror. He could not understand his words.

At forty miles an hour, driving this heavy car, I leaned and slapped his face. I felt his head strike the window.

He began to shout. He kicked. He writhed on the seat, throwing himself around. With my right hand I tried to keep him still, snatching at anything that was my property to snatch at—his hair, the collar of his jacket—I could see that his eyes were closed and his mouth opening and shutting tightly, opening into a high-pitched, furious wail, shutting tightly as if to bite the wail off.

"Stop it! You're crazy!" I cried.

He threw himself forward suddenly and banged his head against the windshield. He banged it again as if trying to butt through it. I pulled him back against the seat, yanking him back by his collar. We shouted toward each other. We were shouting past each other. He jerked away and snatched at the car door, which was locked, and turned to unlock it, pulling up the little safety knob—so fastidious in his desire to die!—and then he opened the car door while I screamed and tore at his jacket, but his strength was greater than mine. He threw himself out of the car.

My car skidded sideways. Something slammed into the front of it. It was like an amusement ride: I was thrown up, thrown sideways. I crawled across the seat, dripping blood, and thought of how heavy and still everything had become—the car itself, the dense air in the car, the sounding of someone's stuck horn right outside my head. . . . I had a few slow seconds before I would crawl out and stagger to my feet, dripping blood, and look back to see what had happened to my son.

An *Interior Monologue*

I am fascinated with that woman. I am a chemist and fascination comes hard with me. I am thirty-one years old, I live alone, my hours are spent concentrating on the cool reality of beakers and statistics, plastics of various types, the icy fuzz of sweat on tubes, the low mysterious hum of machines. Sitting at my workbench, I sometimes glance down at my fingertips, imagining a fine fuzz of ice on them. There is no ice. My fingers are long and lean. I have the idea that they are artistic-looking, though I am not an artist. If I were, I would do something with this laboratory, paint a picture of it, the way it looks at six o'clock in the evening, at quarter after six—glass, enamel, rubber tubes, stoppers, the terrible, powerful pull of vibrations from cooling machines, the terrible power of shadows moving slowly over everything, over me, running right down to my fingertips.

THE MEETING

She and X met in a library. They talk about that meeting often. Out with X in a bar once—where I had only a Coke, since I don't drink—he talked about it in a kind of drunken frenzy, giving me details. "Don't stop, tell me everything!" I wanted to cry out to him. X is a gentle, dark-browed young man, about my age. I say about my age: he is really twenty-eight. His hair falls down onto his forehead when he gets excited.

The essential factor that changed our lives, the lives of all three of us, was that meeting.

She sat at a table, her books sprawled out around her. I can picture that. She is sloppy, self-conscious and a little vain about it—she can get away with being sloppy, other girls can't. All right. She seats herself at the table. She is wearing something light, a cotton dress maybe (they don't give me enough details and I must fill in my own) and her charm bracelet, jingling with silver charms. She takes out her reading glasses and fools around with them, holding them up to the light. Very smudged. Her hair is the color of honey, that vain girl. I hate her hair, her white silly teeth, her nitwit's forehead with its flecks of bangs, all so wearily pretty. . . . Still, she is sitting there. I have to prod myself to keep this vision going. She is sitting there, sitting there, sitting there . . . and X comes in, a stranger, sits across from her, his eyes raw from reading, staying up all night, wasting his young life in bars around the University that are dark at eleven o'clock in the morning. He sits down. He lets his books fall beside him. Aching, his eyes ache, his shoulders ache, his very brain aches with precocious weariness, a young man twenty-three years old and already a few years too old for his classmates, feeding upon sophisticated crap in Philosophy 1A with a hunger they don't share. He notices the girl across from him. He can see right through her, through her head, to the periodical shelf behind her, where magazines from *Review of English Studies* to *Studies in Existential Psychology* are displayed.

Not suave, X, but brilliant and plodding; not glamorous, the young woman, but of a full, essential body and a teasing but kindly smile. They meet. They fall in love. They marry.

A TENNIS MATCH

She is not athletic, even with her frame, and is bored by tennis. X and I play tennis on Sunday mornings, in place of church. He was once a very devout Catholic and, falling away from it, saw the world turn to water, saw gnats swimming through it, lay awake weeping at night with his teeth chattering so that he had to bite the pillowcase to keep all this anguish secret from his family. When I broke away it was easier. I don't think I am less deep than X, but still it affected me less; a few ripples, nothing more. We play tennis on Sunday mornings, in place of church. I like the aggressive swing of an overhand serve, I like the spots of perspiration on my shirt, I like a certain cool freshness to the air, even if this is Detroit's Palmer Park and the junk from last week's picnics lies everywhere. Don't look. Why look? X and I play tennis, calling out our scores. *She* sometimes comes along, carrying the baby. She reads magazines, sitting at a bench, her legs crossed. She wears cotton slacks. She sometimes has her hair brushed back, indifferent, sloppy, a twenty-five-year-old dowdy housewife. No matter: a few strokes of cheap make-up and her cheeks glow again, a few swipes of lipstick and there she is, Miss America, Miss Class of '65, sharp and quick and bright and given to flirting sloppily with me, so casual as to insult me, what does she care? "Here, my love, let me fix your collar behind. This little button—it's broken in half—isn't through the buttonhole." And, while I perspire, standing very straight and forcing myself to think of test tubes, beakers, the cool clean perspiration of metal, she nonchalantly buttons that little button.

NONCHALANTLY

She drives me to use that word! I never use it myself. It isn't one of my words. Nothing is nonchalant with me. I received my Ph. D. degree in chemistry at the University of Michigan, 1964. Back in high school I was considered something of a genius—my chemistry teacher gave me a year's subscription to *Scientific American*. I dress casually but neatly, I try for a quiet, correct, uneventful look; I don't want to stick in anyone's eye.

I'M STILL HERE . . .

She is always there, always there! At the back of my mind, lounging. She was already a woman at the age of twelve, obviously. Knowing everything! Knowing everything at the age of eleven, at ten! Her honey-clear eyes, her curly hair, her sweet stupid smile . . . a little queen of the playground, taunting the boys. Oh, would I like to jet back in time to see her ascend the playground slide, pausing at the top with her queenly intolerant look, and setting herself down like a precious substance, precocious woman, and giving herself a push downward . . . . To rise up from under that slide, leering, an eagle of revenge, to grab hold of her legs at that halfway hump and pull her off! Or, instead, better yet, instead to tip the slide over—a giant heavy rusty thing, falling very slowly, falling on top of her. So much for that.

I'm still here. . . . Yes, I hear her cooing in my mind as I lie awake desperately thinking of ways to mend my life. *Her* life needs no mending. The other night when they had me over to dinner, a spaghetti supper, she said, right in front of X, "Out in California the divorce rate has finally caught up with the marriage rate. I was thinking about divorce, theoretically. I was thinking about how it would shake everything loose, make us see ourselves plainly and terribly. . . ." But she is only toying, only toying with X. She will never divorce him. He will never divorce her.

Or are they both toying with me?

I see her sideways grin, at me. She seems to wink. But she says only, innocently, "Alan, have some more more salad. I made this dressing especially for you."

LANDSCAPE OF NEUTRAL COLORS

She and I are in the supermarket, met by accident. She wears white shorts, the baby is fixed somehow in the shopping cart, pudgy legs stuck through the wire basket. Slight signs of fatigue under her eyes. Freckles on her upper arms, probably on her shoulders and back. Not many on her face: powdered over? There is fine, very fine fuzz on her upper lip, hardly worth mentioning. The small muscles of her arms and legs terrify me.

"Yes, I saw that Bergman movie, I hated it," she says.

"Why? Does madness frighten you?"

"Madness like that, on the screen, is terrible because . . . because you can't get away from it, even if you shut your eyes the sound is still there, and the feeling of madness . . . . It isn't like reading a book, you can close the book up. No. I hated it."

"Is it something personal, do you think?"

"Maybe."

"You could have walked out of the theater."

"I never walk out of theaters—not after I've paid to get in!"

"Did Bob like it?"

"Oh, you know Bob—" with a slight pleased shrug, of course *I don't really know Bob*—"He'll sit through anything. He sits through old late movies on television, James Cagney and Ginger Rogers, all that old crap—he's a very sentimental person."

"But why are you afraid of madness?" I say, pushing my cart along nimbly as I push the conversation back to this topic, feeling myself very much in control and very clever. "Isn't that a certain weakness in you? Shouldn't people want to experience as much as they can?"

"Oh hell."

"Should we turn our backs on any kind of experience?"

Too contemptuous to reply, she flashes me her cool schoolgirl's sideways smile, a smile that could suck my front teeth out, so venomous and delicious and unknowing! I'd like to buy her a balloon, a great pink and white striped balloon, I'd like to dress her up in the long, puffed-out dresses women wore in the paintings of Monet and Manet and Renoir, I'd like to paint very carefully over her cheeks, pinkening them, darkening the blue of her eyes, outlining her stubborn little eyebrows, giving her the glamor of a real woman—someone ageless, ancient, worthy of a man's death. I'd like to—no—make the balloon a giant balloon, put a little wicker carrier beneath it for her to step into, carrying a picnic basket, all blues and pinks and yellows, her pale handsome arms exposed but her legs all covered up modestly—her long brown hair done up in a comely bun, a little frayed, prettily frayed—oh, let her set that sure-footed self into a wicker carrier and I will untie the rope, I'll cut the rope with a giant scissors, and let balloon, carrier, and woman float up into the painted blue sky!

Out in the parking lot, helping her with her grocieries—I as dutiful a husband as X, and as casually thanked—I notice that the pavement is gray, the sidewalk gray, the sky gray, my trousers gray, my hands gray, graying. When I get back to my three-room apartment, in an expensive building with a canopy, overlooking the river, with a doorman, but still only three rooms, I run to the bathroom and look at myself, wanting to weep, yes, for my graying fair hair.

How can I live my life without committing an act with a giant scissors?

CONJUGAL LOVE

There they are, it's after midnight. They sit in their sleazy little living room. X is pursuing his Ph.D. in English but having a slow, dull time of it, his eyes sore again; *she* is dawdling her life away in yawns and complaints, with a shrewd eye for her girl friends' houses in the suburbs, very jealous, with great slovenly strides walking all over his body, grinding her heel in his soft lungs, giving him a wink. It makes me laugh, this marriage! Marriage! My head aches suddenly, after midnight, and I get out of bed to take an aspirin, and suddenly, very clearly, I can see those six miles across town to *their* little living room, where they sit, a mess of crackers on the sofa between them, crumbs and bits of cheese, X getting a little fat with the relief of *her* pulling through the pregnancy, *she* getting sharp-eyed and restless with his thinning hair. Oh, she knows too much! She reads *Cosmopolitan* and the lead article is "How To Get Your Second—Third—Fourth Husbands!" and, frowning, severe, she skims through the article to *find out* where life is being lived, what the details of a remote, secret life must be. Shouldn't I buy her that balloon, really? And set her majestically free up into the sky?

The other evening I dropped in on them, after going to a movie alone, and she scurried around to straighten things up— not knowing how much I wanted to see the mess they lived in ordinarily, being hungry for what they live in *ordinarily*—and I suddenly wanted to embrace her hips, in those unclean unpressed cotton slacks, I wanted to cry out to her, *Have mercy on me!* But instead I talked X into playing a game of chess. *She* hates chess; women hate chess. X is good-natured and likes to waste time, he can be talked into nearly anything, so he is talked into a long, subtle game, dragging on past one o'clock—oh, my good luck!—and she yawns and complains about the baby, what a bother, and finally goes off to the bedroom, walking heavily. I can hear her in there, in the other room. And in the bathroom. A fine icy fuzz seems to form at the tips of my fingers and around my nostrils as I listen to her, listening deeply, sighing with the effort of such listening, imagining her opening the medicine cabinet door—the mirror swinging back, framing her high-colored, bored, puffy face and then losing it—her reaching for a pair of eyebrow tweezers, maybe, or a big jar of cold cream. No: she wouldn't. She'd throw off her clothes and fall into bed, a lazy weight, she'd sleep at once and forget about us. Here we sit out in the living room, bent over a coffee table, worrying about tiny pieces of red and black plastic—the game of chess! X's hair is getting a little thin, yes. He has a grateful, ironic look, a very sensitive young man but coarsening with married life, slack around the middle. I imagine him loitering around a railroad yard as a teen-ager, seeing what he could see. I imagine him with a group of other boys, fooling around at a beach, at an amusement park, with hard, stony faces pursuing girls, united in their pursuit. I imagine him at the back of his classroom, trying to keep awake tomorrow morning, reworking this chess game in his mind, and perhaps evoking me, my several remarks of despair, which seemed to trouble him—

"I wish you wouldn't talk like that," he said to me seriously. He looked at me. "You know you're not going to kill yourself, so why talk about it?"

"I know. I'm sorry."

"You've got everything to live for—a good job, freedom, everything you want—you can go on vacations whenever you want,

you can do anything—" But here he began to falter, casting his
mind about: what do I do with my life? What do I, his best
friend, do in my lonely life?

So, to help him out, I say quickly, "I know it, I'm sorry. I
must sound very self-pitying."

"No, but it's just a surprise. . . . Don't ever talk like that
around *her*," he said, giving an abrupt jerk of his head to indicate
her, sleeping soundly in that double bed. "She wouldn't understand. She's so, you know, so healthy and impatient . . . she
gets mad when I'm sick, even. God! She's really something!"
And grimly, fondly, he began to think about her and stopped
thinking about me, about my desire to die, oh how real, how
deep is my desire to die! and so the game continued.

They sit in their little living room, night after night. They go
into their little bedroom. Everything is crowded in there—furniture piled together—I saw the room once, helping them move in.
I was pleased that they asked me to help them. Afterward we all
went out for a pizza; they bought mine for me. No baby then. I
think she was pregnant, though—how else to explain certain
small jokes and smirks between the two of them? She wore yellow, a yellow sweater. She takes off the sweater in that little bedroom. Their closet must be a mess, with *her* sharing it. X is very
neat, like me. Essentially he is neat. He complained once about
her clothes crowding his out, wrinkling his. He had lived alone
for years. I have lived alone for years, since I left my parents'
house. I wake up at a quarter to one, with a headache. I take an
aspirin, a simple and innocent act. And suddenly I see them—I
imagine them—lying in an embrace, the sheet carelessly over
them, X up on one elbow and joking with her and her joking
back, nothing is serious or sacred between them, they are in love,
in love, in love; I am six miles away suddenly nauseated, living
alone.

Fire, flood, earthquake, all the classic types of sorrow—molten

lava flowing from faucets—the earth itself turned to a giant grid-
dle—a blast furnace of cities burning, enough to melt the painted
rubber of high-sailing balloons—

How am I to be good? How am I to be saved?

I AM NOT THINKING . . .

I am not thinking of her mouth, his mouth. I am not thinking
of their child growing into a human being of its own. I am sitting
in the park, Palmer Park. Shouts from kids nearby playing
shuffleboard . . . slamming the things around, lyric with violence. A man with a sharp stick wanders by picking up papers. A
sharp stick! Picking up papers! I want to say to him, "Why are
you looking at me, you old fool?" But he is not looking at me. I
want to say to him, "You think I'm strange or something, sitting
here?—what do you plan on doing, reporting me? Just who am I
harming here? Isn't this a public park?"

I am not thinking of the cancerous cells that may be in her
womb, her elastic womb. I am not thinking of the skid her car
went into—a whole evening she dramatized it for me, almost
frightening me, while X shook his head with a small strained
smile and had to think, *had to think,* of how close she had come
to dying and leaving him alone. "You should drive more carefully," I told her. I know how she drives: I was with her once
and she nearly ran into a boy on a bicycle. Talking all the time,
fooling around with her hair. No wonder she almost had an accident. No, I am not thinking of her mangled in a car wreck, her
body is too lithe in spite of its disorder for a fate like that. I am
not thinking of the rather prominent veins of her throat. I am
thinking instead . . . of smooth, taffy-colored sandbanks, untouched by human footprints, unsoiled, virginal and lovely,
molded by the wind into flowing tides, blending into the dusty
sky; I am thinking of slow, silent caravans of camels crossing the

sands, with men on them dressed in glaring, absolute white, swaying on the humps of those ugly sleeping beasts, the men's faces veiled, their eyes dark and their brows dark, seeing everything. I am thinking of delicate drops of music, like drops of water. Falling precisely onto my forehead. A drop of crystal reflecting the sand, and each grain of sand pregnant with camels, men in white, swaying veils, the terrible brute power of hidden limbs and trunks and the muscles of both men and camels, blended. . . .

Night comes to the desert all at once, as if someone turned off a light. We are alone. We sleep peacefully.

A STAIRWAY TO THE GALLOWS

In a junk store, an antique store, is a small staircase, four steps high. "A stairway taken from an authentic gallows," says the dealer, a small unconvincing man with a sour line of a mouth. It doesn't look as if *I* would buy such junk! But I linger by it, running my fingers on it, almost hoping for a splinter, thinking, *Yet men have probably walked on these steps who are now dead.* . . .

Later that night I drop in on them. Something in the air, tension? A quarrel? She sits on the sofa, the child is shredding a doll, X is in the alcove of a dining room, at the table, trying to study. They are strangely quiet tonight. I lean over X's shoulder, sympathetic but ironic; he is reading Chaucer. "What of Chaucer's are you reading?" I ask him. He says, "Oh, nothing, it wouldn't interest you," and closes the book. This is a little surprising; but he seems to mean nothing by it. We go into the kitchen. He gets a can of beer for himself and some soda pop for me. Ice falling into the glasses from his fingers. Their ice tray is always a mess. I clean it out for them, put fresh water in it, stick it back in the freezer. Their freezer is always a mess. This gives me time to glance around the kitchen—yes, supper dishes in the sink, a smear of something red on one plate, probably they had nothing better than spaghetti, a frequent dish for them.

Out in the living room we sit and make conversation. *She* is long-legged and sullen. X looks tired. "Is something wrong?" I ask them finally. I am very nervous. "Well, the genius here flunked his German exam today," she says. Bitter and triumphant. I turn to X, flushed with relief, wanting to comfort him. But his face is turned off; no comfort wanted; he sucks at his beer. "Oh, go to hell," he says to her. "I thought you were the genius in this family."

We sit in silence. The little girl frets, has to be taken to bed. X asks me about new records I've bought, pretending interest. I have several thousand records in my apartment, all catalogued and cross-catalogued. I tell him about a new string quartet by a composer he has never heard of. All the time I am aware of *her* padding around in the other room. Finally she comes out, seems to burst upon us, buttoning her coat.

"Walk me to the drugstore, Alan. I've got to get a prescription filled."

I stand at once, such is her power. I follow her out, trying to indicate to X that she has called me, I can't help but obey; she seems to be choosing me over him, to insult him for having failed a foolish German exam; where is love in all this, love, love, love? what does marriage mean?—but he fails to catch my look. She and I go outside. It is November, fairly cold. She walks fast. She says, panting in the cold air, "Why don't you get married yourself? What are you waiting for?"

I am embarrassed. "So many people ask me that. . . ."

"All right, what are you waiting for?"

"A perfect love, I suppose." I smile ironically, to show that this is a joke. She is too grim, too vain to catch the smile.

"Remember that time you and I talked for so long?" she says.

Yes, I remember. We talked for hours. I had dropped in late in the afternoon while X was at his Milton seminar, drowsing through that seminar, and we talked seriously, with a very youthful, naive honesty, about the meaning of life without God. She had said that it lay in human love, in marriage. I had said that each person must find his own meaning. The dialogue, the duet, had stretched out for hours; we had tugged back and forth, this exquisite, powerful, venomous woman, a married woman, the wife of my friend X, and I, rather thin-armed in my sports shirt and no match for her, no match. A few days later I gave her a paperback book, *Psychoanalytic Explorations in Art*; it must have been related to our discussion. She never mentioned it afterward, must not have read it. I would have thought she had forgotten about that talk.

"My life, my life with Bob, is very complicated and very strange," she said. "I think I'm going to have another baby. But I don't think it's his . . . isn't that funny? You know us both, you're our closest friend and practically our only friend, you know that we both love you, sort of . . . I mean we really do love you. . . . But my life is in pieces that haven't fallen apart yet and what's so strange is that I'm very happy, and Bob is happy too, though I'm sure that he knows . . . everything. I wanted to tell you this. I don't know why."

Stunned, I am stunned. Frightened. At the drugstore I turn away from her—but she is turning away from me. She dabs at her eyes. She has been crying, this woman! While she goes to the prescription counter, I try to get control of myself. My heart is frightened, in a mild shock; why has she such power over me? I imagine her and X entwined in bed, their bodies entwined, and her soft pink tongue prodding his ear, telling him about the mysterious caresses of her womb, breaking him down and turning him golden again, my friend X, short broken veins in the whites of his eyes. And I imagine her lazily unbuttoning a blouse, dropping it over the back of a chair, and turning to embrace another lover, who is not a friend of mine and whom I don't know, I don't know. . . .

She is putting change in her billfold, walking vaguely toward me, looking down. She carries a small paper bag—pills of some kind, what kind? But I can't ask. That's too intimate. She glances up at me and our eyes meet and I am filled, suddenly, with a terrible rage. It has something to do with this healthy happy woman striding through a drugstore, a store built just for her, taking her pick of its phony crazy pills, its sugary pills, getting exactly what she wants. Always. Why won't she decide, whimsically, to divorce X? Why won't X decide, in despair and distraction, to move in with me—until "everything is settled"? Why won't she take a false step outside and be thrown fifteen, twenty, thirty feet down the street by a car full of teen-agers. Why not, why not? A fever rises in me. My eyes are feverish. Out on the street I want to scream at her, *Let him go! Isn't one man enough for you?* But I say nothing. I am drowning, suffocating in the heat of my rage. She is speaking lightly to me in a foreign language, I can't understand any of it, chatter, chatter, light and light-brained as a bird, this American woman grown out of an American girl, her own fever leading her on a tightrope of woven gold, stretched out taut and safe for her size-9 golden feet, so skillful. I could scrape that rather ugly mole off her arm and put a culture of cerebral cancer in it, a small neat culture, tape it down, let it set for a few weeks and see what hatches . . . but she chatters on beside me like a woman in a musical comedy. Happy. She is happy and X is happy. They are happy together. I feel as if I am walking suddenly upstairs, up a stairs, struggling with gravity, my heart and my lungs ready to burst, my face filled to bursting with a fever of blood, my brain in a fury to shout at them, *You are predictable, you too! You are statistics! You very nearly don't exist! What does it matter, your loves and your adulteries and your drooling adorable children, your quarrels, your spaghetti suppers, your stained sofas? What does any of it matter?*

THE MACHINE. THE GODDESS.

I stay late every night in the laboratory, working. The hum of a machine is like music beneath my breath. Later on tonight, oh, not too early, but as if by accident, I will drop by at their apartment. It's been a week now; they must think I am offended. They must wonder if something offended me. I will drop by, maybe around ten, ten-thirty, as if by accident, on my way home . . . I will give *her* a tiny charm for her bracelet that I happened to find in a little shop, thinking at once of her, a tiny silver figure of a female skater. Confident, muscled, a kind of goddess, looking wise and militant, able to skate over land and water as well as ice, and over our knuckles, our pulsing hearts. . . . It is all there, in that tiny figure. Women skating over men. Skating over our bare chests, our legs. I will give it to her, a wife, and I will sit on their sofa, in the currents of their marriage, curious and detached and in love, buffeted about, like seaweed or droplets of water, waiting to see what gifts the future may bring me.

What Is the Connection
Between Men and Women?

How does it feel to lie awake all night?

She is a hazy woman, not accustomed to feeling the skin so tight around her face. Hazy, fawnish, not clear to herself . . . if she were to think of herself, she would imagine a woman with a much older face. Her face feels used up. The tight skin, an aching around the eyes, a feverish glow to the cheeks. . . .

How does it feel to lie awake all night?

. . . Her skin is so fine that this lying awake, this misery, will damage it. Small lines have already begun around the eyes. They are pale radiant lines unfolding from the sun, and beneath her eyes are slight shadows, the shadows made by . . .

How does it feel to lie awake all night?

Waiting. She can't sleep. She lies still and her heart races; it is a fever, this racing, this constant thought.

How does it feel to be waiting like this?

A boy in her high school class, many years ago, went insane and they said he died of insanity. His heart raced, his body went rigid and feverish, there was no infection in his body except the infection of madness. A catatonic. He had died of insanity. His body had burned itself up, dried out, in a few weeks. Small wars had gone on in his chest, in his pumping heart, his brain had been terrorized, he had died. He died in a hospital somewhere. People talked about it at school and in the neighborhood.

How does it feel to be waiting?

Now it is eighteen years later. The boy, Fred, has been gone for eighteen years. There is nothing to him now, nothing. Yet he is more vivid to her than the man who will be coming to her to-night . . . a boy who went insane and died eighteen years ago . . . . Back then, they did not believe that eighteen years could pass away from *them.* Not ten years. Not five years. Time was massive and moved slowly; it was not real. Now she is thirty-four years old and if the insane boy were to knock on her door tonight and she let him in, not knowing who knocked, he would be a kid still and she, she would have grown into a woman though she had been a year younger than the boy. . . .

How does it feel to be waiting?

A fever!

What time is it now?

Useless to lie here in bed, waiting. The sheets are damp. Her long hair is damp and awful. Yet there is danger in sitting up too suddenly . . . her room is like an unknown room, like a hotel room in the dark. She should turn on the light. Should get up.

What time is it now?

She sits up suddenly and turns on the light. A momentary blindness—her eyelashes like moths, blinking. *Ten minutes past four.* Behind the Venetian blinds it will be morning before long. Morning is a process that can't be stopped.

How does it feel to lie awake all night?

She thinks of her mother, a mound of sleep. Her mother lives in a small frame house a few miles away, sleeping, her face pained in sleep, her mouth slightly open . . . she is snoring, no doubt. Old women snore violently. They are like bodies into which bizarre animals have crept at night; the animals are vicious, bawdy, noisy. How they snore! There is no shame to their snoring. Old women turn into old men.

How does it feel to lie awake all night?

The telephone will ring. What then? She sits on the edge of her bed, feverish, terrified. There is something she should know: she is terrified.

How does it feel to be waiting for a man?

She was crossing a street, her head bent against the wind, her eyes slits to keep out flying dust. She was carrying a grocery bag that was very light—she recalls how light it was. A car slowed. The sound of a horn. Startled, she looked up and saw a battered old car on the other side of the street, braking to a stop. Someone waved at her. Called her by name. It was an old man she did not know. Then she saw that she did know him, he was one of the men her father-in-law used to hang around with years before. No way to avoid him. And she was ashamed of wanting to avoid him, he looked so pathetic with his big smile, calling out her name across the street. . . . So she stood on the sidewalk and talked with him for a few minutes. Nothing much to say; he lived now with his son's family, he said; he was excited about the baseball game the next day. She told him gently that he was holding up traffic. . . .

How does it feel to be waiting for a man?

Her father-in-law is dead. Dead for years. Her own father is dead, yes, and her husband is dead, permanently dead. She thinks of the three of them, three men, all of them dead and therefore permanent, fixed at the ages of their death, like the high school boy who died at the age of sixteen. . . . She told the old man gently, "I think you're holding up traffic. . . ." A cheerful wave good-by. She watched him drive away. And then she turned to see another man, a stranger, standing near.

"Was that old guy bothering you?"

She shook her head quickly. *No. No.* She passed by this man and he turned with her; she caught a glimpse of his hands— thick, stubby fingers, nails unusually thick and creamy.

"—thought he was going to make trouble for you—"

"No. It's all right."

A few yards away she was struck by something as if by a blow, a fist slammed against her chest; she stopped.

She turned to look back at the man.

He was watching her. He was about her height, his hair was black and thick, his skin swarthy. She had never seen him before and yet she knew him very well. She knew those hands, the way he stood watching her, the look on his face. . . .

"Okay, just take care!" he said, smiling, raising his hand in a brisk, jerky, self-conscious salute. The way he waved at her was familiar too.

What is the connection between men and women?

She went into a store down the street. Her body weak, trembling. She had seen him on the street! He had made a claim upon her. She knew him. In the store was a bin of potatoes that were very dirty. Pale apples. Lettuce wrapped in brown paper, loosely, the leaves wilted and browning, a disappointment. She touched something, picked it up . . . she put it down again. . . . No, she did not know that man; that was a mistake. She had never seen him before. She had no interest in men and did not think about them.

What is the connection between men and women?

Someone had been waiting that day to tell her. A different feel to the vestibule of their building, the smell of bad news . . . the door to the Pedersens' place ajar, so that as she approached it she knew something was wrong. Fat Mrs. Pedersen would jump out at her and complain about the garbage, about the radio! But no. Mrs. Pedersen opened the door gently and behind her stood a man, a stranger, the two of them looking reluctant, grave, important. The stranger was from work. But her husband had not died at work, he had died in an automobile crash . . . this man had been riding in one of the other cars and had been thrown free.

How does it feel to be married?

She is a hazy blond woman. Even her photographs look hazy, blurry. Her hair is sometimes fuzzy and little tendrils lie on her forehead, humidity makes her hair curly, she hates it then. She would like to take a strong-bristled brush and draw it viciously through her hair, forcing the curl out, drawing the hair down straight, straight. Why are the snapshots of her so hazy? She is always standing in too bright a patch of sunlight, or the camera was moved at the wrong moment, or she herself moved at the wrong moment. A snapshot of her and her husband, taken at a picnic, shows her in a flash of white as if a streak of lightning had touched her, only her, leaving her husband erect and frowning a little, his face clear, even the diamond-patterned shirt he wore that day so clear you would think it had some meaning. . . .

How does it feel to be married?

She is married permanently to that man. Married. Married permanently. She is in love with that man yet, a dead man.

Married, In love. When she sleeps, she sleeps with him; his body is next to her, in sleep.

How does it feel to lie awake all night?

Tonight she is wearing an old white slip. She took off only her dress and shoes and stockings, afraid to get undressed. Usually she wears a bathrobe around the apartment; she changes into it as soon as she gets home from work. At night she wears an old faded nightgown, usually. But tonight she was afraid to get undressed.

What is the connection between men and women?

In the store she felt her eyelids closing thickly over her eyes, in terror. Not here. Not in this store. After her husband's death, for almost a year, she had sometimes broken down . . . sometimes right on the sidewalk, or in a store, anywhere . . . and the long shuddering sobs had begun, humiliating her. This had not happened for years, but she was always afraid it might happen. It might happen. In the store she found herself staring at a display of cellophane-wrapped chocolate cup cakes; trying to see them; trying not to break down.

The man came into the store.

She felt him approaching her. The flesh of her body began its long, silent wail. She did not look at him. He was walking slowly over to her, as if this were not planned, walking in that slow, rather heavy-footed way her husband had walked, approaching her in the corner of her eye.

She looked around at him, frightened.

He tried to smile.

A rough, dim face. The smile did not change it. There was something weary about him—soft, slightly discolored skin beneath the eyes. He had an intelligent face but it looked abused; as if he mauled it with his hands. She stood in silence watching him. There was nothing to say. Again he raised his hand in an embarrassed greeting . . . she saw the fingers, the knuckles, the thick, squarish nails. . . .

Why are you following me! she wanted to shout at him.

His face was like a mask, that dark mottled skin. Behind it was another face. Another personality. The mouth was not familiar, but its expression was familiar. He was about to call her by her name.

He saw how frightened she was.

He said, embarrassed, "I come in here sometimes . . . I stop in here sometimes myself. . . ."

He had not said her name. She backed away, nodding. Better get out. Run. Get home.

"I wasn't following you or anything," he said.

She could not move. Her eyes were fixed upon a point behind him, as if hypnotized to that point. He was staring at her openly. Yet she could not move, she could not break the moment. He was staring openly at her, into her face. She seemed to be offering her face to him like a flower.

She thought again that he would pronounce her name.

"I've got to leave—" she said wildly.

She put down the thing in her hand—a can of something— canned tomatoes. She put it down on a shelf without looking at the shelf.

He was staring at her face, her eyes, as if staring at her in sleep. And this was familiar too: his staring at her while she slept.

"I've got to leave," she whispered. She left the store. The store- keeper would think her behavior strange. Why had she come in, if she hadn't wanted anything? Why was she running away? Out on the sidewalk she remembered that she had already stopped at a store, near work, and that she had already bought what she wanted. . . .

She walked home quickly. She felt how she threaded herself in and out of people on the sidewalk, not noticed by them be- cause she was so hurried, so blurred: a woman in a brown coat, her head slightly bent, her eyelids half-closed against the blowing dust.

How does it feel to be waiting like this?

Fever. She runs cold water, puts a washcloth against her forehead. Everything is hot, hot. But the cold water is very cold. It makes her think of the freshness of the air when it touches her face and her body. The pores of her face and body are always open to the air, unprotected. Always open. Anything can happen. Is she still living, so many years later? Her husband died and she is still living. This baffles her. Sometimes, alone, not answering the telephone, she sits in a kind of stupor, baffled at being alive so many years after her husband died. That afternoon he had died. And they had told her about it. And she had heard the words, the news, she had accepted it in her flesh, through the pores of her flesh, thinking that it would kill her. But it had not killed her. She was still alive: she sat for hours, dazed and undreaming, caught up in a kind of unfocused terror, but in the end she would have to come to herself and do something that had to be done. She would have to iron; she would have to make something to eat. Always eat. Eat, Keep living. She had not died.

What is the connection between men and women?

In the daytime it is a world of women. She sees women all the time. She is a supervisor now at the store, in China & Glassware. It is a job that pays well and the work is not physical work; when she thinks of her job, she is satisfied with it. The store is the city's big store. Its dream store. Every day people stream into it, up and down the escalators, up and down the elevators, staring and touching and buying, hypnotized. Up on her floor, the seventh, she sees women all the time . . . but she does not think of them as women, as *women*. She does not think of men as *men*. She thinks of a world of bodies, directed clumsily by thoughts, by darting minnowlike ideas. Come here. Buy this. Walk away from this. Put out your hand. Lie down. Sleep.

What does a woman feel while a man makes love to her?

Barefoot, she is standing at the door. Her hand on the knob. She stands there in her frayed white slip, listening. No one in the hall? No one? She will telephone the police if she hears anything. It is very late at night, too late for anyone to be up. Her heart is pounding with fear. Sweaty terror.

If she goes back to bed, she will lie there; her eyelids will burn. It is not time for her to sleep. She must stand here for a while, listening, her head tilted, the side of her face burning as if someone were standing across the room and looking at her.

What does a woman feel while a man makes love to her?

In the months afterward, she could see her husband out of the corner of her eye. Watching her. And so she walked quickly, furtively, staring down at the sidewalk. She moved out of the apartment they had rented. She got a job selling china. She sat and listened to her mother's complaints—the neighbors, the neighborhood, her mother's ailments, the weather—and out of the corner of her eye she saw her husband, spying on her. She did not talk to men. She did not notice men, really. At night she lay awake and thought of her husband, who was dead and yet who was somehow with her, lying heavily with her, one arm flung out . . . his breathing harsh as it had been when he slept. . . . "Oh, Christ," she said aloud, her voice a surprise to her: clear as a fingernail tapped against a water goblet. She imagined herself used up, her skin tight across her face, her eyes popping out of her head. When she saw herself in the mirror it was always a surprise, after the face she imagined. Why was she still young? Why was she still alive?

She stands at the door, alone, and a feeling of darkness comes over her. Sickness. Her eyes ache. Her body aches. She thinks of someone coming up the stairs—she thinks of the telephone ringing—she thinks of someone knocking at the door. Pounding at the door. He is coming to get her. If she runs out of this place and down the street to the all-night diner, or if she gets a taxi and goes over to her mother's, still he will find her; he will know about her running away.

In a while it will be morning.

Her hair is heavy, it makes her want to weep. "Christ!" she says aloud, angrily. She walks around the room, her living room, striking her hands together, the palms of her hands meeting and recoiling softly, such soft flesh!—she walks into the bedroom, sees the bed, the sheets. What she will do is this: get dressed and telephone a taxi and go over to her mother's. No, telephone her mother first. But no, no. Her mother would make a fuss. Always a fuss. She hates her mother and will not go to her . . . no, she does not hate her mother, but she hates her mother's fussing. As a child she used to stick out her tongue behind her mother's back. Her tongue had strained at its roots, as if trying to get out of her mouth, so angry and so impatient with her mother!—hating her mother! She would strain to see the tip of her tongue then. Pink and wavering. It would not stay still. She thrust it out of her mouth and it trembled with anger, with hatred, while her mother grumbled about something and had no idea what was going on, this angry pink, wavering tip of a tongue straining out toward her as if it would like to touch her.

What does a woman feel while a man makes love to her?

She walked quickly home, threading her way around people. No one noticed. She did not think anyone noticed. She seemed to be pushing her body forward, her head bent so that the top of her head was pushed forward, as if into a wind. Hurry and get home, for Christ's sake. Get off the street. During the day, at the store, she sometimes thought of her life before she had fallen in love; the blank, white china reminded her of that blankness in her life. And then her husband. A man, with a man's needs. His arms, his embrace. His body. Her mind flitted back and forth between the two—herself as a girl, herself as a wife—and she felt guilty that she should so loosely betray him.

A fever. A feverish glow to the skin.

A violent penetration to the very heart: up in the chest. A sense of suffocation. Strangulation. He had held her and penetrated her and, in his embrace, she had lain still with her mind broken up into pieces of white, terrified glass. And then the whiteness had gone away; the terror had gone away. She felt him driving himself in her, the insides of her thighs grown sore from his thighs, their muscular urgency, and the motions of this man were motions she had nothing to do with, really. She loved him and held him in an embrace of her own. She was a quiet, blond, fair-skinned woman, an attractive woman who did not bother with herself, she was a man's wife and in love with him permanently, married to him permanently. There would be no end to the marriage. There would be no end to his love-making.

In that little grocery store he had approached her hesitantly.

In the store he had said something about following her. Not following her.

She had turned to go, blindly. She had knocked against a counter. The man reached out for her and she put out her hand to steady herself, her fingers closing on his arm.

On her way home she had walked quickly, seeing no one.

What time is it?

A noise somewhere. Out on the street. She goes to the window and with her thumb and forefinger carefully pries the Venetian blind open, her eye narrowed to a slit as if it fears seeing something out there. But nothing. No alarm.

It is four-thirty.

Coming home that afternoon, hurrying, she had not once glanced back. She had felt him following her. At a distance, a block behind her . . . he was following her right to this building. Her mind churned. She wanted to think clearly of what she must do: get on a bus? A bus did stop near her and a weary line of people got onto it. But no, she walked by. No bus. For some reason she had not gotten on it. She crossed streets, the grocery bag light in the crook of her arm, her purse grown light, everything breezy and blown with dust; the dust seemed to be inside her head, churning wildly. She did not know if she was frightened or not. Why should she be frightened? He lived around here. He stopped at the store often, so he said. And if he was walking behind her, a block behind her, there was no reason for her to think he was following her.

Her breath came scantily. She was very nervous. She would turn up a street, go into a store, she would hide from him. . . . Or she would turn and look back to see where he was. She would wait for him to catch up to her. She would tell him to go to hell.

But she did nothing, she did not turn away or stop for him. She kept on walking home. It was twenty to six and usually she was home at five-thirty.

Now it is four-thirty in the morning.

By quarter to six she was home. Apartment 2-B. Throwing off her coat, letting her purse fall onto the table, setting the bag of groceries on the counter . . . she rubbed the palms of her hands hard into her face, into her eyes. Was that bastard outside? Out on the sidewalk? Would he follow her into the building and look at the mailboxes, would he figure out which apartment was hers? And then what would he do?

After her husband made love to her she lay beside him and felt her heartbeat slow, ebbing back to normal. But she did not recover, really. He was the only man who had ever made love to her, and she had no interest in other men before him or afterward, she could not force herself to think of them, it was a burden, a waste of time. . . . Men and their nervous laughter! Men and their grins showing stained teeth, their need for women, for her, their clumsy jokes, their jockeying for position as if in a race, wanting women, wanting her! She could not think of them. She carried her body through the crowd of men she had met in the years since her husband's death, not really conscious of men, not interested in them. She was still married. She was married permanently.

If that man telephoned her, she would say to him, *I am married permanently.*

What are the things a woman might do?
All things.

How does it feel to be a woman?
Passing through a crowd of men a woman feels something stab in her, in her loins. A fever, a heat like a knife. She makes her way through the mysterious flow of time, as if swimming, as if pressing herself forward into the wind, angry and impatient and frightened. She feels a desire that is not for one man but for a crowd of men, their faces impersonal and threatening; she puts out her hand accidentally and seizes someone's arm, her fingers closing hard around his wrist.

In love there are two things: bodies and words. The words go along with certain bodies, sometimes the names of those bodies, their "names," and sometimes the words those bodies exclaim.

What are the things a woman might do?
She went out of the kitchen without putting the groceries away. She went into the bathroom and turned on the light and leaned against the sink, so that she could stare into her own face. It was the face that man had looked into so deeply—the dark blond hair combed back from the face, an uneven hairline, tiny strands and tendrils of hair along the temples and in front of the ears, the face itself flushed and hectic, the nostrils oddly prominent. She was always surprised to see that she was really a young woman, still. A young woman after so many years. Her eyes were

wheat-colored, vague, hazy; there were tiny threads of blood in the whites. She was breathing quickly. She could see the process of breathing in her face—the slightly widened nostrils, the blank openness of her skin, her pores, into which anything might flow, any kind of air. It was very warm in this room. She did not know why she had rushed in here, to stare at her own face.

Going crazy had been a temptation years ago. Maybe she had been a little crazy, with that uncontrollable sobbing . . . even out on the street a few times, that sobbing, the scream that formed in her throat . . . the impulse to tear at her face. This fever in her now was a kind of craziness. It might burn her up: her body dehydrated, emptied out. In the catatonic state small wars are waged in the body, acted out, memorized, rehearsed, unleashed, begun again, repeated. She had read that. No, she had been told that. And when she had wept bitterly, in her mother's kitchen, her mother had lost patience and said: "Oh, you! You bawling like hell all the time! You think nobody ever lost a husband but you?"

She rushed out of the bathroom and looked at the telephone. It was on a small table near the television set. She would do this: telephone her mother and say that someone was following her. Had followed her home. She would not say that the man was her husband . . . she would not say that, no, that was crazy, she did not want to be crazy any longer . . . and certainly the man was not her husband, for her husband was dead. Just as she stood staring at the telephone, it rang. "A wrong number," she thought. She reached out at once. A wrong number was no danger; she could answer the telephone if it were a wrong number.

"Hello?"

A moment of silence. She heard the man's breathing—the intake of his breath. Her husband had been silent in that way, waiting for her to speak, drawing in his breath slowly and cagily. She leaned forward, listening, pressing her face forward.

"Hello?"

Finally he spoke. She seemed to hear his words before he actually spoke them. "Hello, is this Sharon?"

"Who is this?"

Her eyelids seemed very heavy. She narrowed her eyes to slits. "This is someone you just met," he said.

"What do you want?"

Silence again. She stood in a kind of stupor, dazzled. She pressed the telephone against her ear and the side of her jaw. "What do you want?" she said shrilly.

She slammed the receiver down.

What is the connection between men and women?

She spent the evening in a state of nervous excitement. She waited for him to come to her. She waited for the telephone to ring again. Hours passed. She felt her body turn light, as if dazzled by thin air, buoyed up by air. She was very lightheaded. Something began to pulsate in her loins, in the secrecy of her dark, moist flesh, that she could not control. She rubbed her hands into her eyes. She sat on the edge of her bed and brushed her hair in hard, fast strokes. She pulled the hairs out of the brush impatiently. She could not stay here in her apartment and she could not leave . . . she could not stay here, she could not leave. She could not stay here all night.

How does it feel to be a woman?

Now the telephone rings again. It is very early in the morning —almost five o'clock. No one would telephone her at this time. It must be a wrong number. She hurries to the telephone, puts out her hand . . . and then stands there, staring, fascinated as the telephone rings. One ring after another. Ringing. Such dazzling sound! It is that man on the other end, *that man,* he has been up all night drinking, he has been thinking about her, he will say to her, *I'm coming up.*

She does not answer the telephone. Agitated, lightheaded, impatient. She walks from room to room. This dingy apartment!—it is the fourth or fifth apartment she has rented since she moved out of that first apartment, wanting a change, always wanting a change. Her heart thuds. It is always thudding, like a fist tapping on her chest. There seems to be electricity in her. Her legs move quickly, nervously. She will have to move out of this apartment too.

How does it feel to be a woman?

Eyeballs: dense white balls of matter. Skin: stretched tight and hot across the bones. She must sit perfectly still so that there will be no sign of her. How can he know she is here? She may have run out somewhere, she may have escaped. . . . Something in the corner of her eye makes her turn. The edge of a table. A lampshade. She folds her arms across her chest as if to contain the beating of her heart.

Is that a tap on the door?

She has heard nothing on the stairs—no creaking. She has been listening so hard that she can hardly hear.

A knock on the door.

It is the sound of his knuckles. His bony knuckles. She sits on the edge of her bed, her eyes closed. The despair rises in her, almost to a wail. He is silent in the hall. She is silent, waiting. Then the knock comes again—three times—the rapping of his knuckles.

She goes to the doorway of her bedroom. The door to the hall is closed. Locked. If there is someone outside she can't see him, can't see his shadow through the door, she can't hear him breathing. But she is so agitated that she can't be sure. What if he calls out her name? He knows her name, he has read it on the mailbox in the vestibule.

Again he knocks on the door. Gently. He does not want to wake anyone in the building.

She steps forward suddenly.

Are you in there?

He said that. He said something—she did not hear it exactly. Her mind churns so that she can't hear, she can't think.

She comes to the door boldly. She puts her hand on the door-knob and stands there, a foot or two away from him.

"What do you want?" she says.

Sharon?

It is like a stab deep in her belly, that name! That name pro-nounced by him! He has been drinking, yes. She can tell. Years ago her husband came home late like this, and she had had to unlock the door to let him in; he had been drinking, he had knocked on the door, on his own door, and she had come to let him in. . . . If she opens the door to this man she will see his eyes and the eyes that are inside them, looking out at her; she will see his hands.

He knocks again, his knuckles barely brushing against the door. It is like a whisper. The two of them are very close, only a foot or so away, leaning together. She will unlock the door, she thinks suddenly. She will unlock and open the door.

Sharon?

She reaches up to slide the little bolt back and everything comes open, comes apart.